More Praise for *Fragments*

"The best novel of the year that you never heard of. . . . Outstanding."

—BarnesandNoble.com

"Prepare to be terrified."

—*Cape Coral Daily Breeze*

"James F. David combines science fiction, mystery, parapsychology, intense action, and even a little romance into a frightening tale that illustrates both his creativity and skillful writing."
—*Post and Courier,* Charleston, South Carolina

"This is a thriller with genuine thrills, part science fiction story, part horror story, part mystery, all excitement."
—*Salem Statesmen Journal*

"A first-rate thriller with a particularly effective climax."
—*Science Fiction Chronicle*

"Where are the new Stephen Kings and Dean Koontses coming from? Former psychology professor James F. David puts himself near the top of the contender's list with his second thriller—an absorbing story that soon leaves implausibility in the dust."
—Amazon.com

Forge Books by James F. David

Footprints of Thunder
Fragments

FRAGMENTS

JAMES F. DAVID

A TOM DOHERTY ASSOCIATES BOOK
NEW YORK

This is a work of fiction. All the characters and events portrayed in this novel are either fictitious or are used fictitiously.

FRAGMENTS

A Tor Book
Published by Tom Doherty Associates, Inc.
175 Fifth Avenue
New York, NY 10010

Tor Books on the World Wide Web:
http://www.tor.com

Tor® is a registered trademark of Tom Doherty Associates, Inc.

ISBN: 0-812-57147-9
Library of Congress Card Catalog Number: 96-53979

First edition: July 1997
First mass market edition: August 1998

Printed in the United States of America

0 9 8 7 6 5 4 3 2 1

ACKNOWLEDGMENTS

My wife, Gale, deserves special thanks for her help with this book. She's moved from spotting typos and spelling errors in my first book, *Footprints of Thunder,* to suggesting improvements in wording and plot in *Fragments*. Can coauthor be far behind? Abby, Katie, and Bethany, thanks for showing my books around school and helping to promote your dad.

Thanks to Carol McCleary, my agent, for her continued encouragement, and to Greg Cox, my editor at Tor, for his support.

PROLOGUE

October 19,1953

The flashing red lights of the police cars lit the crowd that had gathered to see something they could later tell their friends they wished they'd never seen. He joined them, acting curious, planning to stay just long enough to deflect suspicion.

The crowd was thick, and those in the back whispered questions to those in front. What, who, how, and why? the new arrivals asked, and in reply came fact, rumor, and surmise. He joined the crowd and whispered his own questions to a short man with a brown hat. The man turned, anxious to share with a newcomer.

"It's another dead boy."

"College age?"

"Probably. Someone said he has a university decal on his car window."

"Was he killed with a knife?"

"Yeah, just like the others. Cut up, too—you know—especially his private parts. It's the same em-oh. That's what the police call it. Modus operandi, or something like that. My brother-in-law's a cop. He says you can always tell when it's the same killer from the MO."

"Do they know the boy's name?"

"Naw, but they found his body in a '49 Chevy. Know anyone driving a green one?"

He shook his head—a silent lie—then let the man turn to answer the questions of a young woman.

Now he moved on, quickening his pace to a brisk walk. He tried to look casual, like someone out for a walk on a warm October evening—someone going to the twenty-four flavors for a double dip, or down to Hickman's for a cold pop. He strode up the tree-lined street, a feeling of dread growing with every step until it was almost too much to bear.

He rounded the corner at Elm and turned down Lincoln. His house was there on the left, halfway up the block. It was a big house, much bigger than he needed now. Filled once with a family overflowing its six bedrooms, now the house—and his family—was little more than an empty shell.

Every light was on, giving the empty rooms the glow of the living. He liked the house bright. If he couldn't have the people in the house, he at least could drive out the shadowy memories they left behind. He looked up at her second-floor room but saw nothing but her white lace curtains fluttering out the open window. He went up the walk and then the flight of stairs to the porch. The front door was closed and locked, just as he had left it. Entering, he quickly climbed the stairs to the second floor, pulling himself along with the handrail. Checking her room first, he hoped to find her in bed reading, or playing her forty-fives. It was empty, as were his and the other bedrooms. Downstairs he found the living room, library, and den just as empty, so he cut through the dining room to the kitchen. There was an empty glass on the table, lined with a film of dried milk, and a plate with cookie crumbs next to it. He was about to search the side porch when he noticed the back door slightly ajar. The yard was dimly lit by the light coming from the kitchen windows, but there were too many shadows and shrubs for hiding places for him to be sure the yard was empty. Closing the door his hand came away sticky with blood.

Blood drops on the floor led him through the kitchen to the basement door. There was more blood on its handle, and the lights in the basement were on. Softly, he walked down the stairs, trying to avoid the creakiest steps. The basement was filled with bits and pieces of his old life. There were mattresses and bed frames from the now empty bedrooms upstairs, and bicycles that would never be ridden again. Nearly new children's clothes and toys were packed away in boxes—he couldn't bring himself to give them away. His wife's things were there somewhere, too, long since removed from the room they had shared.

When he reached the bottom he could hear the sound of running water. The laundry room was to the right, but the sound was coming from the left—his shop was there, a small room in one corner. He passed through the piles of rummage, careful not to make a sound, and past the shelves for canned goods until he could see. She was there.

Bent over the stainless-steel sink she was washing her hands and arms. She wore a pair of white shorts but no top, only her bra—her blouse on the floor. Her washing was methodical and thorough. Over and over she soaped up her hands and then washed up and down her arms, clear to the elbow. First her right hand and arm and then her left. When done, she started over with her right again. He watched her wash, trying to imagine another explanation for why she might be in the basement doing this, but when she pulled a knife from the bottom of the sink to scrub, he felt all hope drain from him. He recognized the knife—it was from the set in his kitchen. He had used it many times since the murders began. Then he was filled with a terrible resolve.

Slipping back past the shelves, he picked through the rummage until he found an old set of golf clubs. He pulled a driver from the bag, freezing when the other clubs rattled into the empty space. When he was sure the water was still running he crept back along the shelves. Intent on cleaning the knife, she didn't see him coming.

Raising the club above his head, he ran the last few steps, then swung down. She looked up at the last minute, understanding flashing across her face, but there was no fear in her eyes, only surprise that her father could do this to her. But in that she was wrong. He couldn't kill her. At the last second he lost his resolve and tried to soften the blow. The club head came down as her arm came up to deflect the blow. The force left in his swing was too much and her arm was knocked down by the shaft, the club continuing down and contacting her head with a sharp crack.

She crumpled to the floor in a limp pile. He raised the club for a second blow, determined to finish what he had begun; then he saw her face. Her eyes were closed and her blond hair lay loose across her cheek. He'd seen the look many times before, at night when he would check on her and her sisters. His sleeping children always brought out the tenderness in him, and sometimes he would sit watching them until his wife came to drag him off to bed. He knelt now and brushed the hair away from her face. She had that look of a sleeping angel, and he was suddenly transported back to their common past, a time when they both were innocents. There was no murder in him now, no matter what she had done. A small streak of crimson spread through her hair, but it was a small wound and she was breathing strongly. He hoped she would live.

He carried her from the shop, setting her gently on an old mattress, then tied her hands and feet. She was crazy, of course, but not so crazy that she couldn't act normal. That was how she had fooled him and fooled the boys. She would never be his little girl again, or the woman she could have been. He didn't blame her, she didn't ask to be what they made her, but he couldn't let it go on, and he couldn't let the State finish the killing he couldn't do himself.

He went to work in his shop, dismantling the lathe, table saw, and jigsaw and moving them out. He had boxes of tools, a wall full of hooks with more tools, and two vises to move. After he had worked for an hour, she began moaning. A few minutes later she began to talk to him.

"I didn't do anything—" she began.

He hushed her with an angry look. Her pleading expression instantly turned to flashing anger.

"What did you expect? You know what they did to me."

He hushed her again, but she wouldn't be still. She kept after him.

"You didn't do anything. I had to. Someone had to."

He couldn't take it, and he pulled a dishcloth from the laundry basket and wrapped it around her mouth. She screamed and cussed him as he did, using words girls shouldn't know. Then he went back to work dismantling the workbench. He worked through the night until he had the room emptied out. There was no window in the room and it had a sturdy door. He dug through the piles of tools and supplies he had dumped in the basement until he found a hasp and latch and attached them to the door and frame. She was asleep when he finished but she woke when he tried to pick her up. Her struggle made it impossible to carry her, so he dragged her into the room and laid her in the corner. She rolled over, venom in her eyes. He dragged the mattress into the room and then retrieved a blanket from the linen closet upstairs. He tried to move her to the mattress but she wriggled out of his grasp. Instead, he threw the blanket over her and then left, closing the hasp and securing it with a padlock. It was a temporary solution at best. Then he went upstairs and fell onto the bed and slept the sleep of the grieving. He'd just lost another daughter.

He woke to the sound of a distant thumping. He was groggy and his head pounded a painful rhythm in synchrony with the thumping. His mouth was pasty; thick with mucus. He felt like he had a hangover, but he didn't remember drinking anything the night before. He sat on the edge of the bed letting his body adjust his blood pressure to keep himself from blacking out; then he walked to the open window and looked into the street. It was another hot afternoon, and the street near his house was empty except for Mrs. Clayton, who was watering her shrubs with a hose. Mrs. Clayton watered incessantly. It was her way of keeping an eye on what was happening on the street. He turned back to his bedroom, trying to clear his thoughts. Why was he so confused? Then he noticed the thumping again. *What was that pounding?* When he heard splintering wood, he remembered.

Down the stairs he ran at breakneck speed, into the kitchen and down into the basement. He jumped the last four steps and hit the floor running, turning in time to see the shop door kicked open, the frame splintering. She came out screaming in fury. He crashed into her with full momentum. His bulk gave him the advantage and he bowled her over, but he wasn't prepared for her fury. She clawed and bit like a wild animal and he quickly found himself bleeding from a dozen places. He tried wrapping his arms around her to control her, but her violent motions made it impossible to hang on. When he feared she might get away and break to the stairs he hit her. Over and over he pounded at her head. Soon her arms came up, protecting her face. He stopped hitting when he heard the sobs.

She would be manageable for a while and he worked fast. He

carried her into the shop and put her back on the mattress. She turned away from him, curling into a fetal position, her body racked by sobs. He could see bloody circles on her wrists where she had worked at the ropes until her wrists bled, lubricating the ropes. He retrieved the bloody ropes and then left her and checked the door. The frame was split where the hasp had been pulled free. He found a hammer and nails and put the frame back together and then reattached the hasp. It wouldn't be as strong as it was before, so he found a two-by-four and nailed it across the door to keep her in until he got back.

He found what he needed at the hardware store and was back in thirty minutes. He'd dismantled his shop, so he worked on the basement floor. When ready, he pried off the two-by-four and opened the door. She was huddled against the wall, hugging her knees to her chest. The venom was back in her eyes.

"Why are you doing this to me?" Her voice came out in a coarse whisper.

He didn't answer. How do you tell someone they're not sane? Especially when you're not sure you're sane yourself. He ignored her and came in brandishing the two-by-four.

"Turn around or I'll let you have it!"

She hesitated but then turned.

"Put your hands behind you."

"You can't keep me tied up forever."

"Give me your hands or I'll hit you with this!"

Her hands came around and he quickly tied them with rope. Then he tied her feet again. He left the gag off but ordered her not to speak. He went to work with a masonry drill and attached a steel plate to the concrete of the exterior wall. He ran a length of heavy chain through a ring attached to the wall plate and then snapped a keyed lock onto the chain to secure it to the ring. The heavier chain connected to another ring, which had a lighter chain looped through it. He then wrapped one end of the light chain around one of her wrists and secured it with another lock. When he had the other wrist secured the same way he cut the ropes off her wrists and ankles. As soon as the ropes were gone she came after him. He retreated out the door, grabbing his tool-box as he ran. She came screaming, but the length of chain pulled her up short at the door. She stood there pulling on the chains, bloodying her wrists again and screaming at him with foul language. There was none of his little girl left in her now.

He closed the door, shutting out her epithets, and the sight of what she had become. He didn't want to see her this way ever again. He chose to remember her as his little girl, even though somewhere just past childhood that little girl had died, leaving the monster now kicking at the door.

He brought her food but she kicked the tray out of his hands as soon as the door opened. Later he brought her another blanket. She was still only wearing her bra but there was no way to dress her without removing the chains.

The next day he rented a truck and bought a supply of bricks and mortar. Then he went to work in the backyard building a barbecue. When he had a good start he began surreptitiously moving bricks into his basement. He started along the wall of the shop, bricking it from floor to ceiling. It took him three days to do the walls, leaving only the door. She began eating on the third day, accepting the food tray from him. Her attitude had changed, too—she was contrite and apologetic, begging him to forgive her and understand. He couldn't do either.

When he was ready, he entered her room holding the golf club as a weapon and shortened her chain so that she was held back from the door. Then he carried furniture into the room: a bed frame and box springs, a table, and a chest of drawers. Then, as she watched with mounting horror, he took the door from its hinges, busted out the frame, slapped down mortar, and fit the first brick into the opening. Screaming, she lunged at him, but was pulled up short by the chain. Quickly the screaming became soft pleading.

"Please, Daddy. Please don't."

His heart softened but didn't melt and he kept spreading mortar and slapping bricks into place. He paused in his work to build a small wooden frame, which he set in the center of the doorway, and then he bricked up and over the frame. Then he worked nonstop from a stockpile of bricks, quickly filling in the doorway until only the small opening at the bottom remained. When he finished, he heard her voice from the opening at the bottom of the door. Her voice echoed as if from a tomb.

"Why didn't you just kill me quick?"

"Because I love you."

He never spoke to her again.

He waited three days before he slid the keys to the lock through the opening, making sure the mortar was well set. She immediately began pounding on the wall with the chains. He kept her food for two days until she slid the chains and locks out to him. He brought her food three times a day, after that, coming home at lunch to make sure her needs were taken care of. There was waste to be dealt with, too, and he kept her supplied with toiletries. He pushed clothes through the opening regularly and she would push out her dirty clothes. He kept her supplied with books, and when she asked for pencils and a sketch pad he slid those underneath, although no pictures ever came back through the opening.

Her friends called at first, but she had only a few. Most had been driven away after it happened. He told them she had run away to Seattle and they believed him. It helped that she had been morose for some time, and distant. Running away was something unhappy teenagers did. Besides, she was old enough to be on her own anyway. Her friends married and were soon immersed in their own lives and eventually even persistent best friend Jean stopped calling.

Sometimes she would refuse food for days at a time, or send out books and other offerings shredded, but she always came around. It disappointed him in a way. If she had been stronger she could have starved herself to death. But if she had been stronger maybe it wouldn't have happened to her in the first place, and maybe she wouldn't have turned into a monster.

He regretted not putting a radio in the room for her. They were too big to get through the opening, so he took to sitting downstairs and listening to the radio loud enough so she could hear it. She never asked to hear anything in particular, so he mostly listened to news and band music. When TV finally seduced him away from the radio, he would turn the radio on in the evenings, putting it on a rock-and-roll station. He didn't know if she liked the music; she never said. But one day when he came downstairs he thought he heard her singing an Elvis Presley song.

At Christmas he always wrapped gifts and slid them through the opening. On the morning of her seventh Christmas in the room he sat on the floor of his living room and wrapped her presents. He had a pink cashmere sweater, a set of pastel drawing chalk, and a radio small enough to fit through the opening. He wrapped the presents in Santa Claus paper. It was kiddie wrap, but he thought of her as the sleeping four-year-old in his mind, not the eighteen-year-old maniac he'd last seen. When the presents were wrapped with red ribbons and red bows, he put a candy cane on each present and took them down the stairs. He slid the presents through the opening, but when he turned to leave, something slid out. A small package lay on the floor, wrapped in sketch paper she'd colored red. There was even a bow on top made out of shredded paper. He didn't know what to do. He wanted to thank her, but he hadn't spoken in the basement for years and no words would come to him in that environment.

He picked up the small package and carried it upstairs and put it under his tree. It was the only package there. He looked at it for a full hour before he got up to start the ham cooking. He checked on the package off and on all day, not wanting to open it, only to be sure it was there. It was heavy for its size, he knew that, but it might be some cruel joke. He feared he would open it and find it full of human waste or something worse.

At dinnertime he took ham, mashed potatoes, peas, and dinner rolls down to her. He always brought her a glass of milk—she always loved milk as a little girl. When he came to her room in the corner he heard Christmas music coming out of the opening— she was playing her radio. He came back an hour later for the dishes and slid a piece of apple pie into her room.

He couldn't bring himself to open the package that afternoon, although he picked it up twice, feeling it and shaking it like a curious little kid. He brought her more ham for dinner and another piece of pie. The radio was playing rock-and-roll music now.

He turned off the living-room lights and spent the evening holding her package and watching TV by the lights of his Christmas tree. He was still sitting in his chair when the TV went off the air. He watched the test pattern for a half hour and then turned it off and sat in the dark. It wouldn't be Christmas much longer and it would be disrespectful not to open a Christmas present on Christmas. But it was hard for him. When he opened it he would know whether there was any love for him left in his little girl.

He unwrapped it slowly, preserving the paper bow. The paper fell away, revealing a small white statue carved out of a bar of soap. It was a little girl sitting cross-legged in a chair. The detail was amazing and the surface polished smooth. The little girl's face was turned up as if she was looking at someone standing in front of her. The face was the face of his daughter and he imagined she was looking up at him, her daddy, towering above her. The expression was a sad look, a forgiving look; the look she and her sisters gave him after he had punished them. It was a look he knew to mean *I understand, and I still love you.* He began to cry, and he put the statue down, afraid his tears would mar the surface.

It was two in the morning when he had enough control to go back downstairs. The opening to her room was dark, and the radio silent. He still couldn't speak in that place but he slid another piece of pie through the opening. It was a pitiful thank-you, but it was all he could manage. He never got another present, but he didn't care. He knew she was insane and a killer. He knew he was insane, too, or he wouldn't have sealed her in. But in one moment, when they were both lucid, they had connected one last time. The father-and-daughter bond was there, buried in the madness that had enveloped them, and for a brief moment they had found it. He coated the statue with lacquer the next day and then placed it on the nightstand by his bed with her picture.

Six years later he retired and stayed home with her full time. A year after that he experienced chest pain and ended up spending two days in the hospital. He had been so insistent on getting out that they had nearly sedated him. Finally he convinced them to let him go, and they sent him home with nitroglycerin in his shirt pocket. She was famished when he got home, and he fed her generously. He didn't sleep that night, worrying about what would happen to her if he died. Would she starve to death, or would someone find her and release her? If they did, would she kill again? She wasn't sane when he sealed her in; what would she be like now? He got up at 4 A.M. and wrote out a note explaining what he'd done and why, and where to find her; then he went back to bed. At eight he got up and tore up the note.

Six months later he stopped worrying. He came downstairs with breakfast and found her arm sticking out through the opening. Her palm was open as if she was reaching out to grasp something. He touched her arm, keeping away from her hand for fear she would grab him. Her arm was cold. He poked her palm with a finger but got no response. She was dead. He didn't know what had killed her. Perhaps it was suicide, perhaps she'd had a heart attack, or perhaps her appendix had burst. All he knew was that she had lived long enough to crawl to the opening and put her arm out, reaching for something—reaching for him. He sat holding her hand, crying for the little girl that had died twice—once on that terrible night, and then again some time in the early morning.

At noon he gently put her hand down and then drove to the lumberyard to buy more bricks. When he got back he held her hand for a few more minutes, said a prayer for her, and then kissed her palm. Then he gently pushed her arm into the opening. He mixed up the mortar and pried out what was left of the wooden frame. He laid an even layer of mortar and put the first brick into place. It was lighter than the other bricks. It only took a few minutes to fill the opening. When he tapped the last brick into place he felt a rush of relief and sadness. He had finished a painful chapter of his life, but if there was another chapter to come he couldn't see what it would be. She had been the last of his children, and the last of his family. What was left for an old man to do but to spend his days in loneliness and end in some nursing home in the company of strangers? He hadn't spoken to her since he entombed her, but they had shared emotions through the small slot he had just sealed. As long as she had been in the basement he had not been alone—he was alone now.

A week later he returned to the basement and began dismantling the canning shelves and reattaching them to the brick walls of the shop. He worked slowly, only putting in a couple of hours a day. He filled the rest of the south end of the basement with storage bins. When he was done the end of the basement was a maze of storage spaces, neatly hiding her room. Then he moved the contents of the basement onto the shelves and into the bins. The basement looked cleaner than it had in years, and you could actually see the floor again. That empty space made him sad, for he could remember watching his girls tricycle around and around the stairs on that floor. When they were older they played hopscotch and jump rope there on rainy days, or roller-skated—when they could find their skate keys.

He seldom returned to the basement after that. Three years later he suffered a heart attack and was taken to a nursing home.

After a month in the nursing home he realized he would never leave it alive and asked to have some of his personal belongings brought to his room. One of the nurses brought him his pajamas, robe, slippers, toiletries, and a picture of him and his wife and their four daughters. The only other thing he requested was a small soap statue of a little girl sitting in a chair. When he died the house was sold.

1

DEATH BY SUGGESTION

Present day

He never thought of it as murder, since he never once touched his victims—at least not physically. He merely suggested behaviors to them, and those behaviors led to their deaths. He had long since reasoned away his guilt. After all, was it his fault their minds were weaker than his? If they were stronger they wouldn't take his suggestions. He was merely a part of the continuing evolutionary cycle—new genetic characteristics giving an advantage to one subset of the species. He was meant to survive, and those who took his suggestions weren't. He could live with the deaths of evolutionary dead ends and it looked like he might have to make another suggestion. Dr. Birnbaum was acting suspicious. He had taken over from his assistant, and had a determined look on his face.

He had been tested by the best ESP experts in the world, and none of them had yet figured out how he did it. Of course, the different researchers didn't know they were testing the same person, he made sure of that. He also made sure he showed them just enough to keep them interested, but not enough to frighten them. Besides, they were always asking the wrong questions and looking in the wrong places. The eggheads at Ohio State University were typical.

Birnbaum and his graduate students had been testing him in

a typical room for these kinds of experiments. He sat on one side of a table with a screen in front of him, while on the other side was the experimenter. This morning he had been working with a squat female graduate student named Sylvia. She wore wire-rimmed glasses and had a complexion problem. She was all business and totally serious, so he didn't try to kid her along. The screen kept him from seeing her hands or the cards she had in front of her. She had been using a standard set of psi cards. Each card was printed with a different shape. There was a cross, a circle, a star, wavy lines, and a square. The experimenter would shuffle the deck and then turn the cards over one at a time, concentrating on the card. His task was to read the experimenter's mind and indicate which card the experimenter was looking at. By chance anyone could get a match twenty percent of the time. If you could consistently exceed that twenty percent the experts assumed you had telepathic abilities. He made sure his percentage hovered around forty percent. Any more and he would become a sensation and there would be publicity. Any less and they would lose interest in him. At forty percent they paid him to be available for study, and at the same time he picked their brains, trying to learn more about himself and his ability.

He couldn't read minds but he used his ability to convince them he could. It was easy. Parapsychology was a young field, but already rigid in many ways. They recognized only four categories of abilities: telekinesis, the ability to move objects with your mind; telepathy, the ability to send and receive thoughts; remote reviewing, which was perceiving from a distance; and prescience, the ability to see the future. He had none of these talents and that was why they were so easy to fool.

He always insisted that he be tested alone. He told the researchers it was to keep from being confused by the thoughts of others, but it was actually to keep from being found out. The experimenters typically started with a shuffle of the psi cards, and then they would turn them over one at a time and concentrate on the image. He would then either make a guess, which was wrong eighty percent of the time, or he would guess and then make a mental suggestion to the tester that it was a correct response. With just a gentle push the tester would record his response as right and move on to the next card. It worked like a charm and they tested him day after day, ever frustrated in trying to understand how he consistently beat chance.

Like most parapsychologists this tester was an easy mark. She wanted so badly to believe he had psychic ability that it took almost no push at all to get her to record a correct answer. All of the graduate students that had tested him were easy, but they seemed to be getting tired of him here, and he knew that his support money would dry up soon unless he gave them something to get them excited again. He had decided to show them a sudden burst of psychic activity and get seventy percent right. At other universities that had driven them into a frenzy, insuring weeks of continued support. He had worked the scam a dozen times and it worked well—until this morning. Sylvia had been flushed with excitement when she left the room to share her results. But a few minutes later Dr. Birnbaum had come in with that serious look. He was suspicious, and suspicious people were a danger.

Dr. Birnbaum showed no excitement over his burst of psychic power. Instead, he had asked him to be patient for a minute as he worked with the psi cards on the other side of the screen. He could hear the psi cards being worked, and he presumed he was shuffling them. He wished at that moment he could read minds, because he was sure Dr. Birnbaum was up to something. He might have gone too far with that seventy percent success rate and cursed himself for being careless. He considered letting his performance drop to chance, but that might suggest he was hiding something. No, it was better to revert to his forty percent success rate. Then, no matter the outcome, he would be leaving Columbus, Ohio, for good.

"OK, Carl. I'm ready now. Let's begin."

Carl was what he was calling himself now, and he had used his power to ingratiate himself with Dr. Birnbaum—just a suggestion and a push, and Dr. Birnbaum warmed up to him. He was an attractive man with a dark complexion and sharp features, and was generally affable, so with a little push he was everyone's best friend.

Dr. Birnbaum began the test in the usual way, but he held back pushing thoughts into his mind, watching to see if anything was different. Guessing on the first few cards he answered "square," "square," and "ripples." Dr. Birnbaum's face showed no expression. He knew he couldn't wait too long before making his suggestions or else he would have to run a string together right at the end to get his forty percent, and that wasn't his usual pattern. He had no choice but to suggest.

"Card," said Dr. Birnbaum.

"Cross," he replied, and then he thought "correct" and pushed with his mind.

Dr. Birnbaum continued without response.

"Card," Dr. Birnbaum said.

"Circle," he answered and pushed again.

He let the next two cards pass without a push and then he guessed "star" and then pushed a "correct" thought at Dr. Birnbaum. No response. He finished the trials, getting his forty percent. Dr. Birnbaum thanked him and told him that would be all for today. He said his goodbyes and then left the lab and went out past the offices and into the hall. After a few minutes he retraced his steps to Dr. Birnbaum's office. The door was partly open and he could see the crossed legs of one of the graduate students. He crept close and then leaned against the wall as if he were waiting his turn to see the professor. They were talking about him.

"If he's not psychic then how's he getting them right?" one of the students asked.

"That last series was phenomenal. He matched over seventy percent. You think he was reading my face?"

"No, I'm sure of that," Dr. Birnbaum said. "You have a perfect poker face. The truth is I don't think he is getting them right," Dr. Birnbaum said.

His heart started to race. Dr. Birnbaum was on to him.

"No way. We've tested him a hundred times with ten different experimenters."

He couldn't see who was speaking and he didn't recognize the voice.

"Ever wonder why he insisted on being tested alone, and with the simplest procedure?"

"He said other minds confused him. That would be consistent with a weak ability like his," Sylvia said.

"Maybe, but it also makes it easy for him to fake it."

"You think he's cheating?" the male voice asked.

"Not in the way you're thinking. Let me show you what I did in that last session."

He could hear some rustling like Dr. Birnbaum was clearing off his desk. Then he heard the sounds of psi cards being shuffled.

"I presorted the cards before I went in."

"You stacked the decks?" Sylvia asked incredulously. "Doesn't that violate American Psychological Association standards?"

"Get serious," the other graduate student replied.

"Listen!" Dr. Birnbaum commanded. "I sorted one of the decks by symbol and then set out a pile for each symbol on the table in front of me like this." He heard the sounds of cards being moved around. "Then I shuffled the other deck and ran through the series in the normal procedure, except for one difference. This time whenever I turned a card over and concentrated I would reach out and pick up whatever card I heard him respond with and place it in a pile next to the first, and then I would record his answer as right or wrong."

"To double check?" Sylvia asked.

"Yes, but look what happened. Let's go back through the two piles and record the matches. He got forty-two percent, right? That's twenty-one matches. Sylvia, you turn over one pile, I'll turn over the other. Jack, you record the matches."

He listened as they turned over the cards and Dr. Birnbaum called out either match or no match. He knew what they would find, of course, but waited to hear it played out. When they were done Jack added up the score.

"It doesn't make sense. I get only nine matches. That's . . ."

"Eighteen percent," Sylvia finished for him.

"What happened to the forty percent?" Jack asked.

"That's the mystery, isn't it?" Dr. Birnbaum said.

He didn't like the tone of Birnbaum's voice. He sounded smug, like he knew something he was holding back.

"I still don't get it," Sylvia complained. "How'd we get it so wrong in the first place?"

There was silence for a minute and he knew Birnbaum was smiling at his graduate students. He did that a lot. He would sit with a smug smile on his face and let his students wrestle with a problem he could have easily explained to them. When he was sure they were convinced of his superiority he would explain it to them, dribbling it out in tiny morsels, like M&Ms used to reinforce children. He would be doing it to these two soon if he didn't stop him. His mind raced to think of some way to interrupt the meeting, but was distracted when the department secretary brushed past him, and leaned into Dr. Birnbaum's office.

"You've got your phone turned off again, don't you? Well, Dr. Clark called, he asked me to remind you about lunch. You're late."

"Oh yes. Sorry about the phone, but this was important. We'll have to finish this later."

The secretary turned to go and he quickly walked down the hall ahead of her. When he turned toward the exit she called out after him.

"Were you waiting to see Dr. Birnbaum?"

He flinched at the volume of her voice.

"No. Well, I was, but I'll come back after lunch."

The secretary gave him a curious look but shrugged her shoulders and headed back to her desk. He sighed with relief as he left the office complex. Outside he waited by a fir tree for Dr. Birnbaum. A few minutes later the professor came out, still talking with Sylvia. He put his coat on as he walked and then left Sylvia at the bottom of the stairs, merging into the flow of students. He fell in behind the professor, mixing with the crowd, keeping himself within striking distance.

Dr. Birnbaum headed toward High Street and the many restaurants that ringed the campus. That was good—at least better than if Dr. Birnbaum had cut across the campus to the faculty club. You couldn't cause accidents on footpaths. Dr. Birnbaum followed the path between Arps Hall and the parking garage and then turned left, following the sidewalk along High Street. The cars moved along at a good clip between traffic lights on High Street, and the situation had promise.

As Dr. Birnbaum neared the corner he ran the last few steps trying to make the walk sign so he could cross, but it switched to wait and he held back, standing on the curb waiting for the next light. *Perfect,* he thought. Now all he needed was the traffic. He came up behind Dr. Birnbaum but stayed well back, letting people fill in between them. He didn't need to be next to him, but he did need to see him to work it. Having such a limited range was one of the things he wanted to change.

The light turned green for the cross traffic and the cars began to flow past, picking up speed with each shift. The timing had to be just right. Looking left, he saw a bus coming—it would make the light at full speed. He checked Dr. Birnbaum, who was standing on the curb with his head down, staring into the street, lost in thought. It couldn't be a better setup. Sometimes if people were preoccupied, or emotional, it didn't take.

The bus was still coming, and Dr. Birnbaum still stood staring blankly into the street. A few more seconds and he would make the suggestion. Then things went wrong. The bus suddenly swerved to the side and pulled up short of the light to pick up passengers, at the same time blocking the traffic in the curb lane. He cursed to himself—the light would change soon and he would lose his chance. Then to his left he saw a red sports car with two college kids in it zoom around the bus and cut into the curb lane. He didn't hesitate. He thought hard of walking across the street, stared at the back of Dr. Birnbaum's head and pushed with his mind. Without lifting his head out of his stare, Dr. Birnbaum stepped off the curb and took two steps. He was in the middle of the lane when he shook his head clear and looked up, realizing where he was. It was too late.

The timing was perfect and the sports car was on him before the kid at the wheel could hit the brakes. Dr. Birnbaum took the impact at nearly full speed, crumpling under the car's bumper and disappearing under the wheels. The late braking locked the wheels but the car continued over the professor until he was kicked out the back. His body tumbled a few feet, leaving him nothing but a bloody pile of clothes. Screams went up from the crowd, and tires began screeching all over the intersection as bystanders rushed to Dr. Birnbaum's aid.

He watched the crowd form and then turned back toward his dorm. This meant the end of his support, of course, and they wouldn't let him keep the dorm room much longer. It didn't matter. It was time for him to move on. But to where? He was getting nowhere with the parapsychologists. Somewhere somebody must be doing research that could help him develop his abilities into more than just making suggestions.

It was a pleasant fall afternoon and he couldn't face being cooped up in his stuffy room. He decided to walk to the library. He'd found out about Dr. Birnbaum through library research;

perhaps if he broadened his search he could find a new approach. Then the flashing lights of the ambulance appeared and he watched them glide along above the heads of the crowd to stop at the scene of the accident. As the siren changed from a scream to a dying whine, he turned and walked toward the center of the campus.

2

DAPHNE

Daphne sat on the edge of her mattress, rocking back and forth, her hands held out in front of her, fingers rhythmically pounding an imaginary keyboard. She pretended to play because she was afraid—things had changed. The room looked strange. Miriam's half still had her books and knick-knacks on the walls, her dresser was still full, and pictures of her family were still hung over her dresser. Daphne's side was bare, all her possessions pulled from the shelves and drawers and packed away in boxes now neatly stacked in the middle of the floor.

Daphne didn't like change. Any change, no matter how small, sent her running inward to that sheltered hidey-hole deep in her mind. Nothing could touch her there, and that was where she was now.

Her hands soundlessly tapped out the music that could only be heard in the hidey-hole in her mind. The music filled the hole, drowning her, leaving no room for her to think about her empty room, and no thoughts meant no fear. So she played on and on, the pieces flowing together with no pauses. She would play as long as she was afraid and there was little chance of running out of music since she knew hundreds of pieces by heart.

Mrs. Williams and Barney came into the room for more of her

boxes. She didn't look up at them, staring only at their feet. They would talk about her now, as if she weren't there, or as if she were a little baby who couldn't understand their words. In a way she wasn't there, she was in her hidey-hole, but part of her remained aware of everything that went on.

"Man, she's really gone this time," Barney said. "I'm kinda sorry to see her go. She wasn't as bad as some of them. Look at her, will ya? She is really out of it! I hope they haven't sent her over the edge for good."

"Yeah, the poor kid," Mrs. Williams said. "Did you hear where she's going? They're going to use her in some kind of experiment. I wouldn't wish that on a dog."

"What? You mean like cutting her up or something?"

"No, of course not. They want to hook her up with some other mentally retarded kids. Don't ask me what for, I didn't really understand it myself."

They continued talking about her but Daphne pounded on her mental keyboard until she drowned out their voices. Mrs. Williams and Barney were nice to her, but they couldn't let her alone to order herself. When she first came to live there they had persisted in trying to reach her, but it only made it harder for her, and sometimes she would lose control of herself, the whirl-wind of thoughts that made up her mind sweeping her away. Finally, like all the others, they had stopped trying and treated her like she wasn't there. It had been like this with everyone since Grammy died—people treating her like she was a piece of the furniture. Like something to be moved around when it got in the way, and something you could talk about, since everyone knows furniture can't hear or have its feelings hurt. People didn't treat her like that when Grammy was alive.

Daphne's earliest memory was of her mother towering over her, her face contorted in rage, screaming in anger. She was sitting in a small puddle on their dirty kitchen floor. She had wet herself and now she was terrified because she knew what was coming. She wanted to get away, but she was too little to run. She re-membered rocking forward and putting her hands down to push herself to her feet. When she pushed herself up to toddle away from her screaming mother the blows began to rain down on her. The first fist knocked her out of the path of the second, but her mother's miss only made her angrier and Daphne curled into a ball to take the pounding that followed.

How old had she been? She was toddling—maybe eighteen months. Few people could remember that far back, but a special memory could be a curse. Daphne remembered the pain of those early years, as well as the shame she felt. She wasn't old enough to control her bladder yet, but she didn't know that, and she blamed herself for letting her mother down and wetting her pants. The pain faded between beatings, but the shame never left her.

Life was hard then and she lived in fear and pain; one set of bruises seldom healed before her mother bruised her again. She was hungry much of the time, her mother often forgetting to feed her. Sometimes her mother would lock her in the apartment, leaving her alone all day and night. Once she was gone for two days and Daphne drank from the toilet to stay alive. Sometimes her mother would feel guilty for neglecting her and would shower her with affection and gifts, but it never lasted—the beatings always returned.

In those years her only joys were the days spent with Grammy. Her mother would take her to Grammy and leave her for hours sometimes, and for days other times. Grammy didn't have her mother's sour smell. She smelled like the little soap flowers she kept in her tidy bathroom.

Staying with Grammy meant regular meals, plenty of good food, a warm soft bed to sleep in, stories at bedtime, and lots of hugs and kisses. Best of all Grammy loved music, and she had a piano, which she played for Daphne. At night after story time, Grammy would leave the bedroom door open and then play the piano, the music lulling Daphne to sleep. In the morning she would wake to the smell of coffee and oatmeal and hurry to her place at the kitchen table, drinking her orange juice first—she never had orange juice at home. Her oatmeal would come then, a big steaming bowlful, and then the toast would pop up to be buttered and then jellied. Grammy would hover around her, clucking her tongue over the way she wolfed her food down.

Her time with Grammy was always too short and she would cling to her when her mother came to pick her up, crying when her mother pried her from Grammy's arms. Once she was loose, her mother would jerk her by the arm, half dragging, half carrying her to the car, where she would buckle her in to her car seat, yelling at her to knock off the crying or she'd never come back. Often, when they were down the road, her mother would begin to cry, saying, "My own child doesn't love me!" Her tears would stream down her face; then she would get angry and Daphne would duck down in the car seat knowing what was coming, but when you're strapped in, there's no place to go. Soon the blows would come. On a good day one slap across the face would be enough, but on bad days her mother would stop the car to do a better job. Daphne's love of her Grammy was the source of her greatest pleasure and her greatest pain. It was those return trips where she learned to run to her hidey-hole in her mind, and pull the blackness around her, shutting out the world, and most of the pain.

The day her mother died was nothing but a big black hole in Daphne's memory. It was the hole right next to her hidey-hole. She could remember walking around the house, staying away from her mother's body in the living room. How many days did she live with the bloody corpse? She didn't know—two for sure. Her mother's boyfriend found the body when he let himself in. Daphne remembered him carrying her to the kitchen, half starved, and being given a bowl of Cheerios and milk. Daphne was still eating when the police swarmed over the apartment. Finally, a policewoman took her to a hospital, where she spent the night in a clean bed and drank pop from a straw. They gave her soup and Jell-O there—she remembered it was red Jell-O.

The police came the next day and asked her questions. "Did you see anyone? Did you hear anything?" Daphne ran to the hidey-hole every time they asked. Later they asked her to do some drawings for them, but she wouldn't pick up the crayons, her arms hanging limp at her side, her mind safe in its hidey-hole.

Grammy came then and took her home, hugging her liberally. At home she held Daphne, rocking with her for an hour. Grammy was crying and took a long time to stop. Daphne knew something bad had happened because Grammy never cried, but didn't really understand what it was. Daphne pressed her face against Grammy's chest, filling her nostrils with the kind smell of perfumed soap. When Grammy finally stopped crying Daphne asked why she was sad. "Oh, honey, don't you know your mother's dead?" Daphne did know, but she didn't think of it as sad. Grammy's tears told her she was supposed to be sad, and Daphne felt guilty. Then she started to cry—because she didn't love her mother like she should. Together Grammy and Daphne cried, one for a daughter she had loved despite her faults, the other because she couldn't love the same woman.

Daphne and Grammy settled into a comfortable life. Grammy kept her fed and changed. At first Daphne had cringed when Grammy came to her asking if she was wet, but Grammy never did anything but cluck her tongue at her. Daphne knew she was too old to be still wetting her pants, but she couldn't help herself, and for Grammy she tried her best. Daphne had been slow about other things, too. She didn't talk until she was three and then seldom. She surprised everyone when her first words came out in a complete sentence. Daphne was slow to stand, crawl, and walk, and everyone but Grammy called her "that strange little girl."

Grammy supplemented her pension by giving piano lessons and Daphne grew up with the sound of music. In the afternoons Daphne sat next to the piano while Grammy taught her students. They were wiggly children, most wishing they could be somewhere else. Their mothers would sit quietly as Grammy guided her reluctant pupils through the mysteries of the black spots in their music books.

When Daphne was little she would sit surrounded by toys with a baggie of Cheerios and a cup of juice to keep her from getting hungry. Daphne would eat the Cheerios and drink the juice but never played with the toys, not while there was music, even bad music. Music touched Daphne like nothing else could. Its rhythms penetrated deep within her, finding her soul, and Daphne rocked with the rhythm. Music made a beautiful symmetrical pattern in her brain and ordered her tangled mind. When music filled her, even the fumbling music of beginners, Daphne was consumed by the harmonies.

Music was joy to her and when the lessons ended she always suffered withdrawal, suddenly aware of the emptiness inside. Then the tangled thoughts that made up her mind would return and she would turn inward again, away from the confusion. Sometimes running all the way to her hidey-hole, but never to the dark hole next to it.

When Daphne was older Grammy tried to leave her with the TV while she gave lessons but Daphne always followed her to the music room and would sit in her spot by the piano. New students always looked at Daphne oddly at first, trying to understand the strange little girl sitting on the floor rocking like a human metronome. The parents asked about her, too, and Grammy would say proudly, "Why, that's my granddaughter," and nothing more.

On Sundays Grammy would take Daphne to church. At first Grammy tried leaving her in the nursery but the attendants were uncomfortable with Daphne. She didn't like being separated from Grammy and when left she would rock violently. Finally, the attendants told Grammy she was scaring the other children, so Grammy took her to worship with her. Grammy played the piano in the services and Daphne would sit in the front pew by the piano and rock. Daphne loved church: not only did she get to hear Grammy playing the piano but there she also discovered the organ. These rich sounds moved her in new ways and when the choir and organ joined together it was ecstasy.

Daphne's need for music grew, as did her depression when the music ended. One day it became too much for her to bear. It was a Sunday afternoon and Grammy was playing gospel on the piano. There were no music lessons on Sundays, since it was the Lord's day, but on days when it wasn't nice enough to work in her garden Grammy would spend the afternoon playing the piano with Daphne in her usual spot on the floor. It was a rainy Sunday afternoon and Grammy had not been feeling well. After only a couple of songs she put the music away and said she was going to lie down. Daphne was rocking before she was out of the room, saddened by the loss of her afternoon of music.

She tried to hold back the confusion but she wasn't strong enough. The lights in the room began to blur and blend and sounds reverberated through her head. She rocked, letting the motion serve as a poor substitute for the rhythm of the music, but today the rocking wouldn't satisfy her. Soon she was rocking violently—Daphne was losing control of herself, her mind blending into the confusion of the world around her. Her self would be lost soon, indistinguishable from the muted colors that swirled before her eyes.

Daphne closed her eyes tight but that left the soft sounds of the room and the traffic outside. These she could not distinguish from her self, and she began confusing her thoughts with the sounds. Her fear grew. She needed music to order her mind and to find herself again.

Daphne opened her eyes and was blinded by the confusing lights that flooded her mind. She closed them again and reached out for the curved leg of the piano. She thought she touched something, but colors, touch, and sound were the same. Momentarily, she felt as if she were touching green, and then she felt something wood that quickly changed to the sound of a truck rumbling in the distance. She leaned on the sound and pushed herself up, keeping her eyes closed. She kept her hands out, feeling the piano change from the sound of a truck to blue and then quickly to brown. Then the brown became wood and then ivory. She had found the keys. Quickly, before the feel of the keys could become a color, Daphne pushed down, driving the hammer into the string. The sound began in her as a color quickly coalescing into a familiar sound. Daphne could see the sound vibrating in her mind, spreading out like ripples in a pond, clearing away the confusion, but when the sound faded the confusion threatened to return. Daphne pushed the next key and pleasure spread through her again, clearing away the cobwebs. Another key and more pleasure. Soon Daphne was stepping her fingers down the ivories enjoying each sound. Up and down the scale she went in a steady rhythm. She found all the familiar notes and recorded them in her memory like old friends in an address book. When she knew each address she began bringing certain friends together. It was as easy as walking door to door in her neighborhood.

She visited her friends with one hand at first, and then used two, sending them to visit different friends at one time. Daphne had heard Grammy's students complain about how difficult it was to play and how much they hated to practice, but there was nothing but joy in Daphne as she worked the keys, trying different rhythms and different combinations. Then she hit a combination she knew. It was a bit of one of Grammy's favorite songs. She felt a new thrill. She could make music! She knew where the rest of the notes lived for the song and she visited them slowly at first and then more quickly. Then after a dozen repetitions she was playing it without error and the sounds of "Amazing Grace" filled the little house.

Daphne stood at the keyboard and played the song over and

over, enjoying the clarity that music brought to her mind. When she opened her eyes, she saw Grammy staring at her from the doorway. Daphne stopped immediately and dropped to her place on the floor, fearful some punishment might follow. She knew it was Grammy in the room but in her mind she saw her mother and she felt as if she had been caught with wet pants. Soon nothing was left but the confusion and the fear. Then she heard Grammy's voice.

"My goodness, child, you play beautifully and you're only six. Why didn't you ever play before?"

Daphne didn't answer, but she smiled. Grammy wasn't mad, she was happy!

"Would you please play some more? Can I help you?"

Daphne rocked in confusion for a minute and then stood and walked to the piano. Grammy put her hands in her armpits and lifted her onto the piano bench. Then Daphne put her hands on the keyboard and began to play. She played every day of her life after that.

Several happy years followed in Daphne's life. She and Grammy lived together in their little house. Grammy continued to give piano lessons, and Daphne would sit by the piano rocking and listening. Eventually Grammy persuaded Daphne to sit in a chair instead of on the floor, and when the lessons were done Daphne would take her place at the piano. On Sundays and Wednesday evenings Daphne and Grammy would walk to the Baptist church for services where Daphne would revel in the music of the organ and the piano and then rock silently through the sermons. On some Sunday afternoons Grammy's friends from the church would come to their house and listen to Daphne play, marveling at her ability and her repertoire of music. All of it was church music, but Grammy's friends appreciated that, too.

Music was most important to Daphne, but she enjoyed other pleasures, too. Spring and summer she and Grammy tended the flower beds and garden. Grammy grew strawberries, apricots, and plums in her yard and when the fruit was ripe Daphne would help pick it, finding a rhythm in the repetitive crop work. Grammy did the canning, giving Daphne the job of pouring the paraffin on top of the jars. There were vegetables to be harvested, and flowers to tend, and Daphne helped as best she could, wearing her own gloves, carrying her own trowel. Sometimes she would have to flee the garden for the piano, but Grammy understood and never scolded her.

Daphne came to interact with those around her a little, never volunteering anything but responding when asked. Then came a few years of special schooling, where Daphne learned to read and to do math calculations. The teachers were surprised by how quickly she learned but were disappointed by her seeming lack of initiative to use her skills. It was during her school years that they discovered her other unique ability. Daphne was a calendar calculator.

No one knew where Daphne picked up the ability and she never volunteered the information, but like most good things in her life it began with Grammy.

Grammy kept a calendar by her piano to keep track of student lessons and then later used it for figuring up how much the parents of her students owed. For years Daphne listened to Grammy figure out loud the amount owed using the dates when lessons had been given. "There was Tuesday the seventeenth, and then Thursday the nineteenth, and then that make-up lesson on the twenty-third. That was a Monday . . . no Tuesday . . . no Monday."

One evening when Grammy was lying down Daphne had paused from playing the piano and before the confusing buzz of the environment took over her mind again, Daphne began flipping through the pages of the calendar. In the back she discovered a multiyear calendar. She quickly scanned the calendar and then took her place in the chair by the piano, resting until she felt the need to play again.

The confusion attacked the fringes of her consciousness and Daphne began to rock to establish order in her mind. Then she began to play music in her mind, but for a reason she couldn't explain the dates and the days of the calendar swirled in front of her. At first she was frightened by this new confusion but soon a pattern emerged. There was a rhythm to the dates that reminded her of music. Daphne found herself ordered by the dates in much the same way that music ordered her mind. It was comforting and she played with the dates over and over, and the next time Grammy wondered if a date was a Tuesday or a

Wednesday Daphne told her. Grammy was pleased to find Daphne was correct about the dates and soon relied on Daphne to determine days and dates for her. Much to Grammy's surprise Daphne could not only tell her what dates would be Tuesdays next week, but also next year in any given month. She could also do it for the next decade or for a century in the past. Grammy was delighted with Daphne's new ability, and that made Daphne happy.

Daphne's happy years ended when Grammy suffered a stroke. Daphne knew something was wrong when Grammy didn't come in to wake her. Seven days a week, 365 days a year Grammy came in at seven to wake Daphne, but on this morning Daphne woke by herself, confused. Where was Grammy? Daphne rose and dressed, knowing something was wrong, but unable to break from routine without sending herself into a hopeless state of confusion. Daphne went to the kitchen and sat in her usual chair. The kitchen table was bare; there was no oatmeal, no coffee percolating, no glass of juice. Even more afraid now, she sat in her place at the kitchen table and rocked, trying to restore order to her thinking. *Grammy must be somewhere!* she thought. When Daphne could think clearly enough she got to her feet and walked down the hall to Grammy's door. The door creaked open slowly when she pushed on it. The curtains were still drawn and the bed unmade. There was a big lump in the middle of the covers. Daphne walked in one step at a time, pausing to rock between steps. When she reached the bed she rocked for a long time and then reached out and pulled back the covers. Grammy was lying in bed, her eyes open. Daphne cried with relief, then rocked to clear the confusion. When she could think again she realized Grammy wasn't moving.

Daphne stared into Grammy's eyes. The intelligence, the humor, and the twinkle were gone. Daphne feared Grammy was dead but then she blinked. She was alive, but why wouldn't she talk? Why wouldn't she move? Daphne pushed on Grammy's shoulder to rouse her, but Grammy only rocked gently in response. Daphne pushed harder and this time Grammy's mouth opened slightly and a little stream of spittle ran from the corner and down her chin. Daphne ran from the room and to the piano, and played. She was still playing that afternoon when the first of the schoolchildren came for lessons. Daphne stopped long enough to open the door, but then went straight back to the piano to play again. It was the puzzled mother who found Grammy.

Daphne last saw Grammy when they wheeled her out of her home on a stretcher. They took Daphne away that day, too, and she never saw their home again. She spent the next six months in the state mental hospital, where she was tested and labeled autistic. She was uncontrollable for weeks after the forced separation from Grammy, rocking violently and playing a phantom piano with her hands. She might have disappeared forever inside herself if one of the attendants at the hospital hadn't come to understand her hand movements and wheeled her to a recreation room with a piano. Daphne played for six straight hours that day, and they had to drag her away from the piano at bedtime. She got to play every day after that and the staff learned she could be coerced into cooperating by manipulating access to the piano. They released her to her first group home two months later—one with a piano.

The piano helped, but Daphne didn't adapt well to that home or the ones that followed. There was too much coming and going, too much noise, and too much visual clutter. When she wasn't playing she rocked incessantly. She was uncooperative and virtually mute to those around her, never volunteering to speak. Her only contact was through calendar calculations. The attendants always found it fascinating and it was the one way Daphne could order her mind and communicate at the same time. The wonderful rhythm of the seasons comforted her, and out of that comfort she made limited contact. It wasn't enough though, and the well-meaning social workers and psychologists tried to reach her, and the more they tried to break in the more she tried to keep them out.

They moved her to five different homes, looking for an environment she could be comfortable in. It was in the fifth home she met Ralph. Ralph was already living at the home and was the opposite of Daphne. Nothing upset Ralph and everything pleased him. Ralph was mentally retarded and his simple mind comforted Daphne. No complex thoughts or emotions came from him.

Ralph first made contact one day when Daphne was sitting at the piano. Ralph came down the hall walking toward the front door with his long strides. When he passed the living room he paused, and with two steps crossed the room to the piano. Daphne's mind was well ordered that day and when Ralph leaned over and put his face directly in front of hers to speak, she connected with him.

"I'm going for a Slurpee. You want I should bring you one? I gots enough money for two."

Daphne knew what a Slurpee was. Grammy would buy them for her occasionally in the summers. To Daphne's surprise, and to the amazement of those around her, she spoke to Ralph.

"Yes."

Ralph turned to go and then paused and turned back.

"They got two flavors, you know. This month it's Cherry Surprise or Coke. You gotta choose."

"Cherry."

"I could put some of both in. They got this handle and you get to squirt it out yourself. You just push this handle thing and it squishes out in the cup. I could get you some of both but it gets kind of yucky in the bottom. I mixed Very Very Grape and Orange once. Very yucky in the bottom."

"Cherry."

"Okeydokey."

Ralph came back with a cherry Slurpee thirty minutes later.

"Here you go. I didn't suck on it or nothing. I kept it in this hand and I kept mine in this hand. See I always hold mine in this hand. The straw's got a spoon on the other end. It makes it hard to suck out the Slurpee when it gets to the bottom. I can show you how to do it if you get stuck."

"Thanks."

Daphne and Ralph were friends from then on. Ralph walked her to meals, talked to her while she played, or just sat with her in her room. He talked incessantly, but it seemed to have the same calming effect the piano had, so the attendants encouraged it. Besides, it kept Ralph from talking to them. Daphne was happy there with Ralph until they came to tell her Grammy had died. They let her play until bedtime that day, not bothering to try and get her to eat. Even Ralph couldn't reach her that day, or the next. Only when they threatened to hospitalize her did she begin eating, and it was a week before she would do anything but play. Happiness was elusive after that, Ralph being the

                                * * *
source for what little she had.

Mrs. Williams and Barney came in and carried out the last of her
boxes. A minute later Ralph appeared at her door. He was chewing a big wad of gum. Ralph loved gum.

"Time to go, Daphne. I asked them if we could get ice cream
on the way. They said maybe. Think they'll have sprinkles? I
hope they have those pointy cones. You like those pointy cones
don't you? Sure you do. Want some gum?"

Daphne listened to Ralph prattle and let it drown out the confusion and her fear. She could think again, and when she did she
thought of what Mrs. Williams had said. "They're going to use
her in some kind of experiment." It had been explained to her,
but she didn't understand it then and she didn't understand it
now, but nothing could make her more afraid than another move.
Daphne rocked, trying to get her courage up. Ralph stood by the
door watching, talking all the while. Suddenly Ralph's face
wrinkled up into concern and he gave Daphne a worried look.

"You coming, Daphne? We might get ice cream."

Then Ralph held out his hand and smiled. Daphne stood and
took Ralph's hand. Together they walked through the door.

"I'd give you some gum, Daphne, but I chewed it all. Maybe
when we get the ice cream we can get some more gum."

3

FIRST ARRIVALS

D r. Wesley Martin was frustrated. There was a hardware problem somewhere and they couldn't link the EETs with the server, and until they solved the hardware problem they couldn't test the software, and there were always software problems. Eventually Len or Shamita would find a solution, but eventually was too long—his first savant was coming this morning.

"I think I've got it."

Wes looked up to see Shamita's former graduate student, Len Chaikin, holding up a cable. Permanently cheerful, Len had an inexhaustible supply of stupid jokes. He was also the only psychologist Wes knew who also had a degree in computer engineering.

"Wes, unscrew the lock on that cable in the back of the EET," Len said.

Wes looked at the tangled web of cables and reached out.

"No, the one below it."

Dutifully he twisted off the lock.

"What's the color band?"

"Brown, green, green."

"As the wise man said, pickles make juicy bookmarkers," Len said.

"What?"

Shamita traced a cable running to one of the empty cots. "We've got the cables reversed. It should be brown, green, red. Those damn connectors cover the last band."

Wes shook his head at the time wasted. Shamita and Len were already at work at switching the cables when Karon Wilson poked her head in the room. Karon had earned her doctorate under Wes and left a teaching job at Boston College when Wes offered her a chance to join his project.

"Ms. Foxworth is here," she said.

"With Daphne?" Wes asked, anxiously.

"She's alone. She wants to talk to you," Karon said grimly, then pulled her finger across her throat in a slicing motion.

Ms. Foxworth hated the fact that Wes had managed to get permission to use the autistic savants in his experiment. She had complained bitterly that Wes was using them like rats and that it was immoral and dehumanizing. Fortunately, those at the highest level of the Kellum Foundation were interested in his project and with every concern raised by Ms. Foxworth Wes had persuaded the foundation to counter with another benefit for the savants or their families. Ms. Foxworth had stood in his way every chance she could until she saw herself losing the battle, and then, to Wes's dismay, she convinced the foundation board that Wes's grant should carry the condition that she live at the site. Ostensibly it was to assure the safety and comfort of the savants, but Wes suspected she was there to make sure he would fail.

Wes thanked Karon but then decided to load his software while Shamita and Len finished reconnecting the EETs to the server—he wanted to establish the right relationship with Ms. Foxworth. It was his project and Ms. Foxworth needed to know that from the beginning. Fifteen minutes later he decided he'd pushed her far enough—he needed the savants.

The dining room had become their lab, the table and chairs removed to the basement. The living room connected to the dining room, where Wes expected to find Ms. Foxworth fuming on the couch. She wasn't there or in the kitchen either. Frustrated, now Wes searched for the person he had forced to wait.

He found her on the second floor, giving orders and moving furniture. She and Karon were rearranging Daphne's room. The dresser was in the hall and they were wrestling the bed from one end to the other.

"This isn't the time to be redecorating," he complained.

Karon was a small woman, no more than five feet tall with brown curly hair. Her body was unremarkable but her face was inordinately plastic and her every expression exaggerated. Karon used her face to tell him he had just put his foot in it. Even from behind he could see Ms. Foxworth's ears redden to match her hair. Ms. Foxworth was a tall slender woman who nearly matched Wes's six feet, and wore her hair closely cropped. She spun around, her face red with anger.

"Didn't you read my instructions? I told you their environment has to be as consistent with their homes as possible—especially for Daphne. You rip someone out of a stable environment to use them as a lab animal and then don't even make the least effort to minimize the trauma."

Wes tried to answer but she rushed on.

"I sent you explicit instructions on the furnishings and arrangement of Daphne's room and then just a few hours before she is to arrive I find you haven't paid the least attention."

Wes saw an opening and jumped in, ill prepared.

"We furnished this room just like you asked—"

"You purchased the items on the list and then ignored my instructions on arranging. If I didn't care about Daphne I would have let you leave the room like this and traumatize her. It would be weeks before she would be able to sit still for your experiments."

Wes had received the instructions, but irritated by them he had passed on only the purchase list to Len and Karon. Irrationally, he still blamed her for not making the importance of the room arrangement clear. Most upsetting, however, was the possibility of a six-week delay. He had hoped to run the first tests this afternoon.

"Help Dr. Wilson with that end of the bed," she ordered. "It has to be done before Daphne arrives."

Wes walked to Karon's end groping for a way to get the upper hand again. "I suggest we drop the titles—I mean if we're all going to live here it's going to get cumbersome."

Wes was serious about not using titles, but he also liked reminding Ms. Foxworth she didn't have a doctorate and no title to give up. When she didn't respond immediately Karon spoke up.

"We're pretty much on a first-name basis. I'm Karon with an *o.*"

"And I'm Wes with all the usual letters."

Ms. Foxworth stood staring at them, every second of silence more painful than the last.

"All right, I'm Elizabeth."

"Beth?" Wes asked.

"Not Beth! Not Liz! And Liza will get you a black eye!"

They finished moving the furniture, speaking only when necessary, and then helped Elizabeth carry boxes from her car. When Elizabeth began unpacking Daphne's personal belongings Wes offered to help but Elizabeth dismissed him, keeping Karon. Walking back to the lab Wes couldn't shake the feeling he had been given permission to leave.

He worked in the lab for two more hours with Shamita and Len. The cable switch had solved one problem only to reveal more, and they still had to test the liquid-nitrogen lines. Wes realized he would be lucky to get his software running by evening at this rate and wondered how late Elizabeth would let Daphne stay up. Knowing Ms. Foxworth, he realized there would be a rigid bedtime to be adhered to. Gloom settled over him.

"Wes," Karon called from the hall. "Daphne's here."

Wes's heart raced with excitement. It was going to happen—Daphne would confirm that. Wes followed the others to the porch, embarrassed by his excitement. A car pulled to a stop in front and a man got out on the driver's side—Elizabeth greeted him. Wes immediately turned back to the car, watching for Daphne, but instead another man stepped out. "Oh, hi Dr. Martin," the man said. It took Wes a few seconds to recognize Ralph.

Ralph was twenty-eight years old and a big man at six feet tall. From his broad shoulders he tapered to a narrow set of hips and then spread into two muscular legs. His body had the elements of a bodybuilder's, but it was misshappen by his posture. Ralph walked bent over with his shoulders drooping. His strides were the equivalent of two of Wes's and he swung his arms widely like a gorilla. Most unattractive of all was his face. Ralph had an overhanging brow, bushy eyebrows, and large fleshy lips, which he shaped into a protruding pucker whenever he stopped to think. Ralph had no special abilities, and the only reason he was here was because Elizabeth Foxworth had convinced the foundation that Daphne needed Ralph to make the adjustment.

Wes was still confused when he stuck out his hand. Taking it instinctively, Ralph began pumping vigorously. When he spoke he did it in a near shout.

"Nice to see ya. We stopped for ice cream. I had chocolate and lemon sherbert on a pointy cone. Had the chocolate on the bottom. I tried it on the top once but that makes the lemon yucky. Daphne had chocolate-chip mint. You know, that green stuff. I told her it tastes like Scope but she got it anyway. She always gets it. Tastes like Scope ya know!"

"Yes, Ralph, but . . ."

"Nice house," Ralph said, his eyes going wide. "Where's my room? Never mind, I'll find it." With that Ralph strode up the steps.

Wes turned to see Elizabeth Foxworth smiling at him. Wes suspected that she had wrangled to get Ralph assigned to the project just to vex him. Then Wes turned to the stranger. He had expected to see Marshall Cotton, whom Elizabeth had recruited to assist her in caring for the savants. Marshall was nearly as fanatical as Elizabeth, but he was a bit easier to warm up to. Instead of Marshall there was a stranger, a short stocky man with a dark complexion and black hair. He had sharply defined facial features and thin lips, which were curled into a smile. The man looked genial enough, but Wes took an instant dislike to him.

"Dr. Martin," Elizabeth began. "I mean Wes—this is my new assistant, Gilbert Masters."

"What happened to Marshall?"

Elizabeth frowned and softened her voice. "He was killed. Hit by a car. His wife was there, and his daughter. It was awful, I guess. Gilbert showed up a couple days later looking for work. Very fortunate, actually. He's well qualified."

Wes didn't like last-minute substitutions, and he especially didn't like personnel decisions being made without his being consulted. Wes was about to challenge Elizabeth when he saw Gilbert staring at him—Wes decided everything would be fine. After all, this would keep the project on schedule. In fact, now that he thought about it, Gilbert seemed like a nice guy. Wes stuck out his hand and welcomed him.

"Thanks, Dr. Martin. I'm excited about this project of yours."

Now Wes was dumbfounded. What had possessed Elizabeth

to hire someone who approved of what Wes was going to do?

"We're here, Daphne," Elizabeth said, reaching into the back-seat. "Are you ready to get out of the car?"

Daphne whispered back, but Wes couldn't make it out. Elizabeth turned and walked to the door of the house, seemingly forgetting about the savant.

"What about Daphne?" Wes called after her.

Ignoring him, Elizabeth called into the house for Ralph. Seconds later Ralph strode out the front door with his extra-long strides.

"Did you forget about Daphne?" she asked.

Ralph leaned back and folded his arms across his chest, resting them on his protruding stomach. His lips puckered and his brow furrowed, and then he looked lost in thought. Suddenly he straightened and hit himself in the side of the head with his palm. It was a hard blow and Wes could hear the thump.

"How could I be so stupid?" he said, then chuckled and walked to the car door. "Come on, Daphne. I saw your room. It's just like your other one. Mine's different. I like it, though. It has a window. I can see into the backyard. You want to look out my window?"

Daphne emerged from the car slowly and then stood rocking, her head down. Ralph took her arm and led her forward. Wes and Elizabeth followed. To Wes, Daphne seemed stressed, swinging her head back and forth as she walked, oblivious of everyone and everything except Ralph. They entered the house and went straight toward the stairs, but when they passed the archway leading to the living room Daphne stopped, breaking free of Ralph. Frozen in her tracks, she rocked back and forth.

Wes started forward but Elizabeth reached out, holding him back. Elizabeth pointed to Ralph, who turned back and then went into his thinking pose. Once again his hand swung up and he thumped himself on the side of his head.

"How could I be so stupid!" he nearly shouted. "Come on, Daphne."

Ralph took her arm and led her to the piano. Daphne sat, lifted the cover, closed her eyes, and began playing "Give Me That Old-Time Religion." As she played the rocking slowed to a stop. They all listened to Daphne play out the song, and then with a smooth transition she began playing "Throw Out the Lifeline."

Wes became impatient. He wanted Daphne settled into her room, still hoping they could still make a test run that night.

"How long is she going to play?" he asked.

Elizabeth's face reddened. "As long as she wants! You'll get your lab rat when I say she's ready, not before."

Embarrassed by his impatience, but angered by Elizabeth's patronizing manner, he was about to respond when Ralph interfered again.

"She'll play a long time. She plays good doesn't she? I think she does. Do you think she does? Sure you do." Ralph looked around the room briefly and then turned back to Wes. "Got any gum? No? Well, maybe I'll just run down to the Seven-Eleven. Be right back."

Ralph turned and walked out of the room. Too surprised to react at first, Wes sputtered an objection to Elizabeth.

"We can't have him walking out of here just like that."

"Why not?" Elizabeth asked.

"We're responsible for him. I mean, he's retarded—what if he gets lost?"

Suddenly Ralph reappeared and walked up to Daphne. Daphne kept playing while Ralph spoke loudly into her face.

"You want I should bring you a Slurpee?"

"Cherry."

"OK, if they got it. I know what you like if they don't got it. No grape, right?"

Ralph turned to walk out again, and Wes felt panicky. Ralph was a large man, and well muscled, and he didn't relish the idea of wrestling with him, but he couldn't just let him leave.

"Stop, Ralph!" Wes called. Ralph turned back, a smile on his face.

"You want a Slurpee, too? I can carry three. I carried five one time. I spilled one, though. It was lime."

"No, I don't want a Slurpee. Ralph, you can't walk to the Seven-Eleven."

Ralph leaned back with his arms folded on his chest, and then he pursed his lips and nodded his head, a serious look on his face.

"Why not, Dr. Martin?"

"Well, don't you think you might get lost?"

Ralph furrowed his brows into a look of deep concern. Suddenly his eyebrows shot up and his loose features reshaped into a happy face.

"No," he said, and walked out of the room.

Turning to follow him, Elizabeth caught Wes's arm.

"Let him go. He won't get lost."

"How can you say that? He just moved into the neighborhood."

"He never gets lost. You didn't read his file either, did you?"

"I read part of it," Wes replied lamely.

"The part about his cognitive abilities I bet. You can't see past your own twisted experiments. You got the savants on the condition that their needs are taken care of. That means more than just feeding them. Daphne needs to play, so she has the piano. Ralph needs to walk, so let him walk. He won't get lost."

Wes was about to protest but Ralph reappeared. He walked straight to Wes and then stopped. Unnerved by his size and the serious look on his face, Wes shifted nervously from foot to foot. Suddenly Ralph's hand shot out and swung up. Wes flinched but Ralph thumped himself on the side of his head.

"How could I be so stupid? I don't have any money. You got a couple of bucks?"

Elizabeth snickered while Wes sighed with relief and pulled two dollars from his wallet. Ralph took the money and left. Wes and Elizabeth followed him to the door and watched him stride down the street.

"I hope we see him again," Wes said. "Does he have to hit himself in the head and call himself stupid? I wouldn't want someone to think we call him that."

"Worried about your funding?"

Wes hadn't thought of it that way and he was irritated Elizabeth wouldn't give him any credit for having a human side.

"He learned it from his father," she continued. "I think it's cute. Don't worry, I know no one here called him stupid."

Wes took that as a peace offering. If he or his people screwed up, Elizabeth would be on the phone to the foundation immediately, but it was reassuring to know she wouldn't lie to stop the project. Still, Wes worried. If anything happened to Ralph his project would come to an end before it ever got off the ground. The piano music ended, then was quickly followed by "Amazing

Grace." "One walks and one plays! What's next?" he asked absentmindedly.

"Read my reports," Elizabeth said. "You've got some surprises coming."

Unable to imagine what else could happen, Wes stood quietly watching Ralph stride out of sight.

4

TEST RUN

After Dr. Birnbaum's accident he had immersed himself in the library stacks, combing the parapsychology literature. There were the usual reports of investigations into various telekinetic powers, but even the most promising of the reports indicated only subjects with mediocre talent. Only interested in his own abilities, Gil skimmed the reports quickly, exhausting the recent literature. Then he began searching in peripheral areas.

He started with hypnosis, which showed some promise. There was documented evidence of people who were able to eliminate pain through hypnotic suggestion. Childbirth without pain was possible, and even surgery. Appendectomies had been performed using only hypnosis for anesthesia, and even amputations. Of more interest were the reports that some subjects were able to increase physical strength during hypnotic trances, as much as fifty percent. But Gil wasn't interested in physical strength and there were no reports of the technique used with talents like his. The research on hypnotically enhanced concentration intrigued him more.

Under a trance some subjects showed remarkable gains in memory capacity. Gil toyed with the idea of undergoing hypnosis but finally decided he couldn't risk it. Being hypnotized meant giving up control over your consciousness, and he had too many secrets. Gil spent some time with the research in virtual reality but ultimately dismissed it as nothing more than a glorified computer game. The mind-altering-drug research was promising but frightening and he never seriously considered it.

Gil was reading the research on cognitive focusing when he found his lead. Cognitive focusing used a combination of relaxation training and meditation to eliminate sensory distractions and allow one to focus on a single ability. Gil had practiced this informally for years, but these researchers were using sophisticated biofeedback equipment to achieve remarkable levels of concentration. Gil was just finishing an article on the topic when he turned two pages by mistake. His eyes landed on the title of the next article: "Enhanced Intelligence Through Computer-Enhanced Epiphenomena." The Dr. Wesley Martin who had authored the piece was not part of the parapsychology field—Gil knew that field well. The research described in the article excited him as nothing else had.

He bought a plane ticket to Oregon after visiting five ATMs and suggesting that customers forget to take their money. Gil ate dinner at the airport while waiting for his flight and then picked up a *Columbus Dispatch* to read on the plane. An hour after they were in the air, Gil discovered that Dr. Birnbaum had survived. He was in a coma and had lost one leg and an arm, but he was still alive. Gil was uncomfortable leaving unfinished business in a hospital bed, but reasoned it was more dangerous to return. Besides, he rationalized, Dr. Birnbaum's new handicaps would preoccupy him for years.

Now Gil found himself lying on his bed, pleased with his progress. He was part of the project now, and trusted by the others. They would try Daphne on the machine tonight, and soon they would be linking her with the others. He needed a way into that link. If he had to he would use his ability, but it was difficult to manipulate groups, and it was reckless—he couldn't risk detection. He would watch, and wait for an opening. Only if it didn't come on its own would he make one.

Karon tapped at his door and announced it was time for the test run. Gil's pulse raced. He felt closer to mastering his power than he ever had before and was determined to let nothing get in his way.

"Everything's set. Elizabeth wants you to help bring Daphne down."

Gil smiled in an ingratiating way and followed Karon out the door. Elizabeth was waiting by Daphne's door. Ralph was there too, chewing a big wad of gum.

"OK, Gil, you and Ralph bring her downstairs." As Gil passed Elizabeth, she added, "Work your magic on her."

Gil had suggested trust and friendship to Daphne whenever they were alone, and over the last week she had come to depend on Gil, thus guaranteeing him a role in the project.

Daphne was on her bed rocking back and forth.

"Daphne, do you remember what we talked about? The experiment? It's time now, Daphne."

"No."

Daphne rocked harder. Ralph bent to look in her face.

"I'll bet they'll give us ice cream if you do this. Could be chocolate-chip mint, ya know."

"I don't want to, Ralph."

"Well okeydokey then," Ralph said.

"No Ralph, it's not okeydokey," Gil snapped, cursing himself silently for losing his temper. Closing his eyes, he cleared his mind of anger, and then said quietly, "It's important for Daphne to do this, Ralph. Isn't it, Daphne?"

"No."

Gil feared Elizabeth would soon take over if he didn't quickly get Daphne's cooperation. Only Ralph was in the room so he decided to risk using his ability. Gil thought of trusting himself and then stared at Daphne and gave a push. As soon as he pushed, Ralph spoke up.

"Yeah, trust Gil."

Gil was confused—had Ralph received the push by mistake?

"Daphne, you trust me, don't you?" Gil asked.

"Yes."

Gil pictured Daphne cooperating with Dr. Martin in the experiment and pushed. Again Ralph spoke up.

"Yeah, you want to try the speriment, don't you."

Gil looked at Ralph but saw nothing but his big stupid grin. Feeling anxious, he studied Ralph—his comments were just too similar to his pushes to be coincidence.

"Let's go try it, Daphne," Gil said.

"Yeah, let's go. Maybe we'll get ice cream."

Daphne hesitated, but when Gil gently took her arm she stood and walked with him to the door. Elizabeth smiled at Gil as he led Daphne down the stairs. Gil smiled back, hiding his concern about Ralph.

Wes Martin was waiting downstairs like an expectant father. Daphne hesitated when they entered the converted dining room, but Gil pulled her along. Once on the cot, she began to rock again. Then Wes approached, picking up an EET cap.

"Remember this, Daphne?" he asked, holding up the array, which resembled a bicyclist's helmet with wires poking out all over the top. "You tried this on for us before."

"I tried it on, too," Ralph said loudly.

Elizabeth put her finger to her lips and then took Ralph's arm and pulled him to one side. Then she pulled a pack of gum out of her pocket and handed it to Ralph.

"Juicy Fruit," Ralph said, and busied himself with opening the gum.

With Ralph temporarily occupied Wes turned back to Daphne with the scalp array. Daphne kept rocking but didn't resist when they fitted it to her head. Shamita and Len were glued to their monitors. Len's thumb came up but Shamita shook her head and wiggled her hand back and forth. Wes pushed the scalp array down a little farther and then turned back. A minute later Len's thumb came up and a few seconds later Shamita nodded approval. Wes smiled and then turned back to Daphne, picking up an electrode. Then, embarrassed, he waved Karon over, and she attached two electrodes inside Daphne's blouse.

"Daphne, would you please lie down?" Wes asked.

Daphne remained upright and her hands came up and began to play.

Wes's face wrinkled with concern, but quickly Gil stepped forward and put his hand on Daphne's arm.

"Daphne, you trust me, don't you. Please lie down. You can keep playing."

Daphne didn't move, but when Gil pushed gently on her arm she lay down. Then Gil motioned for Wes to take her legs and lift. Daphne's hands remained in the air, playing in silent fury.

"Dr. Martin—I mean Wes. Do you want me to get her to stop playing?" Gil asked.

Wes spoke over his shoulder as he walked to his monitor. "No, it won't matter."

Wes went to work on his terminal and began tapping away while Len and Shamita worked at their own. Karon leaned over Len, her hand on his shoulder, pointing occasionally at the screen. After a few minutes of typing Len spoke.

"Liquid-nitrogen pressure is stable at one atmosphere, super-chips are fifty-seven degrees Kelvin. The computer memory is superconducting. Physiological readings are nominal—her heart's beating like a hummingbird's but it's not dangerous. We're ready here, Kemosabe."

"Not yet," Shamita replied. Then, a minute later: "OK, I'm set to intercept. Whenever you're ready, Wes."

"Right. Relax her, Shamita."

Shamita hit a single key and Daphne's hands stopped playing and slowly sank to her sides. Elizabeth stepped forward, worry on her face.

"What did you do to her?"

"Nothing harmful, Elizabeth," Wes replied. "We've just re-routed her brain waves through the computer."

Elizabeth looked skeptical. "Why did she stop playing?"

"We've selected out psychomotor functions," he said casually.

"What?" Elizabeth asked in exasperation.

"We relaxed her," Len cut in.

The sound of tapping could be heard at Shamita's keyboard. Then Shamita, seemingly oblivious of what had been happening, turned to Wes.

"I'm reading occipital, parietal, prefrontal, the works. It's all routed except the psychomotor. You want me to filter sensory input?"

"Take it down slowly to fifty percent and then hold," Wes responded.

Elizabeth was eyeing Wes suspiciously, making him uncomfortable.

"All we're doing is filtering out the sights and sounds around her," he said defensively. "It's like using a dimmer switch to turn down the lights a little."

"You're robbing her of awareness."

"It's like falling asleep."

"It's unnatural."

Wes gave up. Elizabeth wasn't going to be mollified.

Elizabeth walked over to Daphne and looked down into her face and then turned to Wes.

"People don't sleep with their eyes open."

"I said it was like falling asleep, not exactly the same thing."

"It's like being paralyzed," Elizabeth said, her voice trembling slightly. "It must be horrible."

"Fifty percent, Wes," Shamita said. "She's a beautiful subject. Look at those alpha waves. Almost no spindles. I'm ready to map her. How about you, Len?"

"I was born ready, Shamita."

"What do you mean, map her?" Elizabeth asked suspiciously.

"We need to map out her cognitive functions, and especially localize her calendar-counting ability. Once it's mapped we can select it out."

"Abilities like that aren't localized," Elizabeth said. "It must take the entire cortex to solve those problems."

Elizabeth spoke with authority and Wes realized she had been reading up on brain function. "That's true," he explained. "Most of the cortex is involved, but only peripherally. Key processing functions are highly localized along well-defined neural pathways. We'll select out those pathways."

"You can't eliminate the role of the rest of the cortex."

Wes turned to Elizabeth, unsure of what to say. He was used to her opposition based on humanitarian grounds, but now she seemed to be attacking the scientific basis of his work.

"We've experimented with this, Elizabeth. Any cortex can play a support role as long as its dominance is compatible with the donor cortex."

Elizabeth looked satisfied, but Wes didn't know her well enough to be sure he could read her expressions.

"All right, let's map her . . . I mean map Daphne."

Wes had to constantly fight the tendency to lose himself in his work and to forget he was working with human subjects. Wes made eye contact with Len and Shamita to make sure they were ready and then stood by Daphne's head. Elizabeth moved to the other side and Gil came to stand behind her. Gil's expression was easier to read than Elizabeth's. He was eager.

"Daphne," Wes said gently. "Can you hear me?"

"Yes," she replied softly.

"How do you feel?"

Daphne gave no response, briefly worrying Wes, so he hurried on.

"You feel sleepy, don't you?"

"Yes, sleepy."

Wes wanted to rush into the calendar problems but felt Elizabeth's presence and decided to take extra steps to reassure her.

"Daphne, are you afraid?"

"I'm sleepy."

"You're not scared, are you?"

"No, I'm not scared."

Sure he had satisfied Elizabeth, Wes tried to move on but Elizabeth stopped him.

"Daphne, this is Elizabeth. Do you know where you are?"

"I'm sleepy."

"Do you know who I am, Daphne?"

"I'm sleepy."

"Do you know who I am, Daphne?"

Daphne gave no response and with every second of silence the tension grew. Daphne's answers to Wes's questions made perfect sense but her response to Elizabeth's made her seem disoriented. The look on Elizabeth's face told Wes a storm was coming and he was looking desperately for relief when Ralph distracted Elizabeth.

"I think she went to sleep. Didn't you, Daphne? You went to sleep, huh?"

"Yes," Daphne replied. "I went to sleep."

"See," Ralph said, "she's asleep."

Wes wanted to point out that a sleeping person does not respond to questions, but Len interrupted with another of his stupid jokes.

"Reminds me of the man who went to a talent agency claiming he had a talking dog. The agent said let me hear him. The man asks his dog 'What covers a house?' and the dog says 'Roof.' Then the man asks 'What covers the outside of a tree?' and the dog says 'Bark.' Then the man asks how the ride was over to the agent's office. 'Ruff,' says the dog. The agent throws the man and his dog into the street, where the dog gets up, brushes himself off, and says 'Maybe I should have said bumpity?' "

"Len, be serious," Wes scolded.

"I was. If you think about it, the agent didn't know the dog could talk because the questions could all be answered with dog sounds. We're guilty of the same thing. We believed a reduction in sensory input would mimic falling asleep so all our questions asked if that was what she was feeling. We confirmed our hypothesis rather than looking to disconfirm it. To tell you the truth, Daphne seems disoriented to me."

Len was right. Wes wanted his subjects to be in a harmless state similar to sleep and sure enough he had found what he was looking for. Wes felt naked, like the emperor wearing his new clothes. He hadn't done his homework and now Elizabeth could move in and seriously damage his project. But to Wes's surprise she didn't.

"Len, you're partially right, but I don't think Daphne's disoriented," Elizabeth said. "Just the opposite, actually. She seems highly focused and suggestible. Let me try something. Daphne, you're afraid, aren't you?"

"Yes, I'm afraid."

"Daphne, you're happy, aren't you?"

"Yes, I'm happy."

Everyone except Elizabeth was surprised by Daphne's responses.

"I feel the same way, Daphne," Ralph said. "Kinda happy, angry, sleepy. Maybe some sad, too. Do you feel sad, Daphne?"

"I feel happy."

Wes was surprised by Daphne's answer. "If she feels all those other ways, why doesn't she feel sad?" Wes asked, looking to Elizabeth, who had suddenly become the expert on Wes's experiment.

"You feel sad, don't you Daphne?" Elizabeth asked.

"Yes, I feel sad."

"Oh, I get it," Shamita said.

"Me, too," Karon echoed.

Wes looked to Len, who shook his head knowingly. Wes hated being the only one besides Ralph who didn't know what was going on. "Someone want to let me in on this?" To Wes's annoyance his team turned to Elizabeth, waiting for her.

"Daphne is in a highly suggestible state. When you asked her if she was sleepy you actually suggested to her she was sleepy. I then suggested she was afraid, and she responded she was. In this state Daphne will feel whatever it is you want her to feel. Somehow you've electronically mimicked a hypnotic trance."

"Let's tell her she's a chicken," Ralph suggested, a big grin on his face. "We can make her walk around and cluck and stuff." Ralph put his hands in his armpits when he said it and flapped his elbows up and down.

"No!" Wes said in a near shout.

"We might want to think about that," Len said seriously. Then, when Wes turned and gave him a puzzled look, he added, "We could use the eggs."

Karon laughed but Wes's glare shriveled Len in his chair and Karon covered her mouth. Turning back to Elizabeth, Wes was ready to apologize, but hesitated when he saw a trace of a grin.

"Elizabeth, I . . ." he began.

"Wes, I think it's all right to continue."

It sounded like Elizabeth was giving him permission—again Elizabeth had maneuvered herself into a position of authority.

"You might want to think about what this does to your project," she continued.

Wes was already thinking about it and resented being told to do what he was already doing. His initial analysis suggested it wouldn't make any difference. If anything the similarity to a hypnotic trance could be helpful since to blend several minds into one new mind he needed to shut down certain mental functions in the different brains involved. He planned to do it electronically, but if it could be enhanced hypnotically, so much the better. Wes decided to paper over his anger at Elizabeth and turned back to Daphne.

"Daphne, you're not afraid," he suggested. "You feel fine. You feel relaxed. Now, Daphne, how do you feel?"

"I feel relaxed."

Relieved, Wes returned to his console, and waved Karon forward. She stood in front of Daphne with a set of cards. Each card had a different black-and-white geometric pattern on it. Karon held them up one at a time, waiting until Shamita signaled for the next card. Slowly, Karon showed the entire deck to Daphne. When they began the series again, Elizabeth moved close to Wes.

"What's this about?"

"Well it's kind of complex to explain. . . ."

Elizabeth glared at him.

"We're mapping the visual cortex."

"How can you map a billion neurons?"

"We can't—no one could—and we don't need to. We function at a macro level, not micro. Each of the patterns she is looking at triggers millions of neurons. Fortunately, the neurons make it easier for us by multiplexing. It's a process similar to the way FM radio broadcasts." Elizabeth looked puzzled, so he elaborated.

"Originally it was believed brain neurons functioned in a hierarchical fashion. A single neuron might respond to the angle of a line, another neuron to the line's width, a third to light and dark, and so on. These bits of information would then be passed on, combining to trigger a complex cell. A number of complex cells would combine to trigger hypercomplex cells, and so on. A neat theory, but you were right about the neural activity. Whenever your visual field is active nearly every neuron is firing, all the time. There's no evidence of a hierarchy."

Wes paused when Karon switched to using a tape recorder to map the auditory cortex. Elizabeth was waiting expectantly when he looked back.

"Mapping neural hierarchies proved impossible, but we had better luck with the FM theory. In order to broadcast stereo, frequency-modulated radio combines several waves into a compound wave that can carry more information than the individual waves—it's called multiplexing. The signal is split again at the receiver back into the original waves. The cortex functions in much the same way by compounding signals, and then compounding the compounds—that's multiplexing. We intercept the multiplexed signals and reroute them through fiber-optic lines to the corresponding hemispheric locale in the receiving cortex."

Elizabeth looked thoughtful. "Wouldn't those signals make sense only to the donor mind?"

"There are slight location differences, but we let the receiving brain decide how to split the multiplexed wave. So far every individual we've tested has been able to make sense of the signal if we send it at the multiplexed level."

"Mental telepathy?"

"It's real science," he said defensively.

"Don't get upset. I'm just saying it mimics mental telepathy. But it seems so slow—I mean routing it through the computer and then to another person."

"The signal is routed through the cryogenic computer so we can monitor the brain waves in each donor and reroute signals as we choose. We use the liquid nitrogen to supercool our CPU and the fiber-optic lines. The superconducting chip processes the information faster than the brain itself, which allows us to keep up with the multiplexed brainwaves. Actually neurons fire rather slowly, through a clumsy electrochemical process involving the diffusion of sodium ions across a semipermeable membrane. The distance of the transmission is microscopic so we usually don't notice the slow rate except on a macro level like with reaction times. It can take a quarter of a second to pull your finger off of a hot iron, and that's much slower than our system processes. The light-wave transmission through the supercooled fiber optics is a hundred times faster than that of the neurons—the speed of light, actually. As long as we keep the length of the transmission lines short enough, and we work at a multiplexed level, it works."

Karon had finished with the tapes and was working through the tactile series, poking and prodding Daphne. It was a short series, and she soon finished, Shamita signaling success.

"Looks good, Wes," Shamita said. "She's nominal all the way."

"Great. I'll give her the problems." Wes picked up a yellow pad and stood by Daphne's head. "Daphne, I want to ask you to solve a few date problems for me. You've done these many times before. Are you ready?"

"Yes."

"On what day will July thirteenth fall in 2017?"

Daphne's reply was nearly instantaneous.

"Thursday."

Wes checked the answer on his pad. She was correct. Wes felt relief—it was working.

"What would be the date of the third Thursday in June 1803?"

"The sixteenth," Daphne replied after a few seconds.

"New Year's Day in 1939 fell on what day?"

"Sunday."

All of Daphne's answers were correct. Wes looked at Len and

Shamita. Len was staring at his screen with Karon leaning on his shoulders. Karon looked up and gave a thumbs-up sign. Shamita rocked her hand back and forth in a motion that said "so far so good." Wes returned to his questions.

"On what day would the second Tuesday in February 1901 fall?"

"The twelfth."

"November fifteenth in 2044 would be on what day of the week?"

"Tuesday."

"What year would be the first leap year after 2050?"

"Twenty fifty-two."

Wes ran through his list of questions and Daphne continued to answer correctly, compensating for leap years and never hesitating more than a few seconds. When Wes got a sign from Shamita that she was satisfied with her map, Wes flipped back a few pages in his pad to his special questions. "Daphne, what date would be the fifth Thursday in November 1854?"

"The thirtieth."

"Daphne, what date would be the fifth Thursday in November 1873?"

"There is no fifth Thursday in November 1873."

Wes was pleased. Daphne had instantly recognized his trick question and responded correctly. Wes next tried a new type of question.

"How many Mondays were there in 1826?"

Daphne paused after the question, her eyes flicking back and forth. Then after about twenty seconds she responded.

"Fifty-two."

"What was the first year after 1950 that had more than fifty-two Mondays?"

"1951."

As far as Wes knew, no one had ever asked Daphne to sum the number of particular weekdays occurring in a particular year. Most people wanted to know what day of the week their birthday would fall on in some future year, or what day of the week a holiday like Christmas occurred in the year they were born. When faced with a new type of question Daphne had paused far longer than normal but then responded with her usual accuracy. From then on whenever asked that type of question Daphne never had to pause more than a few seconds. Wes suspected Daphne had taken the time to construct an algorithm to solve the new type of problem.

Wes turned back to his team and got nods or thumbs-up signs from them all, and then they looked at him expectantly. They were ready for the next phase and were waiting for Wes to suggest it. Unfortunately, it required Elizabeth's cooperation. Wes tried to frame his proposal in a diplomatic way.

"Elizabeth, we want to try the next step—just to see if the equipment works. We want to try combining more than one mind. What I mean is we want you and Ralph to volunteer to have your minds combined with Daphne's."

Elizabeth stared at him long and hard before responding. "You want me to submit to an experiment where you can electronically manipulate me into a hypnotic state where I'm susceptible to your suggestions?"

"You make it sound like I have some evil purpose in mind."

"Machiavellian, not evil."

"What is it you think I would do to you?"

"I can think of several possibilities. How about planting a posthypnotic suggestion so when I wake I find myself an ardent supporter of this project."

"Do you really think I would do that?"

"I think you believe very strongly in your work and see me as a threat to your funding."

Wes couldn't tell if Elizabeth really thought he might do something to her, or whether she was simply afraid of something she didn't understand.

"I'd be willing to stand in," Gil interrupted. "Elizabeth's the one who'll get blamed if something happens to Ralph or Daphne. I should be the one to go under, or whatever is the right way to put it."

Uncertain, Wes hesitated. There was something about Gil that bothered him—he was too likable. Everyone seemed to take to him instantly, and Wes didn't believe anyone was that agreeable. Suddenly, he changed his mind. "It's a good idea. Thanks, Gil."

"Yeah," Ralph added. "I think it's a good idea, too, Gil."

Wes watched Gil jerk around to stare at Ralph, then quickly turn back to Wes. Something was going on between them, he realized, but at the moment Wes's experiment was all he cared about.

"Ralph, we can do this with two, but it would be a better test if we had three people. Would you be willing to help us?" Wes asked. "You just have to lie there like Daphne."

Ralph's big smile suddenly dropped into a frown and his eyebrows furrowed. Folding his arms across his chest, he leaned back, thinking long and hard, puckering his fleshy lips. Then in a very serious tone he said, "I dunno. I might be hungry when I get done."

"Wes will buy ice cream when we're done, won't you, Wes?" Elizabeth said.

"Yes. Two scoops. Waffle cones. Whatever you want."

Ralph's expression suddenly changed from a frown to his usual oversized grin. "Well okeydokey then." Smiling, and chewing his wad of gum openmouthed, Ralph stood, swinging his head back and forth.

Pushed into position by Daphne, two cots were angled so the participants' heads would be next to each other. Gil took the middle cot and Len began fitting him with a scalp array. Ralph remained by the wall, grinning and swinging his head. Wes waved him forward but he just stared back blankly.

"Ralph, you need to lie down like Gil and Daphne."

He looked back and forth several times and then suddenly his hand shot out and up and he thumped himself in the head. "How could I be so stupid?" he said, taking three oversized steps and plopping onto the cot. "Can you chew gum and do this?" he asked loudly.

"Not a good idea, Ralph," Len said.

"Okeydokey."

Ralph took the wad of gum out of his mouth and then looked up at the ceiling. When Len followed his stare, Ralph reached under the cot and put the gum on the bottom. It irritated Wes, but he said nothing, making a mental note to have Elizabeth talk with Ralph about his gum-disposal habits. Len fit an array to Ralph and then returned to his monitor. Wes's team bent to their monitors. While they worked Ralph talked.

"Let's go to the Dairy Queen. I want to get a dip cone. Does a dip count as two scoops? I think it should. A dip cone costs less than a double dip at the thirty-two flavors. I like the cherry dip.

Daphne doesn't, though. Daphne likes the chocolate dip. I like
the chocolate dip, too, but I like the cherry dip better. I don't like
the butterscotch dip, do you? Huh? Are you busy, Wes?"

"Yes, I am. Please look at the pictures Karon is holding up."

"Sure, sure. Is it like one of them tests the head doctors do? I
can see a butterfly in that one."

Wes punched up Shamita's display on his monitor, worried
that Ralph's chatter would interfere with the mapping. After several cards, blue lines began multiplying on his display, indicating that the multiplexed waves were being identified and
localized. After what seemed to be an eternity of Ralph's prattle, Wes could stand it no more. "Shamita, is he mapped?" Wes
asked, and then made a slicing motion with his hand. Shamita
waved him off and typed on her keyboard. Wes tried concentrating on setting the program parameters based on the feed he
was receiving on his volunteers, but Ralph's chatter cut through.

"I had a dip cone at Frosty Freeze one time. It was yucky.
They only had chocolate dip. I never got a dip there again. I never
ate there again. I ate a cherry dip at another Dairy Queen one time
that tasted different. I thought all Dairy Queens tasted the same.
Their hot dogs taste different, too. Their hamburgers—"

Suddenly Ralph was silent. Wes looked over at Ralph, who
was now lying quietly on the cot. Shamita flashed him a smile
and wiggled her eyebrows. Wes mouthed a thank-you to
Shamita, then called up a color simulation of Ralph's cortical activity from Shamita's computer. As he expected, there was nothing unusual in his brain-wave activity. That was one of the many
mysteries of the brain. Ralph was mentally retarded, with a func-
tional IQ of sixty, but his brain-wave activity couldn't be distinguished from that of Einstein. Daphne, who was a genius in
music and some math computations, didn't show any particular
differences in brain activity from that of Ralph, or anyone else.
Dozens of researchers had searched for decades for some difference, but had never found any.

Wes reduced the screen window showing Ralph's brain waves
and pulled up Gil's. Wes watched the wave activity with his
practiced eye, but saw nothing peculiar. He felt a presence behind him and turned his head, catching Elizabeth in his peripheral vision. She was standing a few feet behind him, watching
the screen. He knew she was interested, but he suspected she

wouldn't give him the satisfaction of asking for an explanation. Karon was just beginning the deck of visual patterns with Gil, so Wes took the time to explain to Elizabeth.

"Let me show you what we're doing."

Elizabeth came a step closer.

"This screen shows Daphne's brain-wave activity. Here, let me make the image bigger."

Wes doubled the image size and the top view of Daphne's walnut-shaped cortex expanded. Then Wes expanded each of the other views until the three images were side by side. In all three images waves of color washed over the cortexes, expanding from dots to flood large sections of both the left and right cortex, only to be replaced by new waves of color.

"What do the colors indicate?"

"In this mode you're looking at electrical activity. This is essentially an EEG; an electroencephalograph that's been computer enhanced and color-coded."

"I don't see the corpus callosum—where the brain waves spread from one cortex to the next."

"It's deep between the two hemispheres. Here . . ." Wes pointed between the two halves of the walnut shape on the screen. "I can get you a view if you want."

"Maybe later. What you're showing is electromagnetic activity, but there's more going on than just that."

"Right. Here, I'll show you another mode." Wes typed on his keyboard and the image on the screen changed from waves of color to glowing splotches. Most of the brain glowed green, blue, or yellow, but here and there were spots of brown or deep red.

"This is an infrared image. We're measuring the heat content of different regions of the brain," Wes explained. "Red areas are the warmest regions. When an area of the brain is active, the blood flow increases, and it shows as red. That's one way we can tell which regions carry out which functions. Here, I'll show you what we're doing with Daphne. Len! Ask Daphne some calendar questions for me, will you?"

Wes used the computer's mouse to click on the brain labeled DAPHNE and it expanded to fill the entire screen. Another click and the image split in two, providing a separate view of the right and left hemispheres.

"All right, Len, ask. Now, watch the monitor, Elizabeth."

As soon as Len began asking the questions the whole brain changed in color, from bluish green to green and yellow, and here and there new patches of red and brown appeared.

"Notice the red here in the frontal regions, and here in the parietal," Wes said, pointing at the left hemisphere. "Three major centers, and two minor."

"What about the right hemisphere?" Elizabeth asked. "There's not much activity there."

"Calendar counting is primarily a left function; it's based on verbal skills. If these questions were spatial questions—like having her move chess pieces around in her mind—then the right hemisphere might activate."

"I would have guessed she was solving these problems visually. I pictured her rapidly flipping through the pages of a calendar and looking up the dates."

"Really," Wes said in real surprise. "I never thought of it that way. But if she was I would think you would see the right hemisphere working more than it is."

"Maybe," Elizabeth replied. "But you're assuming Daphne's brain has divided functions between hemispheres like other people. What makes her a savant could be having both functions in the same hemisphere."

Wes turned and looked up at Elizabeth, who was towering over him. Wes wanted to see Elizabeth's expression, to see if she was genuine in her speculation or just trying to needle him. Wes saw no guile in her, only sincere interest.

"That's a creative idea," he conceded. "But we've already mapped her, and her hemisphere functions are virtually identical to the norm. Also, remember we enter at a macro level, so unless she rejects the multiplexed waves we send her from the others, her brain will split them into recognizable signals just as other brains do."

Karon finished with Gil, and Len and Shamita indicated they were done mapping the two new volunteers. Wes pulled up the displays of Gil and Ralph, adding them to Daphne's brain-wave activity. Each display had the person's name below it. Next a blank fourth display appeared with the name Frankie below.

"Frankie?" Elizabeth prompted.

"Len's idea." Wes explained. "It's short for Frankenstein. He says our project reminds him of Dr. Frankenstein piecing together body parts to make a whole person. Except our work is cleaner, we're piecing minds together, and we're not working with dead people."

"I see."

Wes detected a note of disapproval in Elizabeth's voice.

"OK, I'm ready," Wes said to his team. "Let's use Gil's pattern as the matrix and overlay Daphne and Ralph."

"Whose verbal center do you want to use? I can connect Ralph up if you want," Shamita said.

"Don't you dare turn him back on!" Wes said in a near shout. Shamita smiled but didn't look up from her monitor. Len started to say something, but Wes cut him off.

"I don't want to hear it, Len," Wes said.

Len acted the shocked innocent, but kept quiet.

"Let's use Gil for verbal," Wes continued. "We want to be sure we're getting integration."

Wes typed in instructions and then used the mouse to select the blank Frankie square. As he typed, the blank square filled with brain waves, colors sweeping back and forth.

"That's Gil," Wes said. "You can see the two displays are the same." Wes pointed at Gil's display and then at the new display below. "Now, here comes Daphne's contribution." Wes typed some more and then used the mouse to click on the Frankie display. The wave pattern changed. "You can see this pattern is different from Gil's and not exactly Daphne's either. Now we add Ralph." Then in a louder voice the others could hear he said, "Let's give Frankie Ralph's sensory input."

"No output from Ralph?" Karon asked, a big smile on her face.

"None," Wes snapped back.

The Frankie display changed again.

"Does everything look good to you?" Wes asked. After everyone indicated agreement, Wes turned to Elizabeth. "Take my yellow pad and go ask Ralph a calendar question."

"Ralph?"

"Yes. He's input."

Elizabeth picked up the pad and walked over to Ralph's cot, standing by his head, her back to Daphne.

"Ralph, can you hear me?"

There was no reply. Before Elizabeth could repeat the question Wes stopped her.

"You're not really talking to Ralph, or Daphne, or Gil, for that matter. It's Frankie, remember."

"Should I call him Frankie?"

"There's not enough of a mix here for that. It's still mostly Gil. Don't call him anything, just ask the question."

Wes could tell Elizabeth didn't like depersonalizing the volunteers, but she went along.

"Was 1492 a leap year?"

There was no response.

"Wait a minute, Elizabeth," Wes said. "Shamita, expand the parameters on verbal. Are you getting all of Broca's area?"

Shamita typed furiously for a minute, then nodded to Wes.

"OK, good. Try it again, Elizabeth."

"Was 1492 a leap year?"

"Yes," came the reply from Gil's mouth.

Elizabeth spun around and looked at Gil in surprise. "That's weird," Elizabeth said.

"You think that's weird," Len said. "If you kiss Daphne, and blow in Ralph's ear, Gil will get an erection."

Karon snickered, but Wes hung his head in embarrassment. "Ignore Len, Elizabeth, we all do. Ask another question."

Elizabeth turned back to Ralph and then bent and whispered in Ralph's ear. Wes understood. She couldn't quite believe that one person could hear the question, a second solve the problem, and a third give the answer. Whispering in Ralph's ear was a simple test. While she was whispering Wes heard Len say to Karon, "She's actually blowing in Ralph's ear."

As soon as Elizabeth finished, Gil said, "Sunday." Elizabeth looked down at the pad and then nodded her head. Wes smiled. Elizabeth whispered more questions, and each time Gil answered correctly. When Elizabeth had satisfied herself it wasn't some kind of trick, she stood up and nodded at Wes, who took it as sign of respect.

"OK, let's shut it down," Wes said.

Elizabeth came over to watch as Wes systematically removed each layer of mind and disconnected from the donor. Finally, only Gil's pattern was left and Wes signaled the others to bring them back out. A few minutes later they sat up one at a time.

Daphne got up immediately and walked out of the room, Elizabeth following. A few seconds later the sounds of "Throw Out the Lifeline" came through the door. When Gil sat up he seemed excited and assured everyone he felt fine, then scampered off to his room. As soon as Ralph sat up his mouth opened.

"Ice cream time. You promised. A promise is a promise."

"Yes, Ralph. We'll go get the ice cream. Just give me a second."

"I'll ask Daphne what she wants. She'll want chocolate dip. She always gets chocolate dip. We going to Dairy Queen?"

"Dairy Queen, fine."

"Not Frosty Freeze."

"I said Dairy Queen, Ralph. It's Dairy Queen."

"Well okeydokey then."

Ralph turned to leave and was nearly gone when Len piped up from behind his console. "Are we still going to Frosty Freeze like you promised, Wes?"

Ralph immediately turned, folded his arms across his chest, and leaned back. His large loose lips formed into a pucker and deep furrows appeared on his brow. Then he walked back over to Wes.

"You said Dairy Queen, Wes."

"Len was kidding, Ralph. We are going to Dairy Queen."

Wes looked at Len, who was hiding behind his console. Karon had her head down next to his and he could hear them snicker every time Ralph spoke.

"I don't like Frosty Freeze. They don't have cherry dip. They only have chocolate. It's yucky. Daphne doesn't like it, either. Daphne likes the chocolate dip at Dairy Queen, not Frosty Freeze."

"Len, tell him you were kidding!"

Wes heard only muffled laughter from behind Len's console. Then Shamita spoke up.

"You're not changing your mind, are you, Wes? I love Frosty Freeze."

Len and Karon burst out laughing and Shamita bit her lip, stifling a giggle. Wes rolled his eyes and waited for what was coming. Ralph crossed the room, pulled a chair up and put his face inches from Wes's.

"Dr. Martin, we've gotta talk."

"It's a joke, Ralph."

"Some things aren't funny, Dr. Martin. Let me explain it to you real simple. I don't like Frosty Freeze."

"I know Ralph."

"The chocolate dip is yucky."

Wes was still listening to the chocolate-dip story when his team walked out to get coffee, holding their sides and giggling.

5

AFTERMATH

Gil lay on his bed, excited and afraid at the same time. He didn't know where he got the courage to actually submit to their experiment, especially after he heard Ms. Foxworth describe it as a hypnotic state. Now Gil was glad he'd had the courage to risk it—his mind felt sharp and clear and he felt confident, and capable. Something was different, and it excited him.

Gil got up and paced his room, trying to do calendar problems like Daphne, then checking them against his wall calendar. He couldn't do it with any accuracy, but still, he was sure in some way he was different.

Flopping back onto the bed, Gil breathed in deeply through his nose and out his mouth, over and over, beginning his relaxation routine. A psychologist taught him the technique a few days before Gil had him step off a subway platform in front of an incoming train. Next he tensed his toes and then relaxed them, then repeated the process with his feet. Working up his body, he slowly tensed and relaxed each muscle group in turn. When he was done he started all over and worked to his head again. Finally satisfied that his muscles were relaxed, Gil worked on clearing his mind.

As he tuned out the sounds of the house Gil felt his mind expand to fill the room. Every sense in his body sent clear sharp signals and Gil could discern even the smallest details of the room. Picturing each breath, he slowly cleared his mind of the room. When nothing else was left in his mind but the breathing, he let the image of his breaths fade away, leaving a void. That's when the whispering started.

It was just a soft murmuring, but it disturbed Gil's meditation. When he opened his eyes to look for the source, the whispering stopped. Gil listened intently but heard nothing. Closing his eyes again, he began his relaxation routine. When he cleared his mind of his breathing image the whispering returned. Again Gil opened his eyes and again the whispering stopped. Gil got up and opened his door—no one was in the hall. Gil walked to the door next to his and knocked. It was Karon's room but no one answered. Gil was frustrated. *Where was the voice coming from?*

Gil returned to his room and repeated the process and the whispering returned. When he tried concentrating on the voice it faded, but when he relaxed it returned. It was too faint for him to distinguish the words, but he listened anyway. It was human speech, he was sure, and it sounded like a woman. *But where was it coming from?* Had the experiment done something to him—improved his special ability? Gil's heart picked up its beat, pounding out his excitement, and again the voice faded.

Now Gil had to be part of the experiment again. If he had to, he would suggest his way in again—then he remembered Ralph. Somehow that retard had heard Gil's suggestions. He would have to deal with Ralph. Then Gil tried to clear his mind to hear the voice again, but found he couldn't think of killing Ralph and hear the voice at the same time.

Ralph led the way down the street with his oversized strides. He was a man on a mission—to get a cherry-dip ice-cream cone. Daphne followed a step and a half behind, running every few steps to keep up. Wes started to shout at him to slow down, but Elizabeth put her hand on his arm to stop him.

"Watch, we won't lose him."

Ralph was only a few strides down the street when he suddenly deviated and crossed the street toward an old woman watering her flowers.

"Afternoon, Mrs. Clayton, how ya doin'?"

Daphne followed Ralph across the street but stayed on the

sidewalk when Ralph walked into the yard to stand by Mrs. Clayton.

"I'm fine, Ralph. Going for a walk?" When she saw Wes and Elizabeth, she added, "Who are your friends across the street?"

"That's Wes and Elizabeth. This here's Daphne. Daphne's retarded but not like me. She's real smart sometimes. That's Wes and Elizabeth. They're doctors. Wes is sperimenting on Daphne. I was sperimented on, too. Well nice talking to you. We're going for ice cream. Bye, Mrs. Clayton."

"Goodbye, Ralph. Goodbye, Daphne."

Mrs. Clayton looked suspiciously at Wes and Elizabeth as they resumed their trip down the street.

"Did he have to tell her we were experimenting on them?" Wes asked. "It makes us sound like mad scientists."

"What do you mean 'we'? Besides, it was honest. Did you want him to lie?"

"Being private isn't being dishonest."

"Nothing is private to Ralph."

Suddenly Ralph deviated to the right into another yard, leaving Daphne standing on the sidewalk. When Wes and Elizabeth caught up with Daphne they found Ralph standing in the yard talking to a bald man holding a rake.

". . . they sperimented on me, too. Now we're going for ice cream. Well, gotta go now. Bye, Mr. Smeltzer."

"Goodbye, Ralph."

Wes waited until they were well away from Mr. Smeltzer before he spoke.

"This is embarrassing. Is he going to tell everyone?"

"Ralph is very friendly. It's in my report."

Wes was stung. He still hadn't read all of Elizabeth's reports. There was no hiding it, so Wes conceded his ignorance.

"I admit I skimmed sections of your reports." Elizabeth smiled at the admission. "What's Ralph's story, anyway? Why is he so . . . outgoing?"

"The intellectually challenged come with just as many different personalities as the rest of us."

"I understand that," Wes said. "But I've never met anyone quite like Ralph."

"He's the only child of a couple who thought they would never have children. His mother was forty-six when he was born and his father fifty-two. They had long reconciled themselves to childlessness and would have lived in a rut for the rest of their lives, dying in the same house they bought as newlyweds, if it hadn't been for Ralph. They made the papers when he was born. Forty-six isn't a record but it is kind of unusual. They loved him dearly, and bought a new house in the suburbs. Just like young couples, they remodeled one of the rooms into a nursery, ready for their little one. His mother told me once that all the kids in the neighborhood called her Grandma. Ralph's father was a carpenter and built him a playhouse that looked like a pirate ship. It's still there. All the kids loved to play at Ralph's house, because Ralph had every toy any kid could want. The once childless couple found themselves the informal parents to a neighborhood full of children. Ralph thrived in that home and had a pretty normal childhood until third grade. That's when it became clear he was going to continue to fall behind."

"They must have been devastated."

"Disappointed, yes. 'Devastated' is too strong—'scared' is a better word."

"They were afraid of Ralph?" Wes said incredulously. Ralph had a muscular physique, but he was the most inoffensive person; annoying, not threatening.

"They were afraid he'd be rejected by the other children. They were afraid of losing their extended family. It didn't happen. At least it happened slowly, the way it should. Ralph fell behind in school, but was mainstreamed wherever possible. His neighborhood friends moved on through the grades without him, but the younger children took their place. Ralph is like a five-year-old; he thinks everyone is his friend. Even you."

"What happened to his parents?"

"His father died when Ralph was thirteen. His mother lived another five years. Toward the end she was too frail to care for him. That's when I first met Ralph and his mother. Just before she died Ralph was put in custodial care and that's where he met Daphne. He's good for her and that's why I insisted he come."

"She is better when he's around," Wes conceded.

"You resent getting stuck with him, don't you?"

"He talks too much."

"He expresses every thought, that's for sure. I know you don't think he's special—not like Daphne and the others—but he is in his own way. Have you noticed that Ralph has only two emotions, concerned and happy? Ralph never laughs, he just grins, and he never cries or gets angry. The closest he can come to a dark emotion is a mild worry and he whips between concerned and happy with no transitional emotions at all. He's very unusual. Many intellectually challenged people have difficulty controlling their emotions, and relating to people—not Ralph. Look at Daphne, so withdrawn most of the time. Ralph, on the other hand, introduces himself to everyone, never self-conscious, never embarrassed. He's not gifted like the savants, but he's special in his own way."

Wes and Elizabeth caught up with Daphne and waited while Ralph stopped a woman carrying groceries and told her he was being "sperimented on." Ralph had just gotten moving again when he reached the corner. The house Wes had rented for his savants and his team was near the University of Oregon and in a neighborhood of large old-fashioned houses, many of which had been taken over by fraternities and sororities. Ralph turned up the walk of the fraternity on the corner and toward a group of fraternity brothers sitting on the steps drinking beer. As soon as they saw him they began shouting.

"Hey, Ralphie!"

"Come on up here, man."

"Hi Steve. Hi Rimmer. Hi Mitch. Hi Bopper. How's it goin'?"

While Ralph told them about the "speriment," Wes stood with Elizabeth. Then three more brothers came out onto the porch, each carrying a can of beer. One of the boys had classic good looks, with dark hair and eyes, and carried himself with arrogance. He frowned at Ralph, then spotted Daphne, and elbowed the boy next to him, whispering something that elicited a snicker. Then to Ralph he said, "Who's the babe, Ralph?"

"This here's Daphne."

"She's cute, Ralph. She your girlfriend?" he said, nudging his friend again.

Ralph grinned wide and shook his head. "I don't got a girlfriend, Billy. We're just friends. We're going to the Dairy Queen to get cones. Dip cones. Want to come?"

"No, Ralphie. You go on without us. See ya later."

"Well, okeydokey."

As they left, Wes noticed Billy and the boys on the porch watching Daphne's back. Daphne wasn't pretty in Wes's eyes, although she wasn't ugly, just plain. The people at the institution kept her hair short for convenience, and Daphne never did anything with it except brush it occasionally. Usually it was just light brown strings that hung limp around her face. Her clothes were mostly baggy dresses that hung below her knees, hiding any figure she might have. He couldn't imagine anyone being attracted to her, let alone fraternity brothers.

It was two more blocks and a half-dozen stops for Ralph before they turned into the small-business district serving the university. Three blocks later they came to the corner with the Dairy Queen. When they walked up to the window Ralph was greeted by name by the middle-aged woman working the counter.

"Back again, eh Ralph?"

"Hi, Ellen."

"Say, this isn't Daphne, is it? It is! Millie, come over here. This here's Daphne!"

A teenage girl walked over, a big smile on her face.

"Hello, Ralph. You finally brought Daphne to see us. I was sure you were eating all those extra cones yourself."

Ralph's smile widened until it threatened to swallow his ears, and his head swung back and forth. Then he remembered Wes and Elizabeth.

"This here's Elizabeth and this here's Wes. They're sperimenting on me and Daphne. Mostly Daphne."

Wes waved at Millie and Ellen but they gave him cold looks.

"We don't dissect them or anything," he said defensively. "It's just some testing . . . really!"

"It better be," Ellen said. "If anything happens to Ralph or Daphne you'll be hearing from my husband."

"Ellen's husband is a police officer," Ralph explained. "He has a gun. He hasn't shot anyone yet but he wants to. I want a large cherry dip. Daphne wants—"

"I know, Ralph. A large chocolate dip. Coming right up. Anything for you two?" Ellen said without the warmth she had shown Ralph.

"Two small vanilla cones," Wes said softly.

Ellen nodded and disappeared into the restaurant. Wes hung his head and worried over his reputation. Elizabeth patted him on the shoulder in sympathy and said, "Remember, tomorrow you get two more."

Daphne was restless and paced back and forth in her room. She felt different. The ice-cream cone had been a nice distraction, but now the change couldn't be ignored. The experiment had done something to her. Her world was different now, a little sharper, a little clearer. It was a small perceptual difference, but to someone who lived in herself, and knew every nook and cranny of her conscious mind intimately, it was a dramatic change.

Daphne welcomed anything that would help her organize herself in the midst of the whirlwind that was her mind. But with clarity also came fear, because she could feel the black hole at the center of the storm. She was terrified by that hole, and if its pull became too strong she would run to her hidey-hole, playing her imaginary piano furiously.

Coming to live with Wes and Elizabeth and Gil had been a good change, too, although it scared her at first. Now she liked it here—she had a piano all to herself and could play anytime she needed. She also had her friend Ralph and now she had Gil. It was all better here and she was happy—until the experiment changed her. Now she didn't know whether to be happy or afraid. The confusion of her mixed emotions sent her running to her hidey-hole, where she dropped inside, her body rocking, slowly at first, then violently until she could think of nothing but the rocking.

In her self-induced hypnotic state her mind was blank and her emotions subsided, the confusing feelings faded. After a half hour she came out of the trance, still rocking, but awareness seeped into her consciousness slowly. With the black hole in her mind safely buried, she relaxed. Sleep helped order her mind sometimes, so she began getting ready for bed.

Wes and his team sat on the porch enjoying the warm September night. Wes and Shamita rocked in the rockers while Len and Karon shared the porch swing. Wes noticed that the two sat in the middle of the swing, their bodies touching. Len leaned over, whispering in Karon's ear, eliciting a giggle. Shamita rolled her eyes at Wes; then she pointed to old Mrs. Clayton, who was across the street watering, keeping one eye on her plants and one on her new neighbors.

"She must be the neighborhood busybody," Shamita said.

"Ralph told her we're experimenting on him and Daphne," Wes said.

"I bet she couldn't wait to spread that around!" Shamita said. "I can imagine what she thinks we're doing over here."

"Ralph told everyone he met," Wes said. "They all think we're mad scientists. Don't expect good service down at the Dairy Queen."

Shamita looked puzzled, but before Wes could explain Elizabeth came out on the porch and leaned against a post. For the first time since they met Wes was glad to see her. She had been pleasant company that afternoon and he hoped the feeling would continue into the evening. He didn't expect the kind of relationship that Len and Karon were developing, but he could use a friend.

"I take it the experiment was a success," Elizabeth said.

Wes was suddenly suspicious. Elizabeth witnessed it, she knew it was successful, so why was she asking the question?

"It went the way we expected. Of course we haven't constructed an entire mind yet, just overlayed two on one."

"But so far so good, thanks to your program," she said.

"Yes, it's a good start, but not just me, everyone contributed."

Wes's team turned and looked at him as if they knew something he didn't. Ever since Elizabeth had arrived he frequently felt he was the last to know what was going on.

"Without Shamita, Len, and Karon I couldn't have done it," Wes added, trying to sound modest. Was that what she wanted? For Wes to concede he couldn't do it alone?

Elizabeth stared hard at him and waited silently. Wes saw Len mouthing something and he stared at his lips. When Wes didn't get it Len added a whisper. Wes heard the words "Daphne" and "Ralph." Then he understood, and the good feeling he had felt for Elizabeth since their walk to the Dairy Queen evaporated.

"I always intended to thank them and give them credit," he said angrily. "Elizabeth, if you have something to say you can come right out and say it."

"I shouldn't have to. You should be caring for Daphne and Ralph yourself. Remember you didn't even want me here. What were you going to do if I hadn't pushed my way in? Lock them in their rooms, bringing them out only for your experiments?"

Wes started to answer, but stopped. She had maneuvered him into a weak position by implying that he had slighted Daphne and Ralph. It wasn't much of an oversight, if any, but he would wait until he was on solid ground before striking back.

"I'll go thank them now." Wes stood angrily, then paused. "Next time you have something to say to me, Elizabeth, just say it. Don't be cute!"

Wes stomped into the house, leaving Elizabeth scowling on the porch. When he was gone she turned back toward the street and then spoke, seemingly unaware of the others on the porch.

"What is it with him? Why does he take everything wrong?"

"Reminds me of a story," Len said.

As soon as Len started to speak Karon scooted away from his side and Shamita sank low into her rocker—neither of them sure of what he would say.

"Did you ever hear of the time the Northern girl met the Southern girl? The Southern girl walks up and says, 'Where y'all from?' The Northern girl replies, 'I was born and raised in Boston. In Boston I went to the finest private schools and at those schools they taught me to speak properly, and I would never end a sentence with a preposition.' The Southern girl looks at the Northern girl and then says, 'I'm sorry. Let me start over. Where y'all from, bitch?' "

Karon's eyes went wide and the blood drained from her face. Shamita sucked in her lips to suppress a laugh, but her body shook with mirth. Elizabeth glared at Len briefly and then walked into the house. As soon as she was in the door the porch erupted in laughter.

Wes was more frustrated than angry. Ever since he had met Elizabeth there had been low-level tension between them that periodically erupted into open conflict. The tension was mild, but like an itch that wouldn't go away, creating constant discomfort. Wes had three months left on his grant, and that meant three months in close quarters with Elizabeth Foxworth. Tonight it seemed like an eternity, and he felt like a scolded child as he scurried up the stairs to thank his participants. He hated the feeling and vowed he wouldn't let her treat him like a child.

Ralph's door was open and Wes found him sitting on the floor staring at a pile of socks. The socks were sorted, and the pairs folded together. Ralph had sorted the socks into three piles, but the piles were mixtures of colors and styles, and Wes could see no pattern. Ralph was looking at the socks with a vacant stare. Elizabeth had described him as having only two emotions, but neither of them was showing here.

"Ralph?"

He turned to Wes and the blank look suddenly reshaped itself into a huge grin.

"Hi Wes. Did ya come to say goodnight? It's not my bedtime yet, is it?"

"Ralph," Wes broke in. "I just came to thank you for helping me with my experiment."

Ralph grinned a little wider. "You're welcome. Thanks for the ice cream."

"You're welcome, Ralph. Goodnight."

Ralph said goodnight and then turned back to his pile of socks, his face immediately going blank.

Daphne's room was next door to Ralph's and Wes walked to it, shaking his head, realizing he didn't understand Ralph any more than he did Elizabeth. Still thinking about Ralph, Wes opened Daphne's door and walked in, stopping in shock. Daphne was topless, leaning over her dresser, looking in a drawer. She shrieked, grabbing a nightgown and covering herself.

Shocked and embarrassed, he backed out the door, turning toward the stairs, not sure of what to do. He started walking but then turned back and closed the door. Wes went down the stairs, trying to get the image out of his mind. Elizabeth appeared at the bottom as he came down.

"What's going on?" she demanded.

"Daphne . . ." Wes began, but was too embarrassed to finish.

Suddenly Daphne burst out of her room, wearing her night-gown, and raced down the stairs, pushing between Wes and Elizabeth. She was crying.

"What did you do to her?" Elizabeth asked accusingly. Without waiting for an answer, Elizabeth followed Daphne to the living room. Wes trailed along sheepishly.

Daphne was playing the piano, but it was angry pounding, not her usual sweet melodies. When Elizabeth put her hand on

Daphne's shoulder, she shrugged it off, pounding even harder, and then running toward the kitchen. A few seconds later they heard the back door slam.

"You better go after her," Wes said.

"Tell me what happened!" Elizabeth insisted.

"I went to thank her, like you wanted me to. She was in her room changing—she didn't have all her clothes on."

"Didn't you knock?"

"I didn't think—"

"You violated her privacy!"

"It was an accident!"

"Would you walk into my room without knocking?"

"Of course not."

"Then why treat Daphne with less respect, unless you don't quite see her as human."

"I never said that! I just wasn't thinking."

"The savants aren't equipment. They're people with feelings that include shame and embarrassment. If Daphne is going to continue in this experiment you are going to respect her privacy. Is that clear?"

"Don't lecture me."

"Then don't act like an ass."

Opening his mouth to respond, he closed it with a snap. He knew he wouldn't be allowed to finish a sentence.

"I'll find Daphne and see how much damage has been done," Elizabeth said.

Wes hoped she was exaggerating. If Daphne was so upset that she would have to leave, the whole project was in danger. The image of naked Daphne bending over her dresser came back and he quickly forced it away. Even so, he now understood why the fraternity brothers had been staring at her, and it gave him one more thing to worry about.

The house Wes had secured for the project was leased from the national office of a fraternity. The local chapter had run into disciplinary problems and been shut down for a year as punishment. Wes's money made the payments and made sure the fraternity brothers would have a place when the suspension was over. The house sat on a large lot with an alley behind it and a separate garage. The house had been leased furnished, and the excess furniture moved into the garage to make space for Wes's experimental equipment. The garage was built in the same Colonial style as the house, with a small cupola on top. There were windows on one side, a small door facing the house, and large double garage doors that opened out to the alley. It was in this garage that Elizabeth found Daphne.

Elizabeth turned the garage light on and found Daphne huddled on one end of a couch, her arms wrapped around her legs, holding her knees to her chest. Her face was red and puffy.

Elizabeth walked to the far end of the couch and sat quietly with Daphne, letting her adjust to Elizabeth's presence. After a few minutes she empathized with her.

"I know what happened. You must have been embarrassed."

"Yes."

"Maybe a little afraid?"

Daphne didn't answer.

"He promised to knock from now on."

"Will he take away my piano?"

"Wes won't punish you. It was his fault. You did nothing wrong. He just didn't know the rules about knocking. Everyone will knock. I promise."

"What if they forget?"

"Then we'll have to punish them, not you." Elizabeth touched Daphne's shoulder, and this time it wasn't brushed away. "Will you come back to the house now?"

"No. I like it here."

"Will you come back soon?"

"I like it here."

"Don't stay much longer, Daphne."

Elizabeth left Daphne in the garage but watched the door from the kitchen window. Fifteen minutes later Daphne came out of the garage and walked straight through the kitchen to the piano. She played until long after the others had gone to bed.

6

ARCHIE

The state took Archie from his mother when he was two. He was too young to remember her, and the only mementos of those first horrible years were the scars on his back from cigarette burns, and scars on his feet where she had scalded them in a bath. The next six years were a series of foster homes for Archie, and then the move to the state institution. He liked it there. No one beat him, or teased him because of his orange hair or his buck teeth. There was always food to eat, there were treats between meals if you minded the rules, and there was something under the tree for everyone at Christmas. Sometimes on holidays he felt bad, because when the visitors came there was never anyone just for him. Those without family were grouped together and kept out of the way. Sometimes church people would come and visit the lonelies, but Archie never liked it. He knew they came out of pity and not love.

Archie knew a lot more than people gave him credit for but no one ever cared to find out so he spent his childhood as an anonymous charge of the state, warehoused with others of his kind. He learned early that it was easier to be like everyone else in the institution, and he adopted the mannerisms of the others, hiding his special talent. So it was that Archie was sixteen before they discovered he wasn't like the others, and they wouldn't have discovered it then if it hadn't been for a broken toilet.

At nights an attendant was always stationed in the hall to make sure no one wandered out of the wards. The attendants mostly read or watched TV, but one night an attendant brought a jigsaw puzzle to work. He spread it out on a card table and sat watching TV, drinking Coke, and working the puzzle. That was the night Archie got up to go to the bathroom. The attendant told Archie to be quick about it, relieved that Archie wasn't one of those who needed to be wiped. In the bathroom Archie noticed one of the toilet handles was stuck down and water was spilling over the sides. When Archie came back he told the attendant.

"Damn, why does this always happen on my shift. Well, what are you staring at? Get back to bed!"

The attendant left Archie standing and stomped off to the bathroom. The toilet was easily fixed but the water took thirty minutes to clean up. When he came back to his station he was stunned to find the puzzle completed. It was a picture of running horses in a field with a rainbow in the background. There were five hundred pieces and the attendant had left it with only about half of the outside edges put together. He reasoned it had to be some kind of joke, but who could put a puzzle together that fast? Eventually the attendant realized the only one near the puzzle had been one of the retarded kids—the one named Archie. The attendant found Archie asleep in his bed and stood watching him. Even in the dark his orange hair looked bright, and his big teeth were poking between his lips. The attendant couldn't believe this clownish retard had solved the puzzle.

He told the morning shift about the puzzle, but they were as skeptical as he. By midmorning it was the talk of the institution and reached Dr. Carmen Hilton. At lunch she went shopping and came back with a new puzzle. Not quite believing the story she selected a 250-piece puzzle. It was a picture of hot-air balloons floating up out of a meadow. She set up a card table and poured the pieces out, spreading them evenly; then she invited Archie over.

"Can you put this together for me, Archie?"

Without a word Archie bent over the table until his face was a few inches from the surface and stared at the puzzle. Then he reached out and picked up two pieces with straight edges, put them together, and set them to his left. Then he scanned the table from about a foot away and picked up a third piece and added it to the first two. Picking up speed, Archie worked quickly, putting the straight edges together. With barely a pause, and never an error, the frame was quickly completed. Then, with another short pause, he began fitting pieces to the outside edges. Only a handful of times did a selected piece not fit. As he worked, with his nose skimming the surface, the staff gathered, whispering and pointing in amazement. Ten minutes later he fit the final piece into the puzzle.

As if Archie's speed weren't enough, two other oddities stood out. Never once did Archie look at the box top to match the colors of the pieces to their location on the box. Experienced jigsaw-puzzle enthusiasts knew this magnified the difficulty. The other oddity was that as the picture began to emerge, it was upside down.

The next day all three of the staff psychologists gathered with a 750-piece puzzle. It was a picture of a harbor filled with fishing boats. Just after lunch they took Archie from making a belt in his occupational-therapy class, and asked him to put the puzzle together. Archie stared for a full minute and then picked up two straight edges and put them together. Then, just as before, with few errors, he systematically put one piece at a time into the puzzle until the harbor and its boats emerged. The puzzle took twenty-five minutes and this time was right side up.

Archie went back to his belt and the amazed psychologists retired to an office for discussion. Archie had been tested before, but he had never shown such ability, and they were somewhat embarrassed that they had missed it. But Dr. Hilton correctly pointed out that Archie had been tested with behavior-oriented tests designed for the educable mentally retarded. Archie had never really been given a challenge like the puzzles. Besides, there might be another reason the staff missed his talent, she pointed out. Archie's posture when solving puzzles suggested that he was visually impaired.

That afternoon Dr. Hilton tested Archie with a standard intelligence test. Archie performed miserably on the verbal and quantitative portions, except for pattern recognition. Using blocks colored red, white, or half red or white, Archie was able to order them into required patterns with blinding speed, his nose skimming the table.

The next morning Dr. Hilton took Archie to an optometrist and had Archie examined—he needed glasses. While they waited for the lenses, Dr. Hilton searched for a pair of frames that went with Archie's face. It was the hardest thing she had ever done. Archie was tall and skinny with orange hair over most of his body. He was balding at an early age and what was left of his orange hair was in three tufts: two on either side and one on the top of his head. His buck teeth protruded noticeably, and were seldom covered by his lips. Everything Dr. Hilton put on his face made him look more like a clown. Archie himself was little help.

"Do you like these, Archie?" Dr. Hilton would say after putting a pair on him. "Yes," he would say after looking in the mirror, and then he would take them off and pick up another pair, twirling them around on his finger. Exasperated, Dr. Hilton tried pair after pair, always getting the same "Yes," and off the glasses would come. Dr. Hilton was about to settle for a plain black frame when the assistant brought out another set of samples.

"These are children's frames. He might like these better."

The frames came in colors and with imprinted designs. Most were too gaudy for Archie's face, but Dr. Hilton began sorting through them. Suddenly Archie dropped the pair he was playing with and picked up a blue pair of frames and put them on. Dr. Hilton looked in the mirror to see Archie smiling at himself. Each side of the bright blue frames was topped with a relief of Mickey Mouse.

"No, Archie. Those look silly."

"They're actually sunglass frames," the attendant added.

Dr. Hilton took off the Mickey Mouse frames and put on a deep blue pair.

"If you like blue, these would look better," she said.

Archie took off Dr. Hilton's frames and put the Mickey Mouse frames back on and smiled at himself in the mirror again. Dr. Hilton tried again, but Archie returned once more to the Mickey Mouse frames. She hated the frames—it made Archie more of a spectacle—but when they left Archie was wearing the Mickey Mouse frames.

That afternoon the ward looked like a psychologists' convention. The word had spread and their colleagues from other institutions had gathered to witness Archie's ability. His Mickey Mouse frames had garnered titters from the psychologists and staff, but the other patients either ignored them or showed delight. Archie acknowledged neither response.

They started with a five-hundred-piece puzzle. Archie worked in his usual fashion, but without putting his nose down to the surface. The puzzle was completed in fifteen minutes, this time upside down. The psychologists buzzed in excitement. The next puzzle was a special one made up of swirling red and white colors. There were no corners to use as anchors and the swirling red and white gave few color cues. Archie completed it in twelve minutes. When he was done they brought out a box nearly overflowing with puzzle pieces and poured it on a bigger table. It was three puzzles mixed together. Archie worked nonstop for fifty minutes and completed all three puzzles. Two were finished upside down. Archie was thanked, given a Three Musketeers candy bar, and sent off with an attendant. The psychologists retired to a conference room to discuss his case. They all agreed that it was fascinating, but because of Archie's other poor skills no change in his treatment, or his residence, was warranted. That night after dinner Dr. Hilton went back to the institution to see Archie. He was in his pajamas and sitting in the recreation room watching TV. Some of the others said hello to Dr. Hilton and then went back to watching the TV. Archie never looked up.

"Archie? Archie, stop watching TV for a second."

Archie turned toward her, his Mickey Mouse glasses perched on his nose, his buck teeth protruding and orange puffs of hair framing his face. Dr. Hilton wanted to talk to him, to ask him how he did what he did, and what other secrets were hidden somewhere inside of his clown head. But the blank stare told her there wasn't enough self-awareness for Archie to answer her questions even if Archie was capable of introspection. Instead, Dr. Hilton dug in her purse and pulled out an old Rubik's Cube she had never been able to solve. Archie's head was drifting back toward the TV, so Dr. Hilton hurried to keep his limited attention.

"Archie? Archie, look at me. This is a puzzle, too. It's a different puzzle. It works like this." Dr. Hilton twisted the puzzle a few times to show Archie how it worked. "You have to get all the colors together. Get all the yellow ones on one side, all the green ones on one side, all the blue ones on one side, and so on. Do you understand?"

Archie never answered; he just began twisting the cube randomly. Dr. Hilton watched him for a few minutes but saw no pattern or progress. When she left he was still twisting the puzzle. Dr. Hilton thought a lot about Archie that night. The next morning when she came to work the solved cube was on her desk. That morning she watched Archie solve a bewildering variety of puzzles brought in by the psychologists and the staff. Nothing stymied Archie as long as it was a spatial task. After dinner Dr. Hilton returned with a new idea. She dumped a new puzzle on the table and then turned all of the pieces facedown so that none of the colors showed. Archie solved it as easily as he did those with the picture showing. That next morning Dr. Hilton called her old college friend Dr. Wes Martin. Dr. Martin came to visit, and a few months later Elizabeth Foxworth came to visit, too. A month later Archie's things were packed and he took the first plane ride of his life, to Oregon.

7

CHURCH

Someone was shaking the bed. It was the gentle rhythmic kind of shaking someone uses when they want to wake you up, but Wes would have none of it. He had been up late the night before listening to Daphne play. Only after he heard her thump up the stairs to bed could he go to sleep. Even then he lay awake worrying whether Daphne would agree to continue in the experiment. Now someone was ending the little sleep he got last night. It seemed like a bad dream, but when Wes heard the voice he knew it was a nightmare.

"Wes? Wes? It's me, Ralph. It's time to get up."

Wes was confused and opened his eyes long enough to check the clock.

"It's only six-thirty, now get out of here, Ralph," Wes mumbled, and then in a louder voice added, "I mean it, Ralph, get out and stay out." Wes waved his hand at Ralph in dismissal and then rolled over, burying his head under his pillow.

"It's time to get up, Wes," Ralph persisted. "We'll be late."

Wes's temper flared and he rolled over, flinging his pillow blindly. The pillow hit the wall by the door and fell to the floor with a soft thud. When the blur of sleep cleared from his eyes he saw Ralph staring at him with his big loose lips curved up in a grin.

"Missed me!"

"Ralph, get out of here! I'm dangerous in the morning, especially when someone wakes me up before dawn."

"It's time to get ready. We don't want to be late."

"Late for what?" Wes shouted in exasperation.

"For church."

"Church?" Wes said stupidly. "What do you mean church? I don't go to church."

"I do."

"Then go," Wes shouted and pointed at the door. "But leave me alone."

Ralph left with the grin still plastered on his face. Wes flopped back down, and his head smacked the mattress—his pillow was on the floor. Too tired to get out of bed and fetch it, he used his arm as a pillow and pulled the covers up over his head. He'd just settled back into the warm feeling that precedes sleep when someone else entered the room. This time there was no gentle shaking.

"Get up, we're going to church," Elizabeth said.

She sounded angry. Wes had taken a beating over invading Daphne's privacy last night, so instead of shouting at her he rolled over and tried to reason.

"I don't go to church, Elizabeth. I haven't since I was a kid. Besides, Archie and Luis arrive today. If you want to take Ralph go ahead and go."

"Daphne wants to go."

Wes knew he had lost. There was more than enough residual guilt left from the night before to allow Elizabeth to manipulate him into doing anything. All Wes could do was lie there looking frustrated.

"You still haven't read my reports, have you?" she said.

"I was going to do it this morning while you were at church."

Elizabeth glared at him so Wes glared back.

"You agreed to honor their routines to protect their psyches. Daphne's routine included church on Sundays."

Wes was flustered and too sleepy to think clearly so he stumbled on.

"Why can't you and Ralph take her?"

"It's your project, as you so often remind me. Of course, if you want to turn over control—"

"Well, why so early? Isn't church at eleven o'clock?"

"We're going to the early service so you'll have plenty of time to get ready for Archie and Luis."

She's clever, Wes thought. She made getting him out of bed at this ungodly hour seem to be for his benefit.

"All right, all right, all right! I'll get up."

"You have time to take a shower. The service starts at seven-thirty."

Wes didn't need an hour to get ready but knew if he stayed in bed he might fall back asleep, and he wasn't going to risk more of Elizabeth's wrath. So he showered and shaved and put on a shirt and tie and met the others downstairs. Ralph was wearing a blue suit that looked a size too big and a gaudy red-and-blue tie. The knot was twisted around and the narrow end of the tie was on top of the wide side. Daphne looked neat and prim in a blue checked dress with a white collar that she wore buttoned tight up to her throat. Daphne kept her head down and didn't look at Wes, but Daphne never looked anyone in the eye so Wes didn't know if avoiding eye contact with him was significant. He wouldn't have looked at her anyway, since he was embarrassed and had trouble keeping the image of her naked out of his mind. Elizabeth was dressed in a simple blue skirt with a white blouse. Even in his foul mood he was attracted to her.

"It's time, Ralph," Elizabeth said. "Show us where the church is."

"OK, I picked out a good one."

Ralph took off with his long strides, Daphne trotting along behind. Elizabeth followed and Wes trailed. He was pouting and meant to walk behind her all the way to church, but she kept slowing so he could catch up and he finally gave up and fell in beside her. They followed Ralph down the block at a fast walk. Mercifully the yards were empty so Ralph made no detours. They turned at the corner where Ralph's fraternity friends lived and into the oldest part of the neighborhood. Wes noticed that the fraternity's yard was filled with debris and a beer keg.

The church was two more blocks and around another corner. It was an old brick church in a classic design, rectangular with a tall steeple. There were cars arriving and people filtering into the church. Many looked as sleepy as he did. Without waiting to see if they followed, Ralph strode into the church. A woman and a man stood at the door greeting those arriving. Ralph grabbed the man's hand and began pumping it.

"Hello, how are you. My name's Ralph and this here's Daphne. Daphne's my friend. She's not my girl or anything. She's pretty isn't she? This here's Wes and this here's Elizabeth. They're sperimenting on me and Daphne. Wes doesn't go to church but Elizabeth got him to come. Gotta go."

Relief spread across the man's face when Ralph released his hand and moved on to the woman, pumping her hand just as vigorously. Daphne shook hands next, never looking up. Wes hung back, letting Elizabeth go first, and then shook the man's hand. Wes's face was red and the man and woman stared at him curiously. He knew they were wondering where this couple with the two retarded children had come from and what exactly they were doing to them. Wes was too embarrassed to explain. He followed Elizabeth into the sanctuary and was dismayed to see how far forward she was walking. He reached out and pulled her arm toward a pew but Elizabeth shook his grip and kept walking. Wes followed sheepishly, not wanting to make a scene in church. When they reached the front pew they found Daphne and Ralph seated at the end away from the pulpit. Wes sat next to Elizabeth, wondering why the front row? It looked like the service would be only half full and there was nobody in the first three rows but them.

A woman walked past and sat at the organ to the left of the end of the pew. When she started to play Wes was overwhelmed by the sound and looked up to see the end of the church filled with racks of pipes. It was a huge organ and Wes knew then why they were in the front row. Wes looked over to Daphne and saw her head tilted up, ecstasy on her face. The rich sounds of the organ were overpowering to Wes but to Daphne it was a narcotic and she was mainlining. Ralph grinned broadly. He had picked this church for her. Guiltily, Wes realized Ralph took better care of Daphne than he did.

The prelude ended and the pastor greeted the congregation. He was a young man with mahogany eyes and hair to match— good-looking, with sharp features and the build of an athlete. Wes imagined the youth group was packed with young Christian groupies. After a few announcements the pastor asked any visitors to introduce themselves and then turned and looked at Wes. Wes hesitated but Ralph didn't.

"Hi, I'm Ralph and this here's Daphne. This here's Elizabeth and this here's Wes. They're speriementing on me and Daphne."

Ralph's voice boomed out the word "speriementing" and now murmurs filled the church. Wes sank lower in his pew in embarrassment while Elizabeth chuckled next to him.

"I see," said the pastor diplomatically. "Welcome to our congregation. Are there any other visitors?"

Wes was mortified and barely heard the rest of the introductions. When they were done the choir sang, accompanied by the organ. Daphne's head tilted up with the first chord, her face glowing through the entire hymn and then her head slowly sinking to her chest when it ended. Daphne responded to the hymn singing in the same fashion, but never joined in.

The sermon was part of a series the pastor had been preaching on stewardship. After the sermon came the offering. The plate came to Wes and he absentmindedly passed it along without putting anything in. Elizabeth dropped ten dollars in the plate and then handed it to Daphne, who dropped in two quarters. When it came to Ralph he put in a handful of change and then to Wes's horror got up with the plate and walked back to Wes.

"I know you don't go to church, so you don't know how it works," Ralph said loudly. "You got to pay something. Except it's not like paying really, cause God don't make you pay, but you should put something in. Me and Daphne put in some money we've been saving from Slurpees. Elizabeth put in a whole lot. Now you got to put something in. I got an extra quarter if you need it."

Wes heard laughter around him and felt his face flame. Quickly he dug out his wallet and pulled out a twenty-dollar bill, dropping it in the plate.

"Wow, that's a lot," Ralph said. "God will like that."

More laughter behind Wes. Mercifully Ralph took the plate to the end of the pew and handed it to the usher.

The service ended with the Lord's Prayer and the Gloria Patri and then the congregation turned to file out. Being in the front meant they followed the rest of the congregation past the pastor, who was shaking every hand. Wes planned on a brief shake and then a quick getaway, but the pastor introduced himself as Phil Young, and he and Elizabeth struck up a conversation.

"These can't be your children, you're too young."

"Why thank you. No, we're their guardians. We're living just a few blocks away."

"I know, you're in the empty fraternity house. What was that Ralph said about experimenting?"

Elizabeth paused and turned to Wes, waiting for him to respond. Wes stepped forward, taking the pastor's hand.

"It's really just testing. Daphne's a savant—"

"What's her ability?"

Wes was surprised by the pastor's quick understanding. "She's a calendar calculator."

"Fascinating. What's your special ability, Ralph?"

Ralph's face wrinkled up into its concern shape, and his arms folded across his chest. He leaned back and looked like he was thinking so hard he was in pain. Before he could come up with an answer Elizabeth spoke.

"His special ability is embarrassing Wes."

"Yeah, bare-assing Wes," Ralph said.

The pastor chuckled and Ralph joined in, hee-hawing even though he didn't get the joke.

"Mind if I stop by sometime?" the pastor asked. "I'm interested in what you're doing."

The pastor looked at Wes when he asked, but his eyes drifted to Elizabeth before he finished the question. Wes glanced at the pastor's left hand; there was no ring. Wes felt a pang of irrational jealousy. He had no relationship with Elizabeth, why would he care whether this pastor had designs on Elizabeth or not? He didn't, he told himself, but still planned to discourage the visit, because it would be disruptive. Before he could answer Elizabeth accepted for him.

"Come by anytime. I'm sure Wes will be glad to show you his work and I'll—"

The sound of music interrupted Elizabeth. Wes realized that Daphne was gone and led the way back into the church. Daphne was sitting at the grand piano playing and the sounds of "How Great Thou Art" reverberated through the church. Wes started forward to stop her but the pastor restrained him.

"I see she has more than one special ability. She plays beautifully."

"She always played at the other church," Ralph offered.

Some of the congregation drifted back in, coffee cups in their hands. Soon a small group had gathered, listening to Daphne play from memory. "Onward Christian Soldiers" followed, and then "Morning Has Broken." When she finished her recital she stood, her head immediately falling to her chest. The audience applauded briefly.

"Remarkable," said the pastor. "I hope you'll bring her back next Sunday. Perhaps you'll let her play in the service?"

"That won't be poss—" Wes started to say.

"Of course we will," Elizabeth said. "Daphne always plays in church. Just let us know what you want her to play. We'll be back next Sunday for the early service again. Won't we, Wes?"

"Yes," Wes said reluctantly. Elizabeth shook the pastor's hand again, holding it longer than necessary. Wes pulled her away and out the door. As they left the church he was hoping something would happen to keep him in bed next Sunday, and Elizabeth away from Pastor Young.

8

WHISPERS

Gil started through his relaxation routine, working through each muscle group, tensing then relaxing, until he felt no tension left. Then he repeated the routine twice more. Next he focused on his breathing, until even that could be filtered from his mind. Now clear, he searched again for the whispering voice—it was there. Gil hoped the voice belonged to one of the others, but Wes and Elizabeth had taken Daphne and Ralph to church and the others were still asleep. There was an urgency to the whispering, not the sound of a sleeper—at least he didn't think so. Still unable to understand the whisper, he gave up, frustrated. He needed to know if the voice was coming from one of the others and reasoned that if he moved farther away from them the whisper should fade.

He tiptoed down the stairs to the living room and lay down on the couch, once again working through his relaxation routine. The voice was there—it was louder but still not comprehensible. The whisper tormented him. He was being teased by something just out of his reach and his interest was turning to anger.

Gil moved to the kitchen, trying to relax in one of the table chairs. It was too uncomfortable, so he put three of the chairs together and stretched out flat. It worked and when his mind cleared the voice was there, louder still. No words could be distinguished but the rhythm was more distinct and the breaks between syllables easier to pick out. He was closer to the source, but where now? Only the basement remained.

Gil went down the stairs into the basement. It was filled with old furniture, suitcases, boxes, and the debris of the fraternity that owned the building. There was little open floor space but Gil found a lawn chair and enough space to fold it open. He stretched out again and soon felt his mind clear and the voice return—but still the words could not be made out. It was most distinct in the basement, but why? Even without the words, he could distinguish emotions—there was a lot of pain in the voice.

Sounds of footsteps above distracted him, silencing the voice. Someone was in the kitchen starting the first pot of coffee—it was time to go. Gil was reluctant to leave. He was intrigued by the mysterious voice, but he was even more intrigued by this new ability. What was it, and how might he use it?

Two more savants arrived today and there was talk of running the experiment again tonight. Gil had to be sure he was a part of it. It would be easy to suggest his way in if it wasn't for Ralph. Ralph would have to be dealt with.

9

LUIS

They found him at a Greyhound bus station in San Diego. Pinned to his shirt was a hand-scrawled note that said simply "My name is Luis. Please take care of me." It was a slow news week and Luis made the local six-clock news. They dubbed him Luis Greyhound, because of where he was found. Physically he looked Hispanic and was likely an illegal, but with no family name to trace he was taken into the state welfare system.

A pediatrician estimated he was two years old, so they began counting his age from the day he was examined. The psychologists found he was nonverbal, even in Spanish, and they based their assessment on his behavior, which was well behind the typical two-year-old's. Even simple holophrastic speech was absent, and he wasn't ready to be toilet-trained. He was withdrawn, seldom making eye contact, so they labeled him developmentally delayed. At four Luis began to speak in one-word sentences, but only in response to questions. At five he was relabeled autistic.

Luis wasn't difficult to work with, he was just asocial, and easy to place in front of a TV and forget. Forgotten for four years, he spent his days in an electronic blur. At eight he was transferred to the Winamakis, who had opened their home to foster children with special needs. They were young, enthusiastic, and idealistic—Luis was their first child.

Mrs. Winamaki enrolled Luis in special classes at the local school, and began home schooling. Luis had learned little, she reasoned, because no one believed he could. Optimism was Mrs. Winamaki's special gift, and she set out to prove that the doctors were wrong about Luis.

Even under her patient tutelage, Luis never learned even minimal social skills. He spoke only when spoken to, and never volunteered an idea or even a feeling. If he was sick the first indication would be vomit or loose bowels, never a complaint. He never asked to eat, or to drink, but would help himself to food or drink if meals were skipped. Her failures with Luis slightly tarnished her shining idealism, but she made up for it by discovering something that all the psychologists, social workers, and teachers had missed. Luis had a very special ability—he remembered virtually everything he was shown.

She discovered that Luis knew the alphabet, and, to her astonishment, that he could read. She discovered it by simply asking him to do it. It happened while she was reading him a story, which she did every day before rest time. Mrs. Winamaki's allergies were acting up and her eyes watered, making it difficult to read. As active as a rock, Luis sat next to her, staring at the book, apparently oblivious of the story. But when Mrs. Winamaki put the book down to wipe her eyes he picked it up. Then she simply said, "You read for a minute, Luis." As she wiped her eyes she heard his slow monotone voice pick up the story.

"The duck was sad. The duck was lost. The duck could not see his brother. The duck could not see his sister. The duck could not see his mother." Without a single error, Luis finished the book.

Mrs. Winamaki introduced more difficult books, discovering that he would stop when he came to a word he did not know, waiting for her to repeat the word. Once told, he continued, always remembering the new word after that. Not once did Luis pick up a book on his own, reading only when asked. The teachers were surprised and enthusiastic at first, but there were many children with more potential, and taking Luis past simple reading wasn't considered the best use of their limited resources. But Mrs. Winamaki had more time, more energy, and her boundless hope.

She began rewarding Luis with M&M's for reading, which he would do all day long if she didn't limit the candy. One day on a long car trip Luis became restless and began reciting the last book she had had him read. Once again the Winamakis were amazed by his letter-perfect memory. When no M&M's were forthcoming, Luis stopped reciting, but as soon as they were home Mrs. Winamaki used candy to entice Luis to recall the entire book. As Luis retold the story Mrs. Winamaki followed along in the book—Luis made no errors.

Mrs. Winamaki told Luis's teachers about his ability and again a brief shower of attention followed. The school psychologist studied Luis and explained that he was "processing information into memory storage in a linear fashion" but could not "deconstruct the information into components and reconstruct it in new combinations." Mrs. Winamaki understood that to mean that Luis had a photographic memory but no creativity. Luis's social worker was equally fascinated but concluded that it didn't alter his situation. Mrs. Winamaki soon agreed. Luis recorded reams of material and recited it perfectly, but never once offered an opinion on what he read. Luis had a gift every student in the world dreamed of, but it was wasted on someone who was incapable of an original thought.

Luis's appearance also added to his troubles—he looked different. He was short and his body was too wide, his head too big, and his lips small. He had been ugly to the point of being unlovable as an infant, and nature's cruel program continued to run its course as he grew. When his permanent teeth erupted they were large and crooked, and his lips could cover them only with effort. With no one to pay for an orthodontist, puberty found Luis with a crooked smile, and then wreaked its havoc on his body. Acne ravaged his face, and his black hair took on a permanent oily sheen. Thick coarse hair sprouted on his face and body, which Luis could not be taught to shave properly, leaving him an ugly troll of a person.

When Mrs. Winamaki found she was pregnant with twins, she and her husband decided to give up their foster child. Luis was no trouble to care for, but it was difficult to attach to someone who showed no interest in your comings and goings. He was as happy sitting in an empty room with a TV as he was holding Mrs. Winamaki's hand during a walk in the park. Mrs.

Winamaki gave the agency six months' notice that they would
have to find a new home for him.

Two months later Dr. Wes Martin came to see Luis. He was
excited by Luis's ability but evasive when Mrs. Winamaki asked
if he was going to be providing foster care. A month after that
Elizabeth Foxworth came to visit. Mrs. Winamaki liked her instantly, finding her to be a warm person who seemed to care
about Luis's well-being.

The Winamakis took Luis to the plane on the day he left for
Oregon. They explained patiently to Luis what was going on
and where he was going, reassuring him that he would like it
there. There was no response. When Mrs. Winamaki hugged
him goodbye, his hands hung limp at his sides. Mrs. Winamaki
walked him onto the plane and buckled him into his seat; then
she combed his hair for him, kissed his forehead, and left. She
paused at the plane's door to see Luis looking at her with emotionless eyes. She waved goodbye but there was no response.
Mrs. Winamaki left the plane crying for them both.

10

NEW ARRIVALS

Gil kept in the background and stayed out of the way. Two more savants would arrive today and the house was a hive of activity. Elizabeth double-checked the room the savants would share to make sure it was properly prepared and then left to pick them up. Acting like an expectant father, Wes puttered around, crabby from lack of sleep. Keeping away from Wes, Gil watched Wes's team as they worked with their equipment, preparing it for another integration. Len was frustrated by a problem with the nitrogen lines, but declined Gil's help, and there was nothing he could help Shamita with. As usual, Daphne was playing the piano and Ralph was parked in front of the TV, changing channels every few seconds, frustrated by Sunday-afternoon TV. Gil sat for a while, watching Ralph, thinking about how to get rid of him, but there was nothing he could do to Ralph here. He needed to get him outside, so he made a suggestion. "Slurpee." Ralph's head immediately snapped around.

"Yeah, Slurpee."

Ralph got up and walked to the piano.

"Hey, Daphne, you want a Slurpee?"

"Cherry."

"OK, if they got it. I won't get you grape."

Gil listened as Ralph found Wes at the kitchen table and

pestered him for money. Wes forked it over willingly and called after Ralph to take his time. Gil watched Ralph go out the front and then waited a minute before going out the back door. There was no danger of losing Ralph, Gil knew, and sure enough when Gil came around the corner of the house he found Ralph halfway down the block talking to a neighbor. Soon Ralph said goodbye and took off with his long strides. Gil followed, watching for an opportunity and worrying at the same time. He had to get rid of Ralph, but if he killed him, Elizabeth or Children's Services could shut down the project. If Gil did nothing he risked discovery. He wanted the project to continue—but how to deal with Ralph?

Ralph talked to more people along the block, calling all of them by name. When he got to the corner he turned and walked up into a yard and out of Gil's sight. Gil crept forward, peeking around a bush into the yard. Ralph was talking to a group of college students sitting on the steps of their frat house. Most were holding beer cans. The college students were raucous and laughing and Ralph laughed with them. Ralph told them about his Slurpee mission and said his goodbyes, then turned down the block. Gil ducked for cover until Ralph was on his way again, but then waited, now knowing what to do. Gil watched the students, picking out one that seemed to be a leader. He was good-looking, and the others deferred to him, laughing at his jokes. Then Gil suggested an idea to him. The boy's face brightened, then he laughed, quickly sharing the idea with the others. Then they all laughed. Gil suggested more ideas that he shared and soon they were laughing and adding their own ideas. More beer was passed around and a party atmosphere spread across the porch.

Gil was still waiting by the fraternity when Ralph appeared, a Slurpee in each hand. Again Gil made the suggestion to the leader, and he shared it with his friends, who erupted with enthusiasm, running down to intercept Ralph. After a little coaxing and a lot of laughing, Ralph followed them into the house.

Wes was standing on the porch when the new savants arrived. Archie stepped out by himself and came to stand on the porch by Wes, but Luis waited in the car to be told what to do. Wes had to smile when he saw Archie, but he was careful not to let Elizabeth see him. The tall, gangly, bucktoothed redhead with the blue Mickey Mouse glasses would make Mother Teresa laugh. Wes looked around to make sure Len wasn't near—he would have something to say for sure.

"Hi, Archie. Do you remember me?" Wes asked.

"Yes."

"Welcome. I'm sure you'll like it here."

"I liked it where I was."

Elizabeth opened Luis's door and asked him to get out and join Archie on the porch. Luis complied, then stood waiting for more instructions. Wes greeted Luis but knew not to expect a reply. When Elizabeth reached the porch she looked around, puzzled.

"I can hear Daphne playing, so I know where she is, but where is Ralph? I can't imagine he would miss this."

Wes hadn't thought about Ralph for hours. He remembered giving Ralph money for Slurpees but then realized he hadn't come back. Wes's heart sank.

"He went for Slurpees," he said.

Elizabeth nodded, then herded Archie and Luis into the house. Wes followed, then called to Daphne. Daphne stopped playing and turned to Wes, keeping her head down.

"Daphne, did Ralph bring you a Slurpee?"

"No. I asked for cherry and I never got it."

Wes turned to find Elizabeth listening, her concern now showing. Elizabeth turned and shouted up the stairs.

"Gil? Gil, come down please!"

Gil appeared at the top of the stairs, a smile on his face. "I didn't know you were back. How are Archie and Luis doing?"

"Gil, have you seen Ralph?"

"He went for Slurpees. Isn't he back yet?"

Elizabeth turned without answering and went through the living room to the lab. Len, Karon, and Shamita all denied seeing Ralph come back. Wes felt his heart sink even lower. He had gotten so used to Ralph's wanderings that he took them for granted. He had forgotten Ralph was emotionally and mentally a ten-year-old.

Elizabeth signaled Gil down and pulled Wes into the hall by the arm.

"I think we better look for Ralph. It's not like him not to come back."

"Elizabeth, I'm sorry . . ." Wes began.

"I'm not accusing you of anything, so don't be defensive. Ralph's gone for Slurpees a dozen times and always come back. Let's just find him now and talk about whose fault it is later."

The three of them went out the door and Elizabeth gave directions on how to split up. She never finished, because Ralph was coming up the block. There was no mistaking his long stride and his rocking gate, but he was a spectacle. He was naked, with red blotches on his body. Several children were following, laughing and pointing, and neighbors were coming out of their houses and down to the sidewalk as he passed. Laughter could be heard as he got closer, with a few indignant voices mixed in. In her yard across the street Mrs. Clayton stood dumbly, the water from her hose raining onto the sidewalk.

Ralph was stripped naked except for his shoes and socks. Concentric red rings circled each of his nipples, making them look like targets. A large red arrow had been painted down his abdomen pointing to his penis. His testicles had been shaved and painted bright red. Just above the arrow across his chest was the word "balls." Wes would have been humiliated, but Ralph came walking up the street with his usual grin plastered on his face. Stopping at the bottom of the steps he smiled broadly.

"Hi Elizabeth, are Archie and Luis here?"

"Yes, Ralph," she replied calmly.

Anything but calm, Wes nearly shouted at Ralph. "What happened? Who did this to you?"

"Did what?" Ralph said.

"Took your clothes, and painted your . . . your body."

"Oh. I got nitiated. I'm a rat brother now—I mean frat brother."

Wes was furious both for what had happened to Ralph and for what this might do to his project. The kids following Ralph were congregated on the sidewalk and Wes shooed them away. Then he urged Ralph into the house.

"Come on, Ralph," Elizabeth said. "You better take a bath."

"Well okeydokey, Elizabeth."

Ralph turned and walked up the steps. When he did Wes could

see his back had been painted with the word "asshole." Above the word was an arrow pointing to his head; just below was an arrow that went down his back and pointed between his cheeks.

Daphne met Ralph just inside the door, seemingly unaware of his nakedness or the paint on his body.

"Where's my Slurpee, Ralph?" she asked.

Ralph stopped and folded his arms across his bare chest and leaned back, with his hips pushed out. His nakedness and painted testicles made it a bizarre sight. Suddenly Ralph's hand shot out and up and he thumped himself on the side of the head.

"How could I be so stupid?" he said. "I forgot it at my frat house. I'll be right back."

Ralph turned to go but Wes jumped in front of him.

"Please, Ralph. A bath first and then clothes."

Ralph looked perplexed for a minute and then broke into a huge grin.

"Well okeydokey." Then he walked up the stairs. Len and Karon came in watching his back disappear up the stairs. Len turned to Wes but before he could say anything Wes cut him off.

"I don't want to hear it, Len."

Len shrugged and whispered in Karon's ear. She guffawed and then slapped her hand over her mouth and ran back into the living room. Len shrugged his shoulders at Wes, smiled broadly, and then followed Karon.

11

FRANKIE

". . . the Lord God formed the man from the dust of the ground and breathed into his nostrils the breath of life, and the man became a living being."

Wes stifled a yawn, fearful Ralph would make a loud comment about him falling asleep. Once again he tried concentrating on the sermon. Pastor Young was a good speaker, his voice rising and falling, punctuating his points with a change in pitch rather than volume. The theme of the sermon was something about the uniqueness of humanity, the pastor arguing that God's breath, in the form of a spirit, set us apart from the animals. If this had been an open forum Wes would have argued with him. The concept of soul was an unprovable hypothesis and simply wrongheaded from Wes's perspective. He was an evolutionist and rejected mystic notions of soul and spirit. In his mind, natural selection was sufficient to account for the development of the great variety of species, and the crowning achievement of that process was the human brain. Ironically, it was that same brain that created gods and religion to explain its own existence. To Wes the only real human mystery left was the mind, and Wes was about to take a giant step forward in understanding it.

The sermon ended and the offering plate was passed. Wes had money ready this time, but still Ralph said loudly, "Remember to put something in the plate, Wes." When the service ended Daphne went forward and played, so Wes waited, being greeted by curious members of the congregation. After a few hymns, Elizabeth led Daphne to the exit, where she shook hands and spoke to the pastor. Wes couldn't hear what the pastor said, but Elizabeth laughed. Wes realized he'd never heard her laugh before.

They walked back to the house like a family, Ralph, Daphne, Archie, and Luis leading the way, Elizabeth and Wes following, making small talk. But when they got to the fraternity that had initiated Ralph, Elizabeth paused.

"Go with the others, Wes. I want to talk to Ralph's fraternity brothers."

"Let me do it," Wes said. He hated confrontation, but they would never be able to keep Ralph in the house and he needed to be able to walk safely through the neighborhood.

"Is that your protective instincts showing? Don't you think a woman can handle this?"

"It's not that—" he said defensively.

Now she smiled. "I'm not serious, Wes. You should see your face."

She laughed again and Wes was embarrassed, but also pleased—it was friendly teasing. Still, Wes wanted to go with her.

"No," she argued. "They'll take this better from me."

Reluctantly, Wes agreed, then followed Ralph and Daphne up the street. Strangely, he kept thinking of Elizabeth laughing—she had a nice laugh.

Elizabeth rapped on the fraternity door several times before someone answered. Elizabeth took an immediate dislike of the fraternity brother. He was good-looking, and knew it, and his eyes said he wasn't a bit sorry for what he'd done to Ralph.

"What do you want?"

"I'm here because of what you did to Ralph."

"I don't know what you're talking about."

Elizabeth stared, unwilling to accept his lie. "What's your name?"

"Go to hell! Why don't you go bother someone else!"

"Like the dean?"

Elizabeth watched his face. He wasn't afraid of her threat; it

seemed more of an inconvenience. Before he could respond
someone pushed past him out onto the porch. He was tall, thin,
and blond, with a ruddy complexion. He was clearly embarrassed.

"I'm Ron Classen, chapter president. We're real sorry about
what happened. It just got out of hand—we like Ralph. Really!"

Elizabeth was sure his apology was heartfelt. "Then why did
you do it to him?"

"When I got back it was almost over. They had been drinking.
I guess it was the beer, but no one hurt him. He seemed like he
was having a good time."

"He loved it!" the good-looking one said, coming out onto the
porch.

"Ron, I think your apology is sincere, but are you speaking for
everyone involved?"

"Yes! Sure. Everyone likes Ralph. We wouldn't hurt him, and
I promise it won't happen again."

Turning to stare at the good-looking one, Elizabeth said
"What about him?"

"Billy, tell her you're sorry!"

Without a word he went inside, slamming the door.

Embarrassed, Classen stammered another apology. "Billy's
got an attitude, but he'll go along. If he messes with Ralph we'll
kick him out. We've already got cause."

Elizabeth accepted Classen's assurance—she trusted Classen.
As long as most of the fraternity boys were like him there
wouldn't be any more trouble, but just in case there were more
like Billy hiding in the nest, she thought it would be best to keep
the savants away from the fraternity.

Archie and Luis had adjusted well to their new room and ate
well, so after a day Wes suggested to Elizabeth that they try another synthesis. To Wes's surprise she agreed.

They parked Ralph in front of the TV with a large Slurpee
from the 7-Eleven. They wouldn't need him for this run, because they had the new savants and Wes wanted him out of his
hair. Daphne was almost eager this time, and Luis was as com-
pliant as a robot. Archie, however, was reluctant. Elizabeth reassured him but he nodded agreement only after he learned he
could keep his Mickey Mouse glasses on.

Shamita, Len, and Karon got busy mapping the newcomers. Their routine was the same, except that they gave Archie a puzzle to work with the picture side down and the brown backing facing up. Elizabeth watched curiously as he put the all-brown picture together and then spoke softly to Len.

"Why is the puzzle facedown?"

"It's not. It's a picture of Los Angeles in summertime," Len said.

Elizabeth punched his arm. "That's a stupid joke."

Len laughed at his own joke. "It doesn't matter to him whether the puzzle is picture side up or picture side down. He solves by shape alone. We put the picture side down to make sure the colors, or images, didn't trigger unwanted memory traces or emotional response. It would contaminate our map."

"Why do you want his puzzle-solving ability?"

"That's what he uses it for, but imagine having that ability when you took geometry, or when playing chess."

"I see. I could have used it in organic chemistry. Constructing models of complex compounds would be easy for him. I suppose an architect or an engineer has this kind of ability."

"No one has the level of ability he has. He's uncanny. If I had his spatial ability I know what I'd do with it."

"Let me guess. You'd devise a three-dimensional programming language."

"Close. I'd invent new positions for sex. I'm tired of the seventy-three I have been using."

Karon snickered and then said, "Seventy-four."

Elizabeth realized this was more than just a private joke—it was an intimate joke. Elizabeth watched Len finish mapping and then signal he was ready. Then Wes surprised them all.

"Gil, would you help us out again?"

Shamita turned to Wes and spoke softly. "We don't need him, Wes. I thought we were going to use Luis for the matrix. We can integrate the rest from the three we have."

"I know. I just want to . . . Well, the program is really designed for more. Let's use Gil for the matrix as we did before."

"We might not get all of Luis's lower-brain functions if he's not the matrix. We could lose his total recall without it."

"We don't know that. Besides, it's just a test."

Unconvinced, Shamita turned back to her monitor, puzzled by Wes's decision.

Karon fit Gil with a helmet, and attached the electrodes to his chest. When Len and Shamita signaled that they had his readings, Wes looked over his savants in anticipation. He'd worked years for this moment.

Luis lay still but Archie was restless, rocking his head back and forth to see what was going on. Len made faces every time Archie's head moved and he muttered something under his breath that made Karon giggle. Waving at Shamita to catch her eye, Wes pointed at Archie and then pretended to strangle himself. Shamita nodded and a few seconds later Archie lay still, breathing in a relaxed manner. Then one by one Shamita reduced the sensory input of each volunteer and selected out their psychomotor functions. When she was done they all lay as if asleep, breathing deep and regular. When Wes got the thumbs-up from all of his team he activated his program which captured the feed from the other stations. Elizabeth came to stand behind him again, showing genuine interest in his work—he liked her near when she was like that.

"Luis's map looks different. It's more diffuse," she pointed out.

"Yes, but see the concentration here and here in the occipital lobes. Luis is unique in this group. He isn't a savant in the usual sense."

"He has a photographic memory, right."

"A better name would be eidetic imagery. He retains everything he sees and then he can read it back as if it's right there in front of him. Of course he has no idea of what to do with the information."

"Don't be too sure. It's more likely he's overwhelmed by all the information he has. If you could reduce the sensory barrage with your computer, he might begin to process."

Wes paused in thought. It was an intriguing idea and Wes's respect for Elizabeth grew. "We might try that later, if you like," he said. "It could lead to a paper. We could publish it together."

"Maybe," she said. "I'm not sure I'm ready to be the bride of Frankenstein just yet."

Smiling, Wes went back to work and began patching together his model intellect. They used Gil as the basic matrix, then overlaid the other pieces of mental function from the donor savants. Daphne's left-hemisphere calendar-counting ability was patched in first, followed by Archie's right-hemisphere spatial skill. Finally, Luis's memory was overlaid. When Wes put the last piece in, Shamita began tapping at her keyboard.

"Hold it, Wes, we didn't get it all. Gil is blocking the integration. Let me reduce the parameters on Luis a bit."

Wes waited while Shamita tapped away at her keyboard. When she signaled that she was done, Wes tried another integration. This time it took.

"We have Frankie," Wes announced.

Len whistled loudly and Karon clapped her hands. Only Shamita stared quietly at her screen.

"What's the matter, Shamita?" Wes said. "That looks like full integration to me."

"I suppose," Shamita said weakly.

"Frankie? You mean this is supposed to be a new person?" Elizabeth asked. "Someone different from Gil, Archie, Luis, and Daphne? I don't see it," Elizabeth said over Wes's shoulder. "It's not any different from what you did before."

"It's more complex, right, Shamita?"

Shamita nodded.

"You define a person in terms of complexity of brain waves?" Elizabeth asked.

"Well, that and uniqueness. These patterns are different from all the donors, hence a unique consciousness. The complexity is equal to that of a person, so we conclude it's a new person."

"What about a sense of self? Isn't that essential for personhood?"

"That's not part of our operational definition."

"It should be, and more."

"We set realistic goals . . ."

"You set low goals and then crow like you've conquered the world and not just the barnyard."

Wes scowled at Elizabeth. "Frankie is much more than you give him credit for."

"Prove it. Prove to me this is Frankie first, and then show me what he can do," Elizabeth challenged.

Wes looked at her for a hard minute and then spoke to Shamita.

"Who has the audition?"

"Gil, just like before."

Wes got up with a yellow pad and walked to Gil. Elizabeth remained watching the readouts on Wes's screen.

"Gil, can you hear me? Gil, if you can hear me respond by saying yes."

A long silence followed.

"Your name is Frankie. What is your name?"

"Frankie."

The voice was Gil's, but it didn't have his inflection, or any rhythm. Wes was pleased, but Elizabeth was frowning.

"Frankie, what is the date of the first Monday in 1892?"

"January fourth."

"What would be the date of the last Tuesday in 2054?"

"December twenty-ninth."

"Want me to go on, Elizabeth?"

"What's the point? I've seen you use Daphne's ability through Gil before. What makes this Frankie?"

"Wait, you'll see. Shamita, give me the selected psychomotor functions."

Wes waited for Shamita to finish typing and give him a nod. Then he turned to Gil and said, "Frankie, sit up, please."

Even though Wes had spoken to Gil it was Daphne who sat up. Wes looked at Elizabeth, who showed only a hint of surprise. Wes pulled a card table over in front of Daphne and took out a small jigsaw puzzle. He dumped it out and then went back to talk into Gil's ears.

"Frankie, would you put this puzzle together for me?"

"Yes."

Daphne worked the puzzle in the same manner as Archie, starting with one edge and attaching a piece to it. Then, systematically and with virtually no error, she put the puzzle together in a few minutes, completing it sideways in front of her. Wes didn't say anything; he just turned to Elizabeth with a "told you so" look. Elizabeth still looked unconvinced.

"You're still just mixing their abilities. This isn't any different than what you did before."

"Just mixing abilities, just mixing abilities," Wes mocked. "Can't you see how incredible this is?"

"I concede it's ingenious, even brilliant, but it's not a person. A person could combine these abilities into a new function, something they have never done before."

"True, and we want that, and more. Let me demonstrate something else. Frankie, can you play chess?"

"Yes."

"You are white and I am black. You open with queen's pawn to queen three. I move king's pawn to king four. How could you threaten my queen?"

"Bishop to knight five."

Wes nodded knowingly at Elizabeth.

"Are you telling me that's right?" Elizabeth asked.

Karon answered before Wes could. "I play a lot of chess. It's not good chess but it's right."

"OK, Elizabeth, are you convinced?"

Looking thoughtful, she said, "Let me ask a question."

Wes hesitated, but then returned to his station.

"Frankie, what move would you make if you were to make the first move in chess?"

"I would move the castle pawn to castle four."

"That's a good move," Karon said. "It frees the castle to protect the front line."

"Yes, I suppose . . ." Elizabeth said, doubtfully. "Let me try something else. Frankie, are you a male or female?"

"Cut it off, Shamita!" Wes shouted. Elizabeth looked at him in surprise. "I didn't mean to shout," Wes said, "but that question could confuse Frankie. Frankie was constructed out of both male and female parts, and it isn't clear how Frankie will think of himself."

"Why? I thought Frankie was a person."

"Frankie's a new person. Gender is complex—you can switch from one to the other as late as age five, with no psychological harm. Think of Frankie as a newborn with adult abilities."

"If Frankie has no gender then why do you use 'he' and 'him' when you're talking about Frankie?"

"I didn't realize I was. What does it matter, since Frankie has no gender?"

"How can anyone be gender-insensitive in this day and age?" she said. "If it doesn't matter then why didn't you choose 'she'?"

Wes swallowed hard, wondering if he would ever run out

of ways of offending Elizabeth. When he had no reply she continued.

"Are you saying I can't ask if Frankie is male or female?"

Wes hesitated. He didn't want to make it look like there was any risk to the savants, and limiting Elizabeth could do that. "OK, you can ask, but be gentle." Wes signaled Shamita to turn Frankie's hearing back on.

"Do you know whether you are male or female?" Elizabeth asked.

"No."

"If you had to guess, what would you guess?"

"I don't know."

Elizabeth walked over to Wes and spoke softly. "Frankie shows no self-awareness. This isn't a person. It is clever, it is amazing, but it's not a person."

"Why? Just because Frankie doesn't sit around with his finger in his navel and explore his feelings doesn't mean he isn't a person. You can't tell me Luis is any more self-aware and you consider him a person."

"Luis is hyperaware, in my opinion, not unaware," she said.

"Elizabeth, you're judging personhood by your own preferences. To you there's a feeling or motive behind every action, so you explore your consciousness endlessly, turning over every rock looking for dark slimy memories to crawl out. There are millions of people out there like you who haunt the pop-psychology sections of bookstores looking for the latest insight into their own behavior, or better yet, everyone else's. Isn't there room for people who aren't as introspective?"

"Everyone is introspective," Elizabeth said defensively.

"Not like you. Take me, for example. I choose not to be self-absorbed."

"You choose not to be self-aware."

Wes gave up. He and Elizabeth were too different, but he didn't want to let her get in the last word. Len solved his problem with another stupid joke.

"Do you know how many psychologists it takes to change a lightbulb? One. But the lightbulb has to be committed to change."

Karon laughed and Shamita snickered, but Wes and Elizabeth just glared at each other.

"I've got more lightbulb jokes," Len offered.

"Got any funny ones?" Shamita asked.

"I have another question, if you don't mind," Elizabeth said, then walked back to the cots. "What are you thinking about, Frankie?"

Wes turned and watched Gil, waiting for a response. There was none.

"When I am not asking you questions, what do you think about?"

"I don't think about anything."

Elizabeth turned and gave Wes an "I told you so" look.

"So Frankie isn't a deep thinker—"

"He's . . . *she's* not a thinker at all. That's the point. There's no independent thought process in your creation. Certainly even you must concede that thought is part of personhood."

"Just because he's not thinking now doesn't mean he hasn't ever had a thought. Frankie," Wes said, turning to speak to Gil. "What was the last thing you remember thinking about?"

"I remember thinking of killing Ralph."

Wes took a step back, trying to regain his composure. It was the last thing he had expected to come from his synthesized intellect. Fortunately, Len helped him put it in perspective.

"Are you sure you didn't mix in a little of yourself, Wes? You're always saying you want to kill Ralph."

Wes forced a laugh. "Yeah, that's right. I've said that myself."

"To know Ralph is to want to kill him," Len added.

Elizabeth didn't join in on the joking, and looked concerned. "Whose thought was that?"

"It's Frankie's," Shamita said, without taking her eyes off of her computer screen.

"But it had to come from someone," Elizabeth countered.

"Not if we have Frankie. It could be an original thought from Frankie," Wes said.

Elizabeth shook her head. "I thought you said Frankie is a newborn. It's scary to think the first thoughts of your Frankie would be about killing someone. Besides, we've seen no evidence of original thought. It's more likely something pulled from one of the donor memories. Any way to tell which one?"

"No," Shamita said. "All we get are multiplexed brain waves.

We can't break them into individual signals, let alone decode them."

"And it's still possible the thought was original. Ralph is awfully irritating," Wes argued.

"He's only irritating to you. He's one of the most universally liked people I know; completely ingenuous. Besides, your Frankie hasn't had a chance to meet Ralph yet."

"But there would be the residual memories that Frankie could access," Wes countered. Wes was going to say more, but he realized he was heading down a dead end. Elizabeth was right about everyone liking Ralph but him. Even his dislike was more of an irritation—Ralph was an extra burden; a burden that picked his pocket endlessly for gum and Slurpees. Wes realized if Frankie was accessing residual memories of Ralph, and if they were all positive, then how could Frankie be irritated enough to react with the thought of killing him? Finally, he just rushed on. "It doesn't matter if it's an original thought or not. We're not done constructing Frankie yet. We still have Yu to add."

"It does matter if someone is thinking of killing Ralph," Elizabeth said.

"It's just an expression, not a threat."

"Maybe."

"When we get Yu into the synthesis we'll get original thought, then you can interrogate Frankie all you want about his feelings about Ralph."

"Her feelings about Ralph," Elizabeth corrected. "Besides, I don't accept your complexity theory. Personhood is more than just brain waves."

"True, it takes memory, reasoning, and synthesis. We'll provide all of these."

"That's a reductionistic machine view of a person. If that's all there was to personhood then computers would generate ideas."

"Computers aren't complex enough," Wes said.

"Complexity again! The most complex computer in the world won't generate thought, because it lacks what really makes a person human—it lacks a soul."

"Elizabeth, you're a mystic!"

"God made man out of the dust and breathed life into him. That breath of life is the psyche—the soul."

Wes recognized the scripture from the sermon that morning.

Elizabeth's theory had no credibility from his perspective and was nothing more than superstitious nonsense, but he was tired of arguing. "Well if Frankie needs a soul, then we'll just have to get him a soul."

"Her a soul," Elizabeth countered with a slight smile.

Yu Tran was the only son of a proud family—a family rich in tradition and culture. Like all the Tran children he was expected to continue the family line and to contribute to the family's prosperity. To help him in his appointed task the course of his life was planned for him before he was born. Yu would be raised to respect his elders, to honor his family, and to honor his country, in that order. Personal honor would come only as a result of the other three. Yu, like his sisters, would learn the value of education beginning in the home. On the day Yu walked into kindergarten he would know how to read and to write, and to do simple math, because his grandmother would teach him. He would speak two languages, and keep his fluency in both all through his life. In school he would be in the talented and gifted program and be accelerated in math. After school he would take music lessons, and then spend the rest of the afternoon doing homework. Most evenings would be spent in the library. In high school he would take the honors courses in math and science and he would earn a scholarship to a prestigious college. He would graduate summa cum laude and go on to medical school, where he would become a surgeon. But Yu wasn't like his sisters, and it became painfully obvious first to his mother, and then to his father, that Yu was destined for a different life path.

Yu could not read when he enrolled in kindergarten, and couldn't count to ten, let alone add. He could write his first name, but that was only two letters. In the spring of that first year his mother was called to a conference, where she hung her head in shame when they told her they wanted Yu to repeat kindergarten. But the shame of that was nothing compared with the shame she felt when she told her husband that night.

Yu's oldest sister took Yu to school after that; his mother could not bear to do it. That was fine with Yu. He had felt his mother's hand grow cold over the last few years, and although he was treated well, something he couldn't understand had come between them—something he had done. There was still warmth in his sister's hand, though, and he clung to it gratefully on those cold walks to school. It was the only human comfort he received from breakfast to bedtime.

After a second year in kindergarten Yu was passed on to first grade, still deficient in even basic skills. By now his mother had lost interest in his education and refused to come to school conferences. When the school insisted, Yu's older sister went and listened to Yu's teachers and the school psychologist recommend a special-education program. Then it was Yu's sister's turn to sit in the kitchen and hang her head in shame and tell her parents what was said. That was a terrible night for the Tran family. The grandparents were called and Yu's aunts and uncles. The meeting went on all night but by morning they had a plan. Yu would not be enrolled in the special-education program. Instead the family would pool its resources and send Yu to a residential school. It was expensive, but family honor was priceless.

Yu clung to his oldest sister the day he was to leave. He cried and pleaded with her, promising to be a good boy if he could stay, but all she could do was hug him and wipe away his tears, promising to write to him and visit whenever she could. Then she handed him an album she had put together with pictures of his family. The first page was a picture of her and Yu.

She wrote every week and the staff faithfully read the letters to Yu. He didn't understand much of what she said about her life, it was so different from his, but he felt the warmth behind the words. One day a letter came that the staff did not read to him. Instead, they took him aside and asked him if he knew what death was. Yu began to cry for his favorite sister and was unable to answer. When he was told it was his mother who had been killed in a car accident, relief swept through him and he smiled. That smile at the mention of his mother's death was noted in his record and worried the staff for years.

Yu was well cared for at the Riverview Residential School. Unlike state institutions, it was well staffed and he received personal attention. Riverview wasn't like a home, not even the best institution could be, but as in a family there were periods of joy and periods of sorrow. Yu's first year was all sorrow as he mourned the loss of his home and family. Riverview was too different for an eight-year-old to adjust to easily, and Yu became sullen and hostile. The staff was patient, however, and Yu slowly accepted his fate, and adjusted to Riverview's routine.

Three months after Yu's arrival a young woman was hired to work with his unit. Her name was Suni and she was short and lithe like Yu's sister. When Suni first came to him she held out her hand and smiled. Yu hesitated, but when he took her hand warmth rushed through him—something he hadn't felt since his sister visited last. Yu went willingly with her, and after that Yu could always be managed by Suni.

Suni never replaced Yu's sister in his heart but she was Yu's security blanket at Riverview. Whenever Yu became morose, or hostile, he was left for Suni to handle. Eventually the staff realized that Yu was becoming manipulative and using his fits of anger and depression to keep Suni near. So one day they transferred Suni to another unit. Yu became depressed and refused to eat. At the end of a week they were forced to choose between force-feeding Yu or bringing back Suni. Suni came back the next day. Yu quickly regained his strength but he was never quite the same. He had withdrawn when Suni left—withdrawn into a place deep inside his mind—and never made it all the way back. Suni still comforted Yu, but he couldn't quite forget that she had abandoned him, just like his family.

By the time Yu was ten he had learned personal hygiene skills and could wash, dress, and feed himself. He had learned to keep his room clean and tidy and became compulsive about it. Everything had a place and everything was kept in that place. When something new, like a sweater or a toy, was given to Yu he would either reject the present or select something in his room that was removed to make space. When someone returned something to

Yu's room they would always ask, "Where is the place this goes?" Yu would direct them to the place and supervise its placement.

When Yu was eleven he began to show remarkable skills at calculating. Yu had learned to add and subtract simple problems, but showed poor ability. But when they introduced multiplication Yu showed an affinity that surprised his teacher. Yu quickly learned to multiply through twelve, and his teacher wanted to stop there because he reasoned Yu would have little use for more complex math. But Suni insisted they test his limits. They introduced more complex math problems to Yu, which he quickly mastered. Soon Yu's ability to compute exceeded the abilities of his teachers.

Over the next year Yu's mental math skills continued to develop, and Suni called Yu's father to come and see what his son could do. Reluctantly, his father came, bringing his oldest daughter with him. Yu clung to his sister's hand through the visit. "Show me," Yu's father demanded as soon as he had arrived. Suni gave Yu the math problems, having him divide and multiply three-figure numbers, multiply fractions, and compute the volume of cubes. Yu's sister applauded in delight and Yu basked in her approval. When the demonstration was over Suni turned to Mr. Tran and asked him if he was proud of his son. Mr. Tran glowered at Suni and then turned to Yu and asked "If a man comes into our store to buy a gallon of milk and pays two dollars and seventy-nine cents, how much change would he get from three dollars?" Yu rocked in his seat, looking perplexed, and then said, "I don't know." Mr. Tran started to leave but Suni stopped him.

"Yu," Suni asked, "what is three hundred minus two hundred seventy-nine?"

"Twenty-one," he replied.

Mr. Tran was unimpressed. "Are you finished?" he asked, and then got up and left. Yu's sister pried her hand loose and kissed him a tearful goodbye.

Everyone expected Yu to sink into depression and become difficult to handle, but he surprised them by continuing to develop his calculating skills and soon could multiply and divide six-figure numbers with great accuracy. Shortly after his twelfth birthday Yu demonstrated a new skill.

It was afternoon break time and Yu and the others in his unit were parked in front of the projection screen TV in the recreation room watching Disney cartoons. Suni was sitting on the couch working a crossword puzzle and called out to a coworker for help.

"What's another word for disobedience?"

"Mutiny," came the reply.

"Starts with an *r.*"

"Revolt," replied the voice.

"Not enough letters. I need nine."

"Rebellion," Yu said quietly, without taking his eyes from the cartoon.

Surprised, Suni found it fit. Then she picked another clue and read it to Yu.

"Someone who teaches, nine letters, starts with a *p?*"

"Professor," Yu replied, his eyes still glued on the antics on the screen.

"No, it doesn't fit. The third letter is an *e.*"

"Preceptor."

Suni had to retrieve a dictionary to confirm that a preceptor was a teacher. She brought the dictionary back with her and began testing Yu's vocabulary. For "transparent" he gave synonyms of "translucent" and "diaphanous." For "treasurer" he gave "bursar," "receiver," and "steward," and for "traveler" he responded with "wayfarer," "vagabond," and "nomad." Suni had never heard Yu use these words in his own speech, and wondered where he could have ever heard some of them.

Suni studied Yu after that, trying to understand where his remarkable vocabulary came from. He read at about a fourth-grade level, and then only when pressured to do so. He never picked up a book voluntarily, and certainly never one that would have words like "wayfarer" or "preceptor" in it. No, Yu was not a reader, but he was a listener. Suni soon realized that Yu listened intently to everything that went on around him. He listened to the staff, to the radio, to visitors, and to the TV. It didn't matter if it was two janitors talking about the latest basketball scores, or the teachers discussing their patients; Yu drank in every word. Yu also soaked up the radio and TV. Whether it was Donald Duck, *Jeopardy, Wheel of Fortune,* or the nightly news, Yu gave it the same intense attention.

Suni began exploring Yu's verbal abilities and found them inconsistent. If Yu was asked for a synonym of a word like "good" he would respond with "benevolent" or "virtuous." But if asked for an antonym of "good," he couldn't even give the common response of "bad." Nor could he define words. He was limited to finding words similar in meaning to the keywords. If you asked him to define the words he would merely shrug and stare at his shoes. If you persisted he would get angry.

The teachers marveled at Yu the human dictionary, but Suni pointed out he was more of a thesaurus than a dictionary. Yu helped solve many a crossword puzzle after that, and his lexicon grew as he learned from dozens of puzzles he helped solve. Suni thought of calling Yu's father again to have him come and witness this new marvel, but decided she would explore his abilities first. Mr. Tran was a hard man to please.

Suni brought in a variety of word games for Yu and found he was completely confused by word-search games where words were hidden among other letters. Scrabble and Boggle were also beyond his comprehension, and he just pushed the letters around aimlessly. One of the teachers brought in a calculator game where the answers to math problems on a calculator spelled out words. The game combined Yu's math ability and his vocabulary skill. Suni watched as the teacher gave the first problem to Yu.

"What did Amelia Earhart's father say the first time he saw her flying an airplane by herself? To get the answer, Yu, you use the calculator. Here, I'll show you. First you multiply three times point-oh-two-three."

"Point-oh-six-nine."

"Yes, Yu, that's correct, but let's do it on the calculator. There, now we add one-oh-one-four-one to the result."

"One-oh-one-four-one point-oh-six-nine."

"Let's do it on the calculator. Now we multiply that by five."

"Five-oh-seven-oh-five point-three-four-five."

"Yes, but look at it on the calculator. Now watch. We turn the calculator upside down and you can read the answer. What did Amelia Earhart's father say the first time he saw her flying an airplane by herself? Read the answer. Let me help you. See, the five looks like an *S* and the four looks like an *h* and the three looks like an *E*. If you read it across it says 'she solos.'"

Yu showed no interest. Suni realized it was at the same time too simple and too complex. Yu was as fast as a calculator so he had no use for them in the first place. Then, to get the answer, which was also a punch line to a joke, Yu had to be able to see the numbers as poorly formed letters. He was too precise to do that.

One day after finishing the crossword puzzle in the paper with Yu's help, Suni noticed that a word-scramble game had been added by the paper. Taking a blank piece of paper, she wrote out the scrambled words in big black letters and then took them to Yu. Suni put the scrambled words WOLOFLS, TEBSI, TRYS-MEY in front of Yu.

"Yu, these words are mixed up. Can you tell me what the words are?"

" 'Follows,' 'bites,' 'mystery,' " Yu said.

Suni tried mixing up her own words with similar success. Suni shared this new ability with the teachers and staff, and soon Yu was helping solve scramble games as well as crosswords. Suni puzzled over Yu's three abilities, calculating, finding synonyms, and unscrambling letters to make words. She could see no connection, however, so she continued to search for more word games for Yu.

One day the newspaper ran a contest to win a trip to Disney World. The task was to find one word that linked three other words. In the example they gave the words "sixteen," "potato," and "heart." The one word that linked all three words was sweet: "sweet sixteen," "sweet potato," and "sweetheart." Suni found Yu in his room straightening things that were in perfect order.

"Yu, I have a new game for you. I will give you three words and then you need to give me one word that connects all three. I know that's confusing, so let me give you an example. If I gave you the words 'sixteen,' 'potato,' and 'heart,' then one word that would connect all three would be 'sweet.' 'Sweet sixteen,' 'sweet potato,' 'sweetheart.' "

" 'Suite of rooms,' " Yu said.

"That's a different kind of sweet. I know it sounds the same. Just give me one word that connects all three. Now try this one: 'house,' 'dog,' 'sauce.' "

Yu swung his head back and forth, in confusion. Suni waited patiently, giving him a chance to figure out for himself what she was asking. A minute later Yu began scuffing his shoe on the floor—it meant he was getting agitated.

"It's 'hot,' Yu. 'Hothouse,' 'hot dog,' 'hot sauce.' "

" 'Hot rod,' 'hot plate,' 'Hottentot.' "

"Yes, Yu. Those all have the word 'hot' in them too. Let's try another one. Find one word that goes with 'port,' 'shell,' and 'gull.' "

Suni waited, and as before Yu stared at his feet. Then softly he said, "Sea."

"That's right, Yu. Very good. See if you can do this one: 'cross,' 'side,' 'out.' "

This time Yu answered with almost no hesitation.

" 'Walk.' "

"That's right, 'crosswalk,' 'sidewalk,' 'walkout.' "

Yu did four more without error and Suni knew he would seldom make an error after that. This new ability seemed so unlike the others that it puzzled Suni. Yu's huge vocabulary was essentially a recognition memory, and his mental math skills were strictly computational. Neither of those abilities could explain the kinds of remote connections he was making between words in this game. Of course, the biggest puzzle of all was why Yu could calculate large problems in his head with lightning speed, have a world-class vocabulary, and make linkages between seemingly unrelated words, and yet couldn't speak more than short sentences, or read above a fourth-grade level.

Suni was still thinking through the mystery of Yu when he looked up at her and said, " 'Cracker,' 'water,' 'jerk.' " Suni smiled in return. He was giving her a problem to solve. Yu's eyes were focused somewhere just below her chin, but he was holding the focus, clearly expecting an answer. Suni thought but couldn't get the connecting word.

"I don't know, Yu. What word connects all three?"

" 'Soda.' "

"Oh, I get it. 'Soda cracker,' 'soda jerk,' 'soda water.' That's very good. Can you do another one?"

" 'Trigger,' 'pin,' 'cut.' "

"Wait, I think I know. Is it 'hair'?"

Yu nodded but didn't speak.

" 'Hair trigger,' 'hairpin,' 'haircut.' "

Yu nodded again and then said, " 'Note,' 'master,' 'horse.' "

Suni was stumped again and said so.

" 'Quarter.' "

"Another good one, Yu. I never would have gotten that. 'Quarter note,' 'quartermaster,' 'quarter horse.' "

Suni played the word game with Yu for twenty minutes, amazed every second at what he was doing. It was the first time she had seen him produce any original thought, and she was sure now that Yu's father would be proud. Suni called him the next day but had to plead to get his father to visit again. Finally he agreed and came two weeks later to see his son's progress. Again his oldest sister accompanied her father and Yu lit up when he saw her. All through the visit Yu held her hand.

Suni demonstrated Yu's vocabulary using a crossword puzzle. Yu's sister praised Yu, but his father only glared and looked impatient. Suni hurried on to the word game.

"Yu, tell me what word connects 'shot,' 'board,' and 'skin.' "

" 'Buck,' " Yu replied.

Yu's father stared, his foot tapping out his impatience. Yu's sister thought for a moment and then said, "I get it; 'buckshot,' 'buckboard,' 'buckskin.' That's very clever," she said, and squeezed Yu's hand. Yu blushed.

"Now, Yu," Suni continued, "give your father and sister one to try."

" 'Town,' 'write,' 'dance.' "

Suni waited, watching Yu's father and sister. His sister's eyes shifted left and right, searching for the answer, but Yu's father only stared.

"I don't know what it could be," his sister said finally.

" 'Ghost.' "

"I never would have guessed, Yu. 'Ghost dance' makes it a very hard one."

Suni was going to continue, but Mr. Yu had heard enough.

"I gave up a day of work for this . . . for tricks!?"

"Don't you see, this is very special. Yu is making these problems up. He's being creative. This is a major step forward for Yu."

Mr. Tran snorted and then turned to his son.

"You are to file the bills for Mrs. White and Mrs. Cramer. Whose bill would be first in order?"

Yu hung his head in response and looked at his shoes. A minute later he began scuffing his feet on the floor.

"That's not a fair question," Suni protested. "It's too hard for him. If you explain what he needs to do I'm sure he could put files in the right order. He knows the alphabet."

"Call me when he can file, and make change, and stock the shelves."

"He'll never be able to work like that."

"Then don't call me! Ever!"

Tears welled in Suni's eyes as she watched Mr. Tran storm out of Yu's room followed by his tearful sister. Suni never called Mr. Tran again.

A year later Suni left Riverview. She tried explaining to Yu about her pregnancy but he seemed oblivious and was completely unprepared for the day she didn't come back.

Yu was hostile and violent for a week after Suni left, and the staff feared they would have to sedate him. Then one morning he got up and began pacing around his room. Around and around he went in circles. Keith, his new unit counselor, watched but didn't interfere. Then, without a word, Yu came out of his room and began walking the perimeter of the recreation room. After several circuits he began walking the halls and in and out of all the rooms. Keith followed him, trying to understand his new behavior. When Yu came to a locked door he became agitated and Keith used his passkey to let him in. Room by room Yu paced the complex. The administrative staff balked at first when Yu came to their offices, but Keith asked them to be patient, and Yu walked the perimeter of each office. When they had gone into every room in the place, Yu walked to the door. Keith hesitated but decided to let his behavior run its course. Yu walked out and down the steps and then along the outside of the building, walking behind the shrubbery where he could. He walked around the entire building and then went back inside and up the stairs to his room, where he sat down on his bed. Keith watched as Yu slowly relaxed.

"Yu," Keith said. "What was that all about?"

"It's all there."

"What's all there?"

"Fifteen thousand sixty-seven square feet."

"That's how many square feet there are in the building?"

"Yes."

Yu never explained the importance of the square-foot

computation to Keith, and the psychologists could only suggest that making the computations kept him from thinking about the loss of Suni.

After that Yu made the computations whenever stressed, and Keith came to accept the explanation of the experts. If they took Yu on a field trip to a museum, he could not relax unless he computed the square feet, even though he spent his time at the museum pacing in and out of rooms. If the furniture in the residence hall was rearranged, Yu would recompute the square footage of the entire building. Yu's pacing and computing was annoying, but no behavior-modification program designed by the psychologists could eliminate the behavior, so the staff resigned themselves to living with it.

Keith was as fascinated with Yu's uneven abilities as Suni had been and experimented with other games and puzzles, but found no new abilities. One day Keith wrote a paper about Yu's abilities and gave it to one of the staff psychologists. The psychologist polished the paper and submitted it to a journal for publication. Shortly after Keith saw his name in print for the first time, a psychologist by the name of Dr. Martin showed up at the school to see Yu. He was refused, since Mr. Tran's permission was needed. The next day Mr. Tran called and approved Dr. Martin's visit and he spent the next few days testing Yu. They didn't see Dr. Martin after that, but one day word came that Yu was being transferred to a new home run by Dr. Martin.

Keith remembered the difficult transition for Yu when he had replaced Suni, and worried about Yu. Suni had left detailed notes about her contact with Mr. Tran over the years, and Keith believed Suni when she wrote that contacting Mr. Tran was useless. Still, he decided the circumstances warranted the call. Mr. Tran was as cold as Suni had described him.

"Mr. Tran, I wanted to talk to you about Yu's move. Disrupting his routine could be very detrimental. It could set him back years."

Mr. Tran snorted derisively into the phone. "Set him back from the fourth grade to the third grade? What a loss."

"It's not just academic ability. There are self-esteem issues too."

"I know you think it is important for him to feel good about being backward, but I do not. True self-esteem comes from doing well, not being told you are doing well. That is a lie."

"It's more than just that. Your son is happy here, well adjusted."

"You will get him back. It is only temporary and then the checks to your institution will come again."

"It's not the money!" Keith was stung by the suggestion he was worried about his paycheck. "But if it's only temporary then why do it at all? Dr. Martin isn't trained to work with the kinds of disabilities Yu has."

"I do it because it is Yu's chance to pay the family back for all they have given him. Dr. Martin will pay us to use Yu in his experiments."

"What?"

"It is done. When the experiments are over Yu will be returned."

Mr. Tran hung up without saying goodbye, leaving Keith listening to a dead line. He tried to find out about the experiments Yu was to be a part of, but found little. When Elizabeth Foxworth showed up to assess Yu and his needs Keith was heartened a little. Ms. Foxworth was a caring, competent professional who listened when Keith described Yu's habits, but Ms. Foxworth shared little about the experiments Yu would be a part of. When Yu left with Ms. Foxworth, Keith was the only one who said goodbye to him. Yu didn't respond, he just climbed into the backseat of the car and sat rocking back and forth. He was still rocking when the car turned out of the drive onto the highway. Keith went back into the residence hall with a sick feeling. A feeling he would never see Yu again.

13

IMPULSE

This time the whispering started when Gil was only halfway through his relaxation routine. It was louder and he could pick out words. "Daddy" was the clearest, and Gil was sure the voice said "I'm sorry." He was also sure that whoever it was was in pain.

Gil went down to the kitchen. He could hear Karon and Len out on the front porch laughing. Wes was bent over printouts at the kitchen table, lost in thought, a cup of coffee by his right hand. Gil wanted to get into the basement to see if the voice was louder but didn't want to explain to Wes what he was doing, so he went past Wes, nodding hello, and out the back door.

Gil sat on the back porch staring into the darkness and working through his relaxation routine until he could hear the voice. He listened, but it was weaker than in the house and he couldn't make out any words, only feel the emotion—but the emotion had changed. It felt angry now, and as he listened he felt himself getting angry. The voice was working on Gil, worming its way into his being, its emotions becoming his emotions. Gil broke the meditative state, feeling genuine anger over the loss of control he was feeling. Self-control kept his special gift a secret, and control kept him out of jail.

Gil left the porch and cut across the yard, turning down the alley toward town, trying to walk off the invading emotion. The alley was unpaved and uneven with mud puddles sprinkled along its two ruts. The only light in the alley came from the porch lights of the old houses that lined either side of the block. As Gil passed he could hear the sounds of family life coming from the homes; TVs and radios blaring, and in one house the sound of a crying child. Gil picked his way through the dark carefully, but stumbled and stepped in the middle of a large puddle, the brown water splashing up his pant leg and then back-washing over his shoe. Angry, Gil kicked the puddle with his other foot, splashing the water up as high as his chest. Gil was about to attack the puddle again when he caught himself—it wasn't like him to be this angry. This wasn't his emotion—it wasn't his anger. "It's that voice," Gil said in an angry whisper.

Gil continued his walk, determined to free himself of his anger. As he neared the end of the alley he heard laughter and voices ahead. Gil slowed, hiding in the shadows. There was a group of people opening the double doors of a garage. The garage belonged to the fraternity Gil had used against Ralph. He had been sorely disappointed the fraternity had only succeeded in getting Ralph lectured, not removed from the project.

The group at the corner disappeared into the open garage doors and came out with a long ladder, and then they started down the alley away from Gil. He followed, his mood darkening to match the shade of the alley shadows. The boys carrying the ladder stopped at the corner while two ran into the street and then signaled the coast was clear. The group with the ladder ran across the street, those in the back fishtailing the end of the ladder and laughing when those in the front cursed them. Gil waited, giving them a chance to get deeper in the alley, and then walked across the street, casually checking to see if anyone was on the sidewalks.

Following their whispered laughter, Gil found them crouched down, peeking through a picket fence at a large two-story house. From his vantage point Gil could see movement in the second-floor window—a sorority sister in a nightgown. Giggling spread along the line of hidden fraternity brothers. It was a fraternity prank, Gil realized. He only hoped they were more successful at this than they had been with Ralph. The thought of Ralph re-freshed the anger he felt toward the fraternity brothers. Gil's breath came more rapidly and he glared at the boys from his shadow.

Two more figures passed by the sorority windows; then the boys climbed the fence, lifting the ladder over. Soon the ladder was pressed flat against the house. The boys paused, making sure they weren't discovered, and then they quietly tilted the aluminum ladder vertically and laid it gently against the side of the house. The second story of the house was smaller than the first by design, and there was a porch outside the back two bedroom windows. A lower roof ran along the side of the house just below the second-story windows. The ladder was leaning against this lower roof. One of the boys climbed the ladder while the others held it at the bottom. The boy climbed slowly and quietly and stepped onto the roof gingerly. He crept along the roof toward the back of the house, stopping at the first window. He peeked inside carefully and then more boldly, exposing his head to full view. Then he turned to his comrades and shrugged his shoulders. The peeping Tom continued to the porch in the back and climbed over the rail, flattening against the wall and creeping to the glass doors that accessed the porch. To Gil the curtains looked fully drawn, but the boy put his eye to the edge of the door and held motionless for thirty seconds. Then he stepped back to the rail and waved excitedly to his friends, making an obscene stroking motion with his hand and setting off waves of quiet laughter.

Feeling his anger grow again, Gil watched intently. Irrationally, he blamed them for not getting rid of Ralph. Even more, he was irritated by their sexual prank. Gil didn't understand sexual motivation, since he had never experienced it, but he was jealous that others could experience something he couldn't. Quietly he left his hiding place and crept closer.

The boys were taking turns going up the ladder now. Two were already up, creeping along the roof to join the voyeur. Two more were climbing up the ladder. Gil positioned himself at the corner of the picket fence, where he could get a clear line of sight on the boys; then he waited for the next one to reach the top. The boy stepped off the ladder and turned toward the porch. Gil stared hard at the boy as he walked carefully along the roof, and when he was halfway to the porch he thought "turn left" and pushed the idea into the boy's head. Suddenly the boy turned and stepped off the roof. When his foot met nothing but air he yelled, pitching forward, his head dipping toward the ground. His arms came out to catch himself but clawed uselessly at the air. Arching his back, he kept himself from going into a dive but ended up in the belly-flop position. A sharp "aaaaaah" sound came from the boy as he hurtled toward the yard below. Wes was waiting for the belly flop but at the last second the boy tucked his head under and turned head over heels like a diver, crashing into the rosebushes flat on his back. A dull thud and the sound of splintering wood sounded the end of the boy's fall.

Satisfied that he was dead, Gil turned away. Shouts of alarm from the others sent Gil hurrying up the alley, fearful a crowd would gather. He was only a short distance away when the screaming started. "Damn, the boy's still alive," Gil thought. First Dr. Birnbaum survived, then he had failed to get rid of Ralph, and now the college punk had survived. Gil listened to the screaming as he walked up the alley trying to judge the level of agony. His victims usually didn't live long enough to scream, so Gil had too little experience to judge whether or not the boy would survive. He hoped not. He didn't like to think he was losing his touch.

14

EXPECTATIONS

It was late but Wes felt wired. He was on his third cup of coffee, but it wasn't the caffeine that had him on edge, it was his experiment. It had gone exactly as he had hoped. Frankie had emerged and answered questions using the abilities of the donor minds. It was a true independent consciousness; at least, it met Wes's criteria. Wes suspected nothing would satisfy Elizabeth.

The printouts were spread in front of Wes and most of the data were close to the predicted parameters. The EEGs from the first and second experiments with Daphne and Gil did show subtle discrepancies, but they were most likely the result of normal variability. Now Wes wished he had used Ralph the second time just for the extra data. More surprising was the EEG run on Frankie. In Wes's previous experiments the synthesized EEGs operated within the range established by the donor brain waves. In this case, however, there was electrical spiking beyond what he had ever seen in any of the donors, and some of the alpha waves were an unusually high frequency.

Elizabeth came in and poured herself a cup of coffee, then sat down at the table opposite Wes. He didn't like her that close to his discrepant data until he had a chance to explain it, so he casually began folding up the printouts. Elizabeth watched him over the top of her coffee cup.

"Anything interesting?"

"What makes you ask?" Wes responded defensively.

"Don't get hostile, I was just curious."

"Sorry. Nothing unusual. Everything's going as planned."

"Let me ask you something, Wes. Let's say you get your Frankie, and let's say it is a fully independent consciousness. Then what? What will you do with it? What's the whole point of this?"

"You didn't read my proposal, did you?" Wes asked to needle her. "The point is to model consciousness. If we can produce it, we can understand it. If we can understand it maybe we can alter it."

"Mind control."

"Why is that the first thing critics always think of? It never occurred to me. I was thinking more of repairing consciousness."

"I would have thought someone with your theory of mind would be a physiologist. Doesn't consciousness depend on brain and therefore to repair consciousness you have to regenerate brain tissue?"

"What about your theory? You think mind depends on soul. If I'm correct then we might be able to transfer functions of mind to other parts of the brain. Neurons are basically electrochemical switches. If we can superimpose a function from a normal brain on an abnormal one, and get the switches to operate in the same way, then that part of the brain may learn the function."

"Very creative."

"You mean fanciful."

"I mean what I say. Stop being so suspicious."

Elizabeth said it seriously, and Wes realized she was sincere. He reminded himself how much his work depended on her and then forced a smile.

"Sorry, it's just that my work is such a big part of my life. I really want this to work."

"The mind repair seems a long way off. What are your short-term goals?"

Wes found himself in a dilemma. He wanted to share with her, but he wasn't sure he trusted her. She had a sharp mind and a sharp tongue, but she could also be compassionate and friendly, not to mention pretty. On his side she would be a formidable ally.

"You're going to think this is weird," he said.

"I already think what you're doing is weird."

Elizabeth said it with a smile and Wes took it as a friendly tease.

"Did you learn about the Swiss psychologist Jean Piaget in your sociology classes?"

"Yes, but everything I learned had a sociological spin on it."

"You know the basic theory, though. Piaget looked at children in a way no one else had at that time. He didn't see them as just short adults who knew little, he saw them as actually reasoning differently from adults."

"I remember the water-jar experiment."

"Right, if you take two short fat jars the same size and fill them to the same level with water, a four-year-old can tell you they have the same amount in them. Then if you take one of the jars and pour it into a tall thin jar and ask the child which has more they will invariably point to the tall thin one because the water level is higher. An older child won't make this mistake."

"I remember, they forget to take into account the diameter."

"Not just forget, they aren't capable. That's an important difference. There's several ways to explain why they make the error, but think of it this way. To compare the two identical short glasses the child only has to compare the height in order to get it correct. To compare the short fat glass with the tall thin glass the child must consider the height of the water as well as the diameter of the glass. To do that the child needs to have two tracks in his mind. More difficult problems require even more tracks. What if we have a child that has to sort blocks on the basis of size, color, and shape?"

"They would need three tracks, and a child has to be older to do that. About ten or so, as I remember," Elizabeth said. "So as we age we have more tracks, as you call them, but what's the point."

"The point is that we don't keep adding tracks; we reach a maximum. There is a limit to the number of concepts we can juxtapose."

Wes sat back, waiting for the implication to register with Elizabeth, but she only stared at him blankly.

"Wes, what are you getting at?"

"Each of our savants is a genius in one part of their mind. Not just genius, more than that. They do things no genius ever could do. Einstein couldn't calendar-calculate or solve puzzles like Archie. It's as if an intellect so great that we can't fathom it was shattered and fragments of that genius sprinkled among the population. What if we could reconstruct that great mind—that superconsciousness—how many tracks would it have? A dozen? A hundred? A thousand? What problems could a mind like that solve if we could knit it together once more?"

Wes realized his voice had raised an octave and he was leaning across the table. She was staring at him in surprise, but when she spoke it was with respect, not mockery.

"It's an interesting theory. Intriguing. You think that a mind that has more tracks has more intelligence?"

"Not in the sense most people think. If two people had the same ability to reason, but one could look at only two sides of an issue at a time, while the other person could look at four perspectives at the same time, then that person would make better decisions and would appear to be more intelligent. Take away those extra tracks and they would perform the same."

"I suppose you've been asked the 'so what' question before."

"I've asked myself that same question many times. There's so many answers I could give. Let me give you one you might appreciate. When I was in college I took a World Religions class to fill an elective. We were supposedly studying different faiths and different cultures, but the professor was a Christian Jew who had his own agenda. One day he got to talking about Christian and Jewish perceptions of God. He said that Christians were always disturbed by the contradictions that belief in an omnipotent God created. Questions like how could bad things happen to good people? If God was all-powerful and the creator of the universe, then didn't He create evil? If He did then isn't He responsible for all the bad that happens in the world? Questions like these create a dilemma for Christians. To resolve these contradictions some argue that God doesn't cause the bad, but allows it to happen. But if you accept that view you could also ask if God has the power to stop something and doesn't, then is that really any different from causing it to happen?"

"I've participated in these kinds of debates. My favorite is the question about whether God can create a rock so heavy he can't lift it."

"Yes, that's the kind of thing I mean. Anyway, this professor said these kinds of contradictions are anathema to Christians and they have spent centuries concocting twisted theological explanations to relieve self-induced stress. Jews, he argued, don't have this problem. They accept God for what God is. God is the source of good and evil and those two thoughts don't give them a moment's pause. I've thought about what he said a lot since then, trying to resolve the contradictions that an omnipotent God poses."

"The easy resolution is there is no God."

Wes wondered if Elizabeth was baiting him, but she looked sincere.

"Belief in a spiritual realm is nearly universal among peoples, Elizabeth. I prefer to think there is a spiritual world that in some way interacts with our world, and that all the different belief systems have come about because when we try to understand the spiritual realm we can only grasp a small aspect of it at a time.

"God probably is good and evil, the creator of everything and the creator of nothing, active in our lives and inactive in our world, a part of nature and apart from nature. People probably do have only one soul and one life, and at the same time are reincarnated. God probably does care about each of us individually, yet lets the child in an abusive home be beaten to death. God is likely all of these things, and more, but we can't understand God, or whatever you want to call the spiritual realm, because we can't hold all these facts together at one time."

"Not enough tracks?"

"Right. But Frankie might be able to make sense of it all."

"You spent years creating all this . . . this hardware, the software, and then pushed through your grant requests, and fought to get the savants, to create Frankie so you could ask it to explain God to you?"

Wes didn't like the way she framed the question. It wasn't just for this, but he had to admit it was in the back of his mind from the first day he conceived of the Frankie project. He wanted to ask all the timeless philosophical questions about truth and the origin of knowledge. He also had questions in his own science to ask. He wanted to try and reconcile the psychodynamic psychologies with behaviorism and cognitive science. He wanted to understand the source of memories, and ultimately what learning was. He even had questions about the origins of the universe, the Big Bang theory, the nature of dark mass, and whether the speed of light was impassable. But when he was honest with himself, which he was now, he had to admit that the ultimate question was the one he would ask first. Is there a God? Wes realized that his eyes had drifted away from Elizabeth's down to the table, and that he had been silent for a long moment. Elizabeth had respected the silence and now he looked her directly in the eyes and answered her question honestly.

"Yes, I want to know if there is a God."

Now it was Elizabeth's turn to be silent. He didn't know what Elizabeth's theological perspective was—she dragged him off to church regularly, but that was for the savants. All the social workers he had met were atheists. There was something about the professional training that drove theology out of people. It was likely that the need to be supportive of all others, no matter what the belief, made it difficult to sustain personal religious beliefs.

Without a clear picture of Elizabeth's beliefs he had no idea how she would react to his admission. Unfortunately, she never got a chance to answer. As she opened her mouth to speak the back door opened and Gil came in. He was flushed and breathing hard.

"Are you all right?" Elizabeth asked.

"Yeah, sure, fine. I stepped in a mud puddle, that's all."

It was a peculiar answer, Wes thought, since it would only explain why his pants were wet, not why he was red-faced and out of breath. Wes offered Gil a cup of coffee, but he excused himself and a moment later they heard him thumping up the stairs. Elizabeth showed no signs of reacting to Wes's admission about his interest in God, so Wes decided to probe. This time the sirens interrupted him.

Sounding faint at first, soon they grew louder. Wes's anxiety grew as the sirens sounded as if they were coming up the block. Suddenly Wes wondered where Ralph was. When his eyes came up and met Elizabeth's it was as if she had read his mind.

"I'll check on Ralph," she said.

As Elizabeth and Wes jumped up, the siren sound abruptly died to a mournful whine and then faded out. The police car was down the block. Still, it didn't relieve their anxiety, since Ralph was a wanderer. Elizabeth started into the next room and nearly ran into Ralph, who was coming through the doorway in his pajamas at full stride.

"There's a ambulance down the street. Let's go see."

Ralph walked away without waiting for a response. Elizabeth and Wes followed, trying to keep up. Len and Karon were on the sidewalk staring down the street and Ralph passed them in two long strides. Ralph wore the kind of pajamas that pinch at the ankle and at the wrist and he made a peculiar spectacle with his V-frame muscular body, his leaning-back posture, and his long strides. It was cold outside and Wes worried about Ralph in only his pajamas, but as they exerted themselves to keep up their bodies warmed.

The ambulance and a police car were only a few houses down the next block. Wes recognized it as one of the sororities. There was a small crowd gathered and Wes and Elizabeth joined in trying to see what had happened. Mrs. Clayton was there—Wes had never seen her without a garden hose in her hand. Ralph sidled right up to her and asked what was going on.

"Oh, hello, Ralph. You shouldn't be out this late."

"It's OK. They're done sperimenting on us for the day. Besides, Elizabeth and Wes are with me." Ralph turned and pointed when he said it. Elizabeth waved at Mrs. Clayton but Wes just smiled vacantly, embarrassed again by Ralph's candor.

"What's going on, Mrs. Clayton?" Ralph asked loudly. "Someone robbed or killed or something?"

Mrs. Clayton responded in a quiet voice. "Someone was hurt when they fell off a roof."

"I fell off a porch once. Broke my arm. Had to wear a cast. It itched. I had a special scratch-back I used to itch inside the cast."

"A backscratcher?" Mrs. Clayton corrected gently.

Ralph stared blankly for a second and then thumped himself on the side of the head and said loudly, "How could I be so stupid? A backscratcher. Yeah, that's what it was. It was a yellow one from Chuck E. Cheese. I won seventy-seven tickets playing Skee-Ball and I got the scratch-back for seventy-five. I had two tickets left over but they didn't have nothing for two. I don't know what happened to the tickets or I would give them to you if you ever went to Chuck E. Cheese."

Another siren announced the arrival of a second police car

with a single officer. Wes used the interruption to leave Ralph in the middle of his backscratcher story and follow the police officer into the yard of the sorority. There were no police keeping back the crowd that had formed on the sidewalk. Wes followed the police officer toward a group of sorority sisters in bathrobes standing in a rose garden. Several of the girls were crying. The rest of the group were college boys with somber faces. When the group parted to let the police officer in, Wes stepped into the space, Elizabeth squeezing in next to him. Three police officers and two EMTs were crouched around a boy lying on his back in the rosebushes. The boy was unconscious, but his chest was rising and falling. The boy was partially obscured by the roses, but Wes realized a wooden stake was protruding from his abdomen. It was covered with blood from its tip to where it disappeared into the boy's stomach. A small amount of steam was forming at the opening, and white pulpy tissue bulged from the hole where it protruded. Wes felt sick. Then the boy woke up screaming.

"He's awake again," one of the EMTs yelled. "Help us hold him down."

The boy's eyes burst open at the same time as his scream and his hands came up to claw at the stake piercing his stomach. The other EMT grabbed one arm and two of the police pushed down on his legs. Another police officer grabbed the other arm, but the boy broke free and grabbed the stake, pulling on it, his hand unable to grip the stake, slippery with his own blood. The police officer pried the boy's hand loose and pulled it away. The struggle with the boy's arms continued, but the officers holding the legs soon relaxed—his legs weren't moving. The boy's screams were constant and more of the coeds began to cry. Talking to their friend, trying to calm him, the fraternity brothers' words were barely audible over the screams. Then suddenly he collapsed again, unconscious.

Wes agonized for the boy on the ground and was frustrated with the police and the EMTs. Why weren't they doing something? Why didn't they put the boy in the ambulance and get him to a hospital? Then a sorority sister came running up to the group carrying a long-handled pair of clippers. She handed it to one of the EMTs, who took it and worked the handles to see how wide the jaws opened.

"This should do it. It might take a couple of cuts. Roll him over a bit, but be careful."

The others did as he said but couldn't move the boy because of the rosebushes. The EMT used the clippers to clip away the growth on one side. Pricked by the thorns, the EMT cursed as he moved pieces of rosebush aside. When the roses were clear they gently lifted the boy and the EMT lay flat, reaching under and working the handle of the clippers. After a dozen tries he pulled the clippers out.

"I think he's free. Let's get the stretcher in here."

The stretcher was moved from the side of the house into the garden and the boy was gently lifted. They tried covering the boy with a sheet but the protruding stake kept the cover at waist level. When he was gone Wes realized there was a large pool of blood on the ground.

Wes followed the crowd out and listened to their talk, Elizabeth standing beside him. After a few minutes they left, pulling Ralph out of a conversation about Slurpees with another neighbor—the old man he was talking to looking relieved. When Ralph was well ahead of them, Elizabeth spoke to Wes.

"Did you hear what happened? The boy was on the roof of the sorority—it was a panty raid or something. Then all of a sudden he just turned and stepped off the roof."

"That's too bad, but he shouldn't have been up there at all. Roofs are dangerous enough in the daylight."

"I guess," she said. "Accidents do happen, but not like that. They said he just suddenly turned and walked off the roof."

Wes didn't know how to respond. From his perspective it was an accident caused by a combination of beer and stupidity, but once again Elizabeth saw things in a different way. "Am I missing something, Elizabeth?" he said.

"It's just peculiar. Remember what happened to my assistant Marshall? He was hit by a car. I remember what his wife said about it. They were walking down the street with their daughter, and suddenly Marshall just turned and stepped into the street in front of a truck. He didn't say anything, they weren't at a corner, there was no reason for him to do it. It was almost like suicide."

"It sounds peculiar, but strange things happen all the time. Stranger than this."

"Maybe, but it's a peculiar coincidence."

Wes could tell that Elizabeth wasn't going to set it aside easily.

"Maybe when you get Frankie up to speed you can ask her about God, and I'll ask her about coincidental accidents."

"You mean him," Wes countered.

"We'll see," Elizabeth said.

15

ENCOUNTER

Daphne stared out the window at the street below. Her head was held high, her ears and eyes wide open, yet there was little of the buzz. Mornings were often like that for her, and that's why Daphne was usually awake before the sun came up. In the morning, things happened one at a time. A door would open, a man would come out, get in his car, and drive off. Then minutes would pass before another person left in the same way. Cars might drive by, but only one at a time. An occasional jogger would pass, but seldom more than one at a time. When the sun rose, it did so like the hands of a clock, too slow to notice. The orange glow of the morning sun lit the neighborhood with a single deep hue, unlike the myriad colors of daylight. Daphne enjoyed the slow change from discrete sensations to complex combinations—she could handle it. As the day wore on, activity picked up and Daphne found it difficult to keep confusion away. It crept in from the sides like a curtain at the end of a show and soon the buzz kept her from the world. Usually by the time Mrs. Clayton came out to water her plants, Daphne would be retreating inward away from the buzz—but today was different. Mrs. Clayton was watering now and Daphne's world was still clear.

It had been this way since the experiment the night before.

She was experiencing the world as others must, able to savor multiple sights and sounds at once. The richness of the world tantalized her—she'd had only fleeting tastes of it before. Sounds from the world didn't reverberate through her head endlessly, blurring with the shadows in her room. This morning noises sounded and faded away as they must for normal people, and light and shadows stayed distinct.

Only the presence of the black hole in her mind kept her from complete joy, but even as she thought of it, it began to open, calling to her. Daphne focused on Mrs. Clayton but still the hole widened, threatening to disgorge its terrible content. The sensations around its edges began to blur, running together. Mrs. Clayton blurred, and soon was indistinguishable from her running hose, and her flowers. Then Mrs. Clayton dissolved into lines, curves, and colors, which were picked up and tossed like leaves in a whirlwind. Around the black hole they swirled, picking up sounds, and smells—any sensation. Soon a roaring tornado of thought surrounded the black hole, preventing Daphne from seeing its contents.

Daphne ran to the hidey-hole in her mind, waiting for the storm to subside. When she felt safe she brought her hands up and began to play, letting the rhythm and melody partition her mind, the storm on one side, order on the other. When the imaginary music could do no more she went downstairs and played long and loud, driving the storm into a corner and hemming it in.

Luis and Archie came down and listened, Archie working puzzles as he did. Ralph turned on *Sesame Street* and Luis and Archie joined him on the floor in front of the TV. After breakfast they watched *Wheel of Fortune*. Luis solved the puzzles before the contestants when only a few letters were in place. Then it was time for classes, and Elizabeth and Gil took them through their lessons, reviewing first reading and basic math, then working on social skills, and especially eye contact. Daphne tried hard, but could look Elizabeth in the eye for only a second.

Luis refused lunch when he saw the Spaghetti-Os and Gil ended up cooking him a toasted cheese sandwich instead. Everyone else was busy after lunch with the experimental equipment, so Elizabeth took the savants to the park. Ralph led the way, stopping to talk with everyone they met. Archie was the slowest and Elizabeth hung back and walked with him. Daphne tried to keep up with Ralph but as usual ended up trailing behind with Luis.

At the park they swung on the swings until a mother complained they were hogging them and were "too big for them anyway." Even through the fog of confusion Daphne was hurt, and left the swings to sit by herself. Ralph sat with her, trying to comfort her.

"She didn't mean nothing, Daphne. We should take turns. I like swinging, don't you? Sure you do. Want some gum? I got some from Wes. He keeps a bunch of it now in his room. I think it's 'cause I ask for it all the time."

Daphne refused the gum, but Ralph's prattle soothed her, taking away some of the hurt and soon she could glance around, seeing the way people were looking at them—she didn't like it. People always stared, especially children. She didn't mind the children as much, except sometimes they made faces when adults weren't looking. The adults weren't as obvious, but gave them the same looks.

The musical bells of an ice-cream truck brought Ralph to his feet.

"I'm gonna ask Elizabeth for some money."

He was off, cornering Elizabeth and talking rapidly. Soon he came striding back.

"She said yes. You want something? I think they got the kind with the nuts on top."

Daphne asked him to bring her one, but stayed on the bench as the others went to the street to wait for their ice cream. The thought of the treat made her feel a little better, but still she kept her eyes on the ground, fighting to stay in touch with the world. Then she was surrounded by legs. She didn't look up, but she recognized the voice.

"You're Daphne, aren't you? Remember us? I'm Billy. Ralph introduced us the other day. I think you met Rimmer, too, didn't you?"

Daphne sat silently, looking at their feet. Then Billy sat next to her, the others closing in around them.

"Ralph was right about you, Daphne. He said you were cute."

The storm in Daphne's mind intensified, pushing on the barrier.

"What are you doing, Billy? She's retarded, man!"

"Shut up, Grant. Don't pay any attention to him, Daphne. I think you look great."

Then he scooted next to her, his hip pressed against hers. Her mind storm howled, the barrier bulging. She filled her head with music—if the barrier broke, she wanted no room for the black hole to empty into.

"I bet guys are after you all the time, aren't they, Daphne? Ralph is, I know. What about that Mexican kid that lives with you? Luis? Didn't you two ever do anything? Play a little doctor?"

He leaned against her and then put his hand on her knee. Involuntarily her hands came up, and she began to play in the air.

"You're making her crazy, Billy."

"I make every woman crazy, Grant. She wants me—see, she wants to give me a massage."

His hand slid slowly up her leg, and she pounded harder.

"Hey, that Foxworth woman's coming back. Let's get out of here before she sees us."

"No massage right now, Daphne. Maybe later."

As he stood he ran his hand along the inside of her thigh. The barrier in her mind nearly broke, but when she felt them leave the pressure lessened, the barrier holding. Slowly control returned and her hands came down. When Ralph arrived with the ice cream she was able to hold it, but it was half melted before she could eat.

16

DISCOVERY

Wes was prepared for the arrival of his next savant—he had spent the night reading Elizabeth's file on Yu. Yu had a history of acting out and could be violent. If his abilities weren't particularly special, Wes would not have included him in the project. As it was, he would be the most difficult of the group, and Wes had gone out of the way to prepare for him.

Elizabeth's report detailed every aspect of Yu's behavior and needs. His daily habits and rituals were described, as were the foods he liked and what he watched on TV. His daily routine was specified, including bedtimes, when rest periods were scheduled, the kinds of physical activity he required. There was even a report, graph, and chart dealing with bowel and urination frequency and regularity. Like Daphne, he needed his room ordered a certain way, but unlike Daphne, Yu's belongings were not to be unpacked—he would do it himself.

Gil, Wes, and of course Ralph were waiting to meet Yu on the front porch. Daphne was playing the piano and the others were waiting just inside so Yu wouldn't be overwhelmed. Even down the block Wes could see Yu was stressed. He was shifting violently in the front passenger seat, rocking forward and back. Elizabeth popped out of the car as soon as she stopped and unlocked the trunk. As soon as the trunk was open, Len and Karon appeared to help Gil carry Yu's things to his room. Before Elizabeth could get around to the passenger side Yu opened the door and stood on the sidewalk, his head bent back and his eyes on the sky. Wes could hear his rapid breathing from the porch and wondered if picking him had been a mistake.

"Ralph will show you to your room, won't you, Ralph?" Elizabeth said.

"Sure I will. What's his name again. Yu? That's a funny name. I never met someone named that before. Well okeydokey, come on, you Yu you." Ralph's smile widened to its full expanse. "Get it? It's a joke. You Yu you."

No one smiled but Ralph was unaffected and turned and walked into the house. Yu followed, swinging his head from side to side. Ralph chattered like a tour guide, pointing out who was in each room. When they disappeared into Yu's room Wes turned to Elizabeth asking for her evaluation.

"I don't know yet. Yu has a well-defined set of adjustment behaviors. We'll have to see if they work for him."

"You mean like ordering his room?"

Elizabeth smiled at Wes when she answered. "You read my report. Yes, he will spend a couple of hours putting his room in order; that will be the first major test of whether he will be able to adjust or not."

"Couldn't we help put his things away? The sooner things are put away the better, right?"

"We wouldn't know where to put his belongings. Even Yu changes his mind periodically. He keeps his room one way for weeks at a time and then suddenly will rearrange. Sometimes it's something little that is changed, like reordering his Dr. Seuss books, and sometimes everything comes off of every shelf and out of every drawer and is placed back differently. He has a unique way of arranging, too. He keeps his underwear and his shoes in the same drawer and his socks are kept in his closet on hangers. Don't ask me why."

Wes was impatient, but knew not to push Yu in any way. Instead, he went to work with his program, trying to understand the anomalies he had found in the last run. An hour later Ralph came in and bummed five dollars for Slurpees.

"Why five bucks?"

"Yu wants one, too, and we decided to get mediums 'cause it's his first day."

Ralph came back a half hour later and handed one to Daphne at the piano and two to Archie and Luis, who sat in front of the TV, then carried the other two upstairs. Two hours later Elizabeth came looking for Wes.

"He's almost done. Everything is out of the boxes and the suitcases. He looks like he's settling down. For some reason he seems to like Ralph."

"Am I the only one that has a problem with him?"

"Virtually," Elizabeth replied. "Ralph kept taking his things out of boxes and looking at them but it didn't seem to bother Yu. He just took them one by one from Ralph and put them away. He even seemed happy when Ralph offered to buy him a Slurpee."

"I bought the Slurpee. I buy all the Slurpees."

"Don't be a grouch, it's cheap therapy. Anyway, he's almost done. Then we'll know better whether he's going to adapt."

It was another hour before Yu came out of his room and began pacing off the house. When he came into the experiment room it looked like a parade. Yu led the way with Ralph trailing along behind. Elizabeth came next and then Gil, who looked perplexed. Wes watched the little parade circle the converted dining room and disappear into the kitchen. When it came back he got up and followed along. Surprisingly, Daphne stopped playing and turned to watch Yu and Ralph lead the parade. Yu went around the main floor again before he discovered the basement door. Wes and Elizabeth waited in the kitchen while Yu worked his way through the junk in the basement to walk the perimeter. Soon he was back and disappeared out the back door. Wes and Elizabeth followed, standing in the backyard watching the parade disappear around the corner of the house.

"He's almost done," Elizabeth announced.

A minute later the parade came back around the corner, with Yu in the front and Gil in the rear. Elizabeth smiled and Gil shrugged his shoulders, following Yu back inside.

"That should do it," Elizabeth said.

Wes expected to find Yu relaxed inside but instead they found him pacing the rooms again, but this time faster. Yu walked the main floor, then the upstairs, and then went back into the basement. When he came back up he went directly outside and paced the perimeter of the house again. When he finished he seemed more agitated than ever and his walking speed increased to a near run. Gil dropped out of the parade and came to stand by Elizabeth.

"He's a machine. I can't keep up."

"I don't understand," Elizabeth said. "He's paced the house—that should relax him. It's a well-established behavior."

Wes didn't like what he was hearing—Elizabeth's worry was evident in her voice. This time when Yu led Ralph outside Wes shouted at him.

"Ralph! Ralph! What's he doing?"

"I think he lost something," Ralph said without losing a step. "He lost something."

"Lost something?" he repeated. Then, turning to Elizabeth, "I don't suppose you took inventory of his things before you brought them?"

"Actually, I did," Elizabeth said. "It was all there. Besides, this isn't his behavior for losing something."

The parade came around the house again and disappeared inside. This time Elizabeth followed it in and up the stairs, Wes trailing behind. When Yu turned into his room Elizabeth stepped in the doorway, blocking his exit. Yu stopped walking, but began rocking back and forth, clearly agitated.

"What's wrong, Yu? Ralph says you lost something. Is that right?"

Ralph took his serious pose, leaning back and folding his arms. "Ya lost something, right?"

"No," Yu replied.

"Then what's wrong, Yu?"

"It's not all there."

"What's not all there?"

"Yeah," Ralph mimicked. "What's not all there?"

"Please, Ralph. Let me handle this."

"Okeydokey, Elizabeth. I was just trying to help."

"What's not all there, Yu?"

"It's supposed to be four thousand eight hundred twenty-two square feet, but it's not. The outside and the inside don't match."

Elizabeth turned and looked at Wes, clearly puzzled. Wes didn't have any idea of what the square footage was supposed to be, but the house seemed all there to him. Still, if it was important to his savant, it was too important to be trivialized.

"Maybe he forgot to account for the thickness of the walls," he suggested.

"Two-by-four studs, plaster and lathe finish inside, two-by-six exterior walls with one-by-six cedar siding," Yu blurted out.

Yu's detailed answer surprised and pleased Wes, making him even more determined to have that ability a part of Frankie.

"Well, maybe there's a room he didn't get into," Wes said. "How much is missing?"

"One hundred and twenty square feet."

Wes and Elizabeth turned and looked at each other, each surprised by the answer. Wes spoke first.

"That's a lot of space. How could we miss all that? The attic . . ." Wes suggested, again knowing it was the wrong answer.

"He didn't get up there, remember," Elizabeth said, looking thoughtful. "Besides, it would be a lot more space than that."

"How could I be so stupid," Ralph said at the top of his voice and thumped himself on the head. "We forgot the garage."

"That's not it," Elizabeth said. "He only paced the house."

"Maybe we should ask Yu," Ralph suggested. "Hey, Yu, do you know where you lost it at?"

"The basement," Yu said.

They followed Yu to the basement and watched him pick his way through the accumulated junk trying to pace the perimeter. The old mattresses, beds, lawn furniture, beer kegs, and miscellaneous debris made it difficult. When he came to the storage bins he opened each of the three doors and peeked inside.

"You know, Elizabeth, he might be miscalculating," Wes said. "He can't actually walk along the wall, and he can't even get in those bins. He could easily be off that much."

"Maybe, but didn't you bring him here because he was a genius at this?"

Wes realized she was right. Yu wouldn't be here without an uncanny ability, and his ability told him space was missing from the basement. Wes looked around, but there was really only one place the extra space could be. One end of the basement was filled with storage bins and shelves and Wes had never really looked into them. "Maybe those shelves and bins back there are throwing off his estimates. Let's get him a better look."

Yu waited impatiently while Wes, Elizabeth, and Gil cleared a path through the junk to get to the shelves. Len, Karon, and Shamita came down and watched from the stairs. Ralph kept getting in the way trying to help until Len offered him a pack of Juicy Fruit to keep him busy. To everyone's surprise Daphne appeared at the top of the stairs, sitting still, eyes on the floor.

When they had some space along the shelves Wes and Elizabeth began removing the old jars and garden tools stored there. Wes found a tire behind a set of jars and pulled it out, turning to hand it to Gil—Gil wasn't there, he was backing up, staring at the shelves. Wes didn't mind if he took a break, but the look on his face wasn't fatigue—he looked scared. Len took Gil's place and Wes and Elizabeth took turns handing things to Len.

"Look at this, Wes," Elizabeth said. "This shelf isn't deep at all."

Wes felt back along the shelf and found it only went back about six inches. The other shelves were much deeper. Wes walked along the shallow shelves and found they went clear to the corner.

"They're shallow clear to the wall and there's brick behind the shelves. I thought those bins were behind here, too."

Elizabeth walked over to the bins and leaned in each door, looking back toward Wes. "They aren't anywhere near that big. Let's take these shelves down."

It took an hour for them to clear off the shelves and begin knocking them apart. Len found a hammer and a crowbar, but it was slow work since the shelves were well made with mitered corners and lips on the shelving to keep things from sliding off. As the shelving came apart it became clear that the missing square feet had been found—there was a brick wall blocking off one corner of the basement, accounting for Yu's missing space.

Everyone was hungry and thirsty before they were half done, so Karon and Shamita disappeared upstairs, reappearing later with tuna sandwiches, chips, and lemonade. Everyone took a break, and for a while the basement atmosphere was that of a picnic. Only Gil and Yu were unable to join in the frivolity, sitting apart, Yu rocking and Gil staring morosely. Wes knew what was bothering Yu, but Gil was a mystery. When they were done

Karon left to take care of the other savants, who were again watching TV.

They resumed work with new energy and cleared the rest of the shelving, leaving a brick wall that ran from the exterior wall of the basement to where the storage bins began.

"Here it is, Yu," Wes said. "It's all here, it's just inside this space."

Yu didn't respond; he just stood, staring and rocking. Wes turned to Elizabeth, already knowing what she was going to say.

"Sorry, Wes, we're going to have to open it up."

Len handed Wes one of the hammers, but it was a pitiful tool to use on a brick wall.

"See if you can find something bigger, Len. It looks like we've got some work ahead of us."

Len looked at Wes blankly and didn't move. Wes waited for the story he knew was coming.

"One day the Lone Ranger and Tonto were out riding on the range—they did a lot of that. Suddenly twenty Indian braves rode up on their right. Then another twenty rode up on their left. Then twenty more rode up in front and behind them. The Lone Ranger looked all around him and turned to Tonto and said, 'It looks like we're surrounded, Tonto.' Tonto looked at the Lone Ranger and said, 'What do you mean 'we,' Paleface?' " Then Len looked at Wes and said, "What do you mean *we* have some work ahead of us? These hands were made for caressing a keyboard, not shattering brick."

"All right, if you find a sledgehammer I'll do the hard work."

"Oh, so finding a sledgehammer is easy. Right, I'll look in the kitchen cabinets."

"Don't look in there, Len," Ralph advised. "I was looking for the Cocopuffs this morning, and there's no sledge in there."

Len thanked Ralph and then groused under his breath all the way up the stairs. Wes took a break and sat down on a lawn chair next to Elizabeth. After a few minutes Elizabeth pointed at the brick.

"There's a different pattern there. That looks like a door, and look at the bottom, that's not the same brick as that on the top."

Wes followed Elizabeth's point and could clearly see the different-colored bricks. Wes got up and squatted down, looking at the bricks.

"What do you think this is? Maybe there's heating ducts behind this wall."

Elizabeth walked along the wall, looking at the ceiling.

"No, the ducts run there and there. Besides, why brick it in?"

Len came stomping back down the stairs carrying a sledgehammer. Wes was impressed; he had been gone only a few minutes. Len held the hammer above his head in triumph with both hands and said, "Mrs. Clayton's husband was in construction. She's got a garage full of great tools."

Wes took the sledge and looked the wall over for a good place to start. The different-colored brick at the bottom made a good target. Wes took the sledge and swung it against the wall. There was a loud smack, but the brick didn't crack or crumble. Wes hit it again with the same result.

"Maybe you should hit it harder, Wes," Ralph suggested. "You'd never win a Kewpie doll like that."

"Maybe you'd like to give it a try, Ralph?"

"He's pulling the Tom Sawyer trick on you, Ralph," Len warned.

"Can I try it? Can I?" Ralph asked, turning to Elizabeth.

Elizabeth nodded and Ralph strode forward and took the sledge.

"It's heavy. I didn't know it was so heavy."

Ralph held the sledge up close to the top with both hands and took a couple of tentative swings. Next he moved his hands back, finding a comfortable position at the end that gave him more leverage. Then Ralph pulled the sledge back and then forward using his well-muscled shoulders. When the sledge hit the wall it wasn't with a smack, it was an earsplitting crunch as the sledge shattered one of the bricks. Ralph smiled a huge grin.

"I bet I would have won a Kewpie doll with that one."

Ralph put the sledge down and spit on his hands, rubbing the spit into his palms. Then he picked up the sledge and buried it into another brick. Settling into a rhythm, he hammered the bricks with one shattering blow after another. Wes, impressed with his progress, didn't notice the smell until Elizabeth shouted to stop.

"Can't you smell it?"

Wes sniffed the air—something smelled foul.

"It's coming from the hole Ralph made," Elizabeth said. "It smells like something rotten."

Karon, who had been sitting quietly on the stairs, got up and stepped forward, looking at the broken bricks at the bottom of the wall. "It smells like something died," she said. Suddenly Gil turned and ran up the stairs.

Wes took the sledge from Ralph and pounded away at the bricks. "Get me a flashlight, will you, Len?" Len went up the stairs without making a joke. While he was gone Wes pulled the broken pieces of brick out of the wall, making a small opening. Len returned, handing the flashlight to Wes, who had to lie down to peek in the hole. The beam lit up the opening, and there on the other side of the wall was the remains of a hand—the skeletal frame lay palm up, bits of dried flesh still clinging to the bones.

17

TOMB

Wes watched the police work from the stairs. Bricks from the wall littered the basement floor, and strobe flashes lit up the hidden room, the police recording the grisly find for posterity. When they removed the remains, Wes set up a fan to air the basement, but the air still had a putrid taint. Elizabeth sat next to Wes, offering a cup of coffee.

"Thanks."

"Have you gotten inside yet?" she said.

"No. I'm not sure I want to. There might be more bodies in there."

"No. I shared some coffee with a nice officer upstairs. There's only one body—actually a skeleton."

One of the officers separated from the others and approached Wes and Elizabeth. His insignia identified him as the chief of police. He was a barrel-chested man of about fifty, with thick salt-and-pepper hair closely cropped on the sides.

"I'm Roy Winston. You're Wes and Elizabeth, right? Ralph talks about you all the time."

Isn't there anyone Ralph doesn't know? Wes wondered.

"My wife works down at the Dairy Queen, and your Ralph's a regular customer." Then, nodding toward the opening, he said, "You want to tell me how you found this place?"

Wes told of Yu's arrival and his need to pace off buildings and compute square footage. Elizabeth explained it as a defense mechanism—a psychological security blanket. The officer took notes as they talked.

"We'll want to talk to everyone in the house," Winston said.

"Some of our savants are noncommunicative," Elizabeth said.

"Not Ralph. I hear you're psychologists or something? Say, maybe you could help us out. Come on, I want you to look at something."

When Roy led them toward the room Wes hesitated, but Elizabeth fell in at his heels. They ducked through the opening and Wes found himself standing in a chalk outline. His nose flared as the stench overpowered him. Swallowing hard, Wes held back his nausea. When he was sure he wouldn't regurgitate he looked around at the bizarre interior.

A thick layer of dust covered everything, but otherwise the room looked neat and tidy. There was a bed in the corner with a flowered bedspread folded open as if someone had just gotten out, a small nightstand sat next to it, and there was a dresser against the far wall. On the nightstand were a lamp and an old-fashioned radio. On the dresser a comb, brush, and mirror sat—all neatly lined up ready to use. On the floor was a pile of sketch pads. Two cigar boxes held a variety of chalks, drawing pencils, and colored pencils. But overwhelming the simple furnishings were the walls. Every surface was covered with sketches—beautiful yet horrifying pencil etchings. There was talent displayed on those walls—also pain.

Many of the sketches showed a young woman walking in open spaces—fields, plains, even arctic tundra. The skies were mostly clear and blue, the only clouds small and puffy. The night skies were sprinkled liberally with stars. The woman in the sketches walked through these scenes, eyes opened wide, a look of wonder on her face. Other sketches portrayed a far different woman, often in a fetal position, her face covered in tears. Most disturbing were sketches of the same young woman with her face contorted in rage, her body tensed, and her fists clenched.

Mixed with the sketches of the young woman were those of other people. Most were of a man; others showed the man and a woman, sometimes with children. As they lifted up layer after layer of sketches they found one of the house. On its porch were the man and woman, and sitting on the steps were four little girls in frilly dresses.

"Her family maybe," Elizabeth suggested. "These are remarkable sketches. She had real talent."

"You're sure it was a she?"

"You can tell by the art, Wes. Most of these are self-portraits. Besides, the policeman upstairs said the skeleton was wearing a nightgown."

"What do you think?" Roy asked. "These pictures tell you anything?"

Wes wanted to protest that he was a neuropsychologist, not a clinician, but Elizabeth jumped right in with an instant analysis.

"She was a very talented woman, who was deeply disturbed—possibly suffering from a dissociative personality disorder."

"What's that?"

"She might have had multiple personalities. Notice the distinct views of herself—innocent in these outdoor scenes, angry in these, and hurting in these sketches. These aren't simply different emotional states, either. These different portraits include different emphases on physical features. Notice also that the happy pictures are less complex, lacking the detail and sharpness of the others. Those showing rage are much more complex, much bolder. The angry drawings are so different it could almost have come from a different person."

Wes listened, and marveled. Elizabeth's analysis suggested expertise Wes didn't realize she had. Officer Winston was equally impressed.

"What do you make of this layout?" he asked. "You think this was her room and someone just walled her up in it after she died?"

"No, I think it's clear she was walled in long before she died. Look at the sketches—notice the recurring theme of openness. This poor woman was trapped in here for a long time. Long enough to drive her mad. Notice the anguish in these, and these. Someone cruelly tortured this woman by walling her in."

Roy was writing Elizabeth's comments on a pad. "This helps a lot. There's no obvious evidence of murder—no holes in the skull, no broken bones, no knife or gun. Her clothes were intact and there are no bloodstains on the floor. It could be someone walled her in and then kept her alive—maybe a love slave or something."

"I don't think so, Officer . . . Roy? That's not reflected in her sketches. Someone kept her alive in here, but they did it with some care. It was a horrible thing to do, but I don't think she was otherwise abused."

The rest of the police had finished packing and were disappearing up the stairs. When Roy thanked them and turned to follow, Wes stopped him.

"Aren't you going to remove the sketches and the other furnishings?" he asked.

"What for?"

"Evidence."

"We've got samples of everything we need. Leave the rest until we can find out who she is and if she has any living relatives."

Wes didn't like the idea of an open tomb in his basement. He was about to suggest that they brick it back up when someone pounded down the stairs. Wes was shoved aside by Yu, who quickly paced the new room and the perimeter of the basement. Then he visibly relaxed, and went softly up the stairs, followed by Karon.

Wes turned to see Elizabeth in the hidden room studying the sketches. Wes joined her for a few minutes, then asked if she wanted to go up for a cup of coffee.

"No thanks, I want to stay a little longer."

She was sitting on the bed staring at the walls when Wes left.

Stretched out on his bed, Gil was clearing his mind to search for the voice, but it's hard to relax when you're afraid. He was afraid of what the voice had been. Was it a ghost from the walled room? He had to know, so he went through the routine again, seeking clearness.

No voice came, but was he relaxed enough? Gil repeated the routine, and still no voice. His fear diminished, then disappeared with repeated failure. It was truly gone. Opening the wall had liberated whatever it had been. Things were at last back on track.

18

QUESTIONS

Adjustment didn't come easily for Yu. After pacing the newly discovered tomb, he spent the next two hours straightening and restraightening his room. One by one, everyone in the house came to watch, looking for the imperceptible disorder in his belongings, and failing. Yet he flitted from object to object, moving them minutely to fit some criteria only he could discern. Even Daphne came to watch, occasionally lifting her head to see what he was doing. Finally satisfied with his room, Yu paced the house, inside and out, again and again. Finally, Yu went to bed.

Yu was just as restless the next day and the next, so Wes didn't bother attempting to map his cognitive functions. Instead, he and his team spent the day working with the results of the last integration. Shamita was fixated on an unusual brain-wave pattern that she had picked out. Wes examined it, then dismissed it as spurious and submerged himself in refining his program. Shamita and Karon tried matching the pattern to digitized records, with no success. Deciding the pattern was a hardware anomaly, Len spent the rest of the day disassembling the equipment and adding to the clutter of the experiment room.

On Wednesday Ralph convinced all the savants to go down to the Dairy Queen for ice cream. Wes was irritated and frustrated, not wanting to go out in the bad weather, but Elizabeth encouraged him by pointing out that Yu seemed interested in the trip.

They left between rain showers, and Mrs. Clayton was there across the street, raking leaves, not bothering to hide her stare and shaking her head in disbelief. Ralph led the way, of course, his long loping strides soon putting him ahead of the others. Daphne trotted along behind him a few steps, followed by red-headed Archie in his Mickey Mouse sunglasses, and Luis's blobish figure. Yu trailed the others, walking head down, with leaden steps.

Ralph met few people on the way and ducked into only two stores to say hello to those working. When he did, his entourage followed, garnering stares from customers and employees. Elizabeth remained amused but Wes couldn't shake his embarrassment.

At the Dairy Queen Ralph introduced Yu to Ellen and Jean, and then they took orders from the savants. Only Archie and Daphne responded to Jean, but Ralph said he knew what Yu and Luis wanted, and that was a chocolate-dip cone.

When Wes took his cone from Ellen, he asked if her husband had found out who the dead girl was.

"I'm not supposed to talk about his cases, but just between you and me he's got an idea. You might be hearing something pretty soon."

Once back at the house, Elizabeth paused on the porch, holding Wes back.

"Wait for Yu."

A few minutes later Yu came through the front door with Ralph following and began pacing the perimeter. After one circuit he went back inside, Ralph pausing long enough to say, "I bet he says it's all there."

When Wes started in, again Elizabeth stopped him.

"Yu will straighten his room now and the others are happy. Why don't we use the time to play detective?"

"Is that anything like playing doctor?" Wes regretted saying it immediately.

Elizabeth frowned but went on. "You want to know who the girl in the basement is, don't you? Well, who's most likely to know the history of this neighborhood?"

Perplexed, Wes stood silent.

"Mrs. Clayton! She's still over in her yard."

Reluctantly, Wes followed Elizabeth across the street and along the side of Mrs. Clayton's house to where she was raking leaves from under her rosebushes.

"Hello, Mrs. Clayton. I'm Elizabeth and this is Wes. We're your neighbors across the street."

"I know who you are. Ralph's told me all about you. You're the one doing the experiments, aren't you?"

"Ralph makes it sound so mysterious—it's just testing, really," Wes said. Because of Ralph, Wes found himself constantly apologizing for his work.

"Well, come in for a cup of coffee and you can tell me about it." As she led the way to the front door, she started pumping them about what was going on in their house.

"Who's the new one?"

"That's Yu Tran," Wes said. "He's a very gifted young man."

"I thought they were all retarded."

"They are retarded," Wes began.

"They are all intellectually challenged," Elizabeth corrected. "But each has a very special ability."

"I know what Ralph's is," Mrs. Clayton said. "He's got the gift of gab. Is that why they're part of you're experiment? Because of their gifts?"

Old, gray, and bent, Mrs. Clayton still had a sharp mind, and Wes found himself liking her directness.

"Yes. Each has an ability far beyond even the brightest scientist. It's as if to compensate for their retardation—their challenges—they developed what few abilities they did have to unheard-of levels."

They followed Mrs. Clayton through a neat little living room to the round dining-room table. A vase of flowers sat in the middle on a crocheted doily. In a minute she was back with a glass coffeepot and three cups.

"So what are you doing to them?"

"I'm not doing anything to them," Wes said defensively. "I'm trying to piece together their abilities—combine them into one intelligence—a very great mind."

Mrs. Clayton's wrinkled face ·showed interest, and she

pumped Wes for more and more information, nodding knowingly even when his explanations became very technical. Two cups of coffee later, Elizabeth found an opening.

"Have you lived in this neighborhood long?"

"We were newlyweds when we moved in. Richard and I borrowed from his parents to buy this house. We were house poor for many years after that. We raised three kids here, and now I've got seven grandchildren."

"Is Richard your husband?"

"My one and only. He died in 1982. Are you two married? No, well you ought to be. I've watched you with those retarded kids over there. They're harder to handle than normal children. I bet you'd make wonderful parents."

Embarrassed, Elizabeth rushed on. "Have you heard about what they discovered in the basement of our house?"

"Oh my, yes. I saw the police arrive. The body was in that plastic bag, wasn't it? Was it really just a skeleton? How awful it must have been. Is it true one of the retarded boys discovered it?"

"Yes, the new one, Yu."

"Is that name Vietnamese or something?"

"Yes," Elizabeth confirmed. "The police are trying to identify the person in the basement. It was the body of a woman, and someone had sealed her into a room. She lived in there for years."

"Someone must have hated her very much to do that to her."

"But loved her, too," Elizabeth said. "They fed her and gave her art materials to sketch with. They kept her as happy as they could in that little room."

"Sounds horrible to me," the old woman said, then sipped her coffee.

"We were wondering, since you've been in the neighborhood so long, if you might have some idea who the girl in the basement might be?"

Mrs. Clayton stirred her coffee and looked smug, enjoying the prestige her years of snooping had earned her.

"Well, many years ago the house was owned by Mr. Watson. Theodore Watson, but everyone called him Ted. He was a nice man, his wife, too. Millie, that was her name. They had four beautiful daughters, but such a tragic life."

Warming her coffee from the glass pot, she let the tension build.

"Their youngest died of polio—she was only three. It was such a tragedy. She was the cutest little thing. Of course, in those days lots of children died of polio. I didn't think anything worse could happen to the Watsons, but then the worst thing of all happened."

Another pause, and a sip of coffee. Elizabeth and Wes knew she was playing them like an audience.

"Mrs. Watson had her two younger daughters in their Buick—coming back from a Girl Scout meeting, as I remember. A drunk man ran a red light and crashed into them. It was a horrible wreck, but worst of all was they didn't die right away. They were trapped in the car when it caught on fire. People who saw it said they could hear them screaming. Mr. Watson, he took it real hard, but that wasn't the end of his misery. He had one living daughter left, and he doted on her. She was a pretty thing, but after her mother died she started running with a wild crowd down at the high school. It led to all kinds of trouble. One night he had to bail her out of jail—drunk, you know! That night I heard them across the street yelling and screaming. What fights they used to have."

"This is very interesting," Wes interrupted. "But I don't see what it has to do—"

"Go on, Mrs. Clayton," Elizabeth said, glaring at Wes.

"Well, as I was saying before I was interrupted, they had some terrible fights. Then something changed. The fights stopped and the house got real quiet. The next thing I heard she had run away. Someone said she had gone to Seattle. Maybe, but maybe not. I never saw her come home again—never. You would think after a couple years they would have made up, but they never did. But maybe she never did run away. Maybe that was her they found down in that basement."

"What happened to Mr. Watson?" Elizabeth asked.

"He lived there a long time, then ended up in a nursing home. That's what will happen to me, I suppose. I met one of the nurses when she came to pick up his things. A while later he died. I went to the funeral. It's a good thing, too, there were only a handful of people there."

"Did anyone live in the house after him?" Elizabeth asked.

"Three families—all with little kids. Then the fraternity bought it. Those boys were too rowdy—had all those parties. I called the police seventeen times on them. Didn't seem to help a bit until last year." A sip of coffee, and then, "The Watson girl is the only one I know of that disappeared from that house."

Elizabeth thanked her and then made excuses to leave. When they left, Mrs. Clayton stood on the porch and called after them.

"If people would come visit more often I wouldn't have to water so much."

Elizabeth turned and smiled at her, then promised to return.

After supper Elizabeth found Wes with his computer, scrolling through lines of programming commands.

"It's Wednesday night," she said.

"So?"

"So, it's church night."

"You're not serious. I mean, going to church on Sundays is one thing, but if you think I'm going two days a week . . ."

"This time I'm asking, not telling. Pastor Young called and asked if Daphne could play tonight. You don't have to come, but all the savants are going."

"I don't want to unsettle Yu—" Wes said.

"He'll be all right; in fact, I think he'll be ready to map tomorrow."

Wes brightened noticeably. Tomorrow all of Frankie's pieces would be together and he felt like celebrating. Normally, church wouldn't be his choice, but at least Elizabeth would be there.

"Maybe I will go with you."

At night the church took on a different aura. The interior felt harsher, because the normally bright stained-glass windows were dark, reflecting only the indoor electric lights. Only half full, the church felt hollow, the few sounds of the congregation reverberating off the hardwoods accenting the interior.

As soon as they entered, the savants were the center of attention. Their unusual behavior and peculiar looks made them a curiosity, and the congregation freely stared. Fearfully, Wes watched for the tittering and pointing the savants often garnered, but there was none; instead the congregation displayed sincere interest.

Ralph, in the lead, greeted those he knew by name and shook hands with everyone within reach. Ralph's energy lit up the room and animated the crowd. Pastor Young was there, dressed informally, and greeted Elizabeth warmly. Then he ushered them to the front row and began the service. The evening service was simple and alternated between prayers and hymn singing. When they got to the place where the sermon would normally go, the program called for Daphne to play. As soon as her name was mentioned, Ralph poked Daphne and she walked to the piano, head down. With a quick adjustment of the piano bench, Daphne began to play "Amazing Grace," rocking forward and back to the rhythm. Daphne's rich playing moved the congregation, and they soon stopped seeing Daphne as a carnival act and began to worship through her music. "Onward Christian Soldiers" followed, and then "How Great Thou Art." Daphne played for twenty minutes, and then, without a word from anyone, stopped and returned to her place in the pew. Only Ralph spoke.

"That was real good, Daphne. You only messed up a little in that one about being built upon the rock."

There was a snicker from a middle pew, then a clap in the back, and soon the church vibrated with the thunder of applause. Wes applauded with the rest, embarrassed over his shortsightedness. His interest in Daphne's calendar-counting ability had kept him from seeing her other gift—the gift of music. It took fresh ears to appreciate it.

Everyone wanted to meet Daphne after that, and Ralph worked the crowd at her side. To Wes's surprise, Daphne took each offered hand in turn, although her head remained down. Yu leaned against a wall, rocking his head back and forth, but Luis and Archie stood in line shaking hands mutely.

Pastor Young shook their hands last, thanking Daphne generously, and then lingering when he held Elizabeth's hand. Wes, at the other end of the line, couldn't hear what was said, but Elizabeth smiled broadly and then giggled. Wes felt his ire rise but couldn't understand why. Elizabeth was nothing to him. Still, on the way back Wes found himself asking questions about the pastor.

"You two sure seem to be chummy. What was he saying to you back there, anyway?"

Elizabeth looked at him curiously. "He was just kidding around. He said we should take our act on the road."

"That all?"

"He asked me out."

"What? That dirty lech."

"What are you talking about? He's a pastor, not a priest. You don't know anything about religion, do you?"

"I know a hypocrite when I see one. He doesn't know what our relationship is. For all he knows we could be engaged or something."

"I told him we just work together."

Wes hesitated, embarrassed by his jealousy. "That's right. We're just friends," he agreed.

"Is that what we are, Wes? Friends? I told him we were colleagues. I wasn't sure we were friends."

Wes had to admit he wasn't sure they were either. "I think we're getting to friendship."

"Yes, I suppose so."

They didn't talk the rest of the way back, but there was a new warmth between them that lasted long after the walk was over.

The next morning Wes came down to see Daphne playing the piano while wearing an EET helmet. Someone had patched together a long cable, and he followed it into the experimental room to find Len, Karon, and Elizabeth hunched over his terminal.

"What's going on?" he demanded.

Ignoring him, they continued to stare at the monitor while Len typed on the keyboard. Wes joined them to see two wave patterns displayed on the screen. In a softer voice he asked, "What are you doing?"

"Sorry, boss man. We borrowed your program for our own little experiment. Elizabeth here had a good idea."

"Elizabeth?" Wes said with more surprise than he intended. Elizabeth scowled at him.

Len chuckled and said, "Smooth boss, you have a way with the ladies. Yeah, it was her idea, our equipment, and your program. Still, you get only fourth author since Karon here has been helping quite a bit."

Karon smiled up at Wes, then turned back to the screen.

"Elizabeth suggested we try mapping Daphne's piano-playing region even though we don't need it for Frankie. Then she suggested we compare it with the region that activates when Daphne plays the imaginary piano. Elizabeth wanted to know if they're the same regions. I bet yes, she bet no. She won."

Wes was intrigued. It was an intriguing question but didn't seem like something Elizabeth would be interested in since there was no practical usefulness. There must be more to it, he thought, but decided to be more diplomatic.

"Interesting idea. Where do you think it will lead?"

"I suspect the two activities originate in two separate regions but play a similar role for Daphne," Elizabeth said. "I thought if we could find a common link we might be able to understand why she works so hard at shutting out the world."

"Look at this, Wes," Len said, pointing to the brain activity displayed on the screen. "This is Daphne playing right now. It's mostly left-hemisphere activity, with some right-hemisphere, mostly from the parietal regions. Now let me bring back what we recorded earlier."

The brain-wave display shrank, and a second display appeared above it. Wes spotted the difference before Len pointed it out.

"See here, Wes. When Daphne plays the imaginary piano it's primarily right-hemisphere and much less parietal."

"That makes some sense," Wes said. "The right hemisphere normally controls spatial abilities. Picturing a piano and the placement of the keys would be a spatial task."

"Right." Len rubbed his chin, then said, "I don't see anything that helps here. Let's display her brain activity when she's not playing."

A third brain appeared, being washed by colors like the first two. After watching for a minute, Len was discouraged.

"I don't see anything. Anyone else? The piano playing just lays over the normal wave patterns. Let's get a cross section."

Len typed and the display changed, the brains appearing as if sliced in half lengthwise. They studied the displays in silence. Then Karon leaned in and pointed.

"Isn't there reduced activity in the thalamus?"

The others watched for a minute, excited by the finding.

"She's right," Wes said. "Take a look lower—in the reticular activating system. That section looks a little more active to me. Len, give us CPS on that." Len typed and the display changed, showing three wave patterns and a digital readout. "That's interesting."

"What's interesting?" Elizabeth asked in frustration. "It was my idea!"

"Sorry, Elizabeth. When Daphne plays, the electrical activity in two particular parts of her brain changes, the activity in the thalamus drops, and the activity in the reticular activating system increases. The thalamus controls sleep and wakefulness and the RAS attention."

"They do more," Len added, "but don't you see the connection? Those parts of the brain control input from the environment. Those regions of the brain are thick with axons bringing input from sensors throughout the body. When Daphne plays it somehow changes the balance between these two regions."

"What effect would that have?" Elizabeth asked.

"Hard to tell," Wes said. "Especially since the activity in the two regions changes inversely. I would guess Daphne would become less aware of some parts of her environment and more aware of other parts."

"That makes sense," Elizabeth said. "Daphne is trying to rebalance her mind by playing. If only we could teach her to do the same thing without the piano playing—maybe with biofeedback?"

The group was interrupted when a smiling Gil came into the room, followed by Yu. "He's hungry," Gil said. "And after breakfast he says he's ready to try on the headgear."

Yu cooperated as long as Gil was near him, and they finished mapping him by afternoon. Wes was anxious to try for Frankie again, but Elizabeth made him wait until evening. The team spent the rest of the day double- and triple-checking their equipment. Len spent most of the day on the floor tracing the fiber-optic lines and checking the seals on the liquid-nitrogen system.

They ordered out for pizza to put the savants in a good mood. Ralph met the driver at the door, calling him by name, and then helped him carry the pizzas into the house. They ate in front of the TV, watching cartoons. When the last of the pizza and soda was gone, they ushered the savants into the experiment room. It was time for a complete integration.

19

THE FRANKIE EFFECT

There were five cots arranged in a semicircle, each with a helmet attached to an EET. A tangle of cables filled every space on the floor. The nitrogen tanks sat in a corner, lines running to the EETs to cool the special CPUs. Daphne, Luis, Yu, and Archie were sitting on four of the cots being fitted with their headgear. Part of the team now, Elizabeth helped Karon with the savants. Only Yu was apprehensive; the others were calm, and even eager for the session to begin. Wes didn't quite understand why Daphne and Archie were eager, but welcomed it. If Yu adapted as well as the others, Elizabeth would have no way of prematurely stopping the project.

"Wes," Elizabeth said. "Do you want Ralph on the fifth cot?"

Momentarily confused, Wes stared at the empty cot. Suddenly it came to him. "No, not Ralph, put Gil there."

Standing in the doorway with a big wad of gum in his mouth, Ralph said, "Gil's right, he's probably better'n me at this. 'Sides, now I can watch what I want on TV." Ralph turned and left.

Ralph's comments about Gil being right made no sense to Wes, but Gil's face was flushed—from anger?

"Wes, we don't really need a fifth," Shamita said. "We planned this for four."

"I know, Shamita, I wrote the grant," Wes said testily. Then, apologetically, he added, "I just thought this would be a better test of the program's potential." Unsure of his own reasons, Wes hurried on. "Take the others under, Shamita, while we get Gil ready."

While Shamita systematically relaxed the donors, Wes thought about Gil. He didn't need the fifth, and Ralph's geographic ability might actually be useful. So why use Gil? Not knowing, he decided to minimize Gil's role.

"Shamita, use Archie for the base matrix." Then, thinking better of it, he added, "No, use Gil for the matrix, just like before."

Len and Shamita looked at him strangely. Then Shamita said, "What about Luis's hindbrain memory?"

"We used Gil before—it'll make a better comparison."

Shamita shook her head, and Karon whispered in Len's ear, eliciting a smile.

Shamita typed and soon Wes had Gil's brain-wave activity displayed on the screen, only the psychomotor functions depressed. One by one she added the brain-wave patterns of the savants, each appearing in a row above Gil's.

"Wes," Shamita said. "Do you see that peculiar wave?"

Wes looked, but suddenly the screen scrambled.

"What was that, Shamita?"

"Power spike, I guess."

"Not with my surge protectors," Len said defensively.

"Check it later, anyway, will you Len? What were you saying about a peculiarity, Shamita?"

"Huh? Nothing. I think I'm ready here. Len, watch the hypothalamic output." Shamita typed for a few more minutes and then pointed to Wes. "The parameters are set as before. I'll configure Yu's after the others are in."

Typing furiously, Wes began patching together Frankie. One by one, the savant abilities were integrated into Gil's brain waves. "All right, Shamita, give me Yu."

"It's going to be a tight fit. He overlaps with Luis quite a bit."

"Your best guess, please. We can toy with it later if we need to."

Wes watched as parts of Yu's right and left hemispheres were deleted from Wes's display, leaving a wave pattern dominated by prefrontal waves.

"That should get Yu's remote-associations ability."

Wes took over and replaced another section of Gil's brain-wave patterns. When he had a functioning whole, Len began applauding. Elizabeth came to watch over Wes's shoulder.

"Is it supposed to be Frankie again?" Elizabeth asked.

"Ask."

"Who do I speak to, Shamita?"

"Luis."

Elizabeth stood by Luis's ear. "Are you here, Frankie?"

A long silence followed. When no answer came, the scientists studied their screens.

"Does the memory from the previous session carry over?" Elizabeth asked.

"I don't know why not . . ." Wes began. "Of course, the memory could have been disrupted by the addition of Yu. It wouldn't hurt to tell him who he is, but I was hoping we'd solved that self-awareness problem."

"You're Frankie. Who are you?"

"I'm Frankie?"

The voice came from Yu.

"Don't you remember? We talked before."

"I don't know if I remember."

Elizabeth paused, looking concerned. "Frankie, how can you not know if you remember?"

"I guess I did talk to you, Elizabeth," Frankie said.

"Shamita, can you turn off the auditory for a minute?" Elizabeth asked.

Shamita typed a few commands and then said, "Frankie's deaf, go ahead, Elizabeth."

"I'm a little concerned. Frankie seems to have a memory of our previous conversation—she called me by name—but it doesn't seem integrated; more like a dissociated memory typical of multiple personalities."

"It may just be adolescent," Shamita said. "Adolescents often don't feel integrated. They're chameleon-like, changing from one person to another depending on whether they're with their friends or their parents. We're working with personalities that never really left childhood. Maybe when you put them together you get adolescent?"

Wes thought for a second and then said, "Personality is mostly a prefrontal function. This might be more Yu than anyone else. Maybe we need to cut down his parameters."

"We could lose the RA ability."

"RA?" Elizabeth prodded.

"Remote associations. That's what we wanted most from Yu—his uncanny ability to see relationships where others can't." Then, to Shamita, "Let's leave it alone for now, and see if we can get Frankie to work for us. Elizabeth, try talking to him again."

"You're sure it's a him?"

"It is if it's mostly Yu talking."

With Luis's hearing turned back on, Elizabeth tried again.

"Frankie, are you there?"

"Yes, Elizabeth."

"What do you remember, Frankie?"

"Nothing."

Wes ran his finger across his throat and Shamita cut off the auditory again.

"Frankie won't have any personal memories, he's only been integrated once before. We need to build a memory set for him. He should have all the procedural memories of the others, however. Try the abilities; then we'll try some creative problem solving."

Elizabeth picked up a yellow pad. "Frankie, on what day does Christmas fall in 2011?"

"Sunday."

"Very good. What one word goes with 'tulip,' 'light,' and 'dim'?"

" 'Bulb.' "

"Correct. Which is farther west, Sacramento or Los Angeles?"

"Sacramento."

Elizabeth looked down at her pad in surprise. "Right again."

Elizabeth asked the rest of the questions, getting only correct answers. Then she nodded to Shamita, who typed on her keypad. Soon Shamita indicated that she was ready.

"Frankie, can you sit up for me?"

Elizabeth waited by Luis, but it was Daphne who sat up.

"Shamita, this gives me the creeps. Couldn't you have made it Luis?"

"Could have, but this is a better test."

Karon brought over a tray covered with pieces of a jigsaw puzzle.

"Frankie, can you put this together for me?"

Daphne looked down and then began picking up pieces one by one and putting them together, first assembling a frame, and then filling in the middle. The puzzle was finished in five minutes.

"Very good, Frankie. Please lie down."

Elizabeth nodded to Shamita, who cut off audition once again.

"Well, Frankie seems to have all the abilities, and she certainly has more life this time. A person, though?—I'm not convinced."

"*He* has more life," Wes corrected.

"Let's settle that now."

"How?"

"I'll ask Frankie if she's a boy or a girl, just like before."

Shamita cut in before Wes could respond. "I'm not comfortable with this. Gender is very complex. It's made up of years of experiences and cultural shaping, mixed with the signals your body begins sending at puberty. Our fully integrated Frankie has too few minutes of personal memories to base a gender concept on, and must certainly be getting mixed body signals."

"Shamita's right, Elizabeth," Wes said. "With Yu integrated in, this Frankie is much more complex. It might be best to let Frankie develop his—or her—own sense of gender."

Thoughtful, Elizabeth stood silent for a minute. "I think Frankie already has a sense of gender. It's Yu's voice, but the tone . . . Well, it seems feminine. Maybe I can get at gender indirectly. There's a simple projective test called Draw a Person. Virtually without fail, a normal person will draw a figure of their own sex."

Wes and Shamita exchanged looks, and then Wes nodded approval.

"Frankie, I want you to sit up again. Here's a pad of paper and a pencil. Will you draw a person for me?"

Vainly Wes and Shamita craned their necks to see. After a few minutes, Daphne handed the pad to Elizabeth, who again signaled for the audio to be cut off. Then she stood unmoving, staring at the pad.

"Well?" Wes prodded to no effect.

Karon walked over and stood behind Elizabeth.

"I can't believe it! Come here, you've got to see this!"

Reaching Elizabeth last, Wes leaned over the others to see a beautifully drawn young woman—something was familiar about the girl. Then it hit him—it was the girl from the walls of the hidden room.

"What does it mean?" Karon asked.

"Nothing," Len said. "Yu walked all over that place and his recall is nearly as good as Luis's. Frankie just tapped into Yu's memory."

"Yes," Wes agreed. "What else could it be?"

"Shamita, turn Frankie's hearing back on," Elizabeth ordered. "I want to ask her directly."

Shamita waited for Wes's approval, then they all returned to their stations.

"Frankie, are you a girl?"

"Yes."

"We call you Frankie. Is that your name?"

Silence filled the room. Then, "I'm Frankie."

Another signal and Frankie's hearing was off again.

"Satisfied, Elizabeth?" Wes asked.

"No. This is too strange." Then, after a thoughtful pause, she had Shamita connect Frankie again.

"Frankie, do you want to kill Ralph?"

"Who's Ralph?" Frankie asked.

Another signal from Elizabeth. "Wes, can you end the session for now?"

Wes was reluctant, wanting to explore Frankie's abilities, but saw no need to worry Elizabeth unnecessarily—not this close to success.

"OK, Shamita, that's it for tonight. I'll separate them for you. Bring Yu up last."

After the savants were settled around the kitchen table eating ice cream, the team gathered in the living room, all silent at first. Wes was first to speak.

"The drawing's just a fluke, Elizabeth. Frankie accessed a memory for a picture and pulled out one of Yu's."

"Isn't artistic ability a right-hemisphere function? Archie contributed most of that hemisphere, not Yu."

"She's right, Wes," Shamita said. "I set the parameters and

there was little of Yu's right hemisphere in Frankie. Archie never saw those photos."

"Episodic memories aren't necessarily stored with procedural memories. I can draw numbers and they're left-hemisphere."

"Bad example," Len said.

"I know. But you get the point." Mildly concerned about his project, Wes nevertheless was enjoying the discussion. There was a puzzle to be solved here. He was also impressed with Elizabeth's insights, no matter how wrong. "I can come up with a better example if you want."

"What about Frankie's response to the question about killing Ralph? Didn't it seem odd to you, Wes?"

"Why? Because Frankie didn't remember saying that before? The memory's there somewhere, we might have accidentally cut it out when we fit Yu's ability in."

"Maybe, but there was something else. Frankie simply asked who Ralph was; she didn't seem shocked by the thought of killing someone."

Wes found Elizabeth's oblique approach to issues fascinating, but also irritating.

"You didn't give Frankie a chance to be shocked." Wes looked around for support, but the others averted their eyes. Then Ralph came into the room.

"You mind if I watch TV?"

The doorbell rang and Ralph crossed the room in three strides to open the door.

"Hi, Pastor Young. Lookee here, everyone, it's Pastor Young."

Elizabeth jumped up and crossed the room. "I'm so sorry, I forgot all about it. I'll be ready in a minute." Then she disappeared up the stairs.

Confused, Wes stood dumbly, then he realized Elizabeth had a date. Jealousy tainted his thinking. "Where are you going?" he asked the pastor.

Amused, the pastor said, "Don't worry, Dad, I'll have her back by midnight."

Len led the others in laughter, while Wes blushed. Daphne came and sat at the piano, distracting the others and sparing Wes any more embarrassment.

"Hello, Daphne," the pastor said.

"Hello, Pastor Young," she said. Then she began to play.

Daphne's greeting to the pastor surprised Wes. To respond at all was unusual for Daphne, and such a strong response was unheard of.

Elizabeth came down with a coat and fresh makeup and soon the two were out the door. Wes waited until the others were occupied and then went out on the porch. Elizabeth and the pastor were walking down the street talking. Suddenly Elizabeth laughed out loud and pushed playfully on the pastor's shoulder. The jealousy came back stronger, and this time he nursed it.

Daphne's mind was clear and she relished the details of her room. Seldom could she enjoy the colors, the textures, the lines and shading. She picked up a yellow pencil and marveled at the sharp detail. Daphne stared out the window, spotting Elizabeth and the pastor walking down the sidewalk. Elizabeth laughed and then touched the pastor. Instantly Daphne remembered Billy's hand on her, sliding between her legs. She panicked and suddenly the black hole was erupting, threatening to spill its memories into her conscious mind. Daphne flopped on her bed, running in her mind to the hidey-hole and hiding deep in it. The black hole was calling to her, so she plunged deeper into the blackness of her hiding place. Then something took hold of her and pulled her deeper than she had ever been before.

She knew! She saw something on that damn machine, and she knew I was different. Gil paced his room restlessly, worried about what Shamita had discovered. He had pushed on her mind to distract her, but he didn't have the power to keep her from seeing it again. Now afraid of discovery, Gil knew he should run—that had always been his way. But neither Ralph's ability to hear his commands nor the voice in the basement had scared him away, and that had given him confidence. Now that he felt his power growing with each session, he wouldn't let Shamita scare him away. She would have to be dealt with—more permanently than Ralph.

Now determined to kill Shamita, Gil found that he could relax, and he stretched out on the bed to clear his mind. Rushing his relaxation routine forced Gil to restart several times before his mind cleared—again no voice. Relieved, Gil began to search for other voices, other people's minds—nothing. Then Gil relaxed and reached out with his mind, seeking to touch others. Suddenly, the person called Gil ceased to exist.

Wes tore off the computer printout and headed to his room. He couldn't concentrate and he didn't want Shamita to think it was because he was jealous. If he was going to stew over Elizabeth's date, he was going to do it in private.

In the living room Archie and Luis were stretched out on the floor in front of the TV. Ralph sat behind them with a bowl of popcorn, looking up when Wes came through.

"Shhh!" he said, a finger held to his big lips. "They're asleep. Want some popcorn?"

Wes shook his head and then went up the stairs and spread the computer printout across his bed. A few minutes later he gave up and stared at the ceiling. "OK," he said aloud, "I'm jealous." Now that he had admitted it, he sat back and enjoyed the feeling.

She paused at the open garage door. She needed something. Turning back, she searched the garage until she found a screwdriver, then tucked it inside her pants under her blouse. Then she left the garage and headed down the alley.

Rimmer was bored and half drunk. Nothing was happening in the whole damn house. The only ones in tonight were studying like freshmen and had brushed Rimmer off when he tried to get a party going. The frat had been a big bore since they had initiated that retard, not to mention that idiot Singleton falling off that roof. Cowed by Elizabeth Foxworth and the administration, half the brothers were too chicken to even tap a keg on weekends. If things didn't turn around soon, Rimmer was going to die of boredom.

Rimmer tossed down the rest of his beer, then pulled another from the fridge. He popped the lid, then swigged down half of it. When he brought the can down he spotted someone walking down the alley. Flipping off the kitchen lights, he could see it was the retarded girl, the one Billy had been trying to feel up in the park. That Billy would do it to any girl, Rimmer thought, even a retard. Even so, as he watched her come down the alley, he realized she wasn't that bad. Billy had screwed some of the best-looking girls on campus, so if he saw something in this girl she was good enough for him. Besides, he thought, it would be sweet to nail one of Billy's girls before he did. Rimmer pulled another can of beer out of the fridge and hurried out the back.

When he came around the corner of their garage he could see her more clearly. It was the same girl, but she looked different. She didn't look that retarded and she was kind of pretty—actually very pretty. He knew her new good looks were the results of the beer, but that was what booze was for—making ugly girls pretty. Rimmer stepped in front of her and held out a can.

"Looking for a party?"

She stopped, her face blank, staring at the can. Then the corners of her mouth turned up into a smile, but her eyes remained dead.

"Yeah. I like to party. Listen to music. Dance." Then she took the beer and drank a swallow.

"All right. Me, too. I'm a party guy. But it's kind of quiet around here right now. How about a private party?"

She nodded and smiled, her eyes still blank.

Excited, Rimmer thought fast. She was going to put out, but where could he do it to her? He could sneak her into his room, but if he got caught with one of Foxworth's retards Classen would kick him out for sure. He decided on using Bopper's van.

"Come on, I'll show you a place."

Rimmer slipped his arm around her shoulder to guide her. She didn't snuggle close, but she didn't shrug him off, either.

He walked her to the corner and then to the back of Bopper's van. Pulling the hidden key from the bumper, he opened the back and helped her in. There was a mattress on the floor and she scooted across and sat with her back against the front seat. Her legs were spread slightly and she looked like she wanted it. Rimmer finished his beer and tossed the can in the yard. Then he climbed in, pulling the door closed.

There was enough light from the streetlamp to see, and she looked good. Her eyes were sparkling now, and her lips moist. Even slumped like she was he could see her plump breasts pushing at her blouse. Rimmer wanted to reach for them but was sober enough to go slow.

Taking the beer from her he took a swig and then set it aside. Then he bent down and kissed her. She didn't kiss back, but her lips parted slightly so he pushed harder and slipped his tongue between her lips. No response, so he pushed it in deeper, touching her teeth. Still she didn't respond but he didn't care.

Rimmer pulled off his shirt, then pulled her down until she was lying flat. Then he kissed her and felt her right breast at the same time. She didn't move, but he knew she wanted it because her nipple stiffened. Aroused and half drunk he pawed at her breasts and then fumbled for her buttons. That's when she moved, pushing him away and down onto his back. Then she straddled him, rocking gently. Rimmer moaned with the pleasure. When she began kissing his chest he put his hands under his head and closed his eyes, enjoying the sensation. The kissing stopped and he saw her unbuttoning her blouse. When she saw him watching she bent and kissed his chest again until his eyes closed. He knew the type. She was shy. That was okay with him, he would look all he wanted when she was naked.

Rimmer was imagining her bare breasts when something plunged through his rib cage and buried in his heart. Pain exploded in his brain, and he opened his eyes to see the yellow handle of a screwdriver sticking out of his chest. His body convulsed, and he lost control of his bowels and bladder. Rimmer's arms moved toward the handle just as she grabbed it and pulled it out. Blood spurted from the hole. His heart was pounding uncontrollably, coming apart in his chest. In his pain he flailed, but she pulled out of reach until his arms lost strength and fell limp. Then his chest seized, never to pull in another breath. Just as the light faded from his eyes he saw the screwdriver bury into his chest again. This time he didn't feel it.

Phil was witty, considerate, good-looking, and good company, but he was a disappointment to Elizabeth. They had gone to a movie, and then out for coffee, and Phil had shown a far-ranging knowledge, conversing with her about classic films, philosophy, and even her profession of social work. But finally the conversation had come around to Wes's experiment, and that was when Elizabeth found out Phil was a psychologist.

Before he felt his call to the ministry he had been a research psychologist. For a time he had immersed himself in his work, but found his life empty and psychology a poor substitute for what he really needed. That was when he decided to follow his father into the ministry. Elizabeth liked Phil the minister better than Phil the psychologist. Still, his interest in the experiment was sincere, and it was a small enough flaw.

It was cool and cloudy, but dry, and they walked slowly, enjoying the stroll, talking as if they were old friends. As they neared their block they could see a knot of people on the corner and the distinct blue flash of police lights. An ambulance roared past them and turned by the crowd. Elizabeth immediately thought of the savants, and pulled Phil into a fast walk.

At the corner they could see police clearing spectators away from a van, and medics climbing into the back. Yellow tape was being stretched around the area to hold back the crowds, preventing her from seeing what had happened. When one of the officers came by stretching out another length of tape, Elizabeth tugged at his sleeve.

"Officer, what is it?"

"Get back, lady, this is a crime scene."

"I live near here. Is someone I know hurt?"

"It's one of the fraternity boys, lady. He's dead. Somebody stabbed him."

"Which one?"

"I'm not supposed to say."

"Please, I knew them."

"Well . . . the kid who found him said his name is Rimmer."

"Oh, no. I did know him."

Pulling Elizabeth away, Phil thanked the officer.

"Are you all right, Elizabeth?"

"I met that boy. I didn't really know him—"

"Let's go home."

Gil woke with a headache. He rubbed his temples and then his eyes—something was strange. He didn't feel as if he'd been asleep, yet he must have been. Three hours had passed, and the last thing he could remember was working through his relaxation routine, trying to explore his ability.

Gil stretched out, running through his routine. Just as he reached clearness, a commotion broke out downstairs. Loud voices disrupted his concentration. Frustrated, Gil forced himself to ignore the voices and work his mind clear again. He was nearly there when someone pounded down the stairs. "Damn," Gil cursed. He was mad now, making getting clear even tougher.

Once again he stretched out and lay back. Three tries later he was just clearing his mind when the door burst open, revealing Ralph.

"Hi Gil. Are you sleeping? You don't have your pajamas on. Do you sleep in pajamas? I do. I used to sleep in my underwear but Mrs. Williams said I shouldn't do that anymore. She bought me some red striped ones. I didn't like them too good. Elizabeth bought me some with rocket ships on them. I like them better. You want I should show them to you?"

"Ralph, what the hell do you want?"

"You shouldn't curse, Gil." Then Ralph folded his arms, leaned back and pursed his lips. "Are you mad or something, Gil?" Then his hand shot out and he thumped his head. "How could I be so stupid? Of course you're mad, otherwise you wouldn't cuss. Barney used to cuss—"

"Ralph! What do you want?"

"Elizabeth is back. She saw a murder or something. You want to come down?"

"No! Now, get out!" Then in a forced softer voice, "Please."

"Well, okeydokey. I'll come back and tell you what's going on."

Ralph left, leaving the door open, and Gil's anger flared. He glared at the door, focusing all his anger—the door moved. It was only a slight movement, as if it had been pushed by a light breeze, but it had moved. Suddenly afraid of his own ability, Gil sat back stunned. *Had he done that?*

Gil stared hard at the door and pushed as if he were making a suggestion. Nothing happened. Next he closed his eyes and pictured it moving. Still nothing. Now Gil pictured himself pushing it closed with his hand, and pushed that image toward the door, but it didn't move. Frustrated, Gil looked away, trying to remember how he had done it before. Then Ralph's voice echoed up the stairs. "Come on down, Gil! It's really interesting." Gil flared again, snapping his head around and staring at the door. It moved.

Anger? He had to be angry to get the power? That prospect

worried Gil. He lost control when he was angry, and control was life to Gil. No, he had to learn to use the power without the anger.

"Hey, Daphne. Come on down and hear this," Ralph shouted.

Suddenly Gil remembered Ralph saying something about a murder. His emotions had clouded his mind—he hated emotions. He should be interested in a murder, or the others would get suspicious. Reluctantly, Gil got up to join those downstairs.

Elizabeth was in the living room telling the others about what they had seen. Another man was sitting next to Elizabeth with his back to Gil—Reverend Young, Gil reasoned. Karon, Len, and Wes were sitting in chairs listening to Elizabeth's story. The savants were glued to the TV—all except Daphne—while Ralph hovered around the group trying to be a part. Gil approached cautiously, listening, but watching the man. He was vaguely familiar.

Elizabeth was telling about a murder on their block. One of the fraternity boys had been stabbed in the back of a van. Compassion was another emotion Gil disdained, and he cared nothing about the death, except that it might threaten the experiment. If the neighborhood appeared unsafe for the savants, Elizabeth might move them.

The murdered boy was from the fraternity Gil used to try to get rid of Ralph. Knowing one was dead made him happy—he regretted not killing the one he'd suggested off the roof. Suppressing his good feeling, Gil sought a way to make the murder less threatening to Elizabeth and the others.

"It's probably drug-related," Gil said. "College kids are into drugs."

When the pastor turned to look at him, Gil recognized him and his face flushed.

"Gil's probably right," Len said, pulling the pastor's attention away from Gil. "There were a lot of drugs around when I was in college."

When Karon agreed, and discussion of college drug experiences broke out, Gil turned and slipped back upstairs. He was panicky now, hoping the man hadn't recognized him. It had been years ago—he couldn't remember which university—but the man had tested him. *It's getting too dicey here,* he thought. First,

Ralph's unexplained ability to hear him, then Shamita detecting something in his brain waves, and now his past catching up to him. He didn't know if the pastor had recognized him, so he would have to act fast. He had to get things under control.

20

INVESTIGATIONS

Officer Winston was back the next day with more questions. Elizabeth met him at the door.

"Hello, Roy. Did you find out who the girl in the basement was?"

"Huh? No, not yet. We have some leads, though."

"It wouldn't be the Watson girl, would it?"

The policeman eyed her warily. "Well, suddenly you're awfully well informed. It may be her, but I'm here about the murder last night. I hear you and Phil Young were at the scene. You mind telling me what you were doing there?"

"You can't be serious. I'm a suspect?"

"Do you know when the last murder was in this town before you people showed up? A long time ago. Now we've got two bodies."

"One is a skeleton."

"True. So where were you thirty years ago?" This time Roy smiled when he said it. "Actually, I'm interested in whether you saw anything that might help us."

"We were coming back from a movie. We passed one or two people by the university, but I don't remember anyone on the block before we saw the crowd."

"Uh-huh," he said, and then wrote in a notebook.

"What are you writing down? I haven't really said anything."

Officer Winston looked at her briefly, then wrote again, saying, "Haven't really said anything." He was smiling again. "One more thing. All your kids in last night? What do you call them?"

"Savants. Of course they were in. They're not allowed out alone that late."

"Sure, sure. Isn't one of them female?" Roy asked without a smile.

"Why are you asking about Daphne?"

"Neighbor said he saw the dead kid"—Roy flipped through the pages of his notebook—"Joshua Ringman, get into the van with a girl."

"There is a university three blocks away. There's a lot of young women to choose from."

"Sure, sure. I was only asking. So, she was here last night?"

"Of course."

"OK, thanks. If you think of anything, give me a call."

Elizabeth watched him leave, but thought about Daphne. She hadn't come down last night when Elizabeth came home with the story about the murder. When Elizabeth did her pre-bed check, Daphne was there, but she honestly didn't know if she had been there all night. Inside she found Daphne at the piano and Ralph with his nose six inches from the TV screen.

"Ralph, can I speak to you a minute?"

"Okeydokey. It's just a commercial for those fruit things that are yucky. Especially the blue ones."

Out on the porch, Elizabeth sat with Ralph on the steps.

"Ralph, did you see anyone leave the house last night?"

"This is a riddle, isn't it? I'm not good at riddles. Except for the one about the polar bear at the north pole. I memorized that one."

"It's not a riddle. Did you see anyone leave last night after I left?"

Ralph pursed his lips, putting on his serious look. "Lemme see. You left. Pastor Young left with you. I don't got such a good memory. Maybe I should get Luis?"

"Excellent idea, Ralph."

Ralph was back in a minute with Luis, who was carrying a bowl of dry cornflakes. Luis ate his cereal dry, with no milk.

"Luis, did you see anyone leave the house last night?"

"Yes."

Elizabeth waited while he filled his mouth with flakes.

"Who?"

"You left with the pastor. Len and Karon left after you."

"Oh yeah," Ralph said. "Now I remember. Karon and Len sat on the swing. They was smooching."

Elizabeth was only mildly surprised to hear about the kissing. "Luis, did you see Daphne leave last night?"

"No."

"He was sleeping watching TV," Ralph said.

"No I wasn't."

"Was too! You fell asleep when that dog show came on."

Whining, Luis said, "I didn't fall asleep."

"Thank you, Luis. You can finish breakfast inside."

"You want me to ask Daphne if she went outside last night?" Ralph offered.

"No, Ralph, I'll do it."

Daphne was still at the piano. When she paused between songs, Elizabeth spoke. "Daphne." She turned, looked up, and smiled. Elizabeth was stunned. Daphne never smiled, and never looked people in the eye. When Elizabeth smiled back Daphne's head dropped to its usual position, her smile folding into a slight frown.

"Yes, Elizabeth," Daphne said.

"You have a nice smile." A fleeting smile was her only response. "Did you go out last night?"

"No."

Elizabeth saw no point in asking anything more, yet she was uncertain. Roy wouldn't have asked about Daphne if he didn't have more than just the vague description of "a girl." But the idea was absurd—Daphne was harmless. Trying to put it aside, Elizabeth left Daphne to work on her weekly reports for the Kellum Foundation, but found it hard to concentrate.

The parsonage attic was filled with boxes belonging to at least three previous pastors. Somewhere in the mess were dusty boxes containing the remnants of his previous professional life. Under the Christmas decorations he found boxes labeled "Files." He moved three of the file boxes down to the kitchen and began sifting through them.

Like viewing an old photo album, searching the files revived long-buried memories, many of them precious, and he lingered over papers and reports, thinking of long ago, of friends made and lost, of successes and failures. He reveled in the nostalgia, but kept himself on task until he located the records on telepaths.

Thirty folders were lined up in alphabetical order. Each folder contained copies of test protocols, results, and evaluations. Phil knew the results—all thirty demonstrated ability when first tested, but only seven had shown even slight ability when experimental controls were introduced. Phil flipped through the names but found nothing under Masters. Then he searched again, looking at first names. There was no Gil. Frustrated, he searched again, opening each file and looking at the pictures of the subjects. Only one file had no picture. The name on the file was Stephen Sacks. Phil read through his old notes, memories of Stephen Sacks coming back in flashes.

As he reviewed the file, the puzzlement he had felt years ago when he had tested Mr. Sacks came back. Mr. Sacks was talented, but his ability came and went in an unpredictable way—sometimes testing strong, other times just above chance. A handwritten note in the back said that Mr. Sacks had missed his last appointment and that his phone had been disconnected. Vaguely, Phil remembered that the man had simply disappeared one day. Was this really the same person as Gil Masters? If it was him, what was he doing working as a social worker with a group of savants? Reading through the records again, he found there was little information. The records had his previous occupation listed as "unemployed." If his Stephen Sacks was Gil Masters, it was odd that he would change his name, but not necessarily illegal. Still, changing a name suggested that the man was hiding something. Perhaps, Phil decided, it was time to catch up on the research in parapsychology.

Gil followed the pastor when he left his house. Keeping to the opposite side of the street, he watched for an opportunity. The streets were too residential here, though, the cars moving too slowly, leaving Gil frustrated. His best hope was if the pastor continued down to the main street—he didn't, instead turning in to the university. Gil trailed him into the psychology building, watching him head down into the library. Gil waited a few minutes, then followed, finding the pastor seated at a computer terminal, searching the psychology literature. After fifteen minutes the pastor moved into the stacks. From a distance Gil watched the minister pull journals, taking notes as he read.

Gil waited until the minister took a bathroom break; then Gil pulled one of the journals from the stack on his table, retreating to a far corner to read. It was a parapsychology journal, confirming Gil's suspicion. The pastor had remembered him. Gil had to get rid of him, but couldn't risk stampeding Elizabeth and the savants from the neighborhood. He needed an accident, and he needed it soon.

Elizabeth found Shamita at the kitchen table, computer printouts spread over the surface.

"Are you working on Daphne's results?"

"Huh? No. Something else."

"Shamita, what did you think about the other night? About that drawing?"

Clearly annoyed at being taken from her work, she said, "I thought it was peculiar, but it could be a memory. Personal memories are impossible to localize. Even with direct brain stimulation, only bits and pieces of personal experience can be located, nothing complex. We do know that it takes time for memories to be consolidated—I mean processed for storage. It's possible that Yu was still processing the images from the basement room and when we picked up his multiplexed signals the image from the dead girl's room was part of that signal and was processed into Frankie's personal memories."

Elizabeth wasn't satisfied, but lacked the knowledge to argue. "What is it you're working on?"

"This. See this wave pattern here. It's a typical alpha wave, which is the dominant brain wave during the waking state. When we integrate brain waves it's normal to have some disruption of alpha-wave activity—at least at first. The alpha waves get deeper and more irregular, and then they return to the normal alpha rhythm. Frankie's brain pattern followed that pattern, except there is something more." Pointing at the printout she said, "You see another weaker wave here."

"Where?"

"It's hard to pick out, but see this line here, kind of an echo of the alpha pattern?"

"It must be more obvious to a trained eye."

"If it was, I would have taken it to Wes. Even I'm not sure I'm seeing it."

"Is it something to worry about?"

"I'm not worried, I'm curious. When I'm working on a problem I get serious."

Elizabeth thought Shamita was too serious, but minded her own business and left her to her work. Gil was back from his walk, so Elizabeth left for the library to find out what she could about the body in the basement.

After supper Karon popped up a big batch of popcorn and they all watched *The Wizard of Oz*. Archie, Luis, and Ralph sang all the songs, Ralph thumping himself on the side of the head when he came to the scarecrow singing "If I only had a brain." When the savants were in bed, and Gil gone for another walk, Wes brewed a fresh pot of coffee, settling at the kitchen table.

Cupping his coffee mug, Wes was excited and disturbed. The emergence of Frankie validated his theories, and guaranteed grants for the rest of his professional life. But odd things were happening around him. Yu's discovery of the hidden room, the body, the murder of the fraternity brother, Frankie's picture drawn from the walls of the hidden room, and even Ralph, his unexpected guest. Now Shamita was acting strange, digging into an anomaly that was incidental and likely spurious. He'd expected difficulty, but difficulty with the experiment, not with life.

Elizabeth came into the kitchen, joining him with a cup of coffee.

"I found something interesting in the library today. I was looking for a clue to who that might have been in the basement room."

"Any luck?"

"Not about that. I did confirm Mrs. Clayton's account of what happened to Mr. Watson's daughters—at least the ones that died with their mother in the car accident. It really was horrible. There was a picture of their wrecked car burned black. It was a terrible accident. Mr. Watson couldn't help but be affected by it. I couldn't find anything about his fourth daughter—the one who supposedly ran away—but there was something kind of interesting."

Wes waited, but Elizabeth sipped her coffee, waiting for his curiosity to take over. "So what did you find?"

Eyes bright, Elizabeth leaned across the table. "About the time Mrs. Clayton said Mr. Watson's last daughter vanished there were a series of murders in town—back in the early 1950s. The press labeled the killer the Stalker."

"You think the Watson girl was killed by this Stalker?"

"I don't know—I doubt it. It's just as likely she's the one in the basement."

"What's the point?"

"The people killed were fraternity brothers, just like Rimmer. I know what you're thinking, but there's more. They were all killed with a knife—one of them in a parked car."

"Rimmer was killed with a screwdriver."

"Yes, but he was stabbed with it, and whoever did the killing mutilated the genitals of the boys."

"Rimmer's genitals were mutilated?"

"Yes. I confirmed it with Ellen at the Dairy Queen."

"It's a peculiar coincidence, but I don't see that they're necessarily connected. Whoever did those killings would be almost fifty years older—too old to overpower a fraternity boy. Besides, wasn't he seen with a girl just before he was killed?"

"I know all that. It just seems strange, that's all."

Wes didn't argue with that, but to him it was just another of the many oddities surrounding his experiment. He could see, however, that Elizabeth's eyes were busy, flicking back and forth, her mind actively wrestling with the mystery.

Gil hid in the alley, watching. After an hour the pastor pulled up in his car and went inside. It was an old house, next to the church and with many overgrown shrubs. Keeping to the shadows, Gil crept into the bushes and peeked into a window—nothing but a dark room. Light from a hall dimly lit the interior of the next room—an empty bedroom. Gil continued around the corner and to a window, looking into the kitchen. He was about to move again when the light snapped on. Ducking, Gil caught sight of the pastor coming in. Gil listened to the pastor rummaging around the kitchen. Pans were banged, water pipes hummed, cupboard doors creaked and banged. When the teakettle whistled the pastor finished up, turning the light off as he left. Gil checked the kitchen again—it was empty.

Hidden by the shrubbery, Gil snuck along the wall, working around to the front and the living-room window. The pastor was watching TV and drinking tea. Gil sat behind a rhododendron and waited, worrying about getting back so late the others would wonder where he had been.

Finally, the light went out, and Gil snuck back along the wall, checking the windows. The bedroom light was on. Gil paused under the window, listening to the sound of water running through pipes. Backtracking, Gil tried the windows—none were open. Gil worked his way around to the far side of the house, finding an unlocked window. Gil pushed it up, cringing with every squeak. When the window was wide open he paused, listening. The room remained dark so he pulled himself through the window and flopped onto a desk covered with papers. Trying not to knock anything to the floor, Gil rolled off and then tiptoed to the door. Pausing, Gil heard the sound of music. When he touched the handle, the water sound died, freezing him. Gil listened, but heard no movements, so he opened the door a crack and peered out. The bedroom directly across was lit, but it was empty. The music drifted down the hall from another bright doorway.

Listening, Gil heard the sound of splashing water—the pastor was in the bath. Baths were fraught with danger, and Gil's hopes rose. Listening to the sounds of washing, Gil slipped up to the door and leaned out until his eye cleared the frame. It was a small bathroom with a tub at the far end. There was a sink and counter along one wall with a toilet at the end by the tub. The tub had a shower curtain pushed back along one side, hiding the pastor's head, while his body was stretched out full length. Most important of all, there was a radio playing on the counter.

Gil studied the radio. It was an old-fashioned clock radio, with hour and second hands. The cord was plugged into an outlet on the counter and then disappeared behind the radio. Gil thought about rushing in and tossing the radio into the tub, but hesitated, worrying the pastor might be fast enough to knock the radio aside. Then the phone rang.

"Not now!" the pastor exclaimed, pushing himself up.

Panicked by fear of discovery, Gil trotted down the hall and turned in to the study just as the pastor emerged, towel around his waist, and ran to the living room. He was on the phone when Gil closed the door and retreated to the window. It had been too close and he was scared. Climbing out, he pulled the window closed, and then headed for the alley. Pausing in the shadow of a bush, he waited, making sure there were no witnesses. His fear subsided as he waited, and his anger returned. The pastor could betray him and had to be stopped, but he had lost his chance for now. Vowing to return, he hopped the back fence and trotted down the alley.

21

CREATIVITY

"Y ou want I should be in the speriment, Wes? I wouldn't mind. You wouldn't have to buy me a ice-cream cone, if you didn't want to."

"No, Ralph. Thanks, but we won't need you this time."

"Want me to put Daphne's helmet on her?"

"Karon will do it, Ralph."

"I could help Yu, or Archie."

"No, Ralph."

"What's this button do, Wes?"

"Don't touch that!" Wes shouted. Then softer, "I know what, Ralph. Daphne and the others will be thirsty when they get done. Why don't you go down and get them all a Slurpee."

"Even in the rain?"

"Sure, sure. Go ahead. It's all right, isn't it, Elizabeth?"

Looking amused, Elizabeth gave her permission.

"Well okeydokey then. I'll need some money."

"Here, Ralph," Wes said, handing him ten dollars.

Ralph turned, then stopped, thumping himself in the head. "How could I be so stupid? I can't carry that many—specially if I get mediums."

"Take a box, Ralph."

Shifting instantly from concerned to happy, "Well okeydokey then."

It took Ralph a few minutes to circulate among the savants, taking orders; then he was off. Wes sighed with relief and then urged his coworkers to hurry.

"You know, Wes," Len said. "You and Ralph remind me of the man who always bought shoes two sizes too small. When asked why, he said, 'Because it feels so good when I take them off.' "

"Do your job, Len."

"You should have put an EET on Ralph, Wes," Shamita said. "I could have turned him off."

Elizabeth scowled at Shamita. "Let's not misuse the equipment, or the savants."

Shamita immediately bent to her terminal, while Elizabeth helped Karon finish up fitting the headgear. One by one Shamita put the savants under, doing Gil last.

As Shamita intercepted the brain waves she fed them to Wes, and they appeared on his terminal. Soon he had a full set of undulating waves. Then, as before, he integrated the functions using Gil as the matrix. Finally he said, "We should have Frankie. Try it, Elizabeth."

"Are you there, Frankie?" Elizabeth said to Yu.

"Hello, Elizabeth."

The voice came from Daphne.

"You recognized my voice?"

"Yes."

"Do you remember drawing a picture for me?"

"Yes."

"Was that a picture of you?"

"Yes."

"How old are you?"

"I'm not sure."

"Where do you live?"

"I live . . . I live . . ."

Wes signaled a cutoff. "You're confusing her, Elizabeth. She's probably filled with memories of the homes of all five of the mind donors. Let's not stress her unnecessarily. We have a special task for her tonight."

"She doesn't sound confused, she sounds disoriented." Then, after a moment of thought, "All right, what is it tonight? Are you going to ask her to explain God to you?"

Wes was hurt that Elizabeth would mock him with something

he'd shared in a private moment. "No, we want to explore the power of her intellect. We're going to ask her to be creative. That was what we designed the program for—to draw on all the powers of the savants to put it to work on a task."

Karon came forward carrying a yellow pad. Reluctantly, Elizabeth moved behind Wes, studying the display.

"Frankie, my name is Karon."

"Hello, Karon. Why can't I see you?"

Karon looked surprised, turning to Wes for direction. Wes mouthed something at her.

"You'll be able to see again soon, but right now we want you to concentrate on what you hear. Can you do that?"

"I can, but I'd like to see you."

"Later. Frankie, I want you to picture a mountain with a temple at the top. Do you know what a temple is?"

"Yes."

"There is a path that winds around the mountain from the bottom to the temple at the top. At sunrise one morning, a monk begins to journey to the temple. He walks at varying speed, stopping many times along the way to rest. When he reaches the top he spends the night. The next morning he leaves again at dawn, but travels much faster going down, again stopping many times to rest. Do you understand so far?"

"Yes, Karon."

"Good. Now, can you prove that there is a point along the path the monk occupies at the same time of day, coming and going."

Elizabeth whispered in Wes's ear. "What kind of problem is that? He'd need calculus to solve it."

As she finished Frankie spoke with Daphne's voice.

"Picture the monk both climbing and descending on the same day, leaving at dawn, one at the top and one at the bottom. At some point they must pass each other, and that is the point the monk would occupy at the same time going up and coming down."

Karon nodded in appreciation. Elizabeth sat quietly trying to understand the solution. Then she said, "It's just a tricky riddle."

"Yes, but it took a creative solution," Wes said.

"You could define creativity that way, but this is just a variation on Yu's ability to make remote associations. Where's the unique contribution? Give this riddle to a hundred people and thirty of them will come up with a solution identical to Frankie's."

"Not thirty, only about ten. But I see your point. We'll get to that eventually."

"You can get to it now if you want."

The voice came from Daphne—it was Frankie. Guiltily, Shamita stabbed at her keyboard and then apologized to Wes.

"I got distracted. I guess I forgot to turn off Frankie's hearing."

His jaw tight, Wes controlled his anger. Frankie wasn't ready for this. She wasn't to know she was being studied like a rat in a Skinner box. Shamita's error jeopardized the whole project. But short of trying to set different parameters around the abilities of the savants to build a different Frankie, Wes had no alternative but to continue.

"There's nothing we can do now," he said. "Turn Frankie back on, but let's be careful. Only one person speak to her at a time. Elizabeth, will you take over? Try to reassure her."

"It's Elizabeth again, Frankie."

"Hello, Elizabeth. Why does my hearing come and go? What about my sight? Can you bring it back?"

"Not just yet. You are a unique person, Frankie, and we're just learning to work with you. When we know each other better I'll be able to explain more."

"I don't understand, but I'll be patient. I've been patient so long."

Puzzled over the last comment, Elizabeth held up her hands and wrinkled her face. Just as bewildered, Wes shrugged back.

Frankie continued, "I can be creative if you want. I do have an idea, but I don't know where it came from. I've been thinking about mental illness, especially schizophrenia. Of all the cognitive disorders it is the most common, and the most common symptom is hearing voices. Most schizophrenics improve with age, or with drugs which control synaptic activity in specific regions of the brain by reducing the sensitivity of receptor sites."

Impressed with Frankie's detailed knowledge, Wes and Elizabeth exchanged puzzled glances.

"Of those that are least helped by medication, there is a peculiar similarity in their symptoms. Many complain of voices trying to control them, or of ideas being placed in their minds.

Ideas so foreign that they must invent new words to represent the concepts—words like circlingology, spectralreverberation, and rectangulight. What if . . ."

Frankie's sentence trailed off.

"What if what, Frankie?" Elizabeth asked.

"What if those poor people who have been labeled crazy and locked up weren't hallucinating? What if, instead, someone decided to believe them?"

Again, Frankie paused.

"Believe that they are actually hearing voices?" Elizabeth said. "But where would the voices be coming from?"

"I can think of three possibilities. First, they could be hearing the thoughts of those around them."

"Telepathy?"

"Yes, at least they should be tested for it. The thoughts of others mixing in with their own could convince anyone they're crazy. But this seems least likely to me. A second possibility is that the voices are coming from a spiritual plane."

"They are channeling?"

"Something like that. However, this too seems unlikely. These people complain of ideas so foreign that they can't express them. Other's thoughts, or the thoughts of the dead, wouldn't seem foreign—dated perhaps, but not foreign. That brings me to the third, and most likely, possibility. It may be that somewhere in the universe another intelligent life-form is trying to communicate with us. Possibly by telepathy, possibly by some technology we can't fathom. It may be these people are receivers tuned in to aliens broadcasting ideas so different from our experience it seems crazy." Then after a long pause, "You wanted creative, so I gave you creative."

Silence reigned until Shamita cut off Frankie's hearing.

"It's OK now," she said.

"This is incredible," Wes said. "This is a person, Elizabeth. You can't deny it now."

"I don't. But it raises a whole new set of ethical problems. Frankie only lives through your machines. Every time you turn them off, Frankie dies, only to be resurrected by another flip of the switch."

"It's not dying like you think of it, Elizabeth. If there is such a thing as a soul, Frankie doesn't have one. When the experiment ends, Frankie ceases to exist. No pain, no suffering . . ."

"No joy, no hope, no creativity, no personhood!"

"But there was none of that before we created her!"

"But it's there now." Then calmer, "Frankie is too much of a person. It's uncanny. Look how much she's changed from just the last contact. Are you sure there's no consciousness when they're disconnected? Could Frankie be a part of one of the donors, hidden away in some corner of the unconscious, like someone suffering from multiple personalities?"

Shamita answered. "It wouldn't be likely. If you watch the displays, Frankie uses the abilities of the donors when she is functioning. Without those, and the memories that go along with them, she wouldn't be anyone at all. You may remember a famous case in the literature of a man by the name of Phineas Gage, who worked at railroad construction in the eighteen-hundreds. One day while he was using an iron rod to pack black powder for an explosion, the powder went off, blowing the three-foot rod through his cheek, behind his eye, and out through the top of his head. The iron rod tore a hole through his prefrontal brain. The doctor who attended him reported bits of bone and brain around the opening in the top of his head. He did recover, but his friends said he wasn't the same person—they said the Phineas Gage they knew had died in the explosion, and the profane, violent man now calling himself Phineas was someone else. Our Frankie isn't Frankie without those brain regions we're using from the donors."

"I see," Elizabeth said thoughtfully. "Let me talk to her again."

Shamita turned Frankie on just as Ralph walked through the door.

"They didn't have Coke, Archie. Only cherry and something that looked like pineapple. Pineapple is yucky. I didn't get it. I got you cherry. I told Sylvia to get new flavors. She said she would when they ran out."

"Ralph, we're in the middle of our work," Wes said.

"You want I should put this in the refrigerator? It's not as good when it's melted. I put one in the freezer one time and it all stuck together. One big lump."

"It's nice to see you're still alive, Ralph."

Frankie's voice silenced everyone but Ralph.

"Was that you, Daphne? Your voice sounds funny," Ralph said.

"No, it's me, Frankie."

"Frankie?" Ralph said.

"Karon, get him out of here," Wes said.

Karon ushered Ralph out on the pretense of helping put the Slurpees in the refrigerator. When he was gone, Elizabeth returned to Frankie, puzzled. "Frankie, last time we talked you said you didn't know Ralph."

"I recognized his voice."

"Why did you say you were glad he was alive?"

"Because I am. I like him, and I know someone wants him dead."

"Who?"

After a long silence, "I don't know, but they want Shamita and someone called Pastor Young dead, too."

Stunned, Elizabeth signaled a cutoff, and Wes ended the session. As they were winding down, he tried to reassure Elizabeth.

"Frankie's just confusing phrases like 'I could kill you,' said in frustration, with actual thoughts of killing someone. Isn't that right, Shamita?"

Shock still showing on her face, Shamita was slow to respond. "I suppose it could be a kind of self-talk. Expressing frustration by saying to yourself 'I wish you were dead.' If so, it could be someone's adaptive way of not acting on their impulses. Although I don't know why one of the savants would feel that way about me. I don't have much to do with them."

"See, Elizabeth. It's easily explained," Wes said.

"I'd still like to know who's having these thoughts. It's got to be one of the donors."

"All of them but Gil know the pastor from church. It could be any of them. I'd guess Archie, or Yu. They're the most sullen," Wes said.

"They're quiet, not sullen," Elizabeth said defensively. "At least not Archie. Yu's got a lot to be angry about, but he's no killer."

"No one's been killed," Wes reminded her; then, looking

around, he saw Gil staring at him. When their eyes met Gil turned away and quickly left.

Wes turned back to Elizabeth to see her watching Gil leave. When their eyes met she just shrugged, and then said, "But someone has been killed, Wes. You're forgetting Rimmer."

"He wasn't on Frankie's list."

"He didn't need to be, he's already dead."

Stretched out on the bed, Gil cleared his mind, looked at his lamp, and pushed with his thoughts. It didn't move. Gil reached deeper, and pushed again—no movement. This time he thought of Ralph's ability to hear him, and his anger swelled, then he pushed. The lamp flew off the table. Surprised, and shocked by the clattering lamp, Gil froze. He listened, but no footsteps sounded in the hall. Quickly he picked up the lamp. The bulb would need to be replaced, but the lamp was unbroken.

He had the power—a real power! Thrilled, he flopped onto the bed, looking for another target. His closet door was open and he pushed, forgetting to get angry. Nothing happened. Giddy, he had trouble summoning anger, but finally he pushed the door closed with his mind. He was telekinetic now, and with his other power he had what he had hoped for. He should leave, he knew, but he couldn't. Like an addict he needed more of the experiment, but unlike an addict, each session strengthened him. Were there new powers awaiting him? Was there any limit on his development? His telekinetic power was much stronger now. What would it be after another session?

He was determined to stay, to develop his new abilities, but he had to clean up the loose ends. They had been talking about people being killed when he came out of the experiment. If only that college kid hadn't been killed it would be easier for him, he could just murder one of his loose ends. But now he needed to make it an accident.

Gil relaxed and began exploring his mind, looking for new powers, and waiting for dark.

Gil was in the bushes when the pastor returned home and headed for his kitchen. The pastor was a man of habit, and Gil waited under the unlatched window while the pastor drank his evening tea. When the pipes hummed with the sound of running water he pushed open the window he had used before and climbed in. He crept to the hall, and as before the bathroom light was on and the radio playing. The taps were closed and then came the sound of splashing. Gil gave the pastor a couple minutes to get well relaxed and then crept down the hall.

At the door he paused, waiting for the sound of splashing to be sure he was still in the tub. Water sloshed and Gil leaned out, stared at the radio, summoned up his anger over the pastor discovering who he was, and pushed. The radio flew across the counter, flying off the end toward the tub—but the cord was too short and the radio was pulled up, dropping to the floor. The surprised pastor sat up, looking around, bewildered.

Gil flattened against the wall. *How stupid!* He had demonstrated his power, alerting the pastor. He might put Gil's presence and the flying radio together. The pastor had to die now, but it had to look like an accident. The sound of water alerted Gil— the pastor was getting out. He felt fear pushing through his anger and knew he had to act. Gil stepped into the open door. Naked, the pastor stood in the tub, startled by Gil's sudden appearance.

"You! I know you!"

Gil stared at the pastor's chest and pushed, hitting him with every bit of anger in his black soul. The pastor slammed into the wall as if hit in the chest with a brick, and dropped into the tub, water showering the bathroom nearly to the ceiling. Then his arms gripped the side and he struggled to push himself up. Again Gil used his mind to push down hard, and the pastor's head went under, the water violently sloshing. Pleased, Gil lost his power and the pastor's head came up, blowing like a whale, then gasping for air. Angry again, Gil pushed at his chest, driving him under, water flooding over the sides. Gil held his anger longer, but once more it weakened and the pastor surfaced, gasping. Gil was about to push again when the pastor panted out a plea.

"God help me! Save me from this demon!"

Pleased at being thought of as a demon, Gil once again felt the power weaken, allowing the pastor to struggle up, pushing himself high out of the water. Frustrated, Gil vowed to end it.

Anger boiling back up, Gil focused tightly on the pastor's forehead and pushed with all the power of his mind. The pastor fell back, plunging into the water, his head slamming against the edge of the tub. Stunned, the pastor could only struggle weakly, and Gil found that his power was strong enough to hold him under, even as his anger slipped toward joy. A pink halo formed around the pastor's head; then his hands came up, pulling at the sides of the tub. Suddenly he slipped deeper, only to come up again to claw aimlessly, pulling the soap and shampoo from the rack into the tub. Then the waving arms sagged into the water. Bubbles suddenly broke the surface, spasms racking the pastor's body. Another spasm and the pastor's bowels loosened, fouling the water. Then all was still.

Gil waited another minute to be sure he was dead; then he left, careful to close the window behind him. He walked back through the alley with a sense of power—the power of life and death.

At home he could barely contain his joy. He fixed the savants chocolate pudding for an evening snack, joking with and teasing Karon, who helped him. After the last of the pudding was licked from the bowls they herded the savants off to bed. The others watched, amused at his energy and good humor. Len suggested that he must have gotten laid when he was out, so Gil smiled and winked, and played along, although he had never had sex. He'd never been capable of it.

Anxious to be alone, he fought the urge and socialized, watching TV with the others. Only Shamita was absent, hiding in her room, studying that day's results. Gil worried about what she was finding, but kept his humor by vowing to kill her as soon as he was sure she wasn't needed to run the experiment.

Finally, the others drifted off to bed, leaving only Karon and Len, who looked like they wished to be alone. Gil left them, then stretched out on his bed, practicing his ability, finding he could pull as well as push his closet door. When he tired of that he tried moving his blanket, finding he could only ripple the limp spread.

Sounds from the next room disturbed him. Giggling at first, and then silence, followed by a rhythmic thumping sound—it was the sound of sex. Len was sharing his bed with Karon. He'd heard the sounds before, and always been irritated and disgusted. But this time he found himself fascinated, and listened as the rhythm built in intensity. When the sounds suddenly stopped, he felt disappointment, and then noticed something. His body had reacted. He felt the unfamiliar swelling, sending pleasure through his body. He couldn't hold the feeling, and soon the pleasure and the swelling were gone, leaving an aching for more.

What other surprises awaited? Gil wondered. First telekinesis, and now a libido. Savoring the memory of the feeling, he tried picturing Karon and Len naked on the other side of the wall. Never capable of sex, he had never seen X-rated movies, or even many R ones. *Playboy* had never interested him, and he had no experience with women, not even touching, so Gil had little success conjuring up erotic images. Soon he gave up, and relaxed. When he did he went blank.

22

STALKER

Janie was drunk and hot, and all they needed was a place to do it. It was past 2 A.M., but the party was still going strong, every bedroom occupied with copulating couples. As a freshman he was low on the pecking order for a room screw—a senior was using his bed right now—but Janie was putting out the signals. Pulling her tight against him, he said, "Come on, let's take a walk."

Janie giggled, letting him pull her along by the hand. He grabbed their coats and then a sleeping bag off the back porch and led her out and down the alley, stopping to kiss her. Her tongue probed deep and she shoved her hands into his back pockets. He wanted to do it right there, but the neighbors might see and call the police. Instead he hurried her along, down the alley and out onto the street.

They walked to the university, stopping to kiss and paw at each other, keeping the passion high. He led her across the first quad to the stadium and then around to the back. There was tall grass there, and it was commonly used by lovers.

When they reached the grass it was damp, but Janie was too drunk to care and now pulled him. They found a patch of smooth ground and while he fumbled to untie the bag Janie began undressing. Dropping her coat to act as a pillow, she then pulled off her sweater, and then unbuttoned her pants. The last knot gave and he spread out the bag, unzipping the side. Janie jumped in when he did, wearing only her bra and panties.

"Hurry up, Scottie, I'm freezing."

Scot pulled off his shoes, leaving his socks to keep his feet warm. When he had his shirt off she hit him in the chest with her bra and then flashed her breasts. Her nipples showed dark and erect, and he hurried to get out of his pants. On his knees, he pushed his pants down, taking his underwear at the same time. Janie giggled and then threw her panties at him, bouncing them off his head. Scot rolled to his back to finish disrobing. When he did, someone came rushing through the grass, a knife flashing in the dim light.

The knife hand struck down, burying into his abdomen just above his genitals. Scot screamed and grabbed for the knife. Janie's screams began as the knife was jerked out and then plunged again. When he grabbed for it again, the knife sliced through his hand, nearly severing a finger. Now his scream drowned out Janie's. When the knife came down again, it buried in his neck, severing his carotid artery. Blood spurted from the wound and Scot reared back, exposing his chest. The knife came again, into the chest this time, and Scot collapsed back onto the bag next to Janie, who scrambled naked into the grass. Blood filled Scot's punctured lung, his screams now bloody gurgles. Then the knife returned to his genitals, hacking and stabbing, but the pain faded, ebbing away with the remnants of his consciousness, and his life.

Elizabeth woke to the sound of running water through pipes. It was too faint to be in the bathroom; she localized the sound to the kitchen. The water stopped, and soon footsteps sounded in the hall. Elizabeth listened to a door open and close, wondering briefly who it was. Free-associating, she quickly forgot about the sounds, drifting from the mystery of the body in the basement, to the subtle changes she'd seen in the savants, to the mysterious conversations with Frankie. Two hours later she finally drifted off.

"Are you asleep, Elizabeth?"

"Ralph, what are you doing? What time is it?"

"I dunno, but it's before *Sesame Street*."

"Why are you waking me up? Get Gil to fix your breakfast."

"I already had some Cheerios. You want I should fix you some? I won't put the sugar on, 'cause I always put on too much. Daphne doesn't let me do the sugar for her. You want some Cheerios?"

"No, Ralph. Let me sleep a little longer."

"Well okeydokey then." Ralph turned to leave, but stopped in the doorway and thumped his head. "How could I be so stupid? Roy wants to see you."

Instantly awake, Elizabeth grabbed her robe and hurried down the stairs. The policeman was waiting at the door but took her to the porch for privacy when he saw Gil and the savants in the living room.

"Sorry to wake you, but I have some more questions."

"About Rimmer's murder?"

"About another murder."

Elizabeth thought of Daphne and wished she'd taken time to make sure she was in her room. Officer Winston was studying her face as if to read her emotions.

"It's another fraternity brother from the same house. Stabbed in the same way. Genitals mutilated just like Rimmer."

"Oh, no. Which one?"

"Scot Salyer. He was a freshman."

Elizabeth didn't remember him but grieved over the loss of a young life anyway. "I didn't see anything this time. This is all news to me."

"OK. I was just asking."

He didn't leave, so Elizabeth knew more was coming.

"Isn't one of your retarded kids an Asian?"

"You know Yu is. Your wife's seen him at the Dairy Queen."

The policeman wrote silently in his notebook, irritating Elizabeth.

"Why are you asking about Yu? You were looking for a woman suspect before."

"Was I? I just said Rimmer was seen with a girl just before he was killed. This time we have a witness at the scene of the murder. Scot was with a girl behind the stadium when someone came after them with a knife. She escaped while the attack was going on. She described the assailant as Asian—actually she said he looked Japanese, but I don't figure she could tell a Japanese from a Vietnamese."

"There's a lot of Asians in a university town."

"Yeah, that's true. You know, she said something else kind of interesting. She said this Japanese guy looked retarded."

Startled, Elizabeth tried to hide the emotion. Yu had the peculiar look of the retarded—the large head and features, the sunken eyes, and oversized lips—but his features weren't as obvious as most.

"Yu wasn't out last night, and he wouldn't do something like this anyway," she said calmly. "Yu's lived most of his life in institutions and has never been in any serious trouble."

"Just minor trouble?" he said, writing in his notebook.

"He has some trouble with emotional control, but he's done very well since we've been here."

"Glad to hear it. Can I speak with him?"

"You're not serious about this?"

"I am."

Elizabeth hesitated but then led him into the living room to where Yu was watching cartoons with the others.

"Yu, Officer Winston would like to talk to you."

Yu didn't look up.

"Gil, I think the TV is too distracting," Elizabeth said. "Let's take Yu into the kitchen."

Gil took Yu by the arm, and walked him to the kitchen.

"Yu, please answer Officer Winston's questions," Elizabeth said.

"Hello, Yu. I was just wondering if you went out last night?"

"No. Can I watch TV now?"

"Not yet," the policeman said. "You were here all last night?"

"Yes."

"Yu doesn't lie, Officer. He isn't capable of it," Elizabeth said.

"Really. You think lying takes a lot of brain power?"

"Yes," Elizabeth said.

"Interesting." Roy wrote briefly in his notebook, again irritating Elizabeth. Then he asked Yu, "Did you see anyone leave the house last night?"

"No."

"Did anything unusual happen last night?"

Yu paused, looking at his hands, then said weakly, "No."

"OK, thanks. Go watch cartoons." When he was gone the officer said, "I may want him to stand in a lineup. The girl was pretty shook up but we ought to give her a chance to identify the killer."

"If you put Yu in a lineup, you better have other retarded Asians in the line or it wouldn't be fair." It came out harsh, and Elizabeth regretted sounding defensive.

The policeman spoke as he wrote in his notebook. "Find five retarded Asians to stand in police lineup."

"Officer, you have linked these murders to those forty years ago, haven't you?"

Surprised, the policeman prodded, "Linked?"

"I'm talking about the similarities—fraternity brothers from the same house murdered and their genitals mutilated. That's quite a coincidence. They never found the killer then, did they? The one they called the Stalker."

"You know they didn't, but there's no connection. It's been too long. No serial killer, not the Stalker, not anyone, starts up forty years later. He—or she—would have to get a day pass from the nursing home to go out on a kill." Roy folded his notebook and put it away. "The way I see it, someone read about the killings and we've got ourselves a copycat. But you did give me an idea. I think I might just check the library records and see who's been reading about the killings. Your name will be there, right?"

Elizabeth nodded, suddenly feeling like a suspect.

"You didn't happen to talk about the killings in front of the savants, did you?"

Elizabeth frowned. Roy was a creative investigator and saw things from an angle she never considered. Elizabeth had mentioned the killings to Wes, but she didn't think any of the savants were around to hear. Still, she realized her library research made Yu a better suspect.

"I didn't discuss it with Yu."

"OK, fine."

As he turned to leave, Elizabeth stopped him with another question.

"Officer, you wouldn't happen to know if any of the fraternity brothers from back in the early fifties live around here still?"

"Are you taking a correspondence course in private investigations or something? Let me be the detective, will ya?"

The policeman left, leaving Elizabeth standing with Gil, who had a peculiar look on his face.

"Let's not discuss this in front of the savants, Gil. I don't want to upset them."

When Gil readily agreed, Elizabeth left him in the kitchen and went to see if Mrs. Clayton wanted to share a cup of coffee.

Wes had never seen Shamita this excited. Her printouts covered the kitchen table and the two of them were leaning across them. Wes studied Frankie's EEG. He could see the peculiar wave, but thought it nothing but interference or harmonics. Shamita, however, felt differently.

"How many EEGs have you looked at, Wes? You ever see anything like this? No, you haven't!"

"It's peculiar, but I don't see what it means. The wave parameters are probably off, and it's just some sort of overlap between donors. Or maybe just plain electronic noise. I'll get Len to check the equipment for leakage."

"It's too regular to be noise, and look how it's getting stronger from session to session."

"Well I can see that, but—"

"Another thing, it's more of a vertical wave, running from the brain stem through the amygdala, then up through the cortex."

"That's not that unusual."

"Odd enough, and why the amygdala? It controls emotions like anger and rage. What are we doing to make Frankie angry?"

"Nothing, of course."

Elizabeth interrupted them before Shamita could respond. To her credit, Shamita knew not to pursue the anomaly in front of Elizabeth and gathered up her printouts and left. After fixing a cup of tea, Elizabeth settled in at the table.

"I just had coffee with Mrs. Clayton."

"Good, you kept your promise."

"She's really quite interesting, and knowledgeable."

Elizabeth smiled knowingly. She was holding something back and waiting for Wes to beg her to share it. Elizabeth's smugness irritated Wes, but she was right about him—he wanted to know what she knew.

"You're not going to tell me until I ask, are you?"

"No."

"All right. Would you please be so kind as to tell me what Mrs. Clayton told you that has made you insufferable."

"Well, since you asked so nicely. You know those forty-five-year-old murders I told you about?"

"Cheerios?" Luis interrupted.

"OK," Elizabeth said. She talked as she filled a plastic bowl with the cereal. "One of the original fraternity members lives three blocks away in that big yellow house, the one with the shutters."

"I know the house. So?"

Elizabeth sent Luis back to the TV with his cereal.

"So, I think we should go talk to him."

"About what?"

"What do you think? Maybe he has some idea of who the killer is."

"We're not the police!"

Exasperated, Elizabeth flopped back in her chair. Then, brightening, she leaned forward. "Officer Winston keeps asking about the savants. Today he wanted to know where Yu was last night. I just thought if we could give him a better suspect he might leave us alone."

Wes felt the threat to his project, and resented being so easily manipulated. Nevertheless he agreed to a visit.

After a lunch of vegetable soup, Elizabeth left Gil in charge of the savants and walked with Wes down the block. It was a cool day, but with a clear blue sky. Neighbors were out raking their leaves or trimming their hedges. Some acknowledged them with a good-afternoon, but most stared curiously. It was a pleasant day and Elizabeth was good company and Wes enjoyed the walk, despite their ultimate destination.

It was a big house, like the one they occupied, but well maintained. A manicured lawn, swept clean of fall leaves, was edged with neat flower beds. Three perfectly spaced cherry trees lined the street in front of the house, and a flagstone walk curved across the lawn, leading to the front porch. An elderly man was sweeping the walk and met them as they entered the yard.

Tom Floyd had aged into the classic grandfather. He was a

pudgy man with a cherubic face, his bald head ringed with white fringe. He wore a red plaid flannel shirt and a pair of blue work pants, dirty at the knees. He had a pair of work gloves in his hand.

"I already bought some Girl Scout cookies, honey," he said, smiling.

"Hello, Mr. Floyd. I'm Elizabeth and this is Wes. We live across the street from Mrs. Clayton."

"You poor things. Come for some sympathy?"

"She speaks highly of you," Elizabeth scolded.

Smile unwavering, he said, "With good reason. What is it I can do for you?"

"I wondered if I could talk to you about what happened forty years ago when you were living at the Kappa house? You know, the murders."

Mr. Floyd's smile sagged into a frown. "I don't want to talk about it. My past starts thirty years ago. That's when I married— I've been happy since then."

"Please, Mr. Floyd. I wouldn't ask if it wasn't important."

"Are you a reporter or something? A writer? I get called every once in a while by some writer or another wanting to cash in on those Stalker murders. They've offered me money but I wouldn't take it from them and I won't take it from you."

"I'm not a writer and I'm not offering money. Do you know about the other murders?"

"I heard there was a killing . . . a boy fell off a roof, too . . . so?"

"There's been two, exactly like the Stalker killings. Fraternity brothers from the same house. They were stabbed and their genitals cut up."

Mr. Floyd sagged against the door, his mouth tight.

"The police suspect friends of mine—ours—and I know they're innocent. I think you can help us. Please, Mr. Floyd!"

Mr. Floyd wasn't listening, lost in some dark thought from his past. Then his eyes refocused, meeting Elizabeth's.

"When I said I had been happy for the last thirty years—well, I lied. I . . . I'll tell you what I know."

Overstuffed furniture filled Mr. Floyd's living room, and they settled in, giving him time to compose himself.

"I was a junior when the killings started. Jimmy Dodson was the first. He was the best football player on a pretty bad team.

Pretty good at basketball and baseball, too. A wild guy—crazy at parties. We used to call him 'Butane Bernie'—Bernard was his middle name. When he got in the mood he'd eat beans all day long, holding in the gas until he'd nearly bust. Then he'd bend over, drop his pants, and cut loose with a huge fart, igniting it with a cigarette lighter. He'd shoot a blue flame a foot. Really!"

"I believe you," Wes said. "There was a guy like that in my fraternity. We called ours 'Tommy the Torch.' "

"We had a lot of parties then. I guess they still do. Anyway, one morning one of the girls at the Epsilon sorority left for class and found Jimmy on their back porch lying on a blood-soaked blanket. He was stabbed so many times nearly every drop of blood in him was spilled out over that porch." His eyes glazed over as he traveled back, resurrecting long-buried memories. "It was a big knife, the police said. His pants were pulled down too, his privates mutilated." Then, after a pause, "Ellie!—that was the name of the girl that found him. She never was the same after that—a pretty girl, as I remember, always had her hair in a ponytail. She dropped out of school." Another thoughtful pause. "I wonder whatever happened to her?"

"Mr. Floyd," Elizabeth interrupted. "Had he been dating one of the girls in the sorority?"

"Jimmy liked to play the field. He dated more girls than the rest of the house combined. The police asked all the Epsilons but none had been out with him that night. They never found any witness, no weapon, nothing." Another long pause. "It was different back then. Murders were rare, especially in a town like this. They're still not that common. Anyway, it scared the whole town, not just the college students. Then it happened again.

"It was Steve Kent this time. His parents were poor and couldn't help him much with school expenses. When spring break came most of the house went home, but some of us headed to California. Steve got a job house-sitting for one of the professors. I can't remember which one—he taught history, I'm pretty sure. Anyway, when the professor and his family got back they opened the door to a terrible stink. His two dogs were nearly starved to death, and there was dog crap everywhere. They found Steve up in the professor's bed cut up just like Jimmy. They never slept another night in that house."

"Any connection between Steve and Jimmy?" Wes asked.

"Same frat house, both stabbed with a big knife, both mutilated. But they weren't drug dealing together or anything, if that's what you're thinking. This was the fifties, remember. Booze was around, but that was about it.

"The police got nowhere with Steve's case either. He'd busted up with a girl a month or so before, and they thought maybe her new boyfriend had done it out of jealousy, or something, but he was in California, too. They did arrest some drifter who happened to be carrying a knife, but they let him go again.

"It was after the second death some reporter started calling it the 'Stalker killings.' The name stuck. Everyone was talking about the Stalker and the town changed—people were afraid, stayed home at night and locked their doors. People don't do that in small towns. Anyway, nothing happened—not for a while. After a couple of months people lost their fear, and started going out again at night. When summer came and school let out, it was pretty well forgotten. But when school started in the fall, the killing started again."

Mr. Floyd sat silently for a long time. There was more emotion connected with this part of the story.

"We were building our homecoming float in a garage down on Second Street. It used to be where the video store is now. We had built goalposts and a big football and were stapling crepe paper all over it. It was one big party, everyone near drunk most of the time. Roger Venutti, me, and a couple other guys worked late one night—drinking a lot of beer. I had to get back because I had a test the next day. Roger had the same class but was still drinking when I left. The next morning I couldn't find Roger, so I figured he passed out in the garage and I went back looking for him. The door was unlocked but all the lights were off. He was lying on the float under the goalposts—like the others. The crepe paper was black with his blood."

Mr. Floyd paused in a sad stare, his tongue running across his lips.

"Mr. Floyd," Elizabeth probed.

"We didn't have a float in the parade that year."

"I didn't know you found one of the victims, Mr. Floyd."

"I left the fraternity then. A lot of the guys quit—the chapter nearly folded."

"If this is too painful, Mr. Floyd, you don't have to continue."

"No, I'm going to finish. There was only one more. After Roger's death there weren't many left in the house and those left wouldn't go anywhere but to class. But a week later they found Nick Colson in his Chevy all cut up like the others. They never got all the blood out of the car. I heard his brother finally scrapped it.

"There weren't any more killings but I never went back to the Kappa house. Somehow it survived, but it was three years before they had a good pledge class."

A shrug, and his story was over. Uncomfortable, Wes struggled for something to say, but Elizabeth silenced him with a glance. Elizabeth valued silence and its healing power, but Wes preferred the distraction of noise. When he could stand it no longer, Wes spoke, the sound of his own voice relieving his tension.

"They never found the killer? No suspects?"

"No. The killings just stopped. No one was ever arrested. Every ten years the paper does a story about the killings, speculating about who the killer might have been, but that's all it is—just guessing."

"Just like Jack the Ripper," Elizabeth said. "Everyone has a theory but no proof."

"Yeah, except I know," Mr. Floyd said.

Confused, Wes said, "You know who Jack the Ripper is?"

"No! I know who killed my friends."

Surprised, Elizabeth and Wes sat dumbly. Before they could recover their speech, Mr. Floyd began again.

"We had some crazy parties in those days. Plenty of beer, and sometimes the hard stuff. Mostly we partied with sorority sisters, but once in a while some of the local high-school girls came by. We knew they were jailbait, but when you're twenty and drunk you don't think too straight." Then with a smile he added, "Drunk and sixty is just as bad." Sadness returned and he continued. "There were a couple of regular high-schoolers. One was a real party girl. She loved to drink and dance—man, could she dance. She loved Elvis Presley. She liked to make out, too, at least she kissed a lot of the guys. Never went all the way, though, always holding back. The guys called her a tease because she frustrated the hell out of them.

"One night we were having a party and she stops by and she's really wild. She was drunk when she arrived and pretty soon couldn't stand up. She ended up passed out in a corner. Sometime that night the last of the girls left—I don't remember what happened next real well, I was drunk, too. Someone found her sleeping in the corner and everyone started kidding around about doing it to her while she was asleep. You know, saying things like 'she'd never know it happened' and 'she's been asking for it anyway.' "

Mr. Floyd paused again, embarrassed and pained. He swallowed hard, looked briefly at Wes and then said, "You know how guys can get when they're drunk." Wes nodded. "We were drunk, like I said. It's not an excuse—I just want you to understand we weren't ourselves." Wes nodded, but Mr Floyd never looked at Elizabeth.

"Someone pulled her out onto the rug and then pulled off her sweater so she was laying there in her bra. Everyone was joking and laughing, but also getting horny. Pretty soon some of the guys started touching her breasts, then someone unhooked her bra and . . . well, took off her bra. We got to looking at her and soon the jokes weren't funny. Next thing I know she was naked on the floor and Jimmy was on top of her. I don't think she even knew Jimmy did it to her, but she woke up when Roger was doing it, and she started to struggle. She was too drunk to fight back. No one paid any attention anyway, and they just kept taking turns. She sobered up quick, though, and started hollering after a while and kicking and hitting. They finally had to hold her down until everyone was done. There were at least eight of us, but I don't know how many for sure—I was drunk, too."

More silence, but this time Elizabeth spoke, an edge to her voice.

"Mr. Floyd."

"Yes, I took a turn. I regret it! Oh God, how I regret it. None of us ever spoke about it after that night. We'd never done that before, or ever again—as far as I know. I never did!

"Her father showed up the next day and threatened us, told us if we ever came near her he'd press charges, but no one ever reported us to the police, so after a while we convinced ourselves she had asked for it, and she liked it." Then with a glance at Elizabeth he added, "We were just rationalizing—we knew what we'd done. The killings started a few months after that. At first

I didn't connect the murders with her. It was only later when I realized the guys getting killed were all there that night, that I saw the connection. That, and because of what she did to their genitals."

"Mr. Floyd," Wes said. "What makes you think it was the girl? Why not her father? You said he threatened you."

"I thought about that, but I couldn't see how he could get that close to them. Especially after the killing started. Everyone was on edge, but a girl—especially a pretty one like her—she could get guys alone on a back porch, or in a car, and if she acted sexy enough they would do just about anything for her."

Elizabeth stood and walked to the window while Mr. Floyd continued.

"The other thing about the killings is they stopped when she left town."

"Did you tell the police about this?" Wes asked.

"I didn't figure it out until later, after the killing stopped. Besides, I felt we were getting what we deserved."

Still at the window, Elizabeth said, "Who was this girl, Mr. Floyd?"

"I think you already guessed. Nancy Watson—you're living in her house."

Lost in thought, Wes and Elizabeth walked back slowly. Mr. Floyd's horror story affected Wes, but he still struggled to see the connection to the current murders. It couldn't be the same girl doing it; she'd been long dead in the basement. No, he thought, this was a dead end, and said so. "Elizabeth, Mr. Floyd's story was horrible, but these have to be copycat killings."

"Maybe, Wes. But they're nearly identical and all from the same fraternity."

"But the murdered boys aren't the ones that raped Nancy all those years ago. Those boys are like Mr. Floyd, grown into old men."

"Two sets of identical killings forty years apart that start just after we find the hidden room in the basement. I don't see the connection either, but it's odd—too odd."

"By moving into the house we probably stirred up some-one's long-forgotten feelings. Maybe finding Nancy's remains released repressed memories in one of the neighbors, and they're looking for revenge."

Elizabeth frowned. "What about Officer Winston's questions about Daphne and Yu?"

"That proves he's fishing for suspects. The killer can't be both male and female."

Another long silence, and then, "This is what we know so far: We moved into the home of a girl who was gang-raped forty years ago. We now suspect this girl killed some of her attackers in a grisly fashion. We know she was imprisoned in her own basement and died there, because we discovered her body. After that discovery similar killings begin again, and the victims are from the same fraternity. And finally, two of our savants are questioned as suspects. And you think there isn't any connection!"

"You're seeing connections when it's only coincidence. It's not logical."

"There's something else, Wes—Oh no!"

Elizabeth broke into a run. Surprised, Wes hesitated until he saw the flashing red ambulance lights in the front of Pastor Young's house. He caught up to Elizabeth by the ambulance just in time to see them slide a covered body in the back.

Crying, Elizabeth said, "It's like some awful curse."

"Elizabeth, we don't know it was Pastor Young. . . ."

"Yeah, it was him," confirmed the police chief, approaching with his arm around a crying woman. "Mrs. Sanchez found him. Go on home now. I'll have Ellen give you a call." When Mrs. Sanchez was gone he turned to Elizabeth. "Another death and again you show up. It's a good thing I don't have a suspicious nature."

Wes watched Elizabeth and Officer Winston lock eyes. Elizabeth's tears dried and her jaw tightened.

"You think I had something to do with his murder?"

"Who said it was a murder?"

Elizabeth's eyes flashed, but she held her tongue. Wes wanted to caution her not to say anything, to keep from feeding the policeman's suspicions, but knew it would only make her look guilty. Instead, he intervened.

"It wasn't a murder?"

Reluctantly Officer Winston turned from Elizabeth to Wes. "I'm not saying it was or wasn't."

"Officer—Roy, what happened?" Wes pleaded.

"Pastor Young drowned in his bathtub. Kind of unusual, but not impossible. It's happened once before that I know of, but that was a ninety-year-old woman. Odd for a young man like Pastor Young, don't you think?"

Elizabeth remained mute, and Wes quickly answered. "He might have slipped in the tub. It's a common accident."

Now Roy looked suspiciously at Wes. "How did you know that's what happened?"

Suddenly frightened, Wes stumbled to explain himself. "I don't know what happened. I've just heard falls in the tub are pretty common."

"Just a guess, huh?" the officer said suspiciously. "He did have a pretty good lump on the back of his head and a cut, but there was something else—kind of strange." Roy paused, waiting for Elizabeth or Wes to blurt out what it might be, but they remained silent. "He had a radio in the bathroom." Again he paused, and again they waited him out. "The radio was hanging by its cord over the end of the counter." Pausing again, he looked them each in the eye as if to search for a guilty conscience. "Doesn't that strike you as peculiar? I mean why would it be hanging like that? He couldn't reach the counter from the tub without getting out, and who would get in the tub with a radio dangling like that?"

Wes thought it peculiar, too, but was afraid to comment.

"I suppose you two are going to be each other's alibi?"

"We were with someone else until ten minutes ago," Wes responded.

"Yeah? Were you together all night?"

"No!" Elizabeth nearly shouted. "We were home last night. Now I expect you're going to ask about the savants. What is it you have against the savants . . . against us? Just what do you think we're doing over there? It's just a science experiment!"

Roy looked pleased he'd elicited a reaction, and pushed her further. "I've got a couple of theories. You want to hear one? Good. I know you're playing with the minds of those savants—doing things no one around here can explain. It sounds like some sort of electronic hypnosis to me. Let's say you use your machines to hypnotize those retarded kids and implant posthypnotic suggestions to kill. Then they go off to do your bidding. I've got

one witness that says she saw someone who looked a lot like
Daphne climbing into the van with that Rimmer kid. The other
one describes someone like Yu using a knife on her lover. I
thought I needed more, but if the killing is going to continue . . ."

"That's nonsense," Wes protested. "That's not what my equipment does. If you want to see I'll be glad to demonstrate. Besides, you can't make someone into a killer with a hypnotic
suggestion."

"I would like to see your experiment. Maybe you're not using
hypnosis. Maybe you're using something else."

"What else?" Wes asked.

The officer merely shrugged. Then he said, "Come on in, I
want to show you something."

Inside they followed him to a back room. Glancing into the
bathroom as they passed, Wes could see a woman dusting a radio
for fingerprints. Wes followed them into a study.

"Take a look at what's on this desk."

Wes leaned over next to Elizabeth. There were Xerox copies
of journal articles stacked along one side. The titles were all
from parapsychology journals. Elizabeth picked up one of the articles and turned to face Roy.

"What's this got to do with us?"

"How about this for a theory? You're using that equipment to
create ESP and then control people. You're using retarded kids
because their minds are easier to control."

"It's nonsense," Elizabeth said. "Besides, why would we use
this power to kill fraternity brothers?"

"I spoke to the fraternity brothers and they told me what they
did to Ralph."

Elizabeth flushed, and then said, "But that's no reason to
kill—"

"Isn't it? You're not one of the researchers, are you, Elizabeth?"

"I'm part of the team—"

"Your job is to protect the retarded kids, isn't it? Just how far
would you go to protect them?"

"I wouldn't kill someone over a stupid prank. Besides, Pastor
Young didn't have anything to do with what the Kappas did to
Ralph. So why murder him?"

"There you go again, calling his death a murder."

"You implied it was murder."

"Now that you mention it, there is a reason you might want him dead. Take another look at that desk. See the yellow pad?"

Wes looked to see a list of names with phone numbers. Some of the names were crossed out, and others had multiple phone numbers. It took him a second to realize the names were from the articles on the desk.

"It looks to me," Roy continued, "that the good pastor was on to you and your ESP experiments, and was trying to find some way to prove it."

"It's nonsense," Elizabeth protested again.

"Are you working on a Department of Defense grant? CIA perhaps?"

"We're supported by the Kellum Foundation—it's well respected," Wes said.

"I'll want to check that out."

Wes's stomach knotted. He doubted any project interested the Kellum trustees enough to risk being associated with murder, but if he tried to stop an inquiry he would only look guilty. He decided instead to try openness.

"Fine, but first let me demonstrate what we're doing—and it has nothing to do with parapsychology—and if you're not satisfied then I'll give you the names of the trustees." Roy agreed and they left, stunned by the bizarre accusations. Outside, Elizabeth started rummaging through her coat pockets, pulling out an old church bulletin.

"Wes, do you have a pen?"

He handed one over and she wrote furiously.

"What are you doing?"

"I memorized some of the names from the list. I think we should call them. Maybe we can find out what Phil was doing."

"We'll only get in deeper, Elizabeth."

Elizabeth looked at him, amused. "Deeper than being accused of being psychic killers, and using retarded people to carry out our murders?"

Wes sighed, admitting it couldn't get any worse—but hadn't he said that before?

"Well lookee here! We found Wes and Elizabeth."

Turning, Wes saw Ralph and the savants. Arms folded across his chest, lips puckered, Ralph was in his concerned mode.

Beside him, Daphne stood head down, glancing up shyly. Short, ugly Luis stood behind Daphne, staring dumbly, crooked teeth protruding. Yu, next to him, stared emotionlessly. Wes could see Archie coming down the block, his puffy orange hair and blue Mickey Mouse glasses a sharp contrast against the muted colors of fall. Behind him trailed Len and Karon.

"What a coincidence, here comes your gang," Roy said.

"Where have you been?" Ralph said to Wes in his concerned voice. Then switching instantly to friendly, "Hello, Officer Winston. We're going to get Slurpees. You want to come? You want I should bring you one? I can carry two. I can carry more than that, can't I Wes. Course I need a box to carry a lot." Thump, he hit himself in the head. "How could I be so stupid? I only have to carry two. You don't want one? Well okeydokey then. See you later."

Wes watched the savants head off down the street and fell in behind them. He felt the policeman's stare all the way down the block.

23

PARAPSYCHOLOGISTS

E lizabeth's short-term memory was good enough to get six
   of the names from Pastor Young's list, and a city for each.
   Each of the cities had a university, and that's where they
started their search, quickly locating three of the professors. Two
of them had talked to "Dr. Young" about their research. He'd
asked about subjects they had tested for ESP. After an hour Elizabeth summarized what they had so far.

"I knew Phil was a psychologist, but I didn't know he was so
well known. He'd researched psychic ability and seemed to be
trying to track down one of his old subjects. He was asking about
a male subject who didn't like to be photographed. I don't know
if he ever found him."

Unenthused from the beginning, now Wes was sure they were
wasting their time. "Elizabeth, I don't think this has anything to
do with what's happening here. Pastor Young was probably pur-
suing a former interest, maybe considering a return to the field."

"He wasn't updating himself on research, he was asking about
a particular person. He was searching for someone—someone
with ESP."

"Someone *tested* for ESP! No one has ever proved it exists,
you know. If you can get someone claiming paranormal ability
to agree to be tested in a controlled environment—which they

normally avoid—the ability suddenly disappears. They have excuses, of course. They claim electromagnetic radiation from the equipment interferes with their ability, or maybe they blame their sudden normalcy on the light from neon tubes, or the phase of the moon. They blame anything and everything rather than face the dreadful fact that they are just ordinary people who will live anonymous lives, then die, quickly forgotten by their friends and family."

"Not demonstrated to your satisfaction is not the same as nonexistent!"

"You've accused me of lacking self-awareness, now look at yourself. In spite of no evidence of a connection with the murders forty-five years ago and those today, you see a relation. There's no connection between Pastor Young's accidental death and the killings and yet you call around the country to find one. No evidence of ESP, yet you believe in it. It's not rational."

Frowning, Elizabeth spoke softly. "Wes, you are a faithful apprentice to the scientific method, but there are other ways of knowing—just as legitimate. I don't have to experiment to know someone's hurting, in love, or angry. I can appreciate a sunset without understanding the orbital mechanics that make it possible. I can read a novel and get more insight into human nature than any battery of psychological tests could ever give. There's a feeling, intuitive side of life and it's just as legitimate a source of understanding as is the scientific method."

Wes paused, not wanting to tarnish the friendship they were developing, then added carefully, "You're right. I know we're different in our approaches, but ultimately we're both seeking truth. Honestly, Elizabeth, I don't see how this helps us."

"I don't either, but I keep thinking about what Officer Winston said about us using psychic powers to turn the savants into killers. I mean, what was Phil calling these people about? Maybe the last three on the list can tell us something."

It was nearing two and the East Coast schools would be closing soon, so they went back to work tracking the other three names. In their first round of calls they found that two of the faculty were not listed at the schools they had called, and one was on medical leave. They decided to ask for faculty in the psychology department with the most years of service, hoping they would know the former professors. Elizabeth discovered that a

r. Leahey had indeed worked at the University of Florida but
ad been killed in an accident a few years ago. When she heard
r. Kinghorn at the University of Connecticut had also died in
n accident, she probed for details. "Well, it was kind of odd,"
is department chair said. "The witnesses said he and his fam-
y were sitting at a railroad crossing waiting for an approaching
ain. Just before it got to them he pulled forward and stopped.
he whole car was demolished. None of them survived. You
ould have thought he did it to commit suicide except anyone
ho knew him, knew he wouldn't do that. He loved those kids!
Vhy kill them?"

After relating the story to Wes, Elizabeth called back to the
Iniversity of Florida to ask for details on Dr. Leahey's death. It,
o, turned out to be an odd accident. "I wasn't there," his col-
ague said, "but it happened out at the airport. Dr. Leahey and
is wife owned a small plane and liked to fly on weekends. His
rife was at the controls warming up the engine while he got
omething out of the car—I heard it was a lunch. He came out
) the plane, got to the door, stopped, then turned and walked
nto the propeller. It was pretty horrible. His wife had a nervous
reakdown."

Wes listened to the story, cringing when he heard about the
ropeller death, but showing no other reaction. Frustrated, Eliz-
beth pointed out the obvious.

"Two deaths, both from unlikely accidents!"

"Accidents happen. Besides, we talked to three who were
ne."

"I only got six names from the list. Who knows how many
1ore accidents there were."

"Or how many accidents there weren't."

"The last name on the list—Dr. Birnbaum—he's on medical
eave. Aren't you curious about why he's on medical leave?"

"Curious? No. Mildly interested is the best I can manage. But
know you well enough to know you won't be satisfied until you
nd out."

Elizabeth smiled and picked up the phone. "Want to bet din-
er it was an accident?"

"You're on. I like steak."

"Be prepared for Chinese."

The department chair at Ohio State University was reticent,

but confirmed Dr. Birnbaum's medical leave, then explained tha
he was hurt in a traffic accident. After gloating, Elizabeth called
directory assistance and found three Birnbaums in the Columbus
area. On the second try Dr. Birnbaum's wife answered, saying
he couldn't take any calls. Despite Elizabeth's pleading, Mrs
Birnbaum would not put the professor on the phone. It was a
dead end.

"OK, so I buy you Chinese food," Wes conceded. "It will be
worth it if you're finally satisfied that there's nothing to this."

"I'm not satisfied. There was something about Mrs. Birnbaum's voice."

"She was probably exhausted, taking care of her injured husband." Then, exasperated, "Won't anything satisfy you?"

"Maybe a talk with Dr. Birnbaum."

"You said he wasn't taking calls."

"That's according to his wife. Next week I'm going back to
Chicago to report to the Kellum Foundation. I think I'll swing
through Columbus and drop in on the Birnbaums."

The mention of the foundation gave Wes chills, but he'd come
to trust Elizabeth and was confident she wouldn't use what had
happened to unfairly end the experiment. They sat at the kitchen
table sipping coffee in silence, Wes watching her face, waiting
for what he could see was coming—he just didn't know what
it was.

"I've been thinking about those accidents," Elizabeth said.
"They were so bizarre. People just don't suddenly drive out in
front of an onrushing train, or just walk into propellers."

"Yes they do. Someone starts daydreaming, loses presence of
mind, and steps off a subway platform. Haven't you absentmindedly touched a hot pan, or driven through a stop sign? It
does happen."

"Sure it does, but I've never come across so many in such a
short period of time to people in the same profession."

"They're spread out over years, Elizabeth, and in widely separated parts of the country. Have you ever checked accident rates
for any profession? Then how can you know this is an abnor-
mally high rate?"

"Maybe it's because of what happened to Marshall."

Wes had forgotten that her first assistant had been killed in an
accident.

"He died like the others—senselessly. He was standing on a urb with his family, waiting for a traffic light, and suddenly he epped out into the street. His wife said he couldn't have timed better if he had planned it."

"Knowing someone personalizes it, making you think it's ore tragic than just another accident."

"I understand that theory, Wes, but how many accidents have happen before they're no longer accidents?"

Knowing better than to try and answer, Wes gave up and let lizabeth try to make sense out of what had happened. Instead, e sipped his coffee, wishing he'd picked a different city for his xperiment.

24

DEMONSTRATION

Two days after Pastor Young's death, Officer Winston came for his demonstration. Ralph met him at the door with hearty handshake and a loud "Hi-how-ya-doin?" When Elizabeth arrived to rescue him from Ralph, the policeman thrust a box at Elizabeth, saying, "Here's the puzzle, what the hell' it for?"

Taking the puzzle, Elizabeth ushered him in to where the savants were being prepared. Wes frowned when the policeman entered. Wes had grown reluctant since the offer had been made but Elizabeth encouraged him to be open and Wes explained liberally. Officer Winston listened politely, but uttered only an occasional "If you say so."

Elizabeth took over the explaining when the savants and Gil were fitted with their helmets. Wes took his station and watched Shamita's brain-wave feeds appear on his screen. Wes started the integration, then hesitated. Typing furiously, he modified the program.

"What are you doing, Wes?" Shamita whispered.

"Let's use Daphne as the matrix, and reduce the parameters on Yu and Luis. We need something from Gil—select out something."

"We won't get Frankie if you do that."

"It's just a demonstration," Wes said.

Shamita knew what he was doing, and said nothing. Soon e wave patterns began to change. Wes was setting up aphne's pattern for the matrix when a flashing clown head appeared in the corner of Wes's screen—Len was sending a message. Then a small plane flew across, pulling a sign behind it ading, *Why are we changing the parameters? We won't get rankie this way, and any new memories will confound the per-nal memories Frankie has been building.* Len stared over his rminal, puzzled. Wes sent back, *We'll make it a brief run and void creating any complex memories.* Wes didn't add that he as afraid Frankie would start talking about killing Ralph or namita again. Then he remembered Elizabeth—would she co-perate?

"Elizabeth, I need your help," he said. "Karon, explain to Of-cer Winston how the EETs work."

Puzzled, Elizabeth came and stood behind Wes.

"I'm going to change the program—use Daphne for the ma-ix, instead of Gil," he said softly.

"Why? What difference will it make?"

"We'll get an integration just like before, but this personality ill be different—more of Daphne, for one thing. Also, because e're modifying the mix, don't call it Frankie—call it Pat or mething."

Elizabeth frowned, but nodded. Shamita finished changing e parameters, then leaned back, sighing deeply. When aphne's matrix was ready Wes set up the integration program piece together a new intellect, then paused.

"All right, Elizabeth, begin the demonstration."

Elizabeth went to each savant in turn and asked them to do a lendar problem, solve a simple puzzle, read a page and recite , and solve a remote-association problem. Only the problem in eir specialty could be solved. The policeman watched quietly, sking no questions. When she was done, Wes ran the integra-on program, piecing together a new intellect.

"Gil will do the hearing, and Yu will speak," Wes explained. "Your name is Pat. Can you hear me?"

"My name is Frankie. You know that, Elizabeth."

Surprised, Elizabeth turned to Wes, who sat openmouthed.

Shamita and Len exchanged shocked looks; then Len whispere
in Karon's ear. Wes quickly hid his surprise when he saw the po
liceman taking in the scene.

Recovering, Elizabeth said, "Of course your name is Frankie
How are you tonight?"

"I feel different."

"I'm sure it's temporary."

"Hey, what's going on here?" Roy asked. "I thought you sai
something about them getting blended together?"

"It's OK, Elizabeth," Shamita said. "I cut off audition."

"They've blended brain functions to create a uniquely func
tioning mind," Elizabeth explained like an expert.

"So why is only one of them talking?"

"It's only one mind, so they have only one voice."

Pleased with Elizabeth's explanation, Wes let her continue.

"Shamita, can you make Luis the voice?" she asked.

After a minute of typing, "OK, try it again."

"Are you there Frankie?"

"Of course, where would I go?" The voice came from Luis'
thick lips.

Unimpressed, the policeman turned to Elizabeth. "So some
one else is talking? So what?"

Signaling a cutoff, Elizabeth whispered, "Try this, Roy. Whis
per a question to Gil, softly so that Luis can't hear you. Some
thing simple." After another signal to Shamita, she added, "/
friend of mine wants to ask you a question. Go ahead, Roy."

Roy bent and whispered a question in Gil's ear.

"No, I don't know Joshua Ringman, or Scot Salyer. Should
know them?" Luis said.

Elizabeth frowned at the policeman, who stared defiantly
After the cutoff signal she said, "I told you to keep it simple."

"Asking if you know someone is as simple as it gets."

"It's also emotionally charged." Then, to the others in th
room, "Those are the boys who were killed."

Wes worried about the effect of the policeman's question o
Frankie—but then remembered it shouldn't be Frankie at all.

Elizabeth took charge of the demonstration again. "Each o
the savants is gifted in a particular way. Daphne is a calendar cal
culator." Roy flipped open his notebook and wrote furiously. Ir
ritated, Elizabeth paused, but the officer continued to write

"Archie's gift is an extraordinary spatial ability. Luis's is total recall—often called photographic memory. Yu's ability is the most unusual for a savant; he makes remote associations—that's the ability to make connections between unlikely events. You saw each of them demonstrate their ability when we began."

Lifting his pen, the policeman said, "What's Gil's special ability?"

"Well, none, actually." Elizabeth paused, unsure of why Gil was still part of the experiment. "We just needed another person, and—"

"What about Ralph? What's his special ability? How come he's not hooked up with the others?"

"Ralph doesn't have a special ability," Elizabeth said without thinking. Then she saw Ralph's face reshape from a smile to concern. Flustered, she searched for a kind thing to say. Len covered for her.

"Sure he does, Elizabeth. Ralph can carry five Slurpees at a time, can't you, Ralph?"

Ralph's face reshaped into his usual lopsided grin. "That's right, Elizabeth. I can carry five. And I hardly spill any. Course the lids help. Want I should get some now? They might be thirsty when it's all over. I know where my box is."

Elizabeth agreed and Wes passed over a ten-dollar bill. Quickly, Ralph was out the door.

"Ralph's here because of Daphne. She needed him to adjust to living here. Ralph's been a stabilizing influence on the others, too."

The policeman stared, uninterested.

"Remember that Yu has the association gift," Elizabeth continued. Nodding to Shamita, Elizabeth whispered to Gil, "What one word connects 'worm,' 'binder,' 'end'?"

" 'Book,' " Luis said. " 'Bookworm,' 'bookbinder,' 'bookend.' "

A single raised eyebrow was the only response from the policeman.

"Roy, when's your birthday?"

"September twenty-sixth."

"Frankie, on what day will September twenty-sixth fall in 2040?".

"Wednesday."

Still the policeman looked unimpressed.

"Frankie, I'm going to read you a passage from a book. Please listen carefully." Elizabeth read Edgar Allan Poe's poem "The Raven." The policeman sat quietly, for once not taking notes. When she was done reading she asked Frankie to repeat it.

" 'Once upon a midnight dreary, while I pondered, weak and weary, Over many a quaint and curious volume of forgotten lore,' " came Luis's voice. " 'While I nodded, nearly napping, suddenly there came a tapping . . .' "

Word by word, line by line, Luis repeated the poem exactly, but emotionlessly. When done, Len applauded softly, and even the policeman nodded appreciation.

"One last ability to demonstrate." Taking the policeman's puzzle, Elizabeth spread it in front of Gil. Signaling Shamita, Elizabeth asked Frankie to sit up. Gil sat up, and then looked around the room.

"I can see you."

"Yes, Frankie. There's a puzzle in front of you. Please put it together for me."

Gil continued to look around, then stopped, eyes on the policeman.

"Frankie, please put the puzzle together," Elizabeth prodded.

Breaking the stare, Gil bent to work on the puzzle. Five minutes later the last piece was put into place.

"It was too easy."

"Yes, Frankie. I know you can do much harder ones. Please lie down again."

With a last look around Gil lay down. Elizabeth signaled the cutoff.

"Now do you see what this is all about?" Elizabeth asked. "Nothing sinister, just a simple experiment."

"Nothing simple about it." Roy replied. "It gives me the creeps—I mean they just lie there like zombies until you make them do something with those machines."

"We don't make them do anything!" Wes exploded. "All our equipment does is allow them to function as one mind. There's no mind control involved!"

"Maybe. But if you've got nothing to hide then why not let me question this Frankie person?"

Hesitating, Wes exchanged glances with Elizabeth and his team.

"You invited me here to convince me that you—and them—had nothing to do with the killings, didn't you? Well, here's your chance. Let me question this Frankie."

Fearing he would look guilty if he didn't, Wes nodded agreement. "All right, but simple questions, and don't suggest anything to her! And whatever you do, don't accuse her of anything!"

"Her? I'm talking to a man, and that boy over there is answering."

"It's a blended personality. It's not any one of them."

"Four boys plus one girl equals a girl? You must be using new math. OK, I still talk to this one, right?" The policeman opened his notebook again, then took his pen from his pocket, poised to take notes. "Frankie?"

"Yes."

"Is that your real name?"

Elizabeth glared at the policeman and mouthed, "No accusations."

"Yes."

"OK. Do you know a Pastor Phil Young?"

"Yes."

The others looked around in surprise. Shamita watched for a cutoff signal, but Wes and Elizabeth let him continue.

"How do you know him?"

"I don't know . . . I've just heard the name. I think I know what he looks like."

"When did you last see him?"

"I'm not sure I've ever seen him. . . . But I must have. . . ."

"Did you see him, or didn't you?"

"I don't know."

Suspicious, Roy wrote in his notebook, the only sound in the room the scratching of his pen. "Have you ever been to Pastor Young's house?"

After a long pause, "No."

"Ever been to the Kappa fraternity?"

"No."

"Have you ever left this house?"

"No."

After writing much longer than it would take to write "no," the policeman folded his notebook and put it in his pocket.

"That's all my questions—for now. Thanks for the demonstration. I'll be in touch."

Elizabeth walked the policeman to the door, then returned to see the savants being disengaged. Gil herded the savants out of the room ahead of him, while the others went through their postexperiment routine. When Wes looked finished, Elizabeth sat next to him.

"I thought you said we wouldn't get Frankie."

"We shouldn't have—not with those changes in parameters. To get their abilities we needed to overlap quite a bit; still, I would have bet money we wouldn't have gotten Frankie and her memories. Perhaps Frankie's memories are stored in the areas where their gifts are localized?"

Shamita joined them. "I didn't see any elevated activity in their gift regions. Besides, memories aren't stored that locally. I wonder how much we could change the parameters and still get Frankie? I have an idea, why don't we—"

"Hey! Come on over here," Len shouted. "You've got to see this."

Karon moved aside so that the others could gather around behind Len's console.

"While the policeman was questioning Frankie I noticed something strange in the physiological readouts—especially respiration, heart rate, and blood pressure." Pointing at the monitor, he said, "Here's Daphne's readings in graphics mode."

Three readouts scrolled across, with a line indicating normal variations up and down.

"Now this is where he asks 'Do you know Joshua Ringman, or Scot Salyer?' "

A Q appeared at the edge of the screen and scrolled across, just above the readout. Behind it the three readouts suddenly elevated, then gradually returned to previous levels.

"See, it's acting like a lie detector."

"I don't know, Len," Wes said. "There could be other reasons for this. Maybe Daphne had a gas pain."

"Keep watching. Here comes the next question. What was that one, Karon?"

" 'Is that your real name?' "

Again, another *Q*, and another elevation.

"Another gas attack, Wes? I don't think so," Len said. "Watch what happens when he asks about Pastor Young."

Another *Q* scrolled by, but the readings remained unchanged.

"No response. But watch the readings as he keeps asking about the pastor."

Gradually, Daphne's heart rate and respiration increased, the blood pressure lagging behind.

"What's coming next, Karon?" Len asked.

"He's asking if she'd ever been to the pastor's house. Next he asks if she'd ever been to the fraternity. Here it comes."

Immediately after the *Q* the readings shot up, remaining high until Len shut off the recording.

"I think the gas-pains theory is pretty well shot."

"You're reading a lot into this, Len," Wes said. "Frankie couldn't know about any of those people, so there would be no reason to lie. Besides, she didn't respond when he asked about Pastor Young. Why the inconsistency?"

"Maybe," Elizabeth said, "because Frankie didn't have anything to do with Pastor Young's death."

"Elizabeth, you're suggesting that Frankie killed the others. Frankie isn't a person! She's bits and pieces of other people's minds. She doesn't exist outside this room. Without this equipment there is no Frankie."

"I know, Wes. But the coincidences are piling up."

"It's all circumstantial."

"You know what they say," Len cut in. "If it walks like a duck, and quacks like a duck . . ."

Gil worked with the savants through the rest of the afternoon, picking up bits and pieces of the others' conversation about the policeman. They were concerned about the policeman's suspicions, but also about Frankie's appearance during the last session. They spent a lot of time analyzing the results of the last run. Gil didn't understand their concern about Frankie, but he shared their concern about the policeman, and more. He still hadn't dealt with Ralph, so he had to be careful not to use his powers to shape their behavior. Also, Shamita was onto something—

something he didn't want her to know. He'd only been able to deal with Pastor Young, but the police were suspicious of his death, and were somehow linking it to the savants. If it wasn't for his new power—his growing power—he would have left long ago.

He helped Karon fix lasagna for dinner, joking and teasing. He felt differently toward her now that he was beginning to feel lust. Len's interest in her had only disgusted him before, but now he noticed things about her—her jeans tight across her bottom, the way her blouse gaped when she leaned over, and the way her breasts reshaped when she reached up to shelves above her. Yes, he was beginning to understand what he'd only scorned, and that was another danger. He didn't care about Karon, or Elizabeth for that matter, but he found himself fascinated by them—like a kid on the edge of puberty. He didn't like the way his body was taking control of his mind and wanted to be well away from here before his urges demanded satisfaction.

After dinner Len and Karon decided to teach the savants to bake cookies. Only Daphne and Ralph would cooperate, and soon the others were back in front of the TV watching *Wheel of Fortune*. Gil laughed and joked with the others in the kitchen for a while, watching Daphne and Ralph try to roll out dough and cut out cookie shapes. Soon, he found his eyes wandering to Karon's form and then to Daphne's, and it unnerved him, so he excused himself and went to his room.

He relaxed on the bed, trying to clear his mind of his lust. Failing that, he tried to summon his power, but couldn't. Frustrated, he felt his anger grow, and with his anger came the power. He nursed the anger, and practiced using it to move objects. Though he never left the bed, he was soon exhausted and lost his anger and his power. Then he was asleep.

A door slam woke him with a start. It was ten o'clock, and he'd not helped put the savants to bed. He checked downstairs, but the savants had already gone. They had gained so much independence in recent weeks, Gil worried they might realize he wasn't really needed.

From the stair he could see Len and Karon sitting on the couch watching TV, Len's arm around Karon, his hand stroking her shoulder. Jealousy filled him—another new emotion. There were too many new feelings for Gil, all of them weakening his self-control. Gil returned to bed and began his relaxation routine, clearing his mind to regain control. Reaching deep into his mind for the cold emptiness that had always been there, he went blank.

25

CONTROL

The yellow house was dark, so she watched from the bushes until she was sure the owners were out. Pulling on a pair of gloves, she broke a basement window, then crawled through onto a stack of lawn chairs. Pausing frequently to listen for sounds of movement, she picked her way through the basement clutter and up the stairs, emerging next to the kitchen, a bathroom directly across from her. Quickly checking, she went from room to room, making sure the main floor was empty. Then she crept up the stairs.

The rooms on the second floor were all empty. The bed in the master bedroom was made, awaiting its owners. One room had a sewing machine and a game table covered with puzzle pieces. Only a few of the pieces had been fitted together. Strangely, she found herself drawn to the unfinished puzzle. Satisfied that the house was empty, she went downstairs to the kitchen and rummaged around until she found a knife, then she returned to the room and sat down to wait, working the puzzle as she did, quickly fitting the pieces together.

Tom Floyd and his wife returned just after midnight from visiting their kids in Portland. It had been a long drive and his wife headed directly upstairs to get ready for bed. Wired from the coffee he had drunk to stay awake while driving, he flopped in front of the TV and began flipping channels, finally settling on a Cary Grant movie. The old pipes rumbled in the walls as his wife started up the shower, and he punched up the volume. A few minutes later a commercial break sent him to the kitchen for a bag of chips and a bottle of beer. His wife wouldn't approve of the beer, but the sound of the shower told him he was safe. Beer and chips in hand, he stepped into the living room to see a man sitting in his chair.

Startled, he staggered back into the kitchen. Starting to speak, but then stopping, he hurried to the wall phone. The line was dead. Frightened, he looked at the back door, ready to make a run for it—but his wife was upstairs, and he could never leave her. Instead, he crept back through the hall, checking to see if the man was still in the chair—he was gone. Now panicky, his eyes darted around the room, looking into every shadow. Seeing nothing he walked quietly to the stairs, his eyes and ears busy. Seeing nothing, he crept up the stairs.

At the top he hurried down the hall to the closet in the sewing room. Opening the closet door slowly, he flinched at every creak the hinges made. Then he lifted a box off the top shelf, opened it, and took out a gun. It was a .38 revolver that he'd fired only once before. He'd bought it for protection when the house next door had been burglarized, but his wife hated it, and refused to have it in their bedroom. He reached deeper in the box and pulled out a box of cartridges. He was still loading the gun when the man stepped into the room holding a knife.

Mr. Floyd trembled, dropping a cartridge on the floor. When the man saw the gun he rushed forward, swinging down with the knife. Mr. Floyd panicked, trying to snap the cylinder into place, then bringing his arm up to deflect the blow. The knife buried into his shoulder before he could and he screamed with the pain, the gun dropping from his limp arm. The man stabbed again, this time into his arm, the knife creasing the bone. While the man was drawing back for another blow, Mr. Floyd looked into his savage eyes and managed a weak "Why?"

Poised for another strike, the man paused, his eyes cold. "You raped me."

"What? I never—"

"You and your friends. You held me down and you raped me."

"You're wrong. . . . I don't know what you're talking about. . . . I'm bleeding."

"I know you, Tom Floyd. You were fourth on top of me. I begged you to stop, to help me, but you didn't, you just kept doing it. Then you held me while the rest did it to me. I can still see their faces, red and panting as they hurt me over and over."

"How could you know?"

"I got Jimmy, Steve, and the others. It was easy. They were all so sure I was a whore who couldn't get enough. They wanted me again, so I let them think what they wanted, then I killed them."

"I don't understand. . . . Who are you?"

The shower stopped, the house suddenly quiet except for the sounds of Mr. Floyd's ragged breathing. He realized his chance and opened his mouth to scream for help, but the knife plunged down into his chest, ripping through his lung, blood pouring into the chest cavity. He drew in a last ragged breath just as the knife plunged into his stomach. As his vision faded he felt the knife stitching its way down to his crotch.

Groggy, Len was heading for a morning cup of coffee when he saw movement in the experiment room. Curious, he stepped in, yawning. Suddenly his mouth snapped shut. Yu, Archie, and Luis were sitting in a tangle of fiber-optic cables, bits and pieces of Len's equipment spread around them.

"What have you done!?" he shouted.

Instantly, their chins pressed against their chests and they rocked in place.

"It's all in pieces. What have you done? . . . Why?"

Looking up briefly, Archie said, "It's too jumbled. It bothers Yu."

"I don't care, this is my equipment. You aren't to touch it. Besides, it needs to be like this."

"No it doesn't," Archie argued. "Here, I drew it out."

Looking past Archie's Mickey Mouse glasses, Len could see sincerity in his eyes. In his hand was a piece of paper. Still angry, Len snatched the page. In crayon were drawn the cots, monitors, computers, nitrogen system, EETs and their helmets, laid out in a semicircle. Between the consoles were neat lines of cables. Still angry, Len nearly tossed it aside, but the detail intrigued im. There was no writing on the page, only symbols he couldn't ecode.

"What's this mean?"

Scooting closer Archie pointed. "This is Dr. Martin's ma-hine. This is yours. This is Shamita's."

"They're mixed up."

Archie began to rock, head down.

Then, gently, "I mean why did you switch them around?"

Archie pointed at the lines connecting Wes's console with one f the EETs. "It's shorter this way."

"Yeah, Archie, but then this one's longer."

"No."

Without a word Luis picked up a cable and walked it to Wes's onsole, then to an EET. Next he walked one from Len's console o the same EET. Both cables had extra length.

"I'll be darned. Are you sure those are the right cables?"

"Green, brown, brown," Luis replied.

Len scratched his head. "Are you sure you remember where verything goes?"

"Yes," all three replied.

"All right, show me some more."

Wes and Shamita were just as angry when they came down, ut Len shooed them out and continued working with the sa-ants. When Elizabeth heard of what Yu, Archie, and Luis had lone, she stood in the doorway and watched for a long time.

Ralph's loud voice woke Gil.

"I'm going to get Wes a paper. Anyone need me to get them omething?"

Voices from all over the house shouted "No."

"Well okeydokey then." Slamming the door, Ralph left.

Gil rubbed his eyes. He felt as if he hadn't slept at all, yet he vas still in his clothes, apparently too tired the night before to ndress. Gil sat up, realizing from the sounds in the house that e was the last up. Rolling to the edge of the bed, he spotted a un on his end table. Frozen in confusion, he sat staring. What vas it doing there? Who would put it in his room?

Searching his memory, Gil tried to remember what he'd done he night before. The policeman had been there, and they had run he experiment. The rest of the day had been normal, up until he fell asleep on his bed. The rest of the night was a blank; he didn't even remember dreaming. He didn't drink, fearing the loss of control, so it wasn't an alcoholic blackout. No, someone else had to put it there.

Footsteps in the hall panicked him and he grabbed the gun, hiding it under his pillow. The footsteps passed, and then he realized the gun now had his fingerprints on it. Gil thought that might be what someone wanted—he'd just incriminated himself. He wasn't going to fall deeper into their trap. He was going to get rid of the gun.

Gil held the gun gingerly. He had never had a use for a gun. It was a simple-looking mechanism: a handle, a cylinder, a barrel, and the trigger. Careful not to put his finger on the trigger, he put the gun in a coat pocket and put the coat over his shoulder.

Strangely, the savants were working in the experiment room with Len, moving tables and stringing cable. He didn't know where the others were, but he suspected they were drinking coffee in the kitchen. Gil went straight out the front door.

He wanted the gun out of the house, but he didn't want to get caught with it, and the farther he took it the greater the risk. Also, if he carried the gun somewhere unfamiliar to get rid of it, he couldn't be as sure that no one would be watching when he disposed of it. Gil wanted to dump the gun as soon as possible— but where? Rounding the corner of the house, he went through the backyard to the alley. It was clear and he turned toward the university, but then stopped, realizing that the closer he was to the school, the more likely he would run into students.

A car passed at the end of the alley, panicking Gil again. The incriminating weapon pulled on his coat, weighing him down. Gil hurried passed the garage and went down the alley. When he came to the garage behind the fraternity he spotted a pile of scrap wood—mostly two-by-fours. Gil pushed a few of the boards apart, creating a space, then looked around. No one was watching, so he dropped the gun in the hole and started to cover it. *Stupid!* he thought, and pulled up the gun, wiping it clean. Then he replaced it in the hole and covered it with the boards, after which he hurried back up the alley to the house.

He joined the others for breakfast, trying to act as if nothing had happened, but he studied the faces of the others, looking for

elltale expressions of who had planted the weapon in his room.
Everyone acted as they should.

Len took the savants back to their lab right after breakfast, and
Gil busied himself cleaning up the breakfast dishes. Elizabeth
was updating the behavioral records of the savants, and he joined
her. Ralph was a pest, as usual, talking incessantly, repeating
what Elizabeth and Gil said, and mimicking their mannerisms.
They were nearly finished when police cars roared up, blue
lights flashing.

Gil thought of the gun. *They found it,* he thought, fighting
back an urge to run. He didn't want to look more guilty than he
already was, but he vowed that if they tried to arrest him he
would use his powers to fight his way out.

Pushing past Elizabeth at the door, Officer Winston thrust a
search warrant at her.

"You can't just come in here like this," Elizabeth protested.

"Read the warrant." Then, to the officers following him,
"Search it top to bottom—and don't forget the garage."

"Hello, Officer Winston," Ralph said, pumping the policeman's hand. "Can I help search? I'm good at finding things. I
found a baseball in a hedge one time and I wasn't even looking
for it. Course I never found my Frisbee."

"No Ralph, this is something the police need to do."

"Well okeydokey then. I can watch though, right?"

"Yes, Ralph," Elizabeth said. "You go watch them."

Ralph turned and followed a policeman up the stairs, asking
if his gun was heavy. Other uniformed men and women fanned
out through the house, and soon the couch cushions were on the
floor and chairs were overturned. Wes and Shamita came out of
the kitchen, and Len and the savants came out of the experiment room, the savants heading up the stairs after the policemen.
When a policeman pushed past him, Len followed him back
into the experiment room.

"What's going on?" Wes complained. "You've got no
right—"

"We have a warrant that gives us the right to search the
premises and the garage in the back."

"But what for?" Wes continued. "You saw the demonstration
yesterday—you know what we're doing here."

"I also know the killing started shortly after you moved to

town. I know that at least two of your retarded kids match de
scriptions given to us by witnesses. I know that there's been ba
blood between you and the fraternity down the street. I know
Elizabeth was close to Pastor Young, and I know that you tw
visited Tom Floyd just a few days ago."

"Oh no! Did something happen to Mr. Floyd?" Elizabeth said

Looking straight at Elizabeth, he said, "Seems like everyon
you go visit ends up dead."

Elizabeth sagged onto the stairs, her chin on her chest.

"You can't suspect Elizabeth!" Wes protested.

"She's the only one who has had contact with all four o
the people killed. Without her these people have nothing i
common."

Flustered, Wes stood silently, the sounds of the search goin;
on around them. He knew that suspecting Elizabeth was ridicu
lous, but he had no alternative explanation to offer. Then Eliza
beth lifted her head and spoke.

"Was Mr. Floyd killed like the others?"

"We're withholding some details of the crime."

"He was, wasn't he? Then you know there is another con
nection."

"The only thing connecting those old murders and these i
you. Pastor Young wasn't even in the state forty-five years ago."

Elizabeth didn't respond, but Wes knew her mind was spin
ning.

"There are a couple of details that I can share. This time th
killer took something—a gun. That's what we're looking fo
now. If you have any guns around the house you can save us th
trouble by turning them over."

"There are no guns here," Wes said. "We wouldn't have then
in the house with the savants."

Out came the officer's notebook, and he began to write a
he spoke. "So your statement is that you have no guns in th
house."

The policeman's tone unnerved Wes, and made him doub
himself. He didn't own a gun, and he had assumed the other
didn't either—but he wasn't absolutely positive.

"What other details were you going to share, Officer?" Eliz
abeth prodded.

"Just one more. Mrs. Floyd is a strong woman, and kept con

rol of herself. She noticed something peculiar in the room where
e was killed. Before they left the house that morning she had
ust started a new jigsaw puzzle. Someone put the puzzle to-
ether while she and her husband were gone. It had to be the
iller. She said it was a real difficult puzzle, and would have
aken hours to put together." The officer paused, letting the im-
lications settle in. "Your assistant was pretty good at putting
uzzles together the other day."

"Gil put the puzzle together, but it's Archie's ability. We
lended them into one mind, remember?"

"Archie, that's the name I was looking for. He's the one that
ooks like a clown, right?"

Reddening with anger, Elizabeth stepped forward. "Don't you
all them names!"

A scream from the top of the stairs interrupted her. Officer
Vinston's hand dropped to his gun as he followed Elizabeth and
Ves up the stairs. More screaming, then Yu emerged from his
oom slapping his head with both hands. Grabbing for his hands,
Elizabeth tried to stop him. Yu was too strong, however, and
ontinued to pound at his head, deafening them with his screams.
Ves tried to maneuver around to get hold of his other arm, but
Yu backed away, pounding himself.

"We've got to stop him, Wes, before he hurts himself," Eliz-
beth shouted.

"I'll try to grab one of his arms, you go for the other," Wes
eplied.

Shoulder to shoulder they approached Yu in the narrow hall.
ust as they reached the door to Yu's room a policeman stepped
ut holding Yu's picture album. Suddenly Yu was driven into a
renzy, pounding himself brutally.

"Get out of the way!" Elizabeth shouted, pushing past the
nystified policeman.

Now the bathroom door opened and out stepped Ralph, zip-
ing up his pants. Lips puckered into his concerned look, Ralph
aused for a moment, then stepped forward and wrapped his
rms around Yu, pining his arms to his side.

"You shouldn't do that, Yu, should he Elizabeth? Doesn't that
urt, Yu? It would hurt me. I'm not squeezing you too tight am
? You're hurting my ears, Yu."

"Don't let him go!" Wes shouted.

Speaking soothingly, Elizabeth tried to calm Yu, but hi
screams only softened to a cry. Then someone held out Yu's pic
ture album—it was Gil.

"It's all right now, Yu. You can put your book back where i
belongs," Gil said. "The policeman won't go back into you
room."

Yu's crying softened to a whimper, then ended with thre
quick sobs.

"Yeah, Yu. Stop crying like Gil says. Can I let go of him now
Elizabeth?"

"Yes. Thanks, Ralph." Then to Gil she said, "Thank you, toc
It must have been the search of his room that set him off. Gil
check on the others, they're probably upset, too."

Yu grabbed his picture album and pushed past them, hurryin
into his room.

Turning, Elizabeth saw Officer Winston at the top of the stair
writing in his notebook. Looking over the top he said, "Not vi
olent, huh?"

"I should never have let you search their rooms like this. You
can't just toss their things around. Most of them have a rigi
need for order. You can't move their things without threatenin
the delicate balance that keeps them in touch with our world."

As he wrote the policeman said, "Become easily unbalance
when someone touches their belongings! Did I get that right?"

Elizabeth snatched his pen and flung it down the stairs. "The
were fine until you and your storm troopers invaded their pri
vacy."

The policeman stared back briefly, then reached into hi
pocket and pulled out another pen, again speaking as he wrote
"Go to store for new pen."

"Go to hell!"

"I'm doing my job."

"Fine, but let me do mine, too. I would have helped yo
search."

"Kind of defeats the purpose, don't you think?"

Glaring as she left, Elizabeth brushed past the policeman int
Yu's room. Yu was moving nervously about the room, puttin
away his belongings, which were in disarray. Astonished by th
mess the police had made, Elizabeth was equally surprised b

Yu's tolerance. He'd watched his room nearly completely dismantled and was broken only at the end when the picture album his sister had prepared for him had been handled. This wasn't the Yu who had joined the experiment only a few weeks ago. And what of the others? Daphne had the second-strongest need for order.

Elizabeth found Daphne in her room, sitting on the floor, surrounded by her possessions. Her bedcovers were tossed off the end of the bed, and the mattress was askew.

"Daphne, are you all right?"

Tears in her eyes, Daphne looked up, a broken glass statuette in her hand.

"It's broken."

"We can glue it, or get you another one."

"It was Grammy's. She can't give me a new one. She's dead. She went to bed one night and she never got up."

Stunned, Elizabeth listened in silence. Daphne had never shared any of this before—she never volunteered anything.

"It sat on her nightstand. I think my mother gave it to her. It's the only thing I have of hers."

Angry at the police, and feeling Daphne's pain, tears formed, and her voice cracked as she spoke. "You loved your grandmother very much, didn't you?"

"She never hurt me."

"Have I hurt you, Daphne?"

"No. Ralph neither. That's why I like him. That's why I like you, too."

Now Elizabeth's tears flowed, and she reached out and touched the back of Daphne's hand. But Daphne pushed it away, leaned over, and hugged her, crying on her shoulder. They rocked together like that, crying a mix of pain and joy. After a few minutes Daphne separated, and stood, her head down in its usual position. Without speaking, she left, and a minute later the sound of "Amazing Grace" reverberated up the stairs.

It was a brief breakthrough, but dramatic and powerful. In all her professional life Elizabeth had never seen anything like it. Then Yu came into the room, interrupting her thoughts, quickly pacing the perimeter of the room, and then leaving just as suddenly. Daphne playing, and Yu pacing; she realized they were slipping back—but they had both shown remarkable progress, progress that could be built on. Drying her eyes, she went to look for Luis and Archie. They were unlikely to be as affected by the police search, but today nothing would surprise her.

26

CONNECTION

i t's time we shut down the experiment," Wes said. "The police won't be satisfied until we do, and besides, we've accomplished most of what we wanted to do."

"Except demonstrate the intellectual powers of Frankie," Shamita reminded him. "We never thoroughly tested that."

"No, but there are ten publications in what we have already— and that doesn't include the patents and spin-offs on the technical developments. The Kellum people will be satisfied and maybe in a year or two we can gather another group of savants together."

Disappointed, they sat quietly, thinking about where they would go next. To everyone's surprise, Elizabeth disagreed.

"There's no reason to disband now. Do you think the police will let us leave town? We're suspects in a series of murders— at least I am. They'll confiscate the equipment, records, notes— everything. You won't publish a thing as long as they suspect us. Heaven help us if they put enough circumstantial evidence together to take this to a jury. Your reputations will be irreparably damaged. You won't get another grant!"

"Is this some new sort of therapy, Elizabeth?" Len asked. "Point out to depressed people that things are always worse than they seem?"

"Sorry. I was trying to be realistic."

"Elizabeth, you were against this project from the beginning—you nearly stopped it from getting funded," Wes said. "You should be happy to shut it down."

Shaking her head, Elizabeth said, "I was concerned for the welfare of the savants, but things have happened to change my mind. I think we should run the experiment again."

The others looked at each other, amazed. Then Karon said, "Yu's still pacing the house, do you think it's wise?"

"I think we should run it without them."

Luis was confused. There was a pain in his chest, but it wasn't any pain he'd felt before. It wasn't from a hurt, or sickness, and it wasn't like a side ache from exercising. It was a dull pain that hurt worse when he breathed. He ran through all the words for pain he knew, and none of them fit. Then he tried losing the pain by straightening his room, ordering his room and thoughts at the same time. That helped a little, but when he stopped the hurt came back. He started around his room again, but when he adjusted a picture of Mrs. Winamaki, his foster mother, the pain shot through him. Then he realized what it was. He felt bad—he felt sad. It was a new feeling for him, before he had only felt confused.

Ordering his room had lost its power, and the dull pain continued. Mrs. Winamaki's face kept intruding, and his flawless memory re-created her kindnesses in excruciating detail. He worked around the room faster, straightening and restraightening his things. Nothing helped. Then he began on the drawers of his dresser. In the first he found a pen and paper and a new urge swept him. Sitting on his bed he began to write about what he was feeling. It wasn't a letter at first, but the more he wrote the more he realized these were things that Mrs. Winamaki should hear.

He started over, addressing it to her, thanking her for her care, and her tenderness. He thanked her for the things she taught him, telling her that he remembered them all. He wrote of the trips in the car with her and how good the memories were, even though he had no feelings at the time. He wrote a page about his memories of eating tomato soup and chocolate pudding for lunch and how good that memory was. Then he wrote about sit-

ting on the Winamakis' back porch swing watching the bug zap-
per flash on summer evenings.

He realized it was getting too long for a letter and ended
abruptly, saying he would write again. Then he wrote "Love,
Luis." After he found an envelope and addressed it, he felt better. Now the pain was gone and he felt even better than when he
ordered his room. As he left to look for a stamp, a new feeling
came to him. He knew the name for this one right away—it was
happy.

Gil packed a small bag with a change of clothes and toiletries.
Tonight he would leave. The gun planted by his bed and the police search had pushed him into the decision to leave, but now
something else was going on. The others were down in the research room getting ready to run the experiment without the savants and without him. The only reason given was that they
wanted to try it with a different set of people—yet, they were
going to include Ralph. Gil knew he was a more logical choice
than Ralph, so they had to be onto him, or at least suspicious. He
suspected Shamita was behind this new experiment—probably
linked to what she had discovered about him.

Gil hid the packed bag in the back of his closet and went
downstairs to resume the evening routine. He was about to fix
the savants their evening snack when Elizabeth stopped him.
Gil could feel his face flush and struggled to keep his face im-
passive when Elizabeth spoke to him.

"Gil, we want to keep them occupied for a couple of hours
tonight. Pop some corn and I'll run to the store for a couple of
videos."

"What's up?" he asked, trying to sound casual.

Elizabeth hesitated, so Gil thought *I can trust Gil,* and pushed.

"We're trying to figure out whether the Frankie intellect is
somehow connected with the killings. During the last run Wes
set the configuration differently, so we wouldn't get Frankie,
but we did. That doesn't make sense, so we're going to try again
with a different group."

"And if you get Frankie it will mean what?"

"I don't know, but we have to start understanding this."

Outwardly, Gil agreed enthusiastically, but silently he
couldn't see the point. That computer generated Frankie couldn't

have anything to do with the killings—certainly not the murder of Pastor Young. Still, they were getting suspicious, and nothing Elizabeth had said reassured Gil enough to stay. He just needed the right moment to slip out.

Gil had two big bowls of popcorn ready when Elizabeth got back with three videos, popping the first in. A feature-length cartoon lit up the screen and the savants were instantly entranced. Gil watched with them for a few minutes, then stood in the doorway watching the experimental preparations.

The experiment room was a different place. Gone was the jumble of cables and nitrogen lines. Now the cots and equipment were arranged in three nested semicircles. Cables connecting the equipment were laid out in neat lines, peeling off one at a time into their respective destination. Len, Archie, Yu, and Luis had worked through the afternoon setting it up. Gil had overheard Len praising Archie's plan, noting that he had been able to shorten half of the cables, improving efficiency.

Shamita was on a cot wearing the helmet, while Wes sat at a console. Len was at Shamita's usual station. They were mapping Shamita for the experiment. Len lacked Shamita's experience, and the mapping was slow. Then Shamita and Len swapped places and the mapping continued. As Gil watched them he realized they didn't even know he was there. Turning back to the living room, he saw that the savants were equally entranced, two videos sitting by the VCR ready to be run consecutively. No one would miss him, not for a couple of hours. He could wait until dark, but if he left now it would be easier to catch a bus to Portland.

In his room he opened his window and dropped the suitcase into the yard, then walked down the stairs, pausing on the landing. The savants hadn't moved, and weren't looking now. The others were still absorbed in the experiment room. Opening the door quietly, he stepped through, softly closing it behind him. He paused, regretting that he had to leave them alive—especially Shamita. She knew too much, and so did the others. Frustrated because he couldn't take the time to kill them, his anger flared. He savored the emotion, having come to enjoy it because it represented power. Turning at the bottom of the steps, he set the porch swing to rocking with one glance and a thought-push.

Feeling invincible, he left for the bus station, swinging his bag and whistling.

It would be an hour wait for the next Portland bus, so Gil stretched out in a chair, his ticket in his shirt pocket. His muscles were tight from anxiety, and would remain that way until he could lose himself in the bustle of Portland. Eyes closed, he alternately tensed and relaxed his muscle groups, slipping into a meditative state. Slowly, his anxiety dissipated, and he savored the relief. Then he felt someone pulling the ticket out of his pocket.

Gil pinned a swastika-tattooed hand against his shirt. He looked up into the eyes of a startled skinhead. Dressed in dirty denim from head to foot, he wore a jacket with cutoff sleeves. Two more skinheads stood behind, snickering. Now caught, he jerked away, leaving Gil's ticket behind.

"Hand it over, greaseball!" he demanded.

Gil's temper flared, and he stared defiantly.

"You deaf, greaseball? I said gimme your ticket."

Gil noticed that the other two were looking around nervously and didn't seem willing to fight for the ticket. His anger red-hot now, he said, "Beat it, asshole!"

Cheeks reddening, the skinhead glared, his lips clamped tight. Gil expected trouble, but then the skinhead looked around at the busy bus station. Unwilling to strong-arm someone in a crowded place, the skinhead opted to save face instead, giving Gil the finger. When he did, Gil snapped.

As the skinhead's hand dropped and he turned away, Gil grabbed his wrist, pulling the hand back to his face. Freezing, the skinhead reached in a pocket with the other hand. Quickly, Gil stared at the offending finger, wrapping his mind around it and pushing. When the finger rose the skinhead looked down, surprise quickly turning to fear. As his finger became vertical the skinhead's other hand extracted a knife, the blade snapping open. The sound energized Gil and he pushed harder than he ever had. The skinhead's middle finger instantly flattened against the back of his hand, the bone snapping loudly.

The boy gasped, and then a soft scream gurgled from his throat. Dropping his knife, he grabbed his injured hand, turning to his confused friends. The others, horrified at the sight of the limp finger flopping around, cursed but did nothing to help. Gil picked up the knife and refolded the blade, dropping it into his pocket. Staggering from the pain, the injured skinhead stumbled through the station, his friends following. A few steps away they caught up and stopped briefly, cussing Gil. He watched until he was sure they were gone.

Now Gil went back to his relaxation routine, once again enjoying relieving the muscle tension. Soon the meditative state returned. Gil deepened his breathing, slipping closer to a transcendental state. Then awareness left him.

Wes checked the connections on Elizabeth's EET helmet, then returned to his station. The feed was clear now. Ralph, Len, Karon, and Shamita were already under, now unaware of what was happening.

"You ready, Elizabeth?"

"You sure this doesn't hurt?"

"You won't even know when it happens. You'll think you fell asleep. When you wake up you might feel a little confused, but that's the worst any subject has ever reported."

"What are you using from me again?"

"Verbal abilities—you'll do the talking. Like usual."

"Funny."

"We're using you as the template, too, so the abilities of the others will be mapped onto you."

"Good. You better not take advantage of me while I'm under."

"I wouldn't think of it. Besides, I don't have to. There is one other effect I forgot to tell you about. Volunteers report feeling horny when the sessions are over."

"Don't get your hopes up—or anything else."

Wes laughed, then shifted to Shamita's station and cut out Elizabeth's sensorimotor functions, mimicking the first stage of sleep. Back at his own station, he began the merge, mixing in abilities from the others, using the parameters Shamita had set up. The merge took, and soon he had integrated brain wave activity. *OK, let's see if you're home, Frankie.*

Placing a tape recorder next to Elizabeth, Wes stood by Len and said, "You're Pat. Can you hear me, Pat?"

"Yes," came the reply from Elizabeth.

"What's your name?"

"Pat."

Wes paused, realizing it wasn't Frankie. It wasn't just that it responded to Pat; the voice lacked emotion. Flat and mechanical, the voice wasn't human in the same way Frankie was. It was more consistent with Wes's previous experiments, and that worried him. Why when the savants were merged did it produce a mind and a personality like Frankie, but with his coworkers it was something less?

Wes continued through the preplanned questions. "Do you know Pastor Young?"

"No."

"Do you know Scot Salyer or Joshua Ringman?"

"No."

"Have you ever been to the Kappa Kappa Kappa fraternity?"

"No."

"Do you remember leaving this house?" There was a long pause.

"No."

"Why did you wait so long to respond, Pat?"

"I was confused."

Since each of the donors had left the house many times, he knew there might have been enough traces of memories to combine to create a personal memory for Pat. But only Elizabeth had actually been to the fraternity, and met the boys who had been killed, so there was less chance of a combined personal memory for that. It was consistent with the way he had hypothesized that the integration would work—personal memories were the basis of personality, so why did Frankie have a personality and Pat not?

"On what day of the week will Christmas fall in the year 2030?"

"I don't know."

"What one word goes with 'dog,' 'potato,' and 'house'?"

"I don't understand."

"I want you to find a word that would go with each of three words I gave you. For example, the word 'hot' would work— 'hot dog,' 'hot potato,' and 'hothouse.' Let's try another one, Pat. Find one word that goes with 'Latin,' 'skin,' and 'pen.' " Another long pause.

"I don't know."

"It would be 'pig.' " Pat certainly didn't have Frankie's intellect, which was a bit surprising. Except for Ralph, there was a lot of intelligence lying on those cots. Wes wondered if Ralph's intellect alone could be dragging the others down.

Wes tried a few other questions and tasks, convincing himself that Pat's intellect was far short of Frankie's, then returned to his station, systematically dismantling the intellect. One by one the others sat up, looking at Wes, who shook his head. Wes brought Ralph back last, dreading giving him back sensorimotor functions. As soon as Ralph was awake, his mouth opened.

"Did you do the speriment? I don't remember it. I'm kinda thirsty though—know what I mean?"

"It's too late to go to the Seven-Eleven tonight. I'll take you for ice cream tomorrow."

"Well okeydokey then."

Ralph remained on the cot, playing with his helmet. Having learned how to deal with Ralph, Wes pulled out a pack of gum and handed it to him. "Share that with the others. They're watching a video."

Ralph's lips puckered, and he stared at the pack in his hand. "Juicy Fruit. Luis likes it lots. He's got a pretty big mouth you know."

Knowing what was coming, Wes handed him another pack.

"Well okeydokey then."

Elizabeth had the tape recorder at Len's station, where they were correlating the questions with the physiological readings. Frankie and Pat's readings were clearly different.

"Pat wasn't lying," Len said. "But it looks like Frankie was."

"That's a bit strong," Wes said. "The readings are different, but there may be other explanations."

Everyone stared dubiously.

"OK, Frankie was probably lying," he conceded. "But why? Frankie isn't someone who can get up and walk out of here—let alone kill someone. Frankie ceases to exist when we stop running the program."

The sound of the front door opening and closing distracted them briefly, and Karon went to check on the savants. After a moment she returned.

"There's something wrong. They're asleep but I can't wake them."

Elizabeth followed immediately, the others trailing. Luis, Yu, and Archie were lying on the floor, on their backs, eyes closed, breathing deeply. Daphne was on the couch, asleep. Ralph sat in a rocker, a big bowl of popcorn in his lap. Wes noticed he was chewing gum and eating popcorn at the same time. Agitated, Karon explained what happened.

"Ralph asked if I would rewind the tape since he'd missed it, and since the others were asleep I said sure. But I tripped over Luis when I tried to get to the VCR. Luis didn't move. I apologized but there was no reaction. So I shook him but he wouldn't wake up. I tried Yu and Archie, too. They won't wake up either."

Elizabeth stooped and shook Luis's shoulder. "Luis, wake up." Luis opened his eyes, looking at Elizabeth and then the blank TV screen.

"I want to watch the movie."

"You can, Luis, we'll start it again."

"I swear I couldn't wake them. They were lying there comatose. Ralph, you saw me try. They wouldn't wake up, would they?"

"I dunno, Karon. I was eating popcorn and it keeps getting stuck in my Juicy Fruit."

"Maybe Gil noticed something," Wes suggested. "Where is he?" No one knew, so Wes went up the stairs looking for him. Wes knocked on his bedroom door, but got no response. Pushing it open, he saw Gil lying on the bed wearing a coat, just waking up. He looked confused, and when he saw Wes he looked startled.

"Are you all right, Gil?"

"Yeah, fine. I was just dreaming. You woke me up."

"I was going to ask you about the savants, but if you weren't down there with them—did you go somewhere?"

"Is something wrong? I only meant to leave them for a minute. I took a walk."

"They're fine. It's just that Karon says she couldn't wake them up. She said it was like they were in a coma. Have you ever noticed them sleeping that deeply before?"

"Can't say that I have."

"OK, thanks."

* * *

Worried that he was going insane, Gil lay on the bed, trying to reconstruct the evening. He'd gone to the bus station to leave town. He'd sat down and then he'd been harassed by those skinheads. Gil felt his pocket, his bus ticket was still there—it hadn't been a dream. Still wearing his coat, he found the switchblade in his pocket, and then his bag in the closet. He'd blacked out and somehow returned home.

Gil lay back down, remembering what had happened, step by step. The last thing he remembered was meditating. Remembering other meditations, he realized the recent ones had been followed by deep, unsatisfying sleep. But what if he hadn't been sleeping? And what had Wes said?—something about being unable to wake the savants. It had to be that Frankie thing. Suddenly sickened, he realized it didn't need the computer to exist. It had been using him. Then Gil remembered the murders, trembling when he thought of the risks Frankie had taken with him. But in the first murder they suspected a girl and an Asian in the second. It wasn't just him; Frankie was using them all, and now she wouldn't let Gil get away.

It wouldn't let him leave, but if he stayed it would keep using him—and eventually he would be caught killing someone. *There must be a way out!* Every muscle in his body was knotted and he couldn't think clearly. Automatically, he began his relaxation routine. Relief spread through him, and soon he could focus on his breathing, clearing his mind. Suddenly he panicked, sitting up with a start. That was how Frankie took him—when he meditated.

If he didn't meditate could Frankie take him over? Was it that simple? What if he got away to Portland; was Frankie hindered by distance? She might not be. He'd read enough parapsychology journals to know that psychic abilities defied normal laws of physics. Then he thought of the experiment, and of another way out.

Frankie was bits and pieces of all the savants, not only him. If he removed a part, could Frankie exist? He doubted it. He might have to remove more than one part, but he didn't care. He was going to be free from this thing, and he was going to be free soon.

                              *   *   *

They listened to the full tape of the experiment at the kitchen
table, Elizabeth raptly listening to herself say things she couldn't
remember.

"Why can't I remember talking to you, Wes? It was only a few
minutes ago."

"They're personal memories—that is, Pat's personal memories."

"But I'm Pat."

"You're part of Pat, but so are Shamita, Len, and Karon—
Ralph, too."

"So why can Pat speak at all? If Pat didn't exist until tonight,
then how could he know how to speak?"

"It's a different kind of memory. Amnesics don't forget how
to speak, or drive a car, but they do forget their past and who
they are." Wes paused, knowing that this wasn't the time for a
lengthy technical explanation. "Notice how long he paused when
asked if he'd left the house. Since each of his donor minds had,
there was likely enough trace to confuse him."

"But Frankie isn't like Pat. There's a spark to her. Why is she
so different?" Elizabeth asked.

"Why is she female?" Karon added. "That policeman is right.
You would think with only one female donor mind that we'd get
a male."

"Remember the savants are different, too," Wes said. "That's
likely why Frankie is unique."

Silent until now, Shamita spread a printout across the table.
"There's still this," she said pointing. "This is the printout from
Frankie, and this is that peculiar vertical wave." Shamita spread
out another printout. "Here's Pat's printout. Notice what's not
here?"

Wes could see the difference immediately, but he had to point
it out to Elizabeth.

"Is that what makes Frankie so human?" Elizabeth asked.

"It's the only difference between Pat and Frankie that can be
measured," Shamita responded.

"That implies there are things that you can't measure—like
what?" Elizabeth asked.

"Nothing," Wes responded. "Anything can be measured once
it's defined."

"What about psychic ability?" Elizabeth asked. "That's what Pastor Young was interested in."

"No such thing," Wes protested.

"Says you!" Elizabeth said.

"Says any respected member of the scientific community."

"We'll see," she said defiantly. "I leave for Chicago tomorrow—let's see what Dr. Birnbaum has to say."

Wes waited while Elizabeth explained to the others who Dr. Birnbaum was. Shamita frowned properly, but Len and Karon lit up with interest. Then Elizabeth spoke like she was in charge.

"Don't run the experiment until I get back. We don't want to give the police any more reason to suspect us."

Frustrated, Wes sighed. It was the worst possible situation. They couldn't leave because the police wouldn't let them, so they would stay, but they couldn't run the experiment. All that was left to them was to analyze old data and baby-sit the savants. Just when he thought it couldn't get any worse, he heard Ralph's voice from the stairs.

"Hey, somebody plugged up the toilet and it's overflowing! And there's turds all over the place!"

Immediately all eyes turned to him, and as he left the room he heard Len say, "Be sure to roll up your sleeve, Wes."

27

DR. BIRNBAUM

Elizabeth's absence meant more responsibility for Wes. Gil took care of the savants—although it seemed to Wes the savants didn't need much care anymore. Still, if something happened Wes would answer to Elizabeth, and then to the Kellum Foundation. He feared Elizabeth's wrath more than losing his funding—it was probably lost already. Because of his heightened sense of responsibility he was sensitized to the comings and goings of the savants and decided there would be few goings. He directed Gil to keep the savants close to the house, and avoid contact with neighbors and especially the police. He immediately had to exempt Ralph from the rule, since it was like penning a wild animal.

Len and Shamita buried themselves in the data, wrestling with Shamita's anomaly, trying to isolate the wave from cerebral static. Every brain wave originated within a neuron somewhere in the brain, and they set out to find the source of the wave. Also intrigued with the anomaly, Wes tinkered with his integration program, trying to find a way to isolate out the unusual wave. He reasoned that if that wave was the source of Frankie, then if he could select it out she should not appear.

Soon Wes was deep into the programming problem and oblivious of those around him. Only when piano music intruded into his consciousness did he become aware of his surroundings again. He tried to ignore the music, to focus on the problem before him, but there was something different about the sound. Daphne's incessant playing had prepared Wes's mind to easily screen it from consciousness, but for some reason he couldn't do it now.

He finally flopped back in his chair and listened. The playing wasn't up to Daphne's usual standards. Near flawless normally, now the rhythm came in fits and starts. There was something else that bothered him, too, but he couldn't put his finger on it. What was different about it? He tried putting a name to the tune. It wasn't played well but he finally recognized it as "My Favorite Things," from *The Sound of Music*. Then the significance hit him. In all the time he had listened to Daphne play, she had never played anything but sacred music.

Curious, Wes left his work at the kitchen table. To his surprise he found that it wasn't Daphne at the piano, it was Archie. Orange hair puffed out, blue Mickey Mouse glasses perched on his nose, Archie was pounding out a fair imitation of the show tune. Confused, Wes stood behind him, trying to decide if this was good or bad. That one of the savants would demonstrate a new skill should be a good thing, but he wasn't sure that Elizabeth would see it that way. Archie had never played the piano before, so it signified something—but what?

Daphne came in, joining Wes behind Archie. Soon her hands came up and she played an imaginary piano behind him. Wes realized he hadn't seen her do that for a long time. Now that he thought of it, life with the savants had changed in many ways. At first they had to be sensitive to the tiniest detail with the savants—nothing could change without triggering a reaction— but now the savants tolerated considerable disruption. Even something as traumatic as the police search had been recovered from quickly, even by Yu. The savants had become more adaptable, Wes decided, and life with them had become easier. The changes were positive, Wes knew, so it followed that Elizabeth would be pleased with Archie's piano playing. Thus reassured, he went back to his work.

Gil didn't care which savant he killed—he would simply take the first opportunity. Unfortunately, Wes had them staying close to the house, and his suggested outings were turned down. But two days after Elizabeth left for Chicago his chance came.

Ralph had been bugging Wes for an ice-cream trip, and when he finally relented Gil volunteered to take them to town. Looking for an opportunity, Gil asked Ralph to cut across the campus so they could walk along the busy street on the other side.

"It's longer that way."

"I know, Ralph. But it's a nice day so let's walk a little farther."

"It's a yucky day."

"It's not raining."

Ralph folded his arms across his chest, and leaned back, puckering his lips. "Are we gonna come back that way? It's longer and I don't like not having ice cream left when we get home. I like to eat the rest on the porch, especially the runny part that comes out the bottom. Daphne likes that, too."

"We'll come back the short way."

"Well okeydokey then," he said, and led off.

Gil followed behind, not expecting to find a killing opportunity. They crossed the quad and then cut between two of the large academic buildings. It was then that Gil noticed the sky-bridge connecting the buildings. The structure was only three stories up, but someone hitting just right might break his neck. Now Gil needed a reason to take them inside and up to the third floor. Gil knew the campus well, and the bridge connected the fine-arts building with the performing-arts complex. Gil remembered a student art gallery on the second floor and decided he could later claim he took them upstairs to expose the savants to art. It was weak justification, but he was desperate to be free.

Calling Ralph back, he convinced him to lead them to the second-floor exhibit area. Ralph headed the strange parade through the building, the odd group turning the heads of students as they climbed the stairs. At the second floor Ralph wandered aimlessly, introducing himself to anyone who would hold still. Finally, Gil herded the group to the gallery and waited impatiently while they wandered around, incapable of even minimal appreciation of the sculptures and paintings. Gil paid scant attention to the collection of modern art himself, but found himself drawn to a painting of a female nude, enjoying the sexual feelings like an adolescent.

Finally, he pulled himself away and testily ordered Ralph to head up the stairs to the third floor. Ralph complied with an "okey-dokey." Trailing, Gil felt his anger grow. He wanted to be free—to be somewhere where he could indulge his new sexuality—but this Frankie thing wouldn't let him go.

Ralph found the skybridge without help, leading the savants to the middle, where they all stopped at the rail to look across campus. Archie, Yu, and Luis stared dumbly, but Daphne and Ralph alternated sides. Under normal circumstances Gil would have killed Ralph, but Ralph wasn't part of Frankie, so he selected Luis. Staring at his head, he suggested he lean over. Luis complied, folding over the rail. Next he suggested to Luis he get on his toes and lean further. Again, Luis complied. His perch was precarious, but he was a short man and the rail was still only chest-high. Now Gil wished he'd picked Archie, who was the tallest, but didn't want to take the time to start over. Instead he suggested that Luis push himself up with his arms and lean out.

"You shouldn't ought to say that, Gil," Ralph said loudly. "Luis might fall off of there. You want I should get him down?"

Gil's anger flared—he'd forgotten about Ralph's ability to hear his suggestions—but his anger gave him power.

"Yes, Ralph, you're right. Would you get him down, please? That does look dangerous."

"Sure, Gil. Luis might hurt himself."

Gil waited until Ralph neared Luis; then he wrapped his thoughts around Luis and pushed hard. Luis's head and shoulders went over, but his hands tightly gripped the rail so he hung inverted for a second, his feet straight up in the air. Ralph lunged for him, but it was too late. Luis disappeared over the edge in a headlong dive. Someone screamed and Gil looked to see Daphne leaning far out watching Luis's fall.

Dr. Birnbaum lived in a new subdivision carved out of the corn-fields north of Columbus. When Elizabeth drove up the cul-de-sac, children scattered and neighbors stared. Pulling into the Birnbaum driveway, she noticed two women across the street whispering and pointing. She felt as if she had triggered the neighborhood watch. She rang the doorbell twice before a haggard middle-aged woman answered.

"Mrs. Birnbaum? My name is Elizabeth Foxworth. I called you last week, trying to speak to your husband. It's important that I see him."

Mrs. Birnbaum stepped out, pulling the door closed behind her. "You can't. He won't see anybody. He was in a car accident—he hasn't recovered yet."

"Just a few minutes—"

"Goodbye." Mrs. Birnbaum stepped inside, closing and locking the door.

Frustrated, Elizabeth sat in her car, devising a plan. Then she drove to a 7-Eleven for a cup of coffee and returned, parking just off the cul-de-sac. She watched the house for two hours before the garage opened and a car backed out. Feeling like a spy, she ducked when Mrs. Birnbaum drove past.

Returning to the 7-Eleven, she called the Birnbaum house. A machine answered with Mrs. Birnbaum's voice. After the beep she said, "Please pick up the phone, Dr. Birnbaum. I'm Ms. Foxworth, and I must speak to you about your work. I'm a friend of Dr. Young. You might remember him, he used to research parapsychology too. He's dead, Dr. Birnbaum, and—"

"This is Dr. Birnbaum. What's this about Dr. Young? I thought he was a priest or something now."

"He was pastoring a church, but he was murdered."

"Murdered? How?"

"Can we talk face-to-face?"

"Come back to the house. The front door will be unlocked. I'll be in the back, but you better hurry before my wife gets home."

Elizabeth found the front door unlocked as promised, and walked through a neat living room filled with antiques, and down a hall. A ramp had been built at the end, leading to a family room, also appointed with antiques. One wall was mostly glass, an atrium on the other side. Amid the many leafy plants was a hot tub, and another ramp led up to it. Dr. Birnbaum was in a motorized wheelchair facing the atrium, turning at the sound of her footsteps. The chair whirred until he faced her.

His empty left pant leg was neatly folded and pinned, and he was missing his left arm, too. His face was heavily scarred on the left and the eye on that side hung low, open but dead.

"My wife doesn't like people to see me like this. She is a

proud woman—some would say haughty—and I was a handsome man. At least I like to think so."

"People can accept anything with time."

"It's not just my looks. She thinks I'm crazy."

"Why?"

The chair whirred and he rolled to a table, picking up a cup of coffee. "You can have a cup if you like, but you have to fix it yourself. I can't reach the coffeepot."

"What makes your wife think you're crazy?"

"Let's talk about Dr. Young. I met him at a conference once. He did some good work, as I remember. I can't say I was surprised when I heard he left the field for the ministry."

"Why is that? Science and religion have little in common."

Dr. Birnbaum laughed. "We like to think they're different, but they're both based on faith. You fail to accept the basic assumptions of science and it all comes tumbling down like a house of cards, just like the religion of a creationist who can no longer deny the truth of evolution. Dr. Young wasn't that different from a priest in the first place. Most of us parapsychologists are like that. We have to be open to what others don't believe exists. Even our evidence is indirect—there's no device to measure what we research. Theologians infer the existence of God based on what they see in the world around us. We do the same," he said, shaking his head. "It's not that big of a step to religion." He sipped his coffee, then turned back to Elizabeth. "Now tell me how he died, or get out!"

"He drowned in a bathtub."

Dr. Birnbaum looked disappointed, dropping his head to his chest. Turning, he rolled down the hall, speaking over his shoulder. "We don't have anything to talk about."

Quickly she added, "It was under very strange circumstances." Dr. Birnbaum turned back expectantly. "Well?"

"He was in the bathtub and he had a head wound, so it looked like he slipped and knocked himself out, then drowned. But there was a radio there dangling by its cord off the end of the counter. The police can't figure out why he would get into the tub with a radio dangling like that. He couldn't reach it from the tub, so he couldn't have pulled it off from in the tub. So how did the radio end up like that?"

Dr. Birnbaum looked interested, but then slowly began to shake his head. "I still don't think I can help you."

"There's more. Dr. Young had a list of names on his desk, all of them researching parapsychology. Your name was on that list, and so were at least six others. I know two of them are dead."

Now interested, Dr. Birnbaum turned back and rolled closer. "Who died?"

"Dr. Leahey and Dr. Kinghorn."

"I knew Kinghorn. What happened to him?"

"He drove his car out in front of a train. It killed him and his whole family."

Dr. Birnbaum's good eye went wide, then his whole body seemed to relax. "Tell me about the other one."

"Dr. Leahey walked into the propeller of his own airplane."

"Yes, it all makes sense. Have there been more deaths?"

Elizabeth felt ghoulish, but she believed Dr. Birnbaum knew something. "My assistant died, too. He stepped in front of a car."

Now Dr. Birnbaum smiled broadly, until he saw Elizabeth staring at him.

"It's not what you think. I'm not happy over their deaths. I'm happy because I know I'm not crazy. You must tell my wife this!"

"But what does it mean? Why so many bizarre accidents to people in your line of work?"

Now solemn again, Dr. Birnbaum spoke deliberately. "Perhaps if you knew what happened to me. We had been testing subjects for telepathy. It was the usual mix of volunteers—most with no ability, but a couple of subjects who consistently performed above chance level. One day a man showed up and volunteered for the study. He was truly unusual. Most of the time he performed like our other talented people, but occasionally he demonstrated remarkable ability, far above anything we had seen. He was so promising we rented him a room and got him a small stipend so he would be available full time. But the more we tested him, the more suspicious I became. I began to think he was faking somehow."

"You were using controlled conditions?"

"Of course. But some of these people are very clever, constantly coming up with new ways of cheating. I got suspicious when I noticed his ability got stronger every time I started thinking about cutting him loose. I decided he was playing with us, baiting us with his power."

"So, was he cheating?"

"You tell me. His ability was inconsistent, but I couldn't see how he was faking it. I watched every session and I tested with different graduate students, and every once in a while his scores zoomed—but I couldn't see how he was manipulating the results. There were two peculiarities, however. He insisted on using the standard set of psi cards—they have simple patterns on them, a cross, a star, a circle, et cetera. He claimed that his ability was too limited for anything more complicated. He also wanted to be able to look at the person sending. He said he couldn't read their minds unless he saw them.

"Finally, I decided to try a slight variation. I sorted several stacks into piles of symbols, then went through the usual procedure with another deck, asking him what card I was concentrating on. When he answered I would take a matching card from one of the stacks and put it in a second pile. That way I could double-check his responses. The odd thing was when it was all over there were hardly any matches in that pile, yet I recorded a forty percent match rate."

"I don't understand. You recorded more matches than there actually were."

"Yes."

Elizabeth thought about the implication, but it didn't fit what she normally thought of as psychic powers. "Somehow he must have affected your thinking."

"Exactly. He would guess and cloud my mind, convincing me he had guessed correctly."

Elizabeth had expected something more dramatic, and looked disappointed.

"Don't underestimate his power until you hear the rest," Dr. Birnbaum said.

Now his face darkened and his voice softened. Elizabeth recognized the symptoms; something painful was coming.

"After that last session with him I met with my graduate students to discuss what I'd done, but before we finished I had to leave for a lunch meeting. I don't remember everything that happened next, but I remember waiting to cross at a light. Suddenly I had an urge to walk into the street. The next thing I knew I was in a hospital—my arm torn off in the accident. The leg they chopped off later." Bitterness clouded his face. "The witnesses said I stepped right in front of a sports car. Sound familiar?"

Elizabeth nodded. "You think he did that to you?"

"I'm convinced. He knew I stumbled onto his secret and he tried to kill me."

"Cheating at cards isn't much of a secret to kill for."

"What if that were only the tip of the iceberg? He made me walk in front of that car, and Dr. Kinghorn drive in front of that train. That alone is an amazing power, but what if that power could be developed into something more?"

"What more is there?"

"That's the question, isn't it?"

Thinking about the implications, Elizabeth stood silently until she saw Dr. Birnbaum staring at her.

"Now, what aren't you telling me, Ms. Foxworth?"

Without hesitation, Elizabeth described Wes's experiments and the bizarre events surrounding them. Dr. Birnbaum listened raptly, occasionally asking technical questions she couldn't answer. She hesitated when it came time to describe the hidden room and the body, but she did, including details about Frankie's drawing, and her discussion with Tom Floyd about the earlier killings. Dr. Birnbaum probed and sifted, asking about every detail.

His wife returned in the middle of the story, glaring at Elizabeth. Dr. Birnbaum and his wife fought briefly over her presence, but then his wife relented, seemingly surprised by her husband's assertiveness. When she was gone Dr. Birnbaum reassured Elizabeth.

"She's not angry, just surprised. I've pretty much let her take over since the accident."

Quickly forgetting the fight, he returned to probing for details. Elizabeth noticed that he kept returning to the basement room, asking about the body and what she'd learned from Mrs. Clayton. After an hour his wife appeared with sandwiches and iced tea. More civil, but unsmiling, his wife sat for a while listening to the discussion. When they were done eating, she cleared the dishes and then left, briefly smiling at Elizabeth when she did.

Abruptly Dr. Birnbaum ran out of questions and rolled to his window, staring out at the atrium. Respecting his need for silence, Elizabeth sat silently, sifting her own thoughts. Finally, without turning, he said, "Describe Gil to me."

"Medium height, dark hair, dark eyes. Looks a little Hispanic, or something. He's quiet, but likable. He's very good with the savants."

"It doesn't sound like him. But it must be."

"You think Gil is doing the killing?"

"I think Gil is my Carl." Then he lifted the stump of his arm. "Yes, he's a killer, but I think you have a bigger problem than that." Lowering his stump, he rolled up to face her. "Take me with you. I'll identify Carl—Gil—whatever name he's using."

"I don't think that's a good idea. . . ."

"I can help you. You need someone with expertise in the paranormal."

"I know what you're thinking, about Frankie and the tomb, but how—"

"Yes, that's it! I want to help."

"I can't take you."

"You need me to help you. We don't know the extent of his powers."

"I couldn't."

Then, raising the stump of his arm again, he said, "He did this to me!"

Elizabeth paused, knowing he might be of some help—especially with Officer Winston—but before she could answer his wife intervened.

"He's not going! He's still not well."

"I'm fine. In fact, I've never felt better."

Elizabeth sat back while a fight ensued, husband and wife arguing back and forth, Elizabeth learning much about their relationship since the accident. Dr. Birnbaum had been suicidal at first, and morose since then. Today was the most animated his wife had seen him since he regained consciousness, and she was grateful to Elizabeth. But she was drained by the last months, and saw his return to life as relief, a chance for her to live her own life again. She admitted it was selfish, but she wanted a chance to live normally again. The argument seesawed, covering the same ground over and over, and finally Elizabeth excused herself, promising to call later.

Back at the hotel she called home.

"Hello, this is Ralph. Who is this?"

"It's Elizabeth, Ralph. How are you?"

"Oh, I'm fine, Elizabeth." Then, after a long pause, "I've got some gum. I'd give you some but you're not here."

"Thanks, Ralph. May I speak to Wes?"

Elizabeth heard the phone clatter on the table, then Ralph shouting for Wes. A minute later Wes answered.

"Hello."

"It's me Wes. I met with Dr. Birnbaum, and he was very helpful."

"What did you find out?"

Elizabeth didn't know how much to reveal. She could share their suspicions of Gil, but what could Wes do? If they shared them with Officer Winston, would he believe them? Without enough evidence to arrest him, they might end up stampeding Gil into harming someone else. If Gil was Dr. Birnbaum's Carl he had to be stopped, but they had to be sure it was him first.

"I think I better wait until I see you tomorrow," she said. "One thing, though. Don't let anyone out of the house without you. I mean no one."

There was a long pause at the other end, and when Wes spoke, he sounded odd.

"Elizabeth, I think you should know . . ."

"What?"

"Nothing. I'll tell you tomorrow."

They said goodbye, but Elizabeth worried about Wes's serious tone. After dinner she called Dr. Birnbaum, who said in a subdued voice that he would try to join her in a few days. Now Elizabeth found herself disappointed—she would have liked Dr. Birnbaum to be there when she confronted Gil.

That night she dreamed Daphne was in the center of a whirlwind that spun faster and faster until it was the speed of a tornado. Objects flew around, circling, accelerating until they spun off into the darkness. Then the savants came, Archie first, then Yu, and finally Luis. Tumbling and twisting, they floated helpless until they shot out into the darkness. Next came Karon and Shamita, followed by Wes and Len. They tumbled around Daphne, reaching for one another, clutching at each other's hands, only to be ripped apart by the powerful winds. Then with a roaring whoosh they were thrown into the void.

She woke with a start, anxious over the dream. Heart pounding, skin clammy with sweat, she sat, breathing deeply. Unable to calm herself she turned on the light, chasing the shadows away and with them the last of her fear. Dream analysis wasn't a part of her training, but she found herself reviewing the images. The savants had been in her dream, and the others with the project. Then she realized two people were missing. She wasn't there, which wasn't uncommon—people were seldom in their own dreams. Gil was the other missing person, which Elizabeth thought significant, but couldn't understand why. She spent a restless night, unable to stop thinking about him.

28

SUSPECT

E lizabeth drove directly to the police station from the airport. It was early and Roy Winston wasn't there yet, but the policewoman called him at home and he asked to meet Elizabeth at a restaurant. He was there when Elizabeth found it, eating a stack of pancakes and drinking coffee.

"You want something? It's on the department."

"Just coffee."

"Well, OK, but I think turning down free food is suspicious."

"You think breathing is suspicious."

"Lack of breathing is what I've been dealing with."

After the waitress brought her a cup she launched into her explanation.

"I might know something that will help you with your investigation."

"Which investigation is that?"

"The murder, of course."

"Which murder?"

Elizabeth glowered at him, realizing he wanted her to connect the killings, possibly to let slip something he didn't know.

Roy poured syrup over the last bite of pancakes and forked them into his mouth. Then he pushed his plate aside and picked up his coffee cup, staring expectantly.

"I might know who killed Pastor Young," Elizabeth said.

"Me, too. Who were you thinking of?"

"I'm not saying I'm sure, but I think it might be my assistant Gil."

The policeman looked surprised. "Why him?"

Elizabeth started with what happened to her first assistant and the other parapsychologists and then moved to Dr. Birnbaum's story. As she spoke, his notebook appeared and he scribbled down occasional notes. During the entire story the policeman's expression never changed. When she finished, he flipped backward through his notebook.

"Lemme see, where was that? Here it is. When I suggested ESP was involved you called it 'nonsense.' Called it that twice actually."

"I was upset. Besides, it is hard to believe."

"It wasn't for me. Now you want me to check out Gil?"

"Of course. That's why I came to see you."

Roy stared blankly.

"I'm telling you the truth."

"Sure. When does this Dr. Birnbaum get here?"

"He said in a couple of days. That's all I know."

"OK, I'll find out what I can about Gil."

"Can't you arrest him and hold him while you check?"

"I don't have any evidence against Gil. I've got more to hold Daphne or Yu on than Gil."

"But he's dangerous."

"Not to your people. They've been living with him for months, and they're all alive and kicking."

Not reassured, Elizabeth pressed again. "If it's him, he's dangerous. Can't you at least post someone outside the house?"

Smiling he said, "It's already been done. Mrs. Clayton's got a guest. He's been checking on your comings and goings. I'll have him park out in front now that you know about it. If Gil's the one we're after it might keep him in line—of course, he might bolt, too."

Both of those alternatives were acceptable to Elizabeth, so she thanked him and left. As she was driving home she began to think about the things Frankie had said about someone wanting to kill Ralph and Shamita and wondered how safe they really were.

* * *

Ralph came out the door as soon as she pulled up, a big grin on his face.

"I'm glad you're home, Elizabeth. Did you bring me something?"

"Thank you, Ralph," she said, pulling out a ten pack of gum. "Did everything go all right while I was gone?"

"Sure, sure," he said smiling. Then his smile was replaced by a pucker, and he looked concerned. "Well there was one thing that happened that wasn't so good."

Before she could ask about it Wes came out onto the porch, a concerned look on his face. Elizabeth's heart picked up its pace and she knew bad news was coming.

"What's happened?" she asked.

"I think you better come inside."

Elizabeth complied, her concern growing. As she stepped in, Daphne trotted to the piano and began playing. Ralph trailed behind, gum smacking in his mouth. Wes led her into the living room. Len and Karon were at the far end, with Gil next to them. Elizabeth stared at Gil briefly, then quickly recovered her composure and spread her gaze among the others. She didn't see Yu, but Archie was sitting on the couch solving a Rubik's Cube, and next to him was Luis—his face covered with scratches.

"What happened to Luis?"

"It's not as bad as it looks. He's just scratched up a bit. Nothing is broken."

"Why should something be broken?"

"Well . . ." Wes began, but Len finished for him.

"It's customary to break something when you fall three stories."

"What? How?" Elizabeth stammered.

"It's who?, what?, where?, when?, and why?," Len said. "Who? Luis. What? Fell. Where? The university. When? Day before yesterday. Why? Gravity."

"Len, please," Wes said, "this is serious." Then to Elizabeth, "I took him to the doctor. They X-rayed and found no breaks."

"Did he really fall three stories?"

"Yes. Gil was there, he can tell you."

Elizabeth forced herself to stay composed and turned to Gil, who responded evenly.

"We took a walk through the university and stopped to take a look at an art exhibit. It was on the second floor. When we left we took a skybridge between buildings on the third floor. We were looking at the view when Luis leaned out too far and fell off."

Elizabeth was suspicious of another accident but couldn't see what Gil would gain by killing one of the savants.

"I didn't fall, I was pushed."

Shocked, Elizabeth turned to Luis, who sat head down. Luis never spoke voluntarily, and now he sat silently, chewing on his lower lip with his oversized teeth.

"Who pushed you, Luis?"

Luis started to answer but then paused.

"Yeah, no one pushed you, Luis," Ralph said. "You just kind of fell—that grave stuff Len was talking about."

"Gravity," Len corrected.

Elizabeth glanced at Gil, noticing his cheeks reddened slightly. "Let Luis answer," Elizabeth said.

Luis began to rock on the couch, licking his lips nervously, his eyes fixed on the ground.

"Luis, were you pushed?"

The rocking increased—Luis was clearly anxious.

"Luis?" Elizabeth prodded.

"I guess I wasn't pushed."

Elizabeth watched Gil out of the corner of her eye while Wes smoothed things over.

"That's right, Luis," Wes said. "It was just an accident—Luis just leaned out too far. Isn't that right, Gil?"

"No one pushed him," Gil said. "I'm just glad he wasn't seriously hurt."

Elizabeth forced a smile and thanked him for his concern, not meaning any of it.

It was bedtime before Elizabeth got a chance to talk to Wes and the others in private. Gil was busy reading a story to the savants, so Elizabeth gathered the team around the kitchen table. She told them about Dr. Birnbaum's experiments and his last subject and the suspected ability. All of them looked shocked when she told of their suspicions of Gil.

"If Gil is the same guy, what's he trying to do?" Len asked.

"We're not sure," Elizabeth said. "He may be trying to better understand his own ability."

"So why kill people? Especially college kids he doesn't even know?" Shamita asked.

Elizabeth shifted uncomfortably in her seat, afraid of sounding crazy. "Dr. Birnbaum agrees with me that there might be a link between the dead girl in the basement and Frankie."

Wes started shaking his head.

"Don't be so quick to judge," Elizabeth said. "Think about what's happened. You integrated Frankie before the hidden room was opened and you got an emotionless, mechanical Frankie—just like Pat. But after the body was discovered Frankie came to life." Pausing to get her courage, she added, "Frankie now has soul."

"Elizabeth!" Wes said. "You can't think Frankie is the ghost of the girl in the basement!"

"Nancy. Her name is Nancy Watson."

"This Nancy is dead, Elizabeth. Dead and buried now. It's tragic what happened to her, but whatever thoughts she might have had died with her. She's not part of our Frankie—no ghost is."

"How do you explain the similarities between the killings?"

"Copycat killings happen all the time."

"I don't know, Wes," Len said. "I think this is stretching co-incidence too far."

Surprised at Len, Wes turned to face him. "But it doesn't make sense. How is Frankie doing the killings, when Frankie doesn't exist without our equipment?"

Len had no response, but Shamita did.

"Maybe it's the odd wave. Maybe that peculiar brain function keeps them together even without your program. I'm not saying I believe in the paranormal, but it would explain—"

"Yes, Shamita. I'm sure it's something like that," Elizabeth said. "Somehow Nancy can bring them all together again—remember how Karon couldn't wake them up? Maybe Nancy was in control."

"But no one died that night. No one even left," Wes protested.

"Gil did," Karon corrected. "He came in just before I tried to wake them. Maybe Nancy was in control and was using

Gil?" Then, softer, she added, "Maybe they haven't found the body yet."

Protesting with a shake of his head, Wes said, "Pure fantasy. There's no concrete connection with our experiment."

"I think I know a way to prove it," Elizabeth said, but then a noise in the living room distracted them.

Fearing it was Gil, they quieted while Karon checked the next room. Turning back relieved, she said, "It's only Ralph."

"Ask him in," Elizabeth said.

Wes frowned and Shamita groaned.

"Hi everybody. Do you do this every night when we go to bed? Are you playing a game?"

"No, Ralph," Elizabeth explained. "We were just talking. Can I ask you a question?"

"Sure! But not hard ones. Sometimes the hard ones give me trouble. Don't ask me addresses. I know where I live but I get the numbers mixed up—know what I mean?"

"Yes, Ralph. You can answer these. Do you like living here?"

"Sure, there's a Seven-Eleven real close."

"Gil's nice, isn't he?"

"Yeah. Except sometimes he buys yucky Slurpees."

"Does Gil ever do anything unusual?—you know, different?"

"I told you about those Slurpees."

"Anything else?"

"I don't think so."

"Well, thanks, Ralph."

"Want me to tell you some things about Wes?"

"Yes, but later," Elizabeth said.

"Well okeydokey then." Ralph turned to leave, but stopped in the doorway. "Oh, yeah. I almost forgot. Gil's a ventilkist. That's unusual, isn't it?"

"You mean a ventriloquist?" Elizabeth offered.

"I think so. Gil can talk without moving his mouth, isn't that one of those people?"

The others looked at each other and then at Elizabeth.

"Gil speaks without moving his mouth?" Elizabeth asked.

"Sometimes. Mostly when someone's upset. Like when Yu was upset when the police were touching his book."

"What does he say to them?"

"He says to calm down—everything's going to be OK—stuff like that."

"Does he ever talk that way to us?"

"He used to, but not much anymore."

"What did he say?"

"I don't remember. It was something about the speriment. I think he wanted to be sperimented on."

Wes lost his skeptical face and looked at Elizabeth incredulously. Elizabeth gave him an "I-told-you-so" look, then turned back to Ralph. "Thanks, Ralph. You should go to bed now."

"Sure, sure."

Ralph left, leaving the others in a solemn mood. It wasn't much evidence but it was another piece of the puzzle. Worse, each of them had to deal with the fact Gil might have been controlling their thoughts. Wes was about to speak when Ralph reappeared.

"Is it OK for Yu to use the phone?"

Surprised, Elizabeth led the way to the hall, where Yu was standing in his pajamas, the receiver held to his ear. Karon started forward, but Elizabeth stopped her with a touch on the arm. They all waited for Yu to complete his call.

"Father! If milk cost two dollars and seventy-nine cents then there would be twenty-one cents left from three dollars. I would file Mrs. Carter before Mrs. White."

Then, without a goodbye, Yu hung up and walked up the stairs.

When he was gone, they gathered back in the kitchen.

"What was that all about?" Shamita asked.

"I have no idea," Elizabeth said. "I understand Yu's father has essentially disowned him, so this might be his way of reaching out to him. Figuring the change for purchasing a gallon of milk is kind of interesting. I wouldn't have thought Yu could solve such a problem." Elizabeth's face darkened. "Actually, I'm sure it's not the kind of thing he could solve. I guess that shows improvement . . . still, very odd. Ralph, go to bed, please."

"Well okeydokey then," he said. "I just thought you should know about Yu. He might have been calling Mars or someplace spensive."

When Ralph was off to bed, they gathered again in the kitchen.

"What was your idea, Elizabeth?" Shamita asked. "You said something about a way to connect the killings with the experiment."

"Yes, I think I know a couple of ways. First, do you have the dates for all the experiments? Good, then let's dig the newspapers out of the basement and match the dates of the murders with the days we ran the experiments."

"I'll get the papers," Len volunteered.

Thirty minutes later they confirmed that the killings started the day the animated Frankie first emerged, and subsequent murders of the fraternity brothers occurred on the same days as an integration, but so did the killings of Tom Floyd and Pastor Young.

"It doesn't fit your theory," Wes argued. "If Frankie is Nancy, then why did she kill the pastor?"

"I believe Gil did that to protect himself from discovery."

"So why wait until after a session?"

"Coincidence. But if you don't believe me there is another way."

The others looked expectantly at Elizabeth.

"We could bring Frankie back and confront her. Ask her if she is Nancy."

No one spoke; instead they sat in silence, thinking of the ramifications. If anyone had an opinion only Wes risked the responsibility of sharing it.

"I don't think we should. I'm not saying I believe what you've been saying, but there is that correlation between the integrations and the killings. If we don't integrate Frankie again, and the killings continue, that vindicates the experiment. If the killings end—well that's for the good, too."

"But what about Gil?" Shamita asked.

"I've shared this with Officer Winston and he's checking up on Gil. If he turns something up he'll let us know. Meanwhile he's going to have someone watch the house." Shamita still looked concerned. "I know what you're thinking, Shamita, but it will only be a day—two at most. Until then we won't leave you alone, or Ralph either. None of us should be alone with him."

Everyone agreed, and then they fell silent, each thinking their own thoughts. As usual, Len's thoughts were a little different.

"This reminds me of the couple who were having trouble delivering a normal baby. The first baby was just a foot. The second baby was just a hand. Finally, they decided to try again. When the nurse brought the baby to the father she said, 'Congratulations, you're the proud father of a seven-pound eyeball.' Devastated, the father said, 'Nothing could be worse than this!' Then the nurse said, 'It's blind.' "

"That's sick, Len," Karon scolded.

"Yeah, but don't anybody say 'it can't get any worse than this.' "

Gil listened from the stairs, trying to pick out what they were saying. It wasn't unusual for them to meet without him but they were talking low, and that was different. He couldn't pick out a single word, but their behavior told him he had to get out of there.

When the kitchen meeting broke up, he scuttled up the stairs to his room, sacking out on the bed. His relaxation routine called to him, but he resisted. He wasn't going to lose himself to that thing again, so he avoided meditating, and he avoided sleep. It would be tough, staying awake until the first savant stirred—maybe he could nap for a couple of hours in the afternoon, but only if at least one of the savants was active.

He listened to the others going to bed around him, using the bathroom, opening and closing doors. It was still for a time; then, on the other side of the wall, he heard Karon's door open. With the house quiet, he could hear whispering through the wall, then giggling. Silence followed, and then the now familiar rocking of the bed.

Gil cursed Karon and Len for teasing him with what he couldn't enjoy. He also cursed the thing that was keeping him trapped in the house. As his anger built he began to move objects around the room with his mind, noticing new strength. When he first learned to control his ability he could move only one object at a time, but now he found he could move two as long as they stayed in his peripheral vision.

The rhythm in the next room reached its climax and then was followed by silence. They would sleep now, he knew, wrapped in each other's arms. That thought tortured him, too, and he nursed his anger to keep his power up to full strength. After a while his head began to ache, and he let the objects sink slowly to the ground. When his mind cleared he found himself thinking about Len and Karon, naked on the other side of the wall. He wanted Karon—or some woman; Ms. Foxworth would be better. He could take one of them if he wanted, it would be easy with his power, but he couldn't until he knew he could escape. Wanting a woman, and knowing Frankie was keeping him from satisfying his lust, helped keep him awake, and he spent the time working on a plan to kill a savant.

29

TRAGEDY

Mr. Tran was on the phone first thing in the morning with Elizabeth, complaining about the midnight call from his son.

"If you can't control him, then I will return him to Riverview. They knew how to keep him from bothering people in the middle of the night!"

"But that call was a significant step in sociability for your son," Elizabeth said.

"Poor manners are no improvement. Teach him respect if you must teach him something."

"Did the milk problem and the filing problem mean anything to you, Mr. Tran?"

"Yes, it meant loss of a night's sleep. See to it I don't lose any more!"

Elizabeth was left with a dead line and another mystery. Yu was no help about the call, once again his mind in a place no one could reach. But Elizabeth felt he would emerge again, and this time she hoped she could keep him in their world.

Elizabeth helped the savants through their morning routine but vetoed the walk Gil suggested. Suspicious, she interpreted even trivial things Gil did, or said, as sinister.

After lunch Gil excused himself, saying he wasn't feeling

well, and went up to his room. Elizabeth took the opportunity for
an outing and quickly got the coats on the savants. Only Daphne
refused the opportunity, choosing to stay and play the piano.
Fearing that Gil might join the walk if he knew they were going,
Elizabeth quickly pushed them out the door. The police car was
there as promised, a young policewoman at the wheel.

Immediately Ralph took the lead, Archie and Yu dogging his
heels and Luis following just ahead of Elizabeth. When they
reached the Kappa house, two fraternity brothers greeted Ralph
halfheartedly and then retreated inside, peeking out the blinds as
they passed. For once Elizabeth didn't mind the shunning of the
savants.

Curious about the accident, she had Ralph lead them to where
Luis had fallen. He protested at first, until she assured him they
wouldn't go up to the skybridge. Elizabeth hadn't spent much
time on the campus since she had been in Eugene and she enjoyed the atmosphere. Old brick buildings mingling with newer
additions created an appealing mix of classic and modern archi-
tecture. Like all of Wes's team she had spent many years on university campuses preparing herself for her profession.

As they passed the student union building Luis deviated toward it, Ralph and the others plodding on, oblivious of Luis's
sudden independence. She called after him, but he continued toward the crowd of students coming and going from the building.
Elizabeth hurried to catch up, curious rather than concerned.
Just before he reached the doors he turned, stopping in front of
a mailbox. Reaching into his coat pocket, he pulled out an envelope and dropped it into the mail slot. Turning back toward his
retreating comrades, he nearly ran into Elizabeth.

"What was that, Luis?"

"A letter."

Letting him pass, Elizabeth fell in next to him, wondering
first what possessed him to write a letter—something he had
never done—and who he would mail a letter to.

"Luis, who is the letter for?"

"My mother."

Elizabeth walked next to him, recalling his file. She knew he
was abandoned at birth, but was it possible his mother's name
and address was buried somewhere in his mind, captured even
as a toddler by his photographic memory? Luis didn't volunteer

more information—it would have been too much to hope he
would—but Elizabeth knew she would explore it further when
they got home.

Gil watched the savants turn in to the university, his travel bag
in his hand. Ever since he spotted the police watching the house
he had been waiting for this. There was no use hiding his ability anymore; they were on to him. But to get away he needed to
make sure Frankie was gone, and there was only one way to do
that.

    Following at a distance, he trailed them into the campus,
knowing Elizabeth was heading for the skybridge. When they
broke out into the quad he skirted to the left, mingling with the
students. He could see the savants being led by Ralph toward the
scene of the accident. Suddenly he realized that Luis had turned
toward the student union building. Briefly he wondered if Luis
was afraid of returning to the skybridge. Had Luis's retarded
brain managed to understand that he was pushed off? Luckily for
Gil he had managed to suggest to Luis he hadn't been pushed—
even if that damn Ralph had heard his thought-push again. Gil
remembered Luis inverted on that bridge, ready to dive headfirst
to the ground, and he chuckled—it was a delicious memory and
he hungered to finish the job.

The skybridge towered three stories above Elizabeth, and directly below it was a brick plaza. Benches were spaced around
the perimeter, many with students talking or reading. Now Elizabeth was faced with another mystery—how could anyone fall
three stories onto brick and have nothing but scratches?

    Ralph was working the benches, introducing himself and talk-
ing about the "speriment." Archie, Yu, and Luis stood together
waiting for the walk to resume. All three of them were more
communicative than when they first arrived and Elizabeth decided to see how much Luis remembered.

    "Luis, is this where you fell?"

    Without looking up he said, "Yes."

    "You fell onto this brick?"

    "No."

    "Where did you land?"

    "I landed in the bushes." Then, looking around and pointing to a laurel hedge along the side of one building, he added, "There."

"So you didn't fall from the middle of the bridge, you fell off one end?"

"No. I fell from there."

This time he pointed up at the middle of the bridge, confusing Elizabeth even more. Finally she called Ralph over.

"Ralph, where on the bridge was Luis standing when he fell?"

"He was in the middle. I was next to him, except I wasn't right next to him. I tried to grab him."

"Do you know where he landed?"

"In that bush. It's still smashed. Want I should fluff it up?"

"No. Thanks, Ralph. Let's get going again."

"Well okeydokey then."

Ralph was soon up to full speed and Elizabeth once again trailed the parade, this time wondering how anyone could fall at such an angle that they could land thirty feet away.

Gil trailed them to the 7-Eleven and waited until they came out eating ice-cream bars. It wasn't an ideal situation, but at least they were distracted by eating. Ralph was peeling the paper away from an ice-cream sandwich as they came to the corner, waiting for the light. The traffic started up on the cross street and Gil watched, looking for a gap just the right size. The cars were too close together at first. Gil watched for a two-length space, building his anger in anticipation. He focused his thoughts on Luis, finding it easy to blame him for his failure at the skybridge.

It was taking too long, and the light would turn soon—he feared he would lose his chance. Then there it was, just before a white pickup truck, the right spacing in the traffic. Gil waited, timing it right, then stared hard at Luis, wrapping his thoughts around him. Then he pushed.

Elizabeth knew what was happening when Luis suddenly straightened, his eyes going wide. Then, as if pushed by an invisible hand, he staggered backward toward the traffic, his arms flung out as if he were trying to embrace whatever was pushing him, his face contorted in fear.

Elizabeth could see the truck coming from her left—there was no time. She bolted forward, lunging toward his embrace.

When she was nearly to his arms he suddenly flew backward, his heels dragging across the sidewalk and off the curb. The truck's tires screamed as the driver locked the wheels. Smoke billowed from the burning rubber, but it was too late. Luis slid backward into the path of the truck.

Luis's thick lips parted in a scream just as the truck plowed into him. His body folded with the blow and he tumbled forward, head over heels. The truck continued over him, the wheels rolling over his legs and chest. The sound of his bones breaking was audible above the squeal of the tires.

Once the truck stopped Elizabeth rushed forward. Only Luis's head and arm were visible; the truck had come to rest on his chest. Helpless, Elizabeth stared as a red wetness spread down Luis's side. Suddenly Ralph was there.

"We got to get him out, Elizabeth!" he said.

Before she could reply Ralph grabbed one side of the truck and lifted, his powerful shoulders knotting under the load—at first nothing, then the truck moved. Elizabeth grabbed Luis, her hand feeling the warm blood, and pulled, but he was still pinned.

"Ralph, lift it higher."

She knew it was an impossible command but then the truck moved another inch and then another, suddenly she realized there were others helping Ralph. As she watched, the wheel cleared Luis's chest, and she pulled with her arms. He didn't budge, so she tightened her grip, planted her feet, and pushed with her legs. He moved, but only a few inches. Suddenly more hands appeared and Luis was dragged from under the wheel.

Luis's chest was soaked in blood and his now crimson shirt pulsed in one spot as if an artery was spilling across his chest. Elizabeth put her palm on the pulsing spot and pushed, her hand sinking—there was a hole in his chest. The futility struck her and she leaned back and watched the pulsing spot until it slowed and then finally stopped. Only then did she feel the extent of her despair, and she leaned back and screamed.

Elizabeth's scream meant he was free, and Gil quickly turned away. People ran toward the intersection, a crowd gathering. They always did, Gil knew, but this time he didn't try to blend in; instead, like a salmon heading upstream, he pushed his way through the gathering gawkers.

"Goodbye Luis, and goodbye Frankie," he said aloud. Then, whistling, he headed toward the highway to thumb a ride to Portland. He had his freedom back now, and his new power, and most important he was in control again.

30

EXPLOSION

Roy Winston questioned Elizabeth, Wes hovering to one side trying to comfort her. The police were now combing the city for Gil and had notified the state police and surrounding communities. Still skeptical, the police were at least willing to hunt Gil down.

Elizabeth's description of Luis being pushed backward into traffic had been confirmed by witnesses, and some had described a person fitting Gil's description leaving the scene—no one at the house had seen Gil since before the accident. There was too much proof not to believe Gil had done it, yet Wes still struggled to accept it. He had to hope for a more rational explanation.

Now mesmerized by the TV, Yu and Archie seemed oblivious of what had happened. Even after witnessing Luis's death they had simply stood, staring blankly. Ralph had been affected, though, bursting into tears—something he had never done in his life. He was quiet now, his eyes red and puffy.

Daphne, too, had suffered, even though she hadn't been at the scene, playing constantly since Elizabeth called with the news of Luis's death. There had been no tears, but Daphne had retreated, pounding the world away with vigorous piano playing.

When he had exhausted his questions, Roy folded his notebook into his shirt pocket and left. Elizabeth headed for the kitchen and a cup of coffee. Wes joined her, not knowing what to say but willing to listen.

"It's my fault. I knew he was dangerous. I should have insisted they arrest him, or at least get him out of the house."

"It might have been worse that way. What if they came to arrest him and he lashed out—the savants could have been hurt. The same could have happened if we had confronted him. There was no right answer to this—the one we came up with was as good a choice as any."

Wes meant it when he used "we." This was his project, and the savants were his responsibility. Going along with a decision was the same as making it.

"I keep telling myself that," she said. "But there must have been something I could have done."

Abruptly the piano music stopped in midstanza, and they could hear Daphne stomp up the stairs and her bedroom door slam.

"Poor Daphne. She's experienced so many deaths for someone so young. Her mother, her grandmother, and now Luis. I hope this doesn't set her back, she was showing remarkable progress—they all were. Did I tell you Luis mailed a letter? Really, he mailed it at the student union. He said it was for his mother, but I know he was abandoned as a baby. Now I'll never know what was in that letter, or who he mailed it to. Poor Luis, he died just when he was reaching out, ready to make contact with people. That's the saddest part—he never really lived life."

"He seemed happy here," Wes said. "He adjusted more quickly than the rest. I think he genuinely liked Ralph—especially the trips for the Slurpees."

"Everyone likes Ralph, except you of course. But you can't really say Luis was happy—I don't know if he was capable of that emotion. At best he wasn't unhappy."

"Elizabeth, I know you're the expert on this, but Luis had an active, full life. I know life here doesn't seem like much, but he was busy, he took walks, he ate meals with people who cared for him, who also took care of his needs like a parent. It was a good life, Elizabeth, and I know in one way that makes it sadder he died, but he also had something many people out there never have. He had a family."

Wes took Elizabeth's silence to mean she was at least thinking about what he said even if she didn't agree with it.

"Wes, I don't want the state to bury him. I want to do it. I'll pay for the funeral. I'll get a plot where my mother is. He'll get visited then."

"We can pay for it out of the grant—"

"No! I'll pay for it."

"I'm sorry . . . I didn't mean—"

"I know. Let's not talk for a while."

Wes sat uncomfortably for a minute, wanting to comfort her physically, but realizing it would be awkward in the kitchen chairs. "Elizabeth, would you sit on the porch with me?"

She smiled briefly and nodded her head. "After we get the others off to bed."

As soon as the savants were in their rooms they settled onto the porch swing, rocking gently. He snaked his arm around her, flashing back as he did to his teen years. She didn't snuggle close to him, it wasn't that kind of mood, but the contact comforted both of them, and they rocked gently, watching the darkness.

Daphne paced her room, wishing for the buzz to block out her thoughts. Luis was dead and they said he was killed by Gil, but she wasn't sure that was true. That other thought was there, poking up from the black hole in her unconscious. Then the memory slithered out of the hole. In a panic her arms came up and she began playing the imaginary piano, the music pouring into her mind—it didn't help now, the memory was unfolding—she mustn't look at it.

Daphne flopped on the bed and spread her arms and legs wide, breathing deeply, but the only images her mind conjured up were of Luis squashed like a bug under a big truck. Daphne dug deeper, picking out good thoughts and warm feelings, but still the Luis picture floated through her head. Then she heard a voice, a soft whispering voice.

It called to her from a part of her mind she had never visited. There was no bad thought there, or image of Luis. It wasn't a good-feeling place but the voice was comforting and seductive. So Daphne drifted down to the voice, hearing it call her name as if from a cave. Down she drifted, the buzz, Luis's bloody image, the bad memory and the world left behind. Over and over she heard her name, growing louder as she fell toward the voice until she heard nothing else, saw nothing else. Then she slipped into the comforting void of the voice.

Gil was tired of listening to the salesman talk and was glad they were nearly to Portland. He would get a bus there, maybe to Seattle, or even to Canada. He needed to let things die down. He'd use the time to develop his new power. After that he didn't know—maybe he'd go back to the parapsychologists and see what else he might develop. Telekinesis wasn't what he'd come looking for, just a welcome bonus, and it made him wonder what other talents might be hidden away.

"You don't mind country, do you?" the salesman asked, turning on the car radio.

Gil hated country music, but smiled and said, "Fine." Listening to the radio was preferable to hearing more about the window coverings business.

"I like just about every kind of music there is, but when I'm traveling I'm always in the country mood. Listen to it night and day when I'm on the road. I bet I could name a country radio station in every major city in the western states."

Gil ignored the salesman's chatter and soon he was humming along with the songs, leaving Gil alone. It was welcome relief, and Gil could finally relax. His breathing deepened and he felt the tension flowing from his body. The rhythm of the highway soothed him and he concentrated on the thrumming sound of the tires on the blacktop. Soon the car sound seemed louder than the music and Gil's mind filtered out the music and then the humming.

Slowly he drifted down, his mind clearing, his body awareness slipping away. The twangy beat of the country music had faded completely from consciousness—he was falling asleep. Taking a deep breath, he exhaled, turning himself over to the urge to sleep. Deeper he drifted, completely losing himself to the emptiness that preceded sleep. Too late he realized it wasn't sleep that was taking him. It was Frankie.

Keith lagged behind Hanson and the other members of the Kappa house. He was sick of going everywhere in groups. Since the killings no one left the house alone, not even in the daytime. It made them look chicken, walking in groups like this, and he was sick of it. Tonight was the worst. They'd gotten a rare invitation to a sorority party and went in a group. The party had been kick-ass and he was making good time with Jenn, when Classen started to mother-hen them and head them back to the house. He wasn't taking that crap, though, and told Classen to shove it, but he kept pushing. Finally, Hanson had intervened and split the group in two, so those who wanted to stay longer could. Having a big fight over walking a few blocks home in the dark was embarrassing and he was fed up—and drunk, and when he was drunk he got brave.

They were almost to the house when he dropped farther behind just to prove he wasn't afraid. Thoughts of dancing with Jenn and how good she felt pressed up against him kept drifting through the alcoholic haze. The more he thought about her the more he wanted to go back for her, and the slower he walked, letting the others plod on without him. Suddenly he staggered off the curb, quickly steadying himself against a car. When he was sure of his footing again, he ducked down behind the car, watching his friends through the windows. "Hello Jenn, here I come," he whispered to himself.

When his fraternity brothers disappeared into the house, he stood slowly, still not quite sure of his balance. When he did he saw someone lying behind the front seat on the floor. It was an unnatural position, and he stared, trying to make sense of it. The person was hidden in the dark between the seats, one arm flopped over his back, one leg hooked over the edge of the back seat where shades or blinds were piled high. Looking closer at the blinds, he could see that one was spattered with red paint— or was it paint?

He tried the back door, opening it and speaking to the man on the floor. "Hey, are you asleep or what?" No answer, so he reached in, pushing gently on the man's back, then harder. "Hey, wake up. Are you OK?" This time he reached in with two hands and rocked him firmly. His hands came away sticky. Staggering back to the streetlight, he could see that it was blood. Dulled by alcohol, he was slow to grasp the implication. "You're dead. Oh man, it's a dead guy."

Turning to run for help, he found himself facing another man.

Startled, he babbled out a plea for help. "He's dead. That guy is dead in there. The guy behind the seat."

"You're from the Kappa house, aren't you?"

"Huh? Yeah, but that guy is dead."

"There's worse things than being dead."

"What are you talking about? We've got to get some help!"

"I've been dead, and there are worse things."

"You're too weird, man. I'm gonna get some help."

"You know what's worse than being dead? Being helpless! Having other people do things to you and there's nothing you can do about it. No matter how much you plead or beg, they just keep hurting you."

"Hell with you!" Keith tried pushing past, but the man shoved him back with a strong arm. Keith's anger flared, but he wasn't scared. Even drunk, Keith knew he could take this guy.

"Keep your hands off of me, or you'll lose them."

"Ever raped a girl? I'll bet you have. You did and you liked it, didn't you?"

"Get out of my way or I'll take you out, man!"

"You and your friends, you like to rape girls like me, don't you!"

Keith knew the man was losing it, so he launched himself into his chest, driving him back. The man staggered from the blow, dropping to one knee. Keith hesitated, seeing the man's vulnerability; then he reared back and kicked him in the chest.

Air exploded from the man, and he was left gasping, but at the same time his hand gripped Keith's ankle, holding it. Keith stumbled, trying to keep his balance and get leverage so he could pull his leg free. Suddenly a sharp pain tore through his leg. Keith looked to see a knife being pulled from his calf. The pain cleared his brain of the alcohol fog and he twisted, trying to pull free. Too late—another stab and the knife was buried in his thigh. As the knife was pulled free he was suddenly loose and he fell to the sidewalk, struggling to get to his feet. His bleeding leg wouldn't support him, though, and he tumbled onto his side.

Rolling over, he saw the man get slowly to his feet, the knife dripping with blood—his blood. Pushing with his good leg and pulling with his arms, he tried to get away. He got to his feet and limped away, every step agony, rivulets of blood running down his leg. Suddenly his hurting leg was kicked from under him and he fell. Turning to look behind him, he saw the man's foot swinging toward his head. A powerful kick to the face turned Keith onto his back, the man towering over him, his face lost in a shadow.

"Now do you know what it feels like to be helpless? To be at the mercy of someone who has no mercy!"

"Please, I never did anything to you."

"But it's not the same. For you it won't last long, the agony will be over soon. You won't have to live with it because you won't live."

Keith screamed when the knife plunged down, burying into his abdomen. Then the stabbing came fast and furious, but the agony quickly faded to a hot burning, and then to no feeling at all.

Wes answered the phone before he was awake, having no memory of it ringing. Then the receiver was at his ear and there was a voice whispering. "Hello? Hello? I can't hear you."

"I said there's someone sneaking around outside your house."

"Who is this?"

"It's me, Mrs. Clayton. I live across the street, remember?"

"Oh yeah!" Wes said, now realizing it wasn't a crank call. "What were you saying?"

"I said there's someone sneaking around your house. He came up the street and then went around to the back. If he had legitimate business he would have rung the bell, wouldn't he?"

"Yes, Mrs. Clayton, thanks for calling us. I'll check it out right away."

Wes jumped out of bed and put his pants on, then stepped into the hall to find Elizabeth waiting for him.

"What's going on?"

"Mrs. Clayton says we have a prowler." Wes didn't need to say more.

"It could be Gil! Call the police."

Wes hesitated briefly, then went back to his room, deciding to report a prowler and let the police handle it. The woman at the other end took his address and name and promised a car would be there in minutes.

Elizabeth was gone when he returned to the hall, but when he turned toward her bedroom he heard a whisper at the bottom of the stairs. Elizabeth was there, gesturing frantically to Wes. Wes's heart rate shot up as he tiptoed down the stairs.

"Someone's in the basement."

Gesturing for him to follow, Elizabeth led him to the kitchen and the door to the basement. The door was ajar, but when Elizabeth pulled the door open Wes stopped her.

"Wait for the police. I'll see who it is."

"Don't go macho on me. Just stay close."

Carefully Elizabeth led the way down the stairs, testing each stair for squeaks before putting her full weight on the step. Halfway down, Wes heard the water running and tapped Elizabeth on the shoulder.

"Do you hear that?"

"Yes, it's coming from over there."

With Elizabeth in the lead they worked their way through the clutter in the basement. Gasping softly, Elizabeth stopped and pointed. "It's Gil."

Wes saw him at the same time, standing in the hidden room. He was at the sink washing something. Elizabeth quickly pushed Wes back and then up the stairs.

"What's he doing here?" she said.

"I don't know, but the police will be here soon. They can arrest him."

Sounds of someone walking up the stairs sent them scurrying for hiding places. They both wedged themselves behind a chair in the living room and waited, listening. The basement door creaked as Gil came through, followed by the sound of the door closing softly. Wes held his breath when Gil walked through the dark living room and went up the stairs. A knife glistened in his hand. Hesitating only until Gil's feet disappeared up the stairs, he followed. When Wes reached the bottom of the stairs he padded up until he could see over the top. Gil stood there, looking from door to door, seemingly confused, the knife still in his hand. Wes felt Elizabeth behind him, her hand on his back. Wes summoned up his courage, getting ready to rush Gil. Then Gil walked to his own room, and went in, closing the door softly. When Wes started forward Elizabeth stopped him with a touch.

"Let him stay there," she said. "You watch his door—I'll wait for the police on the porch." She turned away and then came back, putting her hand on his back again. "Don't do anything foolish, he's got a knife."

Wes appreciated her concern, but was so afraid he wasn't sure he could move even if Gil reappeared.

Gil woke confused. He should have been in a car—the salesman's car—but he was in a room. It was his room—he was back! Gil jumped to his feet, listening hard. The house was silent and the window told him it was night. Then he realized he wasn't free yet. *It had taken him again! But how? He'd killed Frankie when he'd killed Luis.*

He was in danger, he knew that. Luis was dead and he'd disappeared—it had to look suspicious. Listening again, Gil realized they might not know he was home. Frankie had brought him back to the house, but done it surreptitiously. But could he leave now? Why would Frankie let him get away now? *No, he would not get away, not without killing the rest of the savants.* Gil looked around the room and was shocked to see a knife lying on the nightstand, just as the gun had. Picking it up, he had no memory of it in his hand, yet he must have carried it—must have used it. The thought of murder didn't bother him, but the loss of control sent shivers up his spine.

Realizing there was only one way to end this, Gil flipped the knife over into a stabbing position, then thought about Frankie and how she was using him. When his anger was sufficient to energize his power, he stepped into the hall.

His eyes dark-adapted, he studied the doors, making sure they were all closed. He decided to start with Daphne and stepped to her door. Reaching out carefully until he touched the knob, he twisted it slowly, moving like the hands of a clock. A barely audible snap announced that the latch was free, and he pushed the door open until it was wide enough to pass through. Then he raised the knife, ready to step in.

Suddenly someone charged up the steps screaming "No!"— it was Wes. Gil whirled, lashing out with his power, and blindly sending a wall of force at the charging figure. Wes was thrown backward, then rolled across the floor to the stairs. Wes flailed, trying to grab on to something, but continued over the edge and down the stairs. Gil smiled as he heard his body bumping and crashing. Stepping to the edge, he saw Wes spread-eagled at the

bottom. When Wes stirred Gil's anger flared again. He was about
to hammer Wes with another blow when he heard someone behind him.

Turning, he saw Len step out of Karon's bedroom followed by
Karon's head. *They've been screwing again!* Gil's anger reached
a new height. Gil focused this time, picturing a battering ram
aimed at Len's chest, then pushed with all his power. Len was
lifted from his feet, an invisible force pushing him through the
air. He flew the length of the hall, ending his flight when he
smashed into the wall. Len crumpled to the floor, limp, a red
stain spreading across his chest. Then Gil turned his anger toward Karon, who stood screaming in the doorway.

Gil watched her, waiting for her to look his way. He wanted
her to see it coming when he crushed her skull against the door-
frame. Karon was fixated, though, on Len's crumpled form—
frozen in fear and shock. Then her head began to turn, her face
a mixture of fear and disbelief. Gil waited, wanting full eye contact before he struck. As she turned he worked up his anger,
wanting to smash her skull as easily as stepping on an egg—he
was sure now he had that much power.

Karon's eyes met his and he pictured a sledgehammer, and
then pictured it aimed at her head. Her eyes went wide—she
knew it was coming, and that gave him pleasure, but not enough
to weaken his power. It was time. Gil sucked in a deep breath,
ready to send the invisible sledge flying, but then a door opened.

"Oh, hi, Gil," Ralph said. "We thought you was gone. You
missed dinner you know. Course it was just TV dinners. Everyone was kind of upset about Luis. You, too, huh?"

Instantly Gil switched to Ralph, ready to kill him as he'd
longed to do for so long. Stupidly, Ralph stood there in his pajamas, not understanding the danger.

"Ralph, get inside, quick!" Karon yelled.

Gil's anger flared and he lashed out at Karon, but the power
wasn't well focused and he only managed to shove her against
the frame, her head hitting with a loud thump. Karon squealed,
then grabbed her head and staggered inside, closing the door.

Turning back, he saw that Ralph had gone into his concerned
mode—lips puckered—and was staring at Karon's door. Then he
turned to Gil. "Did you do that? You did, didn't you? It's like that
ventrilkist thing you do?" Then, looking around, he spotted

Len's body. "Len! You OK? Hey bud, are you hurt?" Hearing no answer, Ralph swung back around, stepping toward Gil, a new look on his face—one Gil had never seen. "You did that, too didn't you? You shouldn't ought have. Len's funny. He makes me laugh. He makes everyone laugh. You can't be hurting people, Gil!"

Gil's wall of anger cracked as Ralph came toward him. Ralph was stupid, and harmless—at least he always had been—but he was also big. Gil pictured a bowling ball and pushed it at Ralph's stomach, waiting for him to crumple in pain. Nothing happened. Ralph came on unaffected, lecturing him.

"I'm not going to hurt you, Gil. But I can't let you hurt people. Maybe when you're calmed down you'll feel better."

Gil pictured a battering ram and pushed again and still Ralph came on unaffected. Then Gil's anger crumbled under the onslaught of his fear and he bolted to the stairs, racing down two at a time. At the bottom he could see Wes's legs disappearing into the living room. Someone was pulling him out of the way and that meant he was still alive. Disappointed, Gil knew there wasn't time to kill him, so he raced straight to the front door, fumbling with the lock and then crashing through the screen door onto the porch, where he froze. The flashing blue lights of a police car lit up the yard, and coming up the walk were two officers. Surprised, he and they stood staring, and then the police drew their weapons.

"Stay where you are, and drop the knife."

Gil lifted his arm, looking at the knife still held in his locked fingers.

"I said put the knife down," the officer repeated

Panicky now, Gil struck with what was left of his anger, knocking the policemen to the ground. Then he turned back into the house, jumping over Wes's body and running for the kitchen. Suddenly he found himself crashing to the floor—someone had tripped him. When he lifted his head a lamp shattered over his skull, showering him with ceramic shards. Lights flashed in his head and sharp pain stabbed his brain. Quickly, before another blow could come, Gil lashed out with the knife, slicing the air wildly, rolling over as he did.

Elizabeth was there, holding the remnants of the lamp. He wasn't afraid of her, and he felt his anger deep inside him.

Nurturing it, he felt the power coming back, and he stared at Elizabeth. Then Ralph came down the stairs. Frustrated, he pushed with what power he had, knocking Elizabeth to the ground. Then he ran to the kitchen and out the back door.

An invisible punch had knocked the wind out of Elizabeth and she lay gasping on the floor. A policeman appeared, asking if she was all right.

"Yes," she gasped. "Please . . . help . . . Wes."

"My partner's with him. Where did the man with the knife go?"

"Out . . . the . . . back."

"Take a deep breath. Something hit us coming up the walk, do you know what it was?"

Breathing better now, Elizabeth sat up, her stomach aching from the blow. "He has a power. He's telekinetic."

"What? Psychic power? That's not possible!"

Elizabeth didn't bother to argue, she just struggled to her feet. "Aren't you going after him?"

Looking uncomfortable, he said, "Not without my partner."·

Elizabeth stood, holding her stomach. The policeman helped her walk over to Wes, who was sitting up, leaning against the couch. He was holding his left arm across his stomach.

"Are you all right?" She asked.

"I'll be OK, but you better check on Len. Gil hit him pretty hard."

The look on Wes's face sent Elizabeth hurrying up the stairs. Ralph and Karon were at the end of the hall, kneeling by Len, while the other savants stood behind, staring. She could hear Karon crying and Ralph trying to comfort her.

"I'm sure he's just sleeping, Karon. It's nighttime, you know. He's just sleeping—not like Luis. Nope, not like Luis. No sirree, not like Luis."

Elizabeth pushed between them but paused when she reached for Len. His chest was soaked in blood and she suddenly flashed back to Luis. She couldn't bring herself to touch him, so she remained kneeling, emotionally drained—so much pain in so little time.

A policeman came up behind, whistling softly. Then he leaned over and touched Len's neck.

"Unbelievable. This guy's still alive." Then, using the microphone pinned to his chest, he called for an ambulance.

Elizabeth and Karon cried in relief, hugging each other. But when Elizabeth looked again at the blood, she realized she shouldn't get her hopes up.

More police arrived, and after listening to what happened in the house they went in search of Gil. To Elizabeth they seemed reluctant. Elizabeth remained with Karon, quickly coming to understand from her grief how deeply she felt about Len.

The owner of the house had dumped leaves and grass clippings on top of the lumber, and Gil was frantically throwing it to the side by huge handfuls. Finally he reached the boards, but couldn't lift them. Again he threw and kicked grass aside frantically, fearful the police could arrive at any time. When half of the grass had been moved, he grabbed the board and lifted. This time it moved and he dug underneath for the gun. It was there, but when he had it in his hand he didn't find the confidence he expected. If he had to shoot it out with the police he knew he would lose. To escape he needed stealth, or if backed into a corner, his power. He wanted the gun only for Ralph, who was somehow immune to his power.

Gun in hand, he crossed the alley and hopped a fence, cutting between houses to emerge on the opposite side of the block. The street was empty, and he crossed, again cutting between houses and over two fences to the far side of the next block. This time he set off a yapping terrier in the yard next door and an upstairs light came on. Hurrying on, he heard the neighbor yelling at his dog to shut up.

Again the street was empty, and he turned toward town, wanting to lose himself. But it was hours until dawn and no crowd to mingle with. Gil fingered the gun in his pocket, trying to form a plan. The streets were too empty—he was too obvious. When the morning rush started he could mix in and lose himself, but for now he needed to hide. As if to underscore his plan, a police car with lights flashing crossed two blocks away. Reflexively pulling the gun, Gil ducked into a yard, hiding behind a hedge. When he was sure the police car wasn't returning, he hurried down the block, looking for a place to hide.

* * *

The EMTs shook their heads when Elizabeth asked about Len's chances. Then they carried him down the stairs to the ambulance. Karon went with them, riding in the back with Len. Daphne was playing piano when she came back in, Wes talking to a policewoman.

"I'm OK, Elizabeth," Wes assured her. "Put them back to bed."

She left Daphne playing, while Ralph helped her get Yu and Archie in bed again. Neither of them spoke, but they both looked scared. Ralph was helpful, but neither of his moods was showing—not happy or concerned. He was cold now, showing no emotion and talking little.

When Yu and Archie were settled in, Ralph talked Daphne into going to bed, but she sat upright, her arms twitching as if she wanted to play the invisible piano but something was holding her arms down. When Elizabeth tried to reassure her, Daphne interrupted, tearfully.

"It's my fault!"

"It's not your fault, Daphne. It's Gil. He's a bad man. No one's to blame except him."

"It's me."

"Daphne, you can't blame yourself for this. You didn't do it, and you couldn't prevent it."

"You don't understand."

"I know what you're feeling. If anyone is to blame, it's me. I knew Gil was dangerous. I should have insisted the police arrest him."

"I should be arrested."

"Daphne, please don't blame yourself. You've never hurt anyone."

Then Daphne burst into tears, and Elizabeth sat holding her. This time Daphne hugged her back and they sat rocking, taking solace in each other's presence. When she had control again, Daphne let go, rolled over, and pulled the covers over her head. Even through her own pain Elizabeth could see that the breakthrough Daphne had made was continuing—she was coming out, sharing her pain. Unfortunately, Elizabeth wasn't in emotional shape to take pleasure in it.

Officer Roy Winston was with Wes, asking him questions about what happened, and writing in his notebook.

"We were trying to wait for the police," Wes explained, "but when I saw him start into Daphne's room with that knife I didn't think I could. So I charged him. That's when he knocked me down the stairs."

"He did this without touching you? And that's what he did to my officers?"

"He's got the power, all right. I can hardly believe it, even after he hit me." Then, seeing Elizabeth, he asked, "How's Len?"

"Alive, but barely."

Roy gave them a few seconds of silence to think of their friend. Then he motioned for Elizabeth to sit next to Wes on the couch. When she did, Wes winced, holding his arm tighter across his chest.

"He used that power on your friend upstairs?"

"That's what Ralph and Karon said," Elizabeth explained. "Gil sent him flying through the air."

Concerned, Roy looked thoughtful. "Could he stop a bullet with this power?"

Elizabeth and Wes exchanged glances, then shrugged—they didn't know.

"Does a power like this have limited range? I mean, if we can't get close to him can we nail him with a sniper scope and a rifle?"

"We don't know," Elizabeth said. "I've never studied this."

"No one has," Wes said. "There's never been a documented case like this. Many people have claimed to be able to do what he does, but no one could ever demonstrate under controlled conditions."

"Well, if you don't know what you were dealing with, then why in hell were you experimenting with it?"

"My experiment had nothing to do with this! You never understood that."

"I understand there's twenty years' worth of bodies in this town, and somehow you and your experiment are at the center of things. Now, if you know of anything that would help me stop this freak I'd like to hear it."

Wes sat in silent depression; only Elizabeth spoke.

"Maybe Dr. Birnbaum will be able to help. He's studied the paranormal. He said he'd try to be here in a few days."

"Fine, but I need help tonight. There's a psychic killer on the loose in my town and I've got to stop him."

Another officer came in.

"They found two more bodies, Chief. One of them is another of those fraternity boys—stabbed to death."

The policeman turned to Wes and Elizabeth, a dark look on his face. "What kind of evil did you bring to this town?"

31

CORNERED

Wes fell asleep on the couch, and woke only when Archie parked in front of the TV, turning it up loud. He used his good arm to push himself into a sitting position, his other arm throbbing with each move. His elbow was purple and swollen.

"It's broken."

Wes looked up to see Elizabeth staring down at him.

"I'm sure it's not."

"Then stretch your arm out."

"It's a little sore."

"It's broken. We'll get it X-rayed when we go visit Len. He just got out of surgery. He's alive, but he's critical."

Len's name brought back dark images of the night before, and sad feelings. "Did they find Gil?"

"No. But he won't come back here."

"You don't know that. He came back last night—you know why, don't you?"

"He was part of Frankie. But we didn't run the experiment, so how? What triggered the integration?"

Wes shook his head. Luis was dead, Len near death, and he was blaming himself. He couldn't think clearly.

Elizabeth left to help get the savants breakfast and insisted

Wes stay on the couch. He protested, but when he tried to stand he found he was hurting in more places than just his arm. Instead, he lay back down on the couch and closed his eyes, trying to ignore the pain.

"You asleep, Wes?" Ralph asked loudly. "You look asleep on account you got your eyes closed."

"I'm not asleep."

"I didn't think you was. You'd go up to your room if you wanted to sleep, wouldn't you? I would. Course I still got my PJs on. That means pajamas."

"Ralph, I don't feel too well. Why don't you watch TV until breakfast is ready."

"Well okeydokey then." Ralph turned away, then stopped, thumping himself on the head. "How could I be so stupid? That's why you're laying down. You don't feel so good. Want me to get you an aspirin or an Ex-Lax or something?"

"No. I'm fine."

"Want some of that yucky orange medicine Elizabeth makes us take when we got a cold or allergy or something?"

"I just need to lie here quietly."

"Well okeydokey then."

This time Ralph joined Archie in front of the TV, watching a cartoon. Wes was relieved, but also saddened. Ralph had shown concern last night, and even bravery in the way he had gone after Gil. But none of those noble characteristics were with him now—he was just plain retarded Ralph again.

Settling his head deep into the pillow, he relaxed, forgetting about Ralph and trying to split off his guilt and worry to give himself a few minutes of peace—a time for healing and renewal. Then the piano playing started.

Wes gave up and worked himself up into a sitting position. Between the noises from the kitchen, the sound of the TV, and Daphne's piano playing, you would have thought it was a normal day. But the sounds were different, and the atmosphere thick with sadness. Daphne's playing was ragged, and Wes could see her eyes were puffy from crying. He wondered if she had slept at all.

After Elizabeth called them to breakfast, she took time to sit with Daphne, reassuring her that what had happened wasn't her fault. But Daphne wouldn't be soothed and came to the table crying.

Elizabeth had Ralph help Wes to his feet, Wes amazed at the strength in someone who never carried anything heavier than a box full of Slurpees. Once at the table he found it hurt to let his arm hang, so he unbuttoned one shirt button and slipped his arm in, using his shirt as a sling. Ralph watched curiously and then asked, "Are you scratching your stomach?"

The doorbell rang and Ralph bolted, talking to someone at the door. He was back in a minute. "There's a woman and a man in a wheelchair. His name is Dr. Bin-bam."

It was light, but not late enough yet. Gil wanted people around when he emerged. He could suggest his way into a car or use them as hostages if he needed to. With people around he could push them into traffic, creating snarls that would prevent pursuit. If he created enough havoc he knew he could escape. So he waited in his hiding place, startled whenever a police siren sounded in the distance.

Gil fingered the gun again. He thought about leaving it behind, but then he thought of Ralph. Why didn't his power work on that retard? Could there be others like Ralph? If so, he needed to find a way to handle them with his power. Gil leaned out to see the sky. Soon it would be time.

He settled back, practicing his anger meditation. He'd discovered he could get angry and maintain it if he focused on the injustice of what was happening. They were hunting him, yet they were inferior. They didn't have his power, which he considered more than just a genetic fluke. It was a gift—a sign—and he was the one chosen to receive it, and if it was given it was meant to be used. He had only killed when absolutely necessary, and then only in self-defense. If they knew about him—as they did now—they would be jealous. They would lock him up and study him; it would be like the bug studying the humans. No, he decided, they weren't his equal, and hunting him was unjust. Convinced of his personal righteousness, he used it to fuel his sense of persecution. Out of that came his anger. Red-hot, but slow-burning anger. An anger that energized his power.

Elizabeth steadied the front of the wheelchair while Ralph lifted from behind. The motorized chair barely taxed Ralph's strength, and they managed to get Dr. Birnbaum step by step up onto the porch, then into the house. When Ralph saw the chair in action he broke out into a huge, sloppy grin.

"Can I drive your chair? I'll be careful. I won't crash into anything or nothing like that."

"Ralph," Elizabeth explained, "Dr. Birnbaum needs his chair to get around. It's not a toy."

Ralph looked disappointed, and stood staring at Dr. Birnbaum. Then, out of the blue, he asked, "Where'd your other leg go?"

Elizabeth rolled her eyes, but Dr. Birnbaum responded evenly.

"I was hurt in an accident, and they had to amputate it."

"Am-pu-tate. What's that mean?"

"They had to cut my leg off."

"Yuck. Did it hurt?"

"I was asleep when they did it."

"You didn't wake up? Did they cut your pajama leg off, too?"

"Ralph, would you please leave him alone," Wes said, embarrassed.

"No, I don't mind the questions. It's refreshing to have someone be so honest with what they're thinking." Then to Ralph he said, "Amputation is a special operation a doctor does. They use anesthetic so you go to sleep and don't feel a thing. You're naked when they do it so your pajamas aren't cut."

"That's good. I'd hate to ruin a good pair of jamas." Ralph switched his attention from the missing leg to the empty shirtsleeve. "Are you scratching your stomach?"

"What?"

"Wes has his arm in his shirt cause he's scratching his stomach. Is that what you're doing?"

"No. My arm is gone, too."

"You're missing quite a few pieces. Kind of like that jigsaw puzzle Archie put together last week. Archie's good at jigsaw puzzles."

"So I've heard. Now, Ralph, I really need to talk with Ms. Foxworth, if you don't mind."

"Go finish your breakfast, Ralph," Elizabeth said gently.

"Well okeydokey then," and he was off.

"Interesting man," Dr. Birnbaum said. "Is he a savant?"

"No. He's a stabilizing influence," she explained. "I'll tell you about him later. Right now there's some things I have to tell you—something's happened."

Karon took Mrs. Birnbaum to get a cup of tea, while Elizabeth explained all that had happened. Dr. Birnbaum's face darkened as he listened.

"Incredible! He's telekinetic. But it's PK at a level I've never heard of. There's nothing like this recorded in the literature. Dr. Martin, do you have burn marks where the force hit you?"

"Burns? I don't think so. My chest still hurts, but I think it's bruised."

"Please check for burns. Some researchers report an electrical charge associated with telekinesis. Of course it's always been very low-level, but with his power it might create quite a charge."

Wes asked Elizabeth to help him with his shirt. They didn't take it off because of his arm, but they pushed it up, revealing a bright red circle on his chest. Elizabeth poked it with her finger.

"Is it tender?" Dr. Birnbaum asked.

"Feels like a mild sunburn."

"Interesting. Most interesting. Your friend—Len? Was he burned?"

"There was so much blood . . ." Elizabeth said.

"I'm sorry. That was insensitive. It's just that I've spent most of my professional life looking for real psi ability. This sounds real."

"It is," Wes said. "He turned and stared at me and knocked me down the stairs without a touch. Then he knocked Len half the length of the hall and still had enough force to nearly put him through the wall. As he escaped he knocked down two policemen and Elizabeth. It's real all right, and he's a killer."

Dr. Birnbaum looked thoughtful, pulling at his lip with his one arm. "He crushed Len's chest, didn't you say? But he only knocked you down—it was the fall down the stairs that injured your arm, wasn't it?"

"He rolled me along the floor a way, but yes, I hurt my arm when I hit bottom. What are you getting at?"

"I was just wondering why you weren't hit as hard as your friend. You ended up with a sunburn, not a crushed chest."

"I surprised him, and he had to turn pretty quickly."

"Yes, but why would that make a difference? Psi power would operate at the speed of thought. It should be instantaneous."

Wes didn't know anything about psychic ability, but he knew

the research on thought. "You would think so, but thought operates in real time. For example, if you have someone picture a map, and have them picture a line being drawn from one part of the map to another, the farther apart on the map the longer it takes for them to complete the line even though it's just an imaginary map, and it's all done at the speed of thought. I've seen the research on this."

"Interesting. Still, once he decided to use the power on you the thought would have been completed?"

Wes found himself drawn into the problem. "It could be he hit me a glancing blow."

"Yes, but he had more time with the policemen—correct?"

"The police said they stared at each other for a couple of seconds," Elizabeth answered.

"So he had time to aim straight—if that's the right way to put it. I believe you said the police were knocked down, but not tumbled along the walk. Elizabeth's blow was weaker yet—correct?"

Wes could see that Dr. Birnbaum liked to be fed ideas to chew on, so he offered up another. "Perhaps the power diminishes with each use, and he must rest to recharge it."

"A much better hypothesis. It fits with most of the facts. Your friend was nearly crushed with the force, but subsequent attacks were weaker."

"This may be the kind of thing Roy Winston needs to know," Elizabeth said. "He's the officer in charge of the case. He asked if there was some way to stop Gil. I suppose we can suggest that they force him to use his power over and over, until they can subdue him."

Dr. Birnbaum stared at her, a strange amused look on his face. "My dear Ms. Foxworth, they won't subdue him, they will kill him—if they can."

Wes watched Elizabeth's face, but she showed no emotion.

"If you must share our hypotheses, then do so with proper caution," Birnbaum continued. "The police could bet their lives on our speculation and I don't want that responsibility. Besides, there is another possibility. What Wes said about him being surprised by Wes's attack suggests that his powers are narrow. I believe he can project his thoughts to others, and we know he is telekinetic, but he's not a telepath, nor capable of remote viewing. Otherwise you wouldn't have been able to sneak up behind him, and he certainly would have been aware of the police outside. It suggests to me that he needs to look at the person he is trying to influence. The limitation your police friend is looking for may be line-of-sight."

It was an intriguing idea, but Wes couldn't see how it would help. If the police could see Gil, then he could see them.

The doorbell announced Roy's return.

"I need a piece of Gil's clothing," the policeman said. "We're going to track him with a dog."

Elizabeth retrieved a shirt, which they took outside and offered to a pair of hounds tugging hyperactively at leashes held by a man in work boots and wearing a flannel shirt. When the dogs had a noseful the man led them to the backyard and the search began, the dogs quickly leading them past the garage and down the alley.

Wes watched them go, and then Elizabeth took his good arm and led him back into the house.

"It's time to go to the hospital," she said.

The dogs led them down the alley to a garage where they yelped and barked while they dug at a pile of leaves. Roy had his men probe the pile and then search the garage, finding nothing.

"Kelly, you sure your dogs have the scent?"

"Absolutely, Roy. You can tell by the way they bark. He was here all right, and left a pretty good scent. Get your men out of the alley and let me circle the dogs."

Roy ordered his men to line up along the fence, and then Kelly Johnston circled with his dogs. On the second pass one of the dogs jerked toward the far fence, and soon both were yelping, and trying to climb over. Kelly gave them enough lead and they jumped it, nearly pulling him into it.

"It's a hot trail again, Roy. Let's get after him."

The police followed him over the fence and through the yard. Kelly's dogs set the neighborhood animals to barking out turf warnings, and soon neighbors were appearing, watching the police climb over fences and cut through yards. They crossed the next block, but then the dogs turned down the sidewalk, yelping and straining on the leash.

"I think we're close, Roy. You want me to turn them loose?"

"No! Just find him."

"You're the boss, but King and Bud would love to soften him up for you."

The dogs strained harder, and Kelly stumbled along behind, barely able to contain them. They reached the corner, and then the dogs veered right and into a yard, straining toward the porch. As they reached the porch, their yapping changed, and Kelly suddenly pulled them up short.

"They got him treed. I think he's under the porch."

Quickly, Roy surveyed the porch. Ordering Kelly and the dogs back, Roy drew his revolver and motioned his officers to pull back, taking cover behind cars and trees. Rifle bolts working cartridges into place, and shotguns being cocked, were the only sounds on the quiet street. He called for the cars to be brought around and soon the front yard was ringed with police cars. When everyone was ready he sent a man to the back to evacuate the house and the houses on either side. When they were secure, he shouted out an order.

"This is the police. We have you surrounded. Come out from under the porch!"

Neighbors came out of the houses behind them and Roy's men were distracted while they evacuated the newcomers. Once again secure, he repeated his order. Still, nothing happened.

"Want me to send in the dogs, Roy? King and Bud are eager as hell. They mostly track down dead people. This would be a real treat for the boys."

Roy hesitated, not wanting to hurt the dogs but unwilling to risk one of his men either. "He's dangerous, Kelly."

Kelly smiled excitedly. "He's the one's going to get hurt. You just watch King and Bud in action." Then, bending to the dogs, he snapped off their leashes, releasing one and then the other.

The first dog bolted toward the porch with the other close behind. The dog leapt a bush and burrowed down and under the porch, snapping and snarling as he crawled underneath. The second dog jammed its head in the hole, trying to climb over the first. Then the end of the porch exploded.

Splintering wood and the squeals of the dogs were the only sounds, as they were blasted into the air and across the yard. Fragments of the wood that made up the porch whistled through the air like shrapnel, showering the police hidden behind a car. The dogs cleared the car, only to land in the driveway. Both dogs bounced, and tumbled, but only one could get up when they came to rest. It limped down the street, whining pitifully.

"King? Bud? Oh, no! King, come on back, boy."

Kelly chased after the injured dog, which was whining in a human way.

Quickly checking his police, Roy made sure none had been injured. They all turned to him for an explanation. Signaling, he pulled three of them off the line and had them join him for a briefing. Whispering so that the hidden Gil couldn't hear him, he explained the situation.

"I told you those people were experimenting with psychic stuff. That guy under the porch has the ability to knock people around. Campbell here and Lee felt it when he knocked them down."

Campbell nodded, but added, "It wasn't so much."

"Yeah, but you saw what it did to that poor guy with the crushed chest. Now, we can handle him, but we've just got to be careful. Don't take any chances. If he doesn't come out soon we'll fire on his hiding place—it'll give him something to think about."

The officers smiled in anticipation, confident their guns would solve the problem.

The dogs had been too stupid to hold his suggestions, so Gil had no choice but to push them away. He only hoped it would give him time to get away. Crawling back toward the house, he passed through an opening in the foundation and into the crawl-space. Then, belly-crawling, he worked his way under the floor until he found the trapdoor into the house. It came up easily, and he found himself in a closet. Gun in hand, he opened the door quietly, alert for police.

The closet emptied into a hall, and he followed it to a kitchen—empty. The back door was unlocked, but he paused, scanning the yard. No police in sight—they were sure he was still under the porch. Brushing the dirt from his clothes, he then let himself out and trotted across the backyard, climbed the fence, and crossed the next yard out to the street. There were people to his left on the corner trying to see the police action. He joined them, acting curious. He wanted to run but was afraid of suspicion if he went too quickly. Working along the line of people, he found a spot where he could see the police hiding behind their cars. Then he got an idea. Staring hard at two officers he made a suggestion, and then pushed.

The warning not to take chances, and the promise that they would shoot rather than rush the hiding place, reassured the officers, and they smiled, nodded, and moved back to share the briefing with the others. When the word had spread, Roy used a bullhorn to shout out another command to come out from under the porch—again, no reply. While he was waiting for a response, he saw something peculiar. Two of his officers were leaning over a car, shotguns trained on the porch. Suddenly their faces went blank, and they turned toward each other, swinging their shotguns as they did. Roy screamed a warning, but it was too late. Once face-to-face, shotguns at stomach level, they both fired.

He started forward in a futile attempt to help but then realized the danger—they could all shoot each other. "Open fire. Everyone fire at the porch."

Gunfire erupted, and the porch was peppered with bullet holes. Roy reached the officers, but the wounds were too great and their blood flooded the street, red rivulets running under the car they had hidden behind. Angry at himself, he stood, emptying his pistol at the porch. Then he squatted, reloading. He emptied it again, and reloaded before calling a cease-fire. The porch was riddled with holes and more covered the front wall of the house. The front windows were gone.

"Give yourself up. Come out if you still can."

They waited, but no sound came from the porch. Roy knew his situation was worse now. He had no idea if the man under the porch was still alive, and he had limited choices. He could send someone to look under the porch, but if the psychic was still alive whoever he sent would likely be killed. He could wait, hoping the man would finally give up, but he had no idea how long it would take.

He studied the porch, noticing that it ran the full width of the house. The base seemed to be an extension of the foundation, and there was ample concrete to hide behind below the wood that made up the bulk of the porch. He decided that waiting was the best option, then radioed to have tear gas delivered. Now, looking down at the two downed officers next to him, he vowed this killer would never get away—no matter what power he had.

Gil could hear the gunfire behind him as he walked into town. There were people here now and all he needed was the right opportunity. Casually ducking in and out of doorways, he found a stretch of empty parking spaces and then waited for someone to pull up in their car. All he had to do was suggest they leave their keys behind and he would use the car to get out of the city. Normally he wouldn't risk driving a stolen car, but this was an emergency. It would get him away and he would abandon it within an hour.

A car pulled into one of the spaces and Gil pretended to be looking in the store window. Just as the driver turned off the engine he suggested she already had the keys in her purse and pushed. The woman's hand dropped to her purse and she got out of the car, leaving the keys behind, but then she pushed down on the door lock and slammed the door. Frustrated, Gil nearly slammed her with his power.

The sound of distant shooting had stopped now, and Gil worried that the hunt would be on again soon. He might have to hijack a car with the gun if another car didn't turn up soon. Acting casual, he leaned against the side of the building, checking his watch occasionally as if he were waiting for someone. Then he noticed someone watching him from across the street—it was an old lady. He had seen her somewhere before—she was from the neighborhood. She finished staring and then turned into a grocery store across the street. Gil could feel danger as if he were prescient, and hurried away. It was time for desperate measures.

Roy Winston ran his hands through his graying hair, watching one of his men work his way closer with the tear-gas gun. It would be a tricky shot, since the opening was behind the shrubs. The best shot would be if they stood on top of a car, but no one would risk standing out in the open like that. He had ordered his officers to watch each other and if they pointed their guns anywhere but toward the porch to punch each other. No one questioned the strange order.

The officer with the tear gas was nearly in place when a policewoman leaned out of a car shouting to him.

"Do you know a Mrs. Clayton? She just called the station and said she saw this Gil guy in town by the pharmacy."

Briefly frozen, he then turned and sprinted toward the porch, ignoring the shouts of his men. Jumping the shrubs, he ducked down and peeked into the hole. "Damn!" he shouted. "There's a hole into the foundation. He's in town."

Cars were already leaving when he reached his, climbing in next to Chris, who had taken the call. Grabbing the radio, he began giving instructions so that they all didn't converge on the pharmacy.

It was only a few blocks to town and when they arrived, two officers were already inside searching. Other officers were searching the surrounding buildings. When they found Mrs. Clayton, she pointed down the block. Chris didn't wait for a translation; she floored the accelerator, squealing down the street in the direction of her point.

On the radio again Ray gave general directions, sending the patrol cars in a crisscross pattern through the streets. He cautioned Chris to slow down, and they drove up and down the blocks scanning the passersby.

A man in a hurry zoomed his pickup into the 7-Eleven parking lot, and Gil suggested he leave his keys behind. He did, and as soon as he was out, Gil passed him, climbing into his car. The man looked back when he heard his car start, and shouted at Gil. Gil put it in reverse, smoking the tires as he backed up. When he paused to shift into first the man jumped onto the passenger-side running board, cussing Gil and threatening him. He found it easy to be angry that someone insignificant as the man on the running board would dare threaten him. Gil held him in a cold stare, then pictured a rock the size of a basketball, and pushed. The window exploded in the man's face, his head nearly knocked from his shoulders. A woman running to help stopped and screamed when she saw the remains of his face. Gil floored it, drowning her screams in the squeal of his tires, and raced out of the driveway toward freedom.

* * *

Chris was an excellent driver and worked through the intersections expertly, using only her flashing lights as a warning. Up and down the blocks they worked, passing other patrol cars at intersections. They were working out of the business district into the east residential district, and on the other side of that was the freeway. Roy knew that if he had gotten that far he could have hitched a ride and gotten away.

Chris's head snapped back and forth, looking up and down the streets faster than Roy could, but he trusted her young eyes and let her work at her own pace. Suddenly she hit the brakes.

"Did you see that?"

Without waiting for a reply she put it in reverse and backed into the left lane, continuing into the intersection. Pointing across Roy's chest, she said, "Something's going on."

At the end of the block in the 7-Eleven parking lot a man was standing on the running board of a pickup. Suddenly the window exploded, the man's head snapping back and his body tumbling toward a woman coming out of the store.

"Jeez!" Chris said. "It's got to be him."

Before Roy could answer the pickup came roaring down the street. Without waiting for instructions Chris backed out of the intersection, swerving back into the right lane, and then she waited, counting to herself.

"Seven, six, five, four . . ."

Roy grabbed the microphone, giving instructions to other patrol cars.

". . . three, two, one, now!"

With a roar she shot into the intersection, cutting off the pickup, which screeched to a halt inches from their car. Roy found himself staring face-to-face with Gil. Stunned, they both stared, unsure of what to do. Then Roy pulled the shotgun from the dash holder and opened the car door. When he stepped out, the windshield of the pickup exploded and his door was slammed into him, his hip taking most of the force. When the door bounced off his body, he collapsed, quickly pulling his legs out of the opening to keep them from getting crushed. Just as he did the door slammed again, a huge dent appearing over the police emblem.

Roy rolled to his stomach and brought the shotgun up, firing wildly and hitting the truck's grille. Escaping steam whistled and blocked his view, but he fired blindly anyway, hitting the grille again. Still the engine kept running and the pickup went into reverse, racing backward down the street. Bystanders ducked into stores and behind cars to get out of the line of fire.

Roy got to his feet and yanked the door open.

"Get in!" Chris yelled.

Roy barely had his feet inside when she put it in gear and turned, gunning the motor to race after him.

"Are you all right?"

"Yeah. I'll be sore tonight, but not as bad off as he's gonna be," he said coldly.

Chris glanced over at him, then nodded her head. "I'm with you!"

The pickup continued its backward race, heading to the other end of the block. It was nearly there when another patrol car blocked the street, cutting off his escape.

"It's going to get ugly now," Chris said, slowing slightly, watching for his escape move.

Then the door opened and Gil leaned out, looking at the police car blocking his path.

Roy grabbed the microphone to shout a warning but it was too late. The police windshield imploded; then Gil jumped back in and pulled forward. Chris spun the wheel, putting the car into a sideways skid, blocking his advance. Gil swerved right and into the 7-Eleven parking lot, Chris right behind, sliding to a stop. Shotgun in hand, Roy got out, shouting for him to stop. He didn't, but his head turned, fixing Roy in an icy stare. Roy jerked at the trigger just as an invisible wall hit him, knocking him back against the car and slamming the door on his legs. The shotgun fired, but the blast went wide, shattering a window in the 7-Eleven.

Chris leaned across the cab, weapon in hand, and fired as Gil disappeared into the building. Suddenly they were slammed again, Chris knocked back onto the pavement. Roy jerked his legs out of the way just as the door slammed shut.

Screams came from the 7-Eleven and then shouting. Silence followed, and then a shout from Gil.

"If you try to come in I'll kill them! Do you hear me? I'll smash them like flies!"

Roy shouted for everyone to take cover and to call for additional units. Chris leaned in the window, her nose bleeding. "Are you all right?" she asked.

"Nothing broken, but my shin's scraped all to hell. How about you? Your nose is bleeding."

"My wrist is broken, too," she said, then held up her left arm gingerly, her hand hanging limp. "But I'll live."

Roy wished he shared her confidence.

Panicky now, Gil worked at keeping his anger level up. He couldn't afford to lose his power now. Menacing with the gun, he herded the customers toward the back, away from the windows. Ordering them to sit in a circle around him, he squatted, looking fearfully down the aisles, expecting an attack at any minute. After a few minutes he was confident they'd believed his threat and he sat, now becoming aware of his hostages.

There were four men and three women, one the clerk. One of the women was blubbering, and it irritated him, keeping his anger high. The women all averted their eyes when he looked at them, and he knew he had nothing to fear from them. When he scanned the men's faces only one stared back. Gil recognized him. He was from the fraternity he'd used to try and get rid of Ralph. Gil's nostrils flared as his anger flamed. He'd taken some revenge on them, but not enough. More important, this one didn't look scared—wary, yes, but he looked like he was plotting. Gil wanted to kill him then, to smash his smug face in with all his power. He pictured a spiked mace swinging at his head then pictured what the spikes would do to his face and eyes, but held back. He might have a better use for him, and still get revenge.

The 7-Eleven was encircled with patrol cars, police armed with shotguns and rifles. This time there would be no escape. Roy used a bullhorn to call to Gil. Chris stood next to him, holding her left arm to keep the wrist from moving around. She refused to go to the hospital until she could "see him go down." Flipping on the bullhorn, Roy said, "Gil, there is no escape. Come out with your hands up."

A minute later a person appeared in front of the glass door, but it wasn't Gil and he was facing backward.

"He's got hostages," Chris said.

With a bang the doors were blown open and the man was ejected from the store, tumbling across the parking lot toward the police cars, stopping twenty feet away. Two officers moved to help him, but Roy shouted for them to stop.

The man struggled to his feet, breathing raggedly and holding his chest. Roy recognized him, he was from the fraternity where the boys had been killed—Ron Classen, the chapter president. He staggered in a circle, dazed, unsure of direction. The police shouted to him, but the multiple voices confused him and he continued to circle, trying to localize himself. Roy shouted down the other officers, then called out to Ron, giving him directions. Soon he was stumbling toward Roy, following his voice. As he reached the car, he steadied himself on the hood, working around the front. Roy reached out, taking his arm. Suddenly something whistled through the air, the police shouting a warning. Too late, it hit Ron dead center in his back, knocking him into Roy. Together they collapsed, the injured fraternity brother on top. Fearing he was dead, Roy put his ear to the boy's lips—he could hear shallow breathing.

Chris picked up a can of pork and beans that had flattened against Ron's back, shaking her head. "How are we gonna stop this guy? Nuke the Seven-Eleven?"

Thinking of the two dead police officers, and the injured people around him, Roy wondered if even a bomb would stop him.

32

HOSTAGES

Wes was still in radiology when the ambulance arrived with the injured officers. Elizabeth watched in the emergency room while they tried to revive them. Then she listened in horror as a policeman told how he had watched his friends shoot each other. A doctor quickly confirmed that the damage was extensive, shredding their intestines, and severing the spine of one officer.

Wes was in the cast room when an ambulance arrived with two men injured at the 7-Eleven. One was dead, the other unconscious. They were treating Ron Classen for spinal injury and quickly rolled him out of sight. The other body lay on a gurney; the sheet covering the body was bloody around the head. The policemen who accompanied the casualties told of their windshield spontaneously shattering, and other horrors happening around the 7-Eleven.

When Wes's cast was finished Elizabeth hustled him out the door and into the car, filling him in on what had happened. "We've got to do something," she declared. But he didn't know what, and had no response.

Roy Winston pounded on the door, and then walked in before Ralph could open it.

"Hi, how ya doin'," Ralph said in his usual friendly way, extending his hand.

"Is Dr. Birnbaum still here?"

"I call him Dr. Bin-Bam. He likes it though."

"Is he here?"

"Yeah. His wife, too. They're in the kitchen. I can show you the way."

Karon was working with Archie and Yu in the living room, and as soon as Daphne saw the policeman she went to the piano and began playing. Ralph led him to the kitchen, then stood against the wall, his jaw working a mouthful of gum. Dr. Birnbaum was in his wheelchair at the table, drinking coffee with his wife and Shamita.

"Dr. Birnbaum, my name's Roy Winston. We didn't get to meet last night."

"Have you caught him yet?"

"We have him cornered in the Seven-Eleven, but we can't get to him. He's got this power—he can knock you down by just looking at you."

"Telekinesis! But I've never heard of it at his power level."

"He's killed three people we know of—another might die. We need some way to stop him."

Dr. Birnbaum drove his chair up close to Roy. "Tell me what's happened."

Roy began with a summary but Dr. Birnbaum had him start over, describing every event in detail. When he got to the incidents at the 7-Eleven he stopped him.

"You say he leaned out of his pickup and faced the police car behind him? That confirms what I've been thinking. Don't you understand?"

Roy didn't, and shook his head.

"It means he has to see to use his power. And a mirror won't work or else he would have used the rearview mirror in the truck. Does that help you?"

"Maybe, but we have to see him to stop him, and if we can see him . . ." Roy faded out, toying with a couple of ideas. Then he was back. "He got two of my officers to shoot each other when he was hiding under a porch. How'd he see us then?"

"He must have already fled his hiding place. He was in the crowd somewhere when he attacked your officers."

"That figures, I guess," Roy said. "What else can you tell me?"

"For some reason his power seems to come and go. Not everyone that he used it on was as badly injured as that young man last night. He seems to need to recharge."

"It's been pretty consistent today. He's hit us hard over and over."

Dr. Birnbaum looked disappointed. "That's all I can tell you for now. Would you like me to come to the scene?"

Roy Winston didn't want a handicapped man anywhere near the 7-Eleven, but decided he might be useful at the command center a few blocks away. When he agreed to take the professor with him, Dr. Birnbaum's wife objected, worried over his safety. Only after he reassured her that they would keep Dr. Birnbaum at a safe distance did she relent. When he turned to leave he found Daphne standing in the doorway, head up, staring wide-eyed. When he reached out to move her aside, she broke her stare and hurried to the piano, pounding out "Love Lifted Me."

On the porch, Ralph helped lift the wheelchair down the stairs and then into the Birnbaums' van, sitting in the front passenger seat.

"Ralph, you can't go with us," Dr. Birnbaum said.

"I should go. Gil likes me."

"No, Ralph. Gil is very dangerous."

"I should go."

"No," Dr. Birnbaum said firmly.

Folding his arms across his chest, Ralph puckered his lips and assumed his concerned posture.

"Get out of the car, Ralph," Shamita ordered.

Ralph hesitated, then reluctantly got out.

The Birnbaums drove off, following the police car and leaving Ralph on the sidewalk, his arms across his chest, his lip protruded in concern. Once they were out of sight, the others returned to the house. Ralph followed them as far as the porch, where he sat on the top step, lips still tightly puckered. When the others were inside, Ralph hurried down the stairs and down the block toward the 7-Eleven, striding along at full speed.

His hostages knew of his power but it was the gun they stared at—a gun was tangible. Their fear of the gun worked for Gil, because if all six of them bolted in different directions at the same

time most of them would get away. As soon as they darted
around an aisle corner out of his sight he couldn't use his power
on them. Ironically, Frankie had done him a favor by providing
the gun.

Checking his watch, he found it was nearly time to kill another of the hostages. He didn't want to do it. Not because he
valued human life; he didn't. He wanted a human shield around
him when he walked out. Killing one meant more space between
the others, making him more vulnerable to the police snipers.

One of the three women hostages checked her watch and
began crying. She knew it was nearly time. Gil glared at her and
she shrank back, trying to stifle her sobs. She would go next, Gil
decided. He wasn't going to put up with the blubbering—he had
enough to worry about.

Gil studied the building, tracing the rafters, determining which
were the load-bearing walls. The front of the building was almost entirely glass, the other three sides concrete block. He
knew the wall he had taken refuge against was shared with a
video rental store on the other side. There weren't many escape
options and his best hope was still the hostages.

Wes followed Elizabeth into the house, where Elizabeth immediately described Len's condition for Karon and Shamita and
then explained all that had happened. Karon cried at the description of Len's injuries and soon excused herself to her room.
Daphne listened briefly, then settled in at the piano, but her playing was erratic, discordant. Soon she gave up and ran up the
stairs, slamming her bedroom door.

"You want me to comfort her?" Shamita asked.

"No, let's leave her alone. I hate to see her in so much pain,
but at least she's showing what she feels now."

After Elizabeth finished her story, Shamita told them about
Officer Winston's visit. Elizabeth and Wes frowned when they
heard that Dr. Birnbaum had gone to see if he could help. Wes
had an urgent need to help—to do something. He couldn't help
but blame himself for bringing this tragedy to these people.

"I might know a way to help the police with Gil," Wes said.

"What? How?"

"I don't want to do it—I don't think you'll want to either."

"Tell me!" Elizabeth demanded.

"We know that Gil came back to the house because he was Frankie. Even after Luis was dead Frankie still took control. What if we run the integration again and bring back Frankie."

"Of course," Elizabeth interrupted. "If we run the integration it might release Frankie and stop Gil."

Shamita joined the speculation. "Yes, we got Frankie even with drastically changed parameters. The Frankie without Luis wouldn't be as smart, and would be more of someone else, but it would still be Frankie. More important, as far as we know Frankie doesn't have the psychic powers Gil has. Frankie would be a lot easier to handle."

All agreed. Shamita went to set up the equipment—normally handled primarily by Len. Wes herded Archie and Yu into the experiment room, while Elizabeth retrieved Daphne and Karon. Wes was fitting Archie with his helmet when Elizabeth returned.

"Where's Ralph?" Elizabeth asked. "We could use him as part of the integration. Integration of his intellectual functions might lower Frankie's IQ even more. Integrating Ralph's emotions might make Frankie downright gentle." Elizabeth looked around confused. "Karon, where's Ralph?"

"I'm not sure. I haven't seen him since he helped get Dr. Birnbaum's chair out of the house."

"Oh no! He didn't go with them, did he?"

"Shamita wouldn't let him. She told him to get out of the car. The last time I saw him he was sitting on the porch pouting—you don't think he followed them, do you?"

Without replying, she told the others to proceed and then left to find Ralph.

Wes shared her concern, finding he really cared for Ralph. "Let's hurry," he said to the others. "This may be the best chance to stop Gil."

Gil had demanded a windowless van and free passage but Roy had stalled, saying he didn't have the authority to make the decision. Meanwhile he positioned snipers on the roofs surrounding the 7-Eleven. Gil and his hostages were in the back of the store out of sight of the sniper scopes. It kept him safe from a long-distance shot, but it also meant the police could sneak up to the front of the store undetected. That's where two of Roy's officers were now—one ready to fire tear gas, the other to throw smoke bombs. Birnbaum had approved of the plan, saying, "If he can't see, he shouldn't be able to use his power." Neither Roy or the good doctor were entirely confident of their plan, but even if Gil had been an ordinary criminal they wouldn't have given in to his demands. His power created a special revulsion in Roy, a revulsion magnified by the senseless deaths.

His men gave him the thumbs-up sign and then waited, watching Roy. He checked the placement of his men one more time, pulled his pistol, and signaled go.

The *frump* of the tear-gas gun announced the beginning of the action, the cylinder shattering the glass and then disappearing deep into the store. Then more windows were broken and the smoke canisters were thrown in—four, one toward each corner of the store. Another *frump,* and another tear-gas shell bounced off the ceiling and into the store.

Roy counted to ten, letting the store fill with smoke and gas, and then gave the go signal to his waiting men, who rushed forward, guns in hand.

Panic set in when the first shell burst in the next aisle, the gas quickly expanding. Gil screamed at his hostages to freeze, threatening to kill them if they moved. His eyes were already watering when the smoke came, and then another tear-gas shell. Then he knew how much they feared him—they were willing to sacrifice the hostages to make sure he didn't get away. They had no intention of giving him a getaway car and knew he would carry out his threat to kill the hostages. So, they had devised this plan, somehow knowing—more likely guessing—that limiting his sight would limit his power.

He'd anticipated this, and it made him feel even more superior, and that fueled his anger. *How dare they think they could outsmart me! Now they'll learn the truth.* His anger welled up and he nursed it, feeling it reach the levels he needed.

The room was filling with smoke—they would be coming soon. Shouting again at his hostages to hold them in place, he wiped his eyes and listened above their whimpering for the sounds of the police. The sound of more breaking of glass and the pounding of running men announced the attack. *Now I'll teach them!* "Run! I said run, or I'll kill you!"

The hostages looked at him, confused, hopeful, but also fearful. Through tearful eyes he saw the blubbering woman on her knees, too afraid to stand. Pointing the gun at her face, he screamed, "Get up or I'll blow your brains all over the wall!" She wet her pants, and then stood, crying, wiping her eyes, and stumbled through the smoke. Firing the gun into the air, he stampeded the hostages. At the sound of his gun the police ducked for cover. When the hostages had all disappeared into the smoke, he fired the rest of the rounds down the aisles. *Now for more havoc!*

Picturing a wrecking ball, he looked at the ceiling, barely able to pick out the center beam in the gathering smoke. Then he pushed the image with all his might. The beam crumpled and a hole was punched in the ceiling above it, but the ceiling didn't fall. He pushed again and this time the beam fell, bringing big chunks of ceiling with it. Then he turned toward a shelf of ketchup bottles, sending those hurtling into the fog. Somewhere in the gloom the bottles shattered and someone screamed. Jars and canned goods were fired, too, randomly strafing the room. When he was sure the police were either hunkered down or rescuing hostages, he used his power to smash the shelves covering the wall. Then he pictured the wrecking ball and pulverized the concrete block. When the hole was big enough to crawl through, he turned and hammered another of the two remaining beams. The beam bent under the force, then pulled away from the far wall, falling to the floor below. With most of the support gone, the whole ceiling crumpled, slowly at first, then coming down in big chunks. That's when he crawled through the wall into the video store.

Exhilarated by his own power and pleased with his own cleverness, Gil was smiling when he crawled over the rubble into the clean air of the video store. But his smile evaporated when he stood to see Ralph waiting for him on the other side.

With only three savants, they weren't sure integration could take place. Gil had been the matrix, but they used Daphne as a substitute. Leaving as much of Gil's section of the matrix free as they could, they hoped Frankie would fill it in with Gil.

"This won't work," Shamita said. "We can't integrate without intercepting Gil's brain waves."

"Just finish it, Shamita," Wes snapped. "Frankie has integrated

without us before. It must be Gil's psychic ability that links them
without the integration program."

"It's ready, run the integration," Shamita said. "It's sloppy."

"We'll tweak it if it doesn't work. Karon, everything within
parameters?"

Eyes red and puffy, Karon looked up from Len's monitor and
nodded.

"Here we go. I'm running it now." Piece by piece the Frankie
brain took shape, and soon a unique wave pattern was established, but Wes's practiced eye could see that it was different
from Frankie's wave.

"There's no Gil there," Shamita pointed out. "And that sub-
wave is missing. It's not working."

"If only we had Luis . . ."

"Wait . . . it is there . . . here it comes."

Wes watched his own monitor, picking up the peculiar wave,
but realizing it was different in some ways. Without Luis they
couldn't expect it to be the exact same wave, or could they?
More important, could they get Frankie? "Karon, find out if we
have Frankie. Daphne has audition."

Karon walked to Daphne's side. "Are you there, Frankie?"

No answer.

"Frankie can you hear me?"

"Ask if Pat's there," Shamita suggested.

"Are you there, Pat?"

No answer. Frustrated, Wes stared at his screen, wondering
what was happening at the 7-Eleven. Then he saw a subtle shift
in the wave pattern. "Shamita, what's happening?"

"The integration is re-forming. This is better . . . more like
Frankie . . . but not there yet."

Roy watched the debacle, fearing what the body count would be.
Soon after his police rushed in the shooting had started—but
who was getting shot? The smoke had worked for them and
against them, and he couldn't see what was happening. Then a
big chunk of the ceiling was blasted into the sky, telling him the
psychic was still alive. Screaming came from the store and then
one of his officers led a crying woman out of the smoke. Short-
lived relief spread through Roy. More screaming followed, and
another hostage appeared, and another. Then, with a roar, the

ceiling collapsed at one end of the building. Roy started forward with his other men to help, but then realized Gil had to be alive—he had dropped the ceiling for a reason. Roy studied the scene, trying to understand Gil's intentions. The building had collapsed at one end, but the end by the video store was still standing, and that's where Gil had taken refuge—now he understood.

Looking for backup, Roy realized everyone was engaged in rescue, except Chris with her broken wrist.

"Can you hold a gun?"

She smiled and nodded, drawing her weapon.

"Follow me."

Roy led her to the side of the video store, peeking around the corner. The store had been evacuated before they began the assault, but there were two people in it now. Gil was there, facing the big retarded kid, Ralph.

"You've been hurting people again, haven't you Gil?" Ralph said.

"Get out of my way, retard, or I'll hurt you, too."

"It's not nice to call people names, Gil. I don't call you names."

Gil looked right and spotted an emergency exit. It was a way out but he'd have to get past Ralph first, and he wasn't sure he could. He could smash up the video store as he had the 7-Eleven, but that might bring the police—if only he'd saved a couple of rounds from the gun he could put a bullet in the moron's head. Clearly Ralph wouldn't move out of his way, so he stepped sideways, and at the same time sent video cassettes flying. Instinctively, Ralph put up his arms, deflecting the tapes.

"Ow! That hurts, Gil."

More tapes pelted Ralph, and he yelped and complained. Gil worked his way down the aisle, bombarding Ralph with tape after tape, but still Ralph kept abreast in the next aisle—the damn tapes were too light. Ralph was being hurt, but he was too dumb to know how bad. Gil bent low and ran, hidden by the rack of videos, but when he reached a crossing aisle Ralph was there.

"I don't want to play games now, Gil."

Gil turned back, pretending to sprint in the other direction. When he heard Ralph moving he used his power to push, shoving the whole rack back, toppling it onto Ralph and pinning him against the next rack. Then he hammered the rack, over and over, splintering the wood.

"Freeze, or I'll shoot!"

Gil spun, throwing a broadside at the officers entering the store, but one of their guns fired, hitting him in the shoulder. His broadside knocked the cops back out the door, but pain flooded his mind, pushing out the anger. Blood flowed from his shoulder and he pressed on the wound, then turned and staggered toward the back door.

"Stop or I'll shoot!"

Gil turned a corner, squatting at the end of the rack; focused his fading power; then pictured a boulder, leaned out, and pushed. The policewoman took it in the chest, flung backward as if jerked by an invisible string. When he tried to stand and run, lights flashed in his head and he nearly fainted. Blood soaked the front of his shirt now. He pictured another boulder, leaned out, and pushed down the other aisle. A gun fired when his head appeared, the bullet whizzing past his ear. He jerked back, seeing Officer Winston knocked down by his power.

Gil stood, feeling weak, and turned to run, but Ralph was there, his massive arms wrapping around him, picking him up off his feet. Gil found himself staring into Ralph's injured face—dozens of nicks from the video barrage bled down his cheeks.

"Are you hurt bad, Gil?" he asked inches from his face. "Don't you think you should go to the hospital? I could carry you if you want. You wouldn't have to buy me an ice cream or nothing."

"Ralph, let him go. He could hurt you," Officer Winston shouted.

"Naw. He's my friend. He did some bad things, but I think he won't anymore. Isn't that right Gil?"

Gil's hatred of Ralph burned through the pain and he felt the power coming. He pictured a bowling ball, stared at Ralph's face and pushed with all his remaining strength. A hole was blasted through the video rack behind him, and two more beyond, but Ralph stared back, his thick lips in a pucker.

"What was that, Gil? Did something fall?"

Then Ralph turned to look, and Gil found himself looking over Ralph's shoulder at Officer Winston. Searching through his pain he found he could hate the man who had shot him—foiled his bright future—and he searched for his power. He could blast the policeman right through Ralph.

He was weak and barely conscious, but he dug deep, nursing his anger. He pictured a softball-sized rock with jagged edges—edges that would tear and rip human flesh. Then he stared over Ralph's shoulder at the chest of the advancing policeman and summoned his power—but there was something else in his mind; a black hole had opened, its irresistible power sucking everything in. Vainly, he tried to hold on to his anger, but it was sucked into the oblivion and then his pain followed. Finally, his very sense of self was pulled down. As if sinking in quicksand Gil reached out in his mind, clawing at the sides of the black hole, but finding nothing to grasp, and sinking deeper and deeper, until he was gone.

33

HOSPITAL

The policeman who picked Elizabeth out of the crowd said only that she was needed at the hospital. She feared Len was dead, but also worried about Ralph. She never did find him in the chaos around the wrecked 7-Eleven—it had been a war.

The emergency room was a buzz of activity, injured people coming in as fast as the ambulances could bring them. In one corner she found Officer Winston sitting next to a policewoman with her arm in a cast. A nurse was taping his chest.

"Is it Len?"

"No. As far as I know he's still hanging on."

"What about Ralph? We can't find him!"

"Slow down, Elizabeth. Would you let me tell you? Ralph's over there."

Elizabeth turned to see Ralph sitting in a chair, a nurse dabbing at his face.

"He's all right, just some cuts and bruises. He was a big help actually. He grabbed Gil and held him." Nodding to the officer next to him, he said, "Chris and I—and all the others of course—got knocked all over the place, but not Ralph. He just walked up and grabbed him. How do you think he did that?"

"I don't understand," Elizabeth said. "Gil didn't try to kill him?"

"He tried, all right. Isn't that right, Chris? But he couldn't touch him—not directly anyway. He threw things at him, but nothing heavy enough to hurt him bad."

Puzzled, Elizabeth couldn't understand why Ralph would be immune to Gil's power—but she also remembered he had heard Gil's telepathic messages.

"Thanks for taking care of him," Elizabeth said.

"He took care of us, actually. But that's not why I wanted to see you. Something's wrong with Gil. The doctors think he's catatonic, but I'm not so sure. You've been messing with his mind in your experiments, maybe you know what's wrong with him."

Elizabeth's temper flared. She felt a part of the project now and was defensive.

"I thought one of you should check him out," the policeman said.

Still angry, Elizabeth agreed, following the two officers to the second floor, where a policeman stood guard outside a locked door. Inside, Gil lay on a hospital bed, both arms handcuffed to the rails. His eyes were covered in gauze.

"We had a heck of a time convincing a doctor to tape his eyes. He didn't believe in psychic powers. Hell, I didn't either until I saw him use it."

"His shoulder is bandaged."

"Gunshot wound. The bullet didn't penetrate far. He couldn't stop it with his power, but maybe he slowed it down. He bled a lot, but he's gonna live, but what the hell are we supposed to do with him? What jail cell will hold him? He'll just use that psychic power of his and blast a hole in the wall."

Elizabeth understood the magnitude of the problem. If Gil needed to see to use his power, then they could keep him blindfolded, but for how long? Would the state treat him like a modern-day Samson, blinding him and then putting him on display? It was an impossible dilemma, and secretly she was glad she wouldn't have to resolve it.

"You can see he just lies there. He doesn't respond at all. The doctors want to take off the bandages to check his pupillary responses but I won't let them."

"Gil? Gil, can you hear me?" Elizabeth asked. There was no response—no motion, no sound. "Frankie, is that you?"

"Yes, Elizabeth."

The two policemen looked at each other in surprise.

"Frankie, why didn't you talk to the policemen?"

"I was afraid. I don't know where I am. Am I under arrest?"

"You're in a hospital. You've been hurt, but you'll be better soon."

"I was shot."

"Yes."

"Why did someone shoot me?"

"It wasn't because of anything you did."

Elizabeth hushed Roy when he started to protest.

"Was I raped?"

The officers again looked mystified.

"No. Your shoulder is hurt, that's all."

"Thank Ralph for me. He carried me."

"I'll tell him. We're going to step outside now. Go to sleep for a while."

"I don't sleep, Elizabeth. If I sleep I'll die."

Now Elizabeth was surprised but led the officers out of the room.

"What's going on?" Roy demanded.

"When we heard about the trouble with Gil, we hooked up the other savants to our equipment, hoping to pull Frankie together. We thought Gil might disappear if we did. It was probably Frankie that brought him back after he killed Luis."

Roy looked confused but put it together. "So he just blanks out, then thinks he's someone else? A schizophrenic?"

"You're thinking of multiple personality disorder, but this is different. She actually is Frankie."

Roy and the other police looked at her as if she weren't making any sense. Ironically, she found herself defending an experiment she once hadn't believed in.

"I'll try to explain more later, but there's another problem." The police looked at her suspiciously. "You were talking in front of Frankie, and told her she had psychic power."

"So? He—she—whatever, already knew."

"Gil knew. Frankie didn't. Wasn't Frankie easy to handle? I mean, not like Gil?"

"Ralph was holding him when he was still using his power, then he just went limp. Nothing after that until he—or she—

talked to you. But what does it matter? As long as Gil is blind-folded, and chained to this bed, he can't do anything."

"But Frankie isn't just Gil, she's parts of several of the sa-vants, and somehow, even without Wes's equipment, Frankie has been integrating."

"But this is the one that's been doing the killing, right?"

Elizabeth hesitated. She didn't know for sure who had killed the fraternity brothers, and she didn't want to cast suspicion on any of the savants, especially since nothing that happened had been their fault. She decided, as she suspected Roy had, that it was best for Gil to carry all the blame. He had killed, and there was no way to punish a computer program, or a ghost for that matter. But blaming Gil put a terrible responsibility on her. Now she had to make sure Frankie never killed again. "Yes, Gil's the killer."

"Then we'll just have to make sure he doesn't get loose again. I want to talk to Dr. Birnbaum. He might have some ideas on how to keep him under control long-term, or at least through a trial. This is one time I think even the liberals will be happy Oregon has a death penalty."

Elizabeth had always thought death sentences barbaric, but now she found her feelings mixed. Gil had shown no regard for human life and she couldn't imagine what kind of prison could hold him.

She left the police to call Wes and let him know what had happened. "It worked," she told him. "Gil is Frankie now. I've talked to her. Gil did a lot of damage, but they've got him in the hospital now. He's restrained and they have his eyes covered."

"I'm glad, but it doesn't make sense. The integration is set up so that Daphne has the hearing, and yet you talked to Frankie. From here we weren't sure the integration was working at all. The only reason we let the integration run was because the brain-wave pattern resembled Frankie's, but we got no response here. Whatever power Gil has seems to override our integration. When Frankie's integrated she seems to put the savants together in her own way."

"Wes, there might be another problem. Officer Winston men-tioned Gil's powers in front of Frankie. Is there any chance she can access them?"

"I don't know. She seems to be accessing other parts of his

mind we didn't intend, but that could be because the integration is incomplete. Without Luis there may be more flexibility for Frankie to work with."

"Could you set the parameters to isolate Gil's powers so he couldn't use them? That way he would be safe in a prison population."

"He'd have to wear an EET helmet all the time," Wes said doubtfully. Then, after a long pause, "I didn't develop this to use it for mind control. Don't you know that by now, Elizabeth?"

"I didn't mean it like it sounds. I was worried about the police and guards. I should have known you would hate to have it used that way."

"If it's absolutely necessary, we could work on the problem—"

"It's not feasible—sorry I even suggested it."

"I understand," Wes said.

"What about Frankie? Can we keep her from getting to Gil's powers?"

"We can try to localize Shamita's wave, but even if we set it outside the parameters Frankie is hard to keep penned. I'll talk it over with Shamita. You better warn the police, we're going to end the integration soon."

Elizabeth told Roy but he seemed uninterested. Whether the man on the bed called himself Gil or Frankie, made little difference to him. Elizabeth knew the difference was critical, and maybe deadly.

Gil woke confused. There was pain in his shoulder, and his arms were tied down so he couldn't reach his face to uncover his eyes. He listened hard, hearing distant sounds, and he smelled the air. He wriggled his body, discovering a needle in his arm and a catheter in his penis. He was in a hospital.

He remembered being wrapped in Ralph's arms—that stupid retard who'd ruined his plans. He vowed then and there to kill him no matter what risk—with a gun if he had to. He wriggled again, making his shoulder throb. It hurt, but he could still move his arm. He was alive and in good shape, but they knew his Achilles' heel—his eyes were covered. Gil opened his eyes under the bandages. He could see light shining through, and, he realized, he could see the inside of the bandage. He pictured a finger, then gently pushed at the gauze. It bulged slightly, snapping back against his eyes, stinging him. His eyes watered, and he waited, letting them clear before he tried again. Now the door opened. Turning at the sound, he heard the voice of the policeman.

"So you're awake. Are you Gil, or Frankie?"

Frankie had taken him again, he realized, he hadn't fainted. *What must I do to be rid of you?* Then, to the policeman, "Who's Frankie?"

"Fine, be Gil! I don't give a damn. You can be both for all I care. You can keep each other company in your cell."

"Why are my eyes covered?"

"You know why! They'll stay covered, too."

Gil decided to play innocent, blaming everything on Wes's experiment. It was what the policeman wanted to believe anyway. "I don't know what you're talking about. I didn't do anything. Ever since I took part in Dr. Martin's experiment I've been having blackouts."

"Really. So you don't remember killing anyone? You don't remember wrecking the Seven-Eleven? Nothing?"

"I couldn't have done that. I would remember, wouldn't I. What did they do to me? Elizabeth—Ms. Foxworth—assured me it was a harmless experiment."

"They tell a different story."

"They're blaming all this on me? It's just too horrible." Worried he was laying it on too thick, Gil changed direction. "Can't you uncover my eyes so I can see you?"

"Never."

"I have rights, you can't keep me like this."

"I can try. Anyway, soon you won't be my problem. Tomorrow you're going to be transferred to the state prison. They've got a hospital there."

Now worried, Gil thought about the layers of security he'd have to break through to get out of a prison. No, his best chance was here.

"You interested in the body count?" the policeman asked.

"I didn't do anything."

"What was that retarded kid's name? Luis. Do you remember killing him?"

"I loved Luis."

"How many others did you kill before you came to Oregon? Was Dr. Birnbaum one of your victims?"

Startled, Gil twisted his head at the sound of Birnbaum's name.

"Yeah, Dr. Birnbaum's here. He's anxious to see you. He thinks you might be the same one that tried to kill him."

Dr. Birnbaum would surely identify him, and once they made that connection they might trace him to other programs and other deaths. He'd left a trail of false names, but eventually they would uncover it all.

"Nothing to say? You can try the insanity plea, but when a jury sees the video we have on you in action they won't dare set you free."

Gil heard him walk to the door and open it; then he spoke again.

"Don't even think of trying to escape. Every cop on the force thinks the world would be a better place with you dead. I agree. There will be an armed guard outside your door at all times."

Then the door closed, and locked. Gil was alone, and scared. He had to get away! Once they transferred him they would take his picture and those would be splashed all over the country, making it hard for him to disappear. Court might be the easiest place to break out of, but by then the pictures would have been taken. Prison was clearly the worst place to break out of, so it had to be sooner. He could wait until they had him in the ambulance on the way to the prison but they would be sure to have guards in the ambulance, and following in a car. Even injured, now was his best chance to get free.

He worked up righteous indignation, then turned it into anger and opened his eyes again. Imagining a finger he pointed it at an angle and pushed. The bandage moved, up and then down. Pointing the imaginary finger at a sharper angle, he pushed again. The bandage was tight around his head and the push lifted his head off the pillow. With more angle he pushed three quick times in succession. This time the bandage moved up his forehead slightly. Confidence filled him, and his anger at being captured by "average people" built. He pushed three quick times in succession and the bandage moved again. Now he knew he could do it, but it was too soon. He would wait until night, then he would be free again.

* * *

Ralph was treated as a hero at home and got to choose dinner. He picked pizza, which pleased Archie and Yu, and they ate greasy slices of pepperoni pizza while watching his favorite video, *Bambi*. Daphne remained morose, nibbling her pizza, then going to her room. The others ate silently in the kitchen, saddened by the death and destruction that surrounded them. Karla Birnbaum insisted on acting as waitress, getting up and down, and serving the others. Embarrassed, Wes reminded her she was a guest, and she should be waited on, but Elizabeth flashed him a look that told him Karla needed to be busy.

When they were finished, they cleaned up, then sat drinking coffee, listening to the rain. Finally, Elizabeth turned to Dr. Birnbaum.

"Officer Winston thought you might know of a way to stop Gil."

"Kill him. Blind him. A modified lobotomy—if we could localize the source of his ability."

"If it's like most brain function, it could be too widespread to remove," Wes said. "At least not without killing him. But maybe that's a win-win choice."

They sat quietly again until Elizabeth thought about Ralph's immunity.

"How do you explain Gil's power? And what about the way Ralph was unaffected? Did you know he can hear Gil's thoughts?"

Everyone waited for Dr. Birnbaum, the expert.

"I've been thinking about that. Where did the power come from? Genetic mutation? Evolution? Gil wasn't the first to have the power, just the first to have it at this level—maybe you enhanced it with your experiment. I think that's likely. Maybe it's a power we all have in some way. His ability to plant thoughts in people's minds, for example. Why are some people more persuasive than others? What do we mean by a 'forceful personality'? Perhaps some people have always had this ability. Perhaps a few cells, deep in their hypothalamus, give them just a little power over the rest of us. Elizabeth, you seem to dominate the people around you; perhaps you have the power. Perhaps Gil has the same hypothalamic cells as you but they are much larger. Say also that whatever you did with your experiment magnified that power; then you get someone like Gil.

"You don't mind if I continue to use you as an example, do you, Elizabeth? Now, Elizabeth, I said you were dominating—assertive if you prefer—but people tend to see things your way. But I notice that Wes doesn't respond the same way as the others. I suspect you and he get into it now and then. Perhaps Wes and Ralph are alike in some way."

Karon and Shamita snickered, and Wes tried to hide his discomfort.

"I said something funny? Anyway, if we dissected your brain, Wes, and Ralph's, would we find something special in your hypothalamus? Perhaps your own special set of cells that make you resistant to these forces?"

"But Gil used his power on me."

"It's just an example. Ralph can be considered to be like Gil, with an extraordinary ability. Fortunately for us, Ralph's ability is resistance to PK."

Momentarily silent, Wes was thinking about the experiment. "Dr. Birnbaum, what do you think of Frankie? What's the connection with the hidden room downstairs?"

Dr. Birnbaum rotated his chair so he could look Wes straight in the eye. "That, at least, is clear. Your synthesized consciousness is the host for the spirit of the young woman that was entombed in the basement."

Wes was uncomfortable, wanting a different explanation. "A ghost? It can't be—"

"Why not? Possession has been long recognized by a wide range of cultures and throughout history. One person's soul possesses another person's body, and the result is usually devastating—mental and physical disability—as two souls fight for the same body and mind. It can't work and the person is tormented, confused, and labeled insane. But what you have created with your marvelous machines is ideal for possession. A new mind comes into existence without a soul, just waiting to be possessed. All that is needed is a soul looking for a host and you have a match made in heaven—perhaps literally. It's a shame Frankie can't exist permanently. There's no way to sustain the integration without the donors, is there? I didn't think so. What a pity. I wish I could meet this Frankie."

"The experiment's over!" Wes said, but then he saw Elizabeth shaking her head.

"It's not over until the spontaneous integration stops. Frankie is coming together without us." Then she turned to Dr. Birnbaum. "If we knew how Frankie can integrate without our help, it would help us stop it from happening."

Dr. Birnbaum pursed his lips, rubbing them with his fingers. "Most likely it's an extension of Gil's ability to suggest thoughts to people. He can enter their minds and insert his own thoughts. Blending Gil with the others made them receptive to his powers. Perhaps they even share his power to a degree. As to what triggers it, I don't know."

Wes leaned forward, getting Dr. Birnbaum's attention. "You're saying that today when Frankie took over, her soul was part of the mind we synthesized."

"The New Testament says to love God with all your heart, all your soul, and all your mind. You're not a whole person unless you have all three, but if you have to get by with two, you'd be closer to personhood with a soul and a mind, than with a mind and a body. Because of your experiment Frankie gets all three— at least temporarily."

Wes rocked back, letting it sink in. The explanation came hard to an empiricist, someone who worshiped the rational. Wes had never had much use for the emotional side of life, which he saw as inextricably linked to the spiritual. Now, face-to-face with it, he was uncomfortable. Ironically, his rational side now pushed him to accept a nonrational truth. Frankie's animation had surprised him from the first time it appeared, but his ego had fooled him into thinking it was his cleverness that made Frankie what she was. A humbler man might have seen the truth, and perhaps saved lives.

"If that was Frankie's soul in Gil's body, then what if Gil had been killed?" Wes asked. "Would Frankie's soul be released?"

"I love these philosophical questions—I haven't been this happy since before the accident," Dr. Birnbaum said, waving his good arm in the air.

Dr. Birnbaum's excitement cheered the morose group, brightening the kitchen.

"It's a fascinating question, Wes. It might be that both souls are lost if Gil dies. But if the soul is linked to the mind, then if

Gil had died Frankie would have only lost part of her mind. I suspect the soul would have lived on. Frankie would have the lives of a cat, living as long as each of the donor minds lives. Only when all the minds went—each piece killed—could you be sure the soul from the basement would be set free."

"Nancy," Elizabeth said forcefully.

"Excuse me," Dr. Birnbaum said.

"The soul we're talking about is from a young woman who suffered greatly. Her name was Nancy Watson."

"Of course," Dr. Birnbaum said. "The soul of Nancy Watson. Elizabeth, you remind me of something else. Nancy Watson died once already. Perhaps it's her suffering that kept her here—that would be consistent with other similar phenomena—but if so, then there may be no way to send her soul on its way. Not until she's ready to go."

34

BREAKOUT

The muffled hospital sounds were gone now, except for an occasional tap of footsteps down the hall. It was night routine in the hospital—time to begin.

Gil opened his eyes, focusing on the inside of the gauze, then angled a push. He tried several angles until he had the knack again, then push . . . push . . . push. Slowly the gauze worked its way up his face onto his forehead. Looking down, he saw movement—it was his feet under the sheet. He wiggled them again, watching the sheet ripple. Through the slit he looked around the dark room, making sure he was alone. He craned his neck, checking the ceiling corners, and the walls. There were no cameras—not in this hick town.

He worked the blindfold until he could see clearly, but left his eyes partially covered, fearing the guard would peek in. Freeing his hands was more difficult. He studied the cuffs but they were tempered steel and he'd rip his hand off before the chain linking the cuffs would give. Instead, he studied the bedrail, feeling the steel tubing, running his hand along until it met a joint. It would bend if he hit it hard enough, but he feared the noise would bring the guard. Instead, Gil decided to explore the limits of his power.

Thinking of being captured by inferior beings, he rekindled his anger, fanning the flames with images of Ralph and the cop

who captured him. Then he pictured a chisel held against the rail
and pushed slowly and evenly. Nothing. Frustrated, he felt his
anger swell. He pushed again, but too hard, and the steel tube
was crushed, groaning loudly. Flopping back, Gil lay motionless,
listening hard. No guard came to check.

Patience! he reminded himself. He had to be gone by morning but he had time to be careful. Starting over, this time at the
joint, he pushed softly at first, then built slowly, stoking his anger
gradually. He thought of being held captive, of being chained
like an animal. Then he pictured that big policeman and the girl
cop who helped him, and his anger swelled a notch. The steel
tube dented. Then he thought of Wes and Elizabeth, and the
other so-called scientists, and the way they thought of him as an
inferior, ordering him around. His anger notched up again and
the dimple in the tube spread. Then he thought of Ralph and his
hatred reached its zenith. The tube slowly flattened. He continued to push, bending the flattened tube until it folded in half,
pulling out of the joint.

Elated, Gil slid the handcuff off the tube. *You can't hold me—
you can't stop me!* he wanted to scream in defiance, but instead
he turned the emotion to anger and went to work on the other
rail.

Daphne had no crutch—the sounds of the piano no longer filled
her, ordering her thoughts, bringing structure. The imaginary
piano did no better, and she was at the mercy of the swirling
thoughts in her head. But the confusion of the swirl was nothing
compared to the horror that was the eye of her mental hurricane.
Having long feared being swept up in the buzzing confusion in
her mind, she longed to be carried away by it. Anything was
better than what waited at the core.

Daphne paced the room, pounding away at the keyboard in
her mind. *I won't remember, I won't!* But in saying it she realized
she did remember—her conscious mind now pained by what
had tortured her soul most of her life. The pain was unbearable,
and she fell down on her bed sobbing.

Wes asked the Birnbaums to stay and they put them in Len's
room for the night. Ralph carried the motorized wheelchair up
the stairs and then returned for Dr. Birnbaum. "You're not as

heavy as some people. That's because you're missing some parts, isn't it?" Dr. Birnbaum laughed, and Karla Birnbaum beamed at Wes. *At least some good is coming out of this,* Wes thought.

With the Birnbaums settled, Wes found Elizabeth standing outside Daphne's door. As he approached he could hear crying. Elizabeth shushed him when he started to speak, and took his arm, leading him down the stairs. He warmed at her touch, and found he was less anxious. At the bottom she let go, but he reached out, taking her hand. She squeezed his hand in response, and they sat on the couch, sides touching, still holding hands.

Wes waited silently, enjoying the feel of Elizabeth next to him. He was concerned about Daphne, but selfishly didn't want the moment with Elizabeth to pass. It was a few minutes before she spoke, releasing his hand and then rocking sideways to look at him.

"Daphne is very upset."

"She has good reason to be."

"Yes, but this isn't simple grief. She's suffering terribly."

"Is she worried that Gil will come back?"

"No, this is personal pain. Daphne's never been like the other savants. Luis, Yu, and Archie are true savants in that they are retarded in all areas except where they have their special ability. Ralph is retarded in the same sense. In most cases like Ralph, something goes wrong in prenatal development, and the brain gets wired wrong; intellectual functions are depressed. In savants, though, another wiring fluke gives them their special ability. But there's another developmental path to becoming a savant, and Daphne took it. Daphne isn't retarded at all in the usual sense, and her special ability is more of a defense mechanism."

"It's a real ability."

"Certainly, but I suspect calendar-counting didn't come naturally to her. She uses it to keep from thinking about something else. Did you ever have a song that popped into your head unpredictably? Most people have. That song isn't just some random tune, it serves an important function. It keeps you from thinking about something else. When something from your unconscious comes bubbling up—something anxiety producing—here comes the song to fill your mind, leaving no space for the uncomfortable thought. Daphne uses music that way, and calendar-counting. Let me put it in computer terms for you. Imagine how much RAM it would take to solve Daphne's calendar problems."

Wes knew a simple program could solve those problems, but understood the point. For the human mind to calculate as she did would take every available space in memory.

"Daphne developed calendar-counting by focusing her abilities on the task. She could do this because she's autistic. She doesn't care about the world, and can shut it out, leaving every bit of her mind to solving the problem. We could do the same thing if we wanted to sacrifice all social contact."

"In some ways that's what I did, Elizabeth," Wes confessed. "I've done nothing but study and do research since I entered college. I had friends, but they were psychology majors, like me, equally focused. I even got most of my general-education classes waived. I thought art, history, and literature were a waste of time. Besides, I knew if I could publish as an undergraduate it would give me an advantage. It did. Graduate school was the same. The grants came easy after that, and this project is career-making research—at least it was. You see, I was just as focused as Daphne."

"You didn't sacrifice everything. You have friends. Len and you get along well."

"We only see each other in the lab. I don't think I knew what I was missing until we became like a family here. And when we lost Luis it hurt like he was my own child."

They were silent then and Elizabeth moved back over, leaning against Wes. His arm was in a cast or he would have put it around her, willing to risk rejection, but unwilling to hide his feelings anymore.

Standing against the wall, Gil peeked out, then flattened back. The policeman was sitting reading a book. Preferring to take the policeman by surprise, Gil wanted him to come in. A nurse would check on him at some point but when she did the policeman would be on his guard, knowing how dangerous Gil could be. Besides, the nurse might not come until morning—maybe with the morning rounds. It would be crowded then and that could work for him, but he couldn't be sure they wouldn't come to transfer him to prison first thing.

Instead, Gil leaned against the wall, looking out the window on the far side. It was covered with wire to prevent escape, even though they were three stories up. It gave him an idea. Picturing a battering ram, he focused his anger and his power, then pushed hard. The window shattered, sending the screen flying into space. Then he hugged the wall, waiting.

The lock rattled; then the door handle turned, the policeman rushing in with gun drawn, running straight to the window. Gil could have left, but his anger was honest. He hated the policeman—he was one of those who had imprisoned him and he would make him pay.

"Looking for me!" he said.

Startled, the policeman turned slowly. Gil enjoyed the look of terror on his face. When his gun came up, Gil hit him in the chest, driving him through the empty window frame. He screamed all the way to the ground.

Gil turned to leave and ran into a nurse. He lashed out, knocking her back through the door. In the hall more people were running and he cleared the hall, knocking them down like bowling pins. Then he spotted an exit and ran toward it, throwing shock waves ahead of him and sending carts racing down the hall, crashing into people and walls. Running barefoot in his hospital gown, he pounded down the stairs toward freedom.

Elizabeth picked up the phone before Wes, but he hung on, listening to the conversation.

"He got away about an hour ago. It will be light soon. If he isn't out of town already, he'll probably hide like he did before, maybe until night. We'll try to get some more dogs and go after him but it's been raining pretty good."

"Did anyone get hurt?"

"Yeah. One of my people is dead. I have to tell you he's killing this town—literally. Everyone's related to everyone else, or knows someone. Most of them had families." Then, a long pause, where Wes could feel his pain. "My department's not that big—everyone is either scared or out for revenge. I'm not saying we're going to shoot him on sight, it's just that my people are pretty upset. Anything could happen—just keep Ralph away this time."

Roy was being honest—there was little chance Gil would be taken alive. Wes understood and found he had few qualms about killing Gil; in fact, he found himself thinking, *The sooner the better.*

"He knows he's got to get out of town as soon as he can," Roy said. "If you're worried I can have one of my people stay with you."

"Thanks, but I know you're shorthanded. I'll feel safer when he's caught, and you need everyone for the search."

"Yeah. Thanks. The state police are helping, and we've got volunteers coming in from other departments."

"Do you still want to talk to Dr. Birnbaum?"

"It's too late for that, but would you folks stand by to do that trance thing? I don't want any more of my people hurt."

Wes hung up after they did, wondering how safe they really were. Would Frankie let Gil get away?

He couldn't go back to sleep, so he showered and then started a pot of coffee. Elizabeth was there just as it finished the drip cycle.

"Gil escaped."

"I know, I listened in."

"Is there anything we can do?"

"I've been thinking about it. We could be proactive. Let's put Frankie together again. Maybe we can find Gil through Frankie."

"How? Frankie took control of Gil last time."

"Frankie might not know the danger and come out in public. But there's another way. We can put someone into the matrix— one of the team."

"But wouldn't they become part of Frankie?"

"I can adjust the program. I might be able to keep them conscious."

Wes watched Elizabeth's face, knowing she would realize the danger.

"But that would put two minds in one person. I can't imagine what that would be like. The psychological stress would be enormous."

"I'll keep the contact brief. If we can integrate Frankie then we'll insert the informer briefly to see if they can sense where Frankie is."

Elizabeth looked thoughtful a minute, then said, "I'll do it."

"No. It's my idea. I'll do it."

"It doesn't make sense for you to go in. Without Len you're needed more than ever. You know I'm the only one who can be spared."

"We could send Ralph."

"It wouldn't be ethical. He's not capable of making an informed choice."

Wes hesitated, carefully wording what he wanted to say next. "Elizabeth, Ralph might fare better sharing a mind, since . . . well, he has space in a sense. Besides, he has a lot less to lose than you do."

Wes knew if he had said that when they first met she would have been offended, but now she stared back with kind eyes.

"Ralph's mind is complex in its own way, and even if it is simpler you can't judge human worth on IQ. If we used him, and something went wrong, I couldn't forgive myself."

Wes wanted to say he wouldn't forgive himself if Elizabeth were harmed either, but instead he nodded his head. "I better get started on modifying the program." Knowing Elizabeth was the one taking the risks motivated him to make it as safe as he possibly could.

Daphne sat motionless on her bed, her hands in her lap. She'd cried herself out, the sobs finally subsiding to sporadic tremors. She stared out her window, seeing only the tops of trees, but in her mind she replayed the violent scene over and over. She could see the body flying across the room and hitting the wall, and then the head being slammed against the wall over and over. When the body was finally a lifeless pile, the image replayed. It began with the anger, and the pain, and then came the pounding and again the body flying across the room hitting the wall. She'd been replaying the scenes all night long, and as she did her sadness deepened but at the same time the swirling storm that was her mind slowed and gradually dissipated into order. She could visit her memories now, and the world around her, without fear, without confusion. But the price was pain and guilt. And sadness. Sadness greater than she felt even at Grammy's death.

A knock she didn't answer announced Elizabeth, who came in tentatively, walking around to face her. When Daphne made eye contact surprise spread across Elizabeth's face.

"Daphne, can I help?"

"No."

"Would you like to talk?"

"I can't now. Maybe later."

"Do you still blame yourself for what happened?"

"It is my fault."

"What Gil did had nothing to do with you, and anything that happens next won't either."

"What happens next?" Daphne asked, fearful of the answer.

"Gil got out of the hospital. They're looking for him again."

The image of the body flying through the air haunted her. "I don't want any more people hurt!"

"Daphne, it's not your fault, and there's nothing you can do."

Daphne shook her head; then her lips tightened and her eyes narrowed. She couldn't let it happen, but she was afraid of losing control if she tried to help.

"There's nothing we can do," Elizabeth said. "We're not letting Ralph go near him either."

Daphne stared defiantly, her jaw set in determination.

"Do you hear me? There's nothing you can do," Elizabeth repeated.

"I hear you," she said, making no commitment. Then, turning, she stared out the window, signaling Elizabeth to leave—but Elizabeth stayed.

"Daphne, we are going to do something and I think you should know about it because it involves you. When we run the experiment, we mix together pieces of your mind and the others, and we get a new mind called Frankie."

Daphne had heard the explanation before, but guessed there was more to it.

"Yesterday when I wasn't here, they ran the experiment because Gil is part of Frankie. When a part of you is Frankie, then Frankie is in control. It's the same with Gil. We thought that if Frankie was in control that Gil would stop hurting people. It worked. We want to do that again—turn Gil into Frankie. Are you willing to do that? It is one way you can help."

"No one asked me before, why now?"

"Because you're different now. Don't you feel different?"

Daphne did feel different—her center was pain now, not con-fusion. But Elizabeth was right, it was a way to help, and until she knew a better way, she would cooperate. "Let me know when you're ready."

Elizabeth thanked her, then reluctantly left. Daphne sat at the window, thinking about the past and the future, afraid of both. Then she stretched out on the bed, trying to relax, but revisiting the painful image of the head pounding against the wall. She was tired, and exhausted, her body's defenses running constantly to ward off the effects of her anxiety. Forcing herself to think of other things, she let her consciousness skip from thought to thought. Soon she didn't have to force her mind to change im-ages, and her consciousness flowed past, and then, like crossing a stream by jumping from rock to rock, she carefully picked out good thoughts, standing on those, letting the painful memories flow around her. Then she heard a distant voice—alluring, promising protection from the pain around her. Turning her mind's eye, seeking the voice, she skipped toward it.

Blood loss, lack of sleep, and the physical and emotional stress of the last couple of days left Gil drained. His hiding place was comfortable, and he was pretty sure no dogs would track him this time. He'd fled the university hospital in the rain, stealing a coat and a bike and riding off, still wearing his hospital gown. He'd have to get clothes before he could get away clean, but he needed dark for that. His immediate problem was sleep— Frankie was always a threat.

Gil's eyelids were heavy, and he dozed, suddenly snapping awake, realizing what had happened. Gil sat up, but knew he had to stay low. Walking around was too big a risk, so he waved his arms around and stretched his legs. The movement helped, but soon he found his eyelids sagging again. Painfully pinching his cheek helped, but only briefly. He was losing the battle against sleep and soon his head sagged. He snapped awake again, only to nod off once more. Finally, he gave up and lay back, promis-ing himself only a short nap—a promise he had no way to keep.

A thump in the bathroom stopped Wes, and he knocked on the door. "Are you all right in there? Hello? I'm coming in." The door opened a crack before it hit something. Wes could see a pair of legs blocking the way. He pushed harder, moving the legs out of the way, then leaned in. Yu was unconscious on the floor.

"Elizabeth, come quick."

Squeezing in, Wes reached for Yu's neck, but realized his chest was heaving and he was breathing deeply. Then Elizabeth's head appeared.

"Check the others—it may be Frankie," Wes said.

Pulling Yu out of the way, Wes rolled him over, checking for injuries. When he was sure there were no wounds he checked his eyes, watching the pupils constrict. He shook Yu but he wouldn't wake. Then Elizabeth was back.

"Archie and Daphne are unconscious, too. It's Frankie, isn't it? But that's good, we were going to try and do it ourselves anyway."

"Maybe, but this way we may not find out were Gil is."

"It won't matter if they capture him as Frankie."

Wes agreed, but worried anyway. He preferred being in control. "Let's move them downstairs so we can monitor. If we have to we can still go through with the insertion."

Wes couldn't lift Yu by himself, so Elizabeth went to find Ralph. Wes meant to share the load, but Ralph scooped up Yu, and carried him down the stairs, the others trailing.

Seeing Dr. Birnbaum at the bottom of the stairs, Ralph said, "He's not as heavy as your chair, but he's heavier than you. Course he's not missing any parts."

Dr. Birnbaum laughed, then followed them to the experiment room, whirring around in his chair, watching Elizabeth fit the EET helmet to Yu's head. Ralph returned with Archie; then Dr. Birnbaum rolled around to inspect the terminals, pestering Karon and Shamita with questions. When he rolled up to Wes's terminal, Wes began a running narrative, describing function and theory. He accompanied every move he made with another explanation. Dr. Birnbaum sat enthralled.

Karon finished with Archie, then moved to Len's terminal, checking the physiological readings. Elizabeth joined Dr. Birnbaum, listening to the explanation. Everyone was submerged in their work, so it was a long time before they realized Ralph was standing behind them chewing gum.

Irritated, Wes turned to Ralph. "You were supposed to carry

Daphne down, Ralph. If you want a Slurpee to do it, I'll gladly buy you one. A large one!"

"Would you, Wes? I can drink a large, but I usually don't buy them. Too spensive, you know."

"I'll make it a special treat. Now, would you please bring Daphne down?"

"I will as soon as she gets back."

"What? She's gone."

"She's not in her room. I looked in the bathroom for her. I didn't just walk in. I knocked first. Daphne doesn't like me to walk in when she's in the bathroom."

Elizabeth squeezed Wes's shoulder. "Oh no! Frankie has Daphne."

35

PARTY

When Classen was injured at the 7-Eleven it left a power vacuum at the Kappa house, and Billy took control. Classen had lost support with each brother who left the fraternity anyway. Only a half-dozen brothers were left, and three of them were Billy's toadies. Sammy Chow was intelligent but didn't give a damn about school, living to party with Billy. He was skinny as a rail, but still some of the girls went for his Eurasian looks. Emil Loprenzi was large and soft, with a Roman nose and curly brown hair. Only the ugly girls went for him, but he didn't care, usually dating two or three at a time. He'd been Rimmer's best friend until he'd been killed, but now he hung with Billy's group. Billy's best friend was Grant Brewster, who was nearly as good-looking as Billy, and the two of them did everything together, Grant always willing to follow Billy's lead.

The house would have to close by fall if the members didn't come back, but for now Billy could lead—if only he knew which direction. Everyone was too scared to go out, and no one would come to the house to party. Frustrated, Billy paced the living room, kicking at the newspapers spread on the floor. Grant watched from the couch, a football game playing on the TV.

"Want to play some basketball?" Grant asked. "Emil and Sammy might get into it as long as we didn't leave the driveway."

"No, I don't want to play basketball. It's boring."

"How about some racquetball? Want me to call for a court?"

"No! Jeez, you're boring. I want to have some fun."

"Having fun gets you killed, or didn't you notice?"

Billy was frustrated. "It's those damn mad scientists. They did it. We had a bitchin' good time around here until they came."

Then they heard someone pounding on the back door.

Billy led Grant through the kitchen and saw a girl through the back window. It was the retarded girl—the one they suspected of killing Rimmer. Billy's teeth ground together as he looked her over. She didn't look dangerous—he could take her easy, and with Grant it would be a piece of cake. She wasn't a beauty, but she wasn't bad either. Her hair was pulled back into a ponytail, and she'd tied it with a blue ribbon like a little girl. He could only see down to her waist, but her figure was decent. When he lifted his eyes from her breasts he saw her smiling, and then she winked. Curious, he reached for the handle. Grant slapped his hand away.

"What the hell you doing?" Grant demanded. "You know who she is?"

"Yeah! So? I mean what is she gonna do? There's two of us and she's only a girl."

"Remember how strong Rimmer was? He's dead, man!"

"Don't be a wuss! We don't have to let her in. We'll just see what she wants."

Reluctantly Grant stood aside.

Opening the door, Billy said, "What do you want?"

"I'm looking for a party," she said, smiling.

With the door open Billy could look her over top to bottom. She was wearing a blue sweater over a white blouse, and a navy pair of pants. The pants were loose so he couldn't see her legs well, but the sweater fit snug, showing off her breasts. Aroused now, he didn't bother sneaking peeks at her body, he stared openly, then looked her in the eye. "Funny you should ask about a party, we were just getting ready to start one."

"Are you nuts, Billy? You know what Classen will do if he finds out?"

"Now think about that, Grant. Just where is Classen?"

"Oh yeah. But it could be dangerous."

Billy shook his head sadly, then turned to the girl. "My friend here is afraid of you. He thinks you might be some psycho killer."

"Now my feelings are hurt," she said. "How could you say such a thing about me?" She smiled and swung her hips. "But if you'd feel safer you can search me." Then she lifted her arms in the air, inviting them to pat her down.

"Oh, man," Grant said, stepping forward. But Billy cut in front, putting his hands on her hips, then sliding them up and around her waist and down onto her bottom. He felt her muscles tighten as his hands cupped her buttocks. Then he dropped to his knees, starting at her right ankle, feeling up her calf, and then slid his hands up her leg to her thigh, one hand between her legs. He pressed firmly at her crotch and then repeated it with the other leg. Now his breath came in short rapid breaths and his heart was pounding.

She kept her arms above her head when he stood, and he put his hands back on her waist, sliding them up until he could feel her bra under her clothes. Bringing his hands around, he slid them across her back and then around to the front, coming slowly toward her breasts, expecting her to stop him at any second. She didn't, and his hands soon cupped her breasts where he lingered.

"Satisfied?" she said, smiling.

"It's a start. Come on in, let's party."

Billy turned and pushed Grant ahead of him, whispering, "She's hot, Grant. Really hot."

Behind them she stepped in, dropping her arms, catching a knife as it started to slip from her sleeve. Pushing it back, she shivered as she remembered his hands on her. Feeling the cold of the knife along her arm, she smiled in anticipation.

Wes, Elizabeth, and Karon raced to the street, spreading out up and down the block, looking for Daphne. When they couldn't spot her, Elizabeth took the car, slowly driving up and down the blocks. Karon went to the neighbors while Wes ran for the fraternity house, bounding up the steps and pounding on the door. No one answered, but he could hear rock music and he pounded again. Finally, he saw a shadowy shape coming down the hall. The boy who answered looked Asian and he was frowning.

"What the hell do you want?" he said.

Wes could smell beer on his breath. "I'm looking for one of the kids staying with us. Her name is Daphne."

"She's not here. We don't want those retards around here."

"It's important we find her. . . ."

"The cops say you and those retards are behind all the killing."

"That's not true. Let me explain. . . ."

"Get the hell out of here!"

The door slammed in Wes's face, but at least he knew the fraternity brothers were on edge and Daphne wouldn't get near them. Yet Wes wanted them to understand that it wasn't their fault—his fault. If they would listen to him he might be able to explain that to them—but first he had to find Daphne. Chills rippled along his spine as he thought of what she might be doing.

Roy Winston was at the station laying out a search pattern when the call came.

"It's Ms. Foxworth. She says it's important," Chris said.

Speaking as soon as he said hello, she sounded frightened and out of breath.

"Daphne's missing and we think Frankie is in control. You've got to help us find her."

"I thought Gil turned into Frankie."

"They're all Frankie! We've explained this to you before and I don't have time to do it again now. The important thing is to stop Frankie."

"Gil is top priority," he replied. Silence followed, and Roy began to wonder if she had hung up.

"Roy, you should know that Frankie is really Nancy Watson." The name was familiar, but he couldn't quite recall it.

"She's the girl from our basement—actually it's her spirit. Dr. Birnbaum believes the mind we create with Wes's synthesis program provides a host for Nancy's spirit."

Roy had accused them of using psychic powers to control their retarded kids but there was an aura of science about psychic research. He was unprepared for a supernatural explanation.

"That's hard to believe."

"Harder to believe than Gil's power?"

Like a slap in the face, Elizabeth's comment cleared Roy's

thinking. Why was a ghost story any harder to believe than a psychic killer decimating his police force?

"I'll put the word out on her, but we've got to stop Gil."

"Nancy—Frankie is a killer, too."

"Yeah, but she knifes them one at a time. Gil can kill them by the carload."

Roy wished he could do more, and promised himself he would end both reigns of terror, but Gil was still first priority.

Frankie swayed around the room, feigning a drunken dance. Four of them watched. Billy was killer-good-looking, but his eyes were cold, as if he had never known love—she wanted him dead most of all. Grant and Sammy were nothing by themselves, but she knew their kind were nothing more than extensions of Billy. They would do it to her if he wanted them to. They were probably thinking about it right now. The biggest one was Emil—dumb and brutal, she thought. Another stupid college jock who thought every girl wanted him. *Well this one does want you—wants you dead!* she thought.

She danced past Billy, wiggling in front of him and grabbing the beer out of his hand. He grabbed at her sweater but she danced out of reach, circling the room, teasing each of the boys. The music ended and she paused, swigging at the beer, remembering how much she had loved it. "Boy it's hot in here," she complained, then pulled her sweater off over her head.

"Take it all off," Emil shouted. She winked at him, then said, "What kind of girl do you think I am?"

Emil leaned over and whispered something to Sammy, who chuckled and nodded his head. She knew the kind of things boys like this said. Her father told her she shouldn't go with boys like these. He had been right, but she didn't know it until it was too late. Fraternity boys were exciting, daring. They made her feel grown-up, like the woman she was, not the little girl her father saw. But she had paid the price for associating with boys like these, who had no mercy, and now she would repay them.

"Play something from Elvis," she asked.

"You've got to be kidding. The King is dead," Billy said, picking out another CD.

The music came on loud, pounding out its rhythm deep in her bones. She waited, picking out the beat, then started her dance again, planning to get them alone, and one by one make sure they would never hurt anyone the way she had been.

"Elizabeth, are you sure you want to do this?"

"Yes. We need to find Daphne. Frankie could get her killed."

"OK. Shamita, double-check the parameters I set for Elizabeth. Karon, watch her physiological signs. You can expect elevated pulse, pressure, and lowered GSR, but I'll pull the plug on this if you think it's too high."

"What can I do, Wes?" Dr. Birnbaum asked.

"Me, too, Wes," Ralph added.

Wes wanted to send him for Slurpees to get him out of the way, but knew he wasn't safe on the streets.

"Dr. Birnbaum, you will need to talk to Elizabeth and ask her where she is. Ralph, you stay with Dr. Birnbaum. He might need your help."

"Well okeydokey then. I'm a good helper."

"But Ralph, if you are going to stay you have to sit quietly. No talking unless I say so. Do you understand?" Wes said it firmly. Ralph babbling in Elizabeth's ear would trigger her cognitive functions and possibly alert Frankie to their presence. It could also make it harder for Elizabeth to subsume her own mind and allow Frankie to use parts of her brain functions.

"I'll sit right here and not say a word. Unless you say it's okeydokey. My lips are sealed." Then, with exaggerated motion, Ralph pursed his lips and locked them with an imaginary key, pretending to drop the key in his shirt pocket.

Shamita fed Elizabeth's, Archie's, and Yu's patterns to Wes, and he initiated the program. Frankie was already integrated, and he hoped they could at least eavesdrop.

"What you're getting is the active sections from Yu and Luis," Shamita explained. "Frankie has the rest pretty well shut down."

"It looks like our integration," Wes said.

"Nearly identical, except the parameters are broader. She's taken more from each of the others because of Luis being . . . well, not available. We'll have to guess what she's getting from Gil and Daphne, but I can do a pretty good estimate. I'll use the parameters from our last integration. I needed to modify your parameters for Elizabeth a bit."

"Yeah, I see. OK." Shamita was even more cautious than Wes

and had set the parameters so that Elizabeth would be sensing at a subliminal level. Wes doubted it would work, but knew it was safest to start there. "Let's go with these. Elizabeth, are you ready?"

"Yes. It's just like last time, right?"

"Right. But for you it will be like having a vivid dream. You might just get feelings at first, but eventually you should share what Frankie is seeing and hearing. It will seem disconnected, but just think of it as a dream. You'll also share thoughts, and that's what we're concerned about. Your thoughts will mingle. You could confuse her thoughts with your thoughts, but more likely you'll feel very confused, or even disoriented. Don't try to fight it, just let your mind go. Let her do the thinking."

"I'll be able to talk?"

"Yes. You'll be able to hear us but we don't want to talk to you unless we have to. We don't want Frankie to know we're breaking in. It would be best if you give us a running narrative of what you're seeing and doing. Tell us what Frankie is thinking as much as you can. As soon as we get a key to your location we'll pull you out."

Elizabeth nodded, shaking the wires from the helmet. "Let's go and get back."

"Put her under, Shamita."

As Wes watched, Shamita lowered the electrical activity of Elizabeth's brain and she settled down, her breathing becoming slow and rhythmic. Then Wes integrated Elizabeth into the mind pictured on his screen. Soon the bits and pieces of mind functioned as one on his screen.

"Pulse rate and BP are climbing, Wes," Karon said. "Steady increases."

"Elizabeth's respiration has quickened, too," Dr. Birnbaum reported. "They're all breathing hard."

Wes checked the integration—it seemed normal. "Shamita, what's going on?"

"Look at the activity in the motor cortex," Shamita said. "Frankie is very active. Is she running or something?"

"Dr. Birnbaum, try to get Elizabeth to start talking to us. But do it gently."

"Elizabeth? Can you hear me?" he whispered.

"Yes."

"Why are you breathing so hard?"

"I don't know."

"Can you sense anything?"

"No. I only hear your voice."

Wes and Shamita exchanged glances and shrugs. The integration seemed normal but he'd never seen this kind of physical reaction before. "Karon, how are the physical signs?"

"They've leveled off. Nothing dangerous."

"Watch them close. Shamita, we've got to integrate more of her."

Shamita frowned, but sent over new parameters, closer to those Wes had originally set. Wes typed in the adjustments, then integrated slowly.

"I can hear music. Rock music. It's loud. Something's not right. I feel funny—dizzy. I can taste something too. Tastes like . . . alcohol . . . beer. I'm drinking beer. I can see faces swirling by, but they're blurry. Everything is bouncing. I'm moving—I'm dancing. I'm dancing at a party. I'm drunk."

She'd drunk too much beer, and she was losing control. She stumbled as she twirled around, and kept shaking her head to think clearly. Her eyelids felt thick and heavy, and she had trouble seeing. Her thoughts cleared momentarily, and she knew it was urgent she get them alone and kill them soon. Dancing closer to Billy, she ran her hands up and down her body. He took a sharp breath as she touched herself. Then, leaning close, she said, "I have to go to the bathroom. Can you show me the way?"

"Yeah. Sure. This way."

The others shouted at him to bring her back but he told them to shut up and put his arm around her waist, pulling her close. Being close to him nauseated her, but she let him hold her. He took her past the bathroom on the main floor and upstairs, then through a cluttered bedroom to another bathroom. The bathroom connected two bedrooms, and had two sinks, a toilet, and a combination shower and tub. Towels littered the floor, and the vanity was cluttered with razors, soap, and cans of shaving cream. Stepping in she tried to close the door but he held it open.

"Hey, a girl needs a little privacy," she protested.

"Security rules. No visitors are allowed in bathrooms by

themselves." Leering at her, he added, "If you don't want me watching, I could go get Emil."

She leaned against the door, putting her face close to his, hiding her arm behind the door. "I'm kind of shy. Can you at least turn your back?" As she spoke she shook her arm, working the knife out of her sleeve into her hand.

"Gotta watch everything."

Forcing a big smile, she said, "OK, then. Come on in." Then she leaned back.

She hated his kind more than he would ever know, and her smile faded as he walked past her. Her whole body shook as she remembered what boys like him had done to her, and the muscles in her arm tightened. Memories of the boys on top of her flashed through her mind, clearing the alcohol fog from her brain, and when she saw his back she lifted her arm, stroking down with all her might. But just as she swung she saw their reflection in the mirror over the vanity—he was watching.

He lunged forward away from the blow, and in her drunkenness she couldn't adjust quickly enough, the blade just creasing his back. Still, he screamed as if she'd buried it six inches deep. She recovered her balance and lunged again, but he was turning, deflecting the thrust from his stomach. He screamed again, this time calling for help. Suddenly the music downstairs died. She swung the blade wildly, slicing through his shirt as he jumped back, falling into the tub. His screaming was continuous now. Staggering forward she lifted the knife, concentrating on one good downward thrust that would cut through his hand to find his soft belly. Then she could neuter him as she had the others.

He cowered in the tub, pulling his legs under him and trying to get to his feet. The terror on his face was satisfying, and his squealing for help was an echo of her own unanswered pleas. Just as she was about to swing, he reached out, pulling the shower curtain across, blocking her view. Pausing, she ripped it aside. He was coming up now, trying to stand, holding his arms out to ward off the coming blow. She could see a red streak on the tub from the wound on his back. Pleasure flooded her— pleasure over his fear, pleasure over his pain, and pleasure over his pleadings. Then she lifted her arm, ready for a near erotic burst of joy as she stabbed him. Suddenly a dark stain appeared in his crotch. She hesitated, momentarily confused. He'd wet his pants! She smiled broadly and leaned in to strike, but then she heard the voice—small and distant, screaming for her to stop. The voice mingled with her thoughts, but the voice wasn't hers. Mad with blood lust, she cocked her arm to strike. Suddenly she was engulfed by a huge set of arms.

"What did she scream?" Wes asked.

"She said don't kill him," Dr. Birnbaum said.

"Oh no. We're too late."

"He won't let go of me," Elizabeth said.

"Dr. Birnbaum," Wes said. "Talk to her. We've got to find out where Frankie is."

"Wes, her heart rate is climbing again—all her signs are up," Karon said.

"Elizabeth, can you hear me?" Dr. Birnbaum asked.

"I cut him."

"Who, Elizabeth? Who did you cut?"

Flailing with the knife, she tried to reach whoever was holding her. Swinging low, she stabbed a leg, eliciting a scream, the arms loosening.

"Hold her!" Billy screamed, standing in the tub. He reached out and tried to grab her arm.

Swinging at Billy, she drove him back into the tub, but the arms still held her and were dragging her back. She reached up, and sliced the arm—it released. Turning, she faced big Emil, who was backing out the door, his arm bloody. Slashing and stabbing, she drove him out the door into the bedroom.

"I cut them—she cut them. They're bleeding. I'm sorry. No, don't hurt them!"

"Who, Elizabeth? Can you see their faces?"

"Billy—"

Dr. Birnbaum looked at Wes, who shrugged helplessly. Turning back to Elizabeth, Dr. Birnbaum asked, "Who else is there?"

"Don't hurt them."

"What is the other one's name?"

"It's Emil."

Again Dr. Birnbaum turned to Wes, who shook his head. Panicky now, Wes knew Frankie was somewhere trying to kill two

people, but he didn't know where. Then he saw Ralph's hand
waving in the air like a grade-school child trying to get attention
in class. Irritated, Wes ignored him, turning away. But Ralph
leaned out, shaking his hand in his face. Then Wes remembered
that Ralph knew everybody in town.

"Ralph, do you know who she's talking about?" Wes shouted.

Ralph nodded, then reached into his shirt pocket and pulled
out the imaginary key and unlocked his pursed lips, putting the
key back in his pocket. "I know a Billy and a Emil. They nitiated
me. We're rat brothers . . . frat brothers."

"But I was there—he lied to me. I'm going down to the fraternity. Karon, call the police!"

Before Wes could move, Elizabeth froze him in his tracks
with a scream.

Billy had tackled her from behind, and she screamed in rage,
crashing to the floor with him on her back. The knife was pinned
under her and when she pulled her arm out Sammy jumped on
her wrist, holding her hand to the floor. He pulled at her fingers,
trying to free the knife while the others held her to the ground.

"Get the knife, Grant!" Sammy screamed. "I'll hold her arm!"

Grant kneeled, pulling at the fingers tightly wrapped around
the handle.

"Hold still, you bitch!" Billy screamed, as she kicked and
shrieked.

Then the knife was free and Grant tossed it out the door, letting it clatter down the hall.

"Good job, Grant," Billy said. "Go get something to tie her up
with."

Even with Grant gone, she couldn't break loose. They merely
had to sit on her, their bulk pressing her to the floor so she could
take only short shallow breaths. Then Grant was back with curtain cord and they pulled her arms up on her back, tying her
wrists together. When Grant wrapped a cord around her ankles,
Billy stopped him.

"Don't do that."

"She kicks like a mule!" Emil protested.

"Yeah, but if you tie her legs together we can't have any fun."

She went into a frenzy then, screaming and flopping around
on the ground, flailing wildly with her legs. They jumped back,

letting her tire herself out. She slowed physically, but the
screams continued. Then Billy sent Grant for a towel, and they
held her while he tied it across her mouth, muffling the sounds.

"Help me carry her to the bed," Billy said.

Each taking an arm or a leg, they lifted her, ignoring her
weakening gyrations, and tossed her onto the bed. Focusing her
remaining strength, she kicked at them, but they easily snagged
her legs, Sammy holding one, Grant the other. Finally she collapsed, her rage turned to despair, and now fear. Helpless on the
bed, memories flooded back. She saw the faces around her
laughing at first, then leering. Then one by one the faces appeared close up as they hurt her—raped her. She began to cry,
her tears blurring her vision. Then Billy's face appeared.

"You cut me, bitch, but now it's my turn."

Then she felt his hands on her, pulling at her pants, and she
dissolved in tears. Waves of fear rippled through her mind, building to a tidal wave of horror. Submerged in the horror, she sank
deeper and deeper, slowly dissolving in the acid of her fear.

"No! No! They're raping me!" Elizabeth screamed.

"The police are on their way, Wes!" Karon said, returning to
her monitor. "Wes, her signs are at dangerous levels! Bring her
out!"

"I'm trying!" Wes aborted the program, expecting the integration to disintegrate, but it didn't. Frankie was holding it together. Suddenly, Elizabeth went limp, and Frankie's wave
pattern dissolved, re-forming into a new pattern.

"What happened, Shamita?"

"I don't know—the integration is different. The parameters
are—it looks like Frankie changed the parameters."

Then Elizabeth started crying.

Billy had her pants half off when she suddenly went stiff. He
looked up to see her looking around, confused, as if she were
seeing her surroundings for the first time. Then she lifted her
head and stared hard at Billy, as if she wanted to bore a hole
through him.

"As they say, relax and enjoy it," he said with a smile. Then
he returned to pulling her pants down.

Suddenly he was flying through the air. When he hit the wall it was like being smashed between two giant bricks and his ribs compressed nearly to the breaking point, his breath exploding from his body. He slid to the floor, dazed, gasping for breath and dizzy from the pain. Dumbly, the others looked from him to her. Then it was Emil sailing across the room, landing on a dresser and tumbling to the floor. The dresser fell on him, the lamp from the top shattering on the floor.

Grant backed away from the bed, holding up his hands, but Sammy ran for the door. When he was three feet from it the door slammed loudly, Sammy crashing into it. Unhurt, he yanked at the handle, desperate to escape. Then, as if he were pushed with an invisible hand, he was slammed against the door so hard it cracked down the middle. Then twice more he was smashed into the door, each time the crack getting bigger. Then he staggered back a few steps, his hands holding his bleeding face, only to be slammed against the door again, this time crashing through it. He lay motionless in the hall.

Grant ran for the hole in the door but was knocked sideways, hitting the wall instead, his left arm crumpling as he tried to stop himself—the crack of the bone audible above the crash. Grant slid to the floor screaming.

Looking around wildly, Billy saw Emil crawling toward the door. Suddenly she sat up. Billy closed his eyes to a squint, pretending to be unconscious. She was working at the cord holding her wrists. Soon they were free and she took the towel from her face and stood, pulling her pants up and calmly buttoning them. Grant stood, backing away from her, holding his arm and begging her not to hurt him. She backed him toward the wall and then suddenly he was flying through the air and crashing through the window, screaming as he fell to the patio below.

Sobbing, Emil crawled through the shattered door, across Sammy's body, and into the hall. Billy froze as she looked at him briefly, and then followed Emil into the hall. Billy got to his feet, but each step racked his body with pain. Slowly he walked to the bathroom and through to the other bedroom. *Hide or run?* He couldn't run, he hurt too bad. Then he heard the sirens. The police were coming, they were saved. A scream and a crash told him it was too late for Emil, but he could be saved—he was still alive.

He opened the closet, working his way through the clothes,

and pulling the door closed behind him. The sirens were muffled, but still coming. *Hurry, please hurry.* He stood still, listening now for her sounds. It was quiet—he hoped she was gone. He dared think about being safe, and telling the police about what had happened. He began constructing a lie about how she had come to them, asking to use the phone, but then had attacked them. She was a freak—a mutant, or something—maybe a creation of those crazy scientists. Then the door opened.

The clothes parted by themselves, and then she was staring at him. Her stare was unwavering; she held him transfixed with her eyes.

"I didn't mean anything—" he began.

He was pushed to the wall, held by an invisible hand.

"Please don't hurt me," he begged with his last words.

He felt his head gripped by an invisible hand, which tightened, threatening to crush his skull. His eyes wide with fear, he clawed at his head but there was nothing to grip. Slam, his head hit the wall of the closet. Lights flashed behind his eyes and the pain made him weep. Then slam, slam, slam, over and over, his head pounded the wall—he was powerless to resist. His head battered the Sheetrock until it crumbled, but the stud behind it held, cracking his skull. Then his lifeless body was allowed to slip to the floor, leaving a bloody streak down the wall.

36

CONFRONTATION

Birnbaum, talk to her," Wes shouted. "She should be able to hear us."

"Elizabeth? Do you hear me, Elizabeth?"

"I'm not Elizabeth."

"Yes you are. Your name is Elizabeth Foxworth."

"I'm not . . . I don't know . . ."

"Wes, do you see it?" Shamita shouted.

"Yes." The integration changed, the brain-wave patterns swirling; then suddenly the integration failed, the minds separating. The savant patterns returned to normal, followed by Elizabeth's. "Bring her out, Shamita." She was already working, Elizabeth slowly coming back to full alpha-wave function. When the equipment was shut down, Wes hurried to Elizabeth. Dr. Birnbaum pulled the helmet from her head. Her eyes were open but she stared blankly.

"Are you all right, Elizabeth?" he asked.

Slowly her eyes looked around at the faces above her, her face showing confusion.

Gil woke with a start, bumping his head on the bottom of the table. The pain helped clear his mind. He was groggy, but he knew it wasn't from sleep. *It was that damn Frankie again!* He cursed and swore she'd done it for the last time. He rolled out from under the table, looking out the window at the house. It had been a good hiding place. No one would suspect he'd come back here, but no hiding place was going to help him unless he could be free of Frankie. He'd been so close to having it all: the power, his freedom, unlimited control of others. But Frankie had taken that from him—there was only one way to be free—they all had to die. He stepped out of the garage, searching through the shrubs until he had a handful of rocks. Then he stormed toward the house.

Elizabeth's confusion lingered, her eyes darting around the room as if they were unable to focus. Suddenly they opened wide with fear. "Daphne!" Elizabeth shouted. "We've got to help her. They're hurting her!"

"We called the police," Wes said.

Elizabeth slid off the cot, heading for the door, Wes holding her arm to support her. They stopped on the porch when they saw Daphne coming up the walk with Officer Winston. Daphne's eyes were fixed on the ground. The policeman's face was haggard.

"She's all right. We found her down by the fraternity."

Elizabeth hugged her, putting her arm around her waist and leading her into the house. Wes hung back to talk. The policeman opened up as soon as Daphne was inside.

"Gil got into the fraternity house. He must have been hiding out there or something."

Wes hesitated, unsure of what to disclose.

"Gil was there?"

"Had to be. Four boys are dead. Smashed up just like my officers."

Wes was quiet, wondering what really happened in the frat house.

"We're fanning out now, using the dogs to track him."

The policeman turned to leave but the sounds of splintering wood and shattering glass came from the house. Running up the steps two at a time, they raced in, just in time to see Karon, Yu, and Archie running from the experiment room. Suddenly they were knocked down by a silent blast, tumbling across the floor toward them. Yu rolled into the wall next to them, hitting it hard and then lying still. Archie came to rest on his stomach and then pushed himself to his hands and knees. Crying, he crawled about searching for his glasses. Daphne stood with Elizabeth, frozen in the middle of the living room, Karon lying at their feet. Then Gil stepped into the room, his face contorted in rage. Roy drew his gun, but was instantly knocked back against the wall, his gun clattering to the floor. Karon and the others struggled to their feet, backing away as Gil advanced, Dr. Birnbaum rolling backward. Then Gil turned on Dr. Birnbaum, as if noticing him for the first time. Dr. Birnbaum glared back defiantly.

"I know you!" Dr. Birnbaum said, his voice trembling. "You did this to me!"

Shaking with anger, Gil used an invisible push to send Dr. Birnbaum hurtling backward, crashing into an end table. Dr. Birnbaum tipped, rolling out onto the floor, trapped under the heavy chair. Wes could see him pushing with his stumps trying to free himself. Gil advanced on Dr. Birnbaum, and then Ralph stepped between them.

"You hurt him, Gil. I told ya you can't do that to people!"

"I'm not afraid of you, Ralph!" Gil said.

Ralph moved forward, spreading his arms. "I'm gonna have to hold you again, Gil. I won't hurt you, I promise."

Gil gave him a cold look, but held his ground. Then he held up his hand and dropped a rock. When it reached eye level, it shot forward like a bullet, burying in Ralph's shoulder. Ralph jerked with the blow, but didn't cry out. Standing still, he looked at his right shoulder, then slowly brought his hand to it.

"Ow! That hurts, Gil!" Ralph said.

Gil's hand raised again and he dropped another rock. Ralph ducked this time, and the rock whizzed across the room, burying into the wall with a loud *whump*. Quickly Gil dropped another rock, this time firing it like a bullet into Ralph's leg. Ralph reacted slowly again, sinking to the floor, now holding his bleeding leg.

Wes looked around, not knowing what to do. He noticed that Roy was sitting up, but the policeman looked dazed. The gun was on the floor and Wes measured the distance to it, then looked back to Gil, estimating his chances. Ralph was struggling up now, holding his right shoulder. Up came Gil's hand, ready to drop another rock, when suddenly he flew backward, disappearing into the experiment room, followed by crashing sounds.

Stunned, everyone stood still looking at each other. It was as if Gil's power had backfired. Wes didn't understand what had happened, but he realized it was their only chance. He jumped for the gun and rushed to the door, pausing to peer in. Gil was there on hands and knees trying to free himself from a tangle of cables. Wes pointed the gun at him, advancing slowly.

"Don't turn around, Gil. I have a gun."

Gil paused, then went back to freeing himself from the wires. Wes didn't know what to do. Only Ralph could hold him, but he was injured. Once he turned around Wes would be at the mercy of his power, but he couldn't bring himself to shoot a man in the back. While Wes wrestled with a course of action, Gil finished freeing himself of the cords and then stood.

"Get back down!" Wes shouted. "Lay facedown."

"I'm picturing a telephone pole and when I turn around, I'm going to ram it right through you."

"I'll shoot!"

"Then we'll both die."

Suddenly Gil jumped over the table in front of him. Wes fired a gun for the first time in his life, the revolver's shot passing over Gil as he slid across the tabletop. Now on his hands and knees, Gil crawled toward the kitchen. "Stop!" Wes shouted. When Gil kept crawling, Wes fired, the bullet hitting the floor in front of Gil. Quickly, Gil turned and knocked Wes backward, but he had little power. When Wes sat up he saw Ralph walking in full stride, but with a limp. His leg and his shoulder were bloody.

Ralph circled the tables, trying to cut Gil off. Gil spotted him, but had lost his rocks in the fall. He ripped a cable from a computer, sending it flying toward Ralph. With one end connected, it whipped across Ralph's face. Smarting with the pain, Ralph stumbled back. Gil stood and ran into the kitchen. Wes fired again, but Gil was through the door and the bullet went wide, striking the wall. Then Wes was up and scrambling over the table, but Ralph was ahead of him.

When Wes ran to the kitchen he found Gil cornered and Ralph advancing.

"Get out of the way, Ralph!" Wes shouted. "I've got a gun."

"It's not nice to shoot people, Wes. I'll just hold him like before."

"It's too dangerous," Wes argued, but Ralph ignored him.

Gil stood perfectly still, leaning against the counter, not making a move to run. It unnerved Wes, who knew he was planning something. Then Gil reached down and pulled open a drawer, and extracted a knife.

"Get down, Ralph!" Wes shouted, jumping to the side.

Ralph ducked just as a butcher knife whizzed over his head, sticking into the wall. Then Ralph rushed forward, reaching for Gil. Gil grabbed another knife, holding it, slashing at Ralph, who took the blow on his arm. He didn't react, but kept coming, wrapping his arms around him. But there was little strength on his injured side and it was a wrestling match, Ralph trying to control the knife arm while Gil tried to break free. Wes aimed the gun, but they were a tangle of arms and legs.

Wes rushed forward to help, but suddenly the toaster was launched at him. He turned, taking it on the shoulder, then turned again. Canisters machine-gunned off the shelf. They flew wide, ricocheting off the refrigerator. Wes came on and then was punched in the stomach with an invisible blow. Wes buckled but was amazed he was alive—Gil's power was weak. Hurrying before Gil could recharge, he reached into the mass, trying to grab an arm, but couldn't hold one using only one hand. Stuffing the gun in his waistband he reached with both hands.

Gil lashed out wildly now, smashing cabinet doors, and sending dishes and canned goods flying. Still he and Ralph held on. Gil's head twisted toward Wes, so he danced around, keeping out of his field of view.

"Stop it, Gil," Ralph scolded. "You're hurting me."

"I'll kill you, you moron!"

"It's . . . not . . . nice . . . to call people names."

Suddenly Gil freed an arm and transferred the knife to his free hand. Before they could react, the knife plunged down into Ralph's shoulder. A few seconds later Ralph yelped, his arm releasing, hanging limp. Gil twisted, sending Wes backward with a blow to the chest, then turned toward Ralph, murder in his eyes. Ralph sank to his knees, holding his bleeding left arm.

"At least I'll get you, you bastard!" Gil screamed, and raised the knife.

Wes threw himself forward, tackling Gil. When they hit the floor Wes crawled up his back, holding Gil's head toward the cabinet so he couldn't look at him, trying to watch the knife. Gil shattered the cabinet with his power, the splintered wood showering Wes. Wes cringed in shock, and Gil half rolled, turning his head toward Wes. Wes couldn't stop him now, Gil was turning over. Wes reached to his waistband but the gun was gone. Then he saw Gil looking at him. Wes could feel the power building behind those eyes—he was going to die.

Suddenly a small automatic pressed against Gil's temple. He froze, eyes fixed on Wes. It was Roy, and the policeman's eyes were cold. Silently, he held the gun, watching Gil's eyes. Slowly the policeman pulled back on the trigger, Wes tensing, waiting for the gun to fire. But then the trigger finger stopped, just before the point of releasing the firing mechanism.

"If you look at me, you die," the policeman said.

Gil's eyes were still locked on Wes, but he knew Gil was estimating his chances of knocking the gun away before Roy could fire it. The standoff continued, neither man's eyes moving, or even blinking. Then Gil's eyes flicked toward Roy, the gun firing at the same time, blowing his brains against the shattered cabinet.

EPILOGUE

Ralph was on Luis's cot, filling his place in the integration. Wes slowly pieced together the segments fed by Shamita. When the Frankie intellect was functioning, he signaled Elizabeth. Turning, she spoke softly to Daphne.

"Frankie, are you there?"

"Yes, Elizabeth." Her voice was shaky, not confident like before.

"We know it's you, Nancy." Silence followed. "You hurt a lot of people, Nancy."

"Not people, they were animals. They hurt me."

"That was long ago. You killed them, didn't you?"

"They raped me!"

"Your father found out and he put you in the basement, didn't he?"

"He didn't do anything about what they did. He said I was asking for it. He didn't understand."

"It's over, Nancy. It's been over for a long time. The boys you've been killing didn't do that to you."

"They're all alike . . . they tried to do it again."

"It's time for you to sleep, Nancy."

"I'm afraid. I have nightmares."

"You won't now, Nancy. It's time to sleep."

"I don't want to be alone. I'm afraid. I was alone so long."

"Your father's waiting, your mother and sisters, too. You'll be a family again." A long silence followed.

"There's a light."

"Go toward it, Nancy."

"It's bright . . . it hurts."

"They're waiting, Nancy."

"I can see someone . . . Daddy!"

Elizabeth reached out and took Daphne's hand. As Wes watched, the integration flickered and a wave he'd never seen swept the cortex, and then the integration dissolved.

"She's gone, Elizabeth." Nodding to Wes, she held Daphne's hand until they were all awake. As soon as he was up, Ralph used his good arm to scoot off his cot into his motorized wheelchair. Then he rolled around the room, banging into the furniture. Archie and Yu watched him enviously.

"Ralph, can I have a turn?" Yu asked.

"Me, too?" asked Archie.

"I suppose. But I get to drive it when Dr. Bin-bam comes."

Rolling into the living room, he transferred to a chair. Archie drove around the living room backward.

Daphne stayed behind, holding Elizabeth's hand.

"Would you sit on the porch with me, Elizabeth?"

On the porch they rocked slowly, watching Mrs. Clayton rake leaves.

"It was me, Elizabeth. I hurt those boys."

"Don't start that again, Daphne. You aren't to blame any more than the rest of us."

"I'm different now, Elizabeth."

"Yes. It's a remarkable change."

"I can remember things—terrible things from when I was little. My mommy used to treat me bad."

"You don't have to talk about this, Daphne. There's been so much pain lately."

"She used to hit me. Sometimes because I was bad, like when I wet my pants, or when I would cry too much. But mostly she hit me when she was drunk. I was so afraid of her, but she was my mommy, and after she beat me she would hug me, and hold me, crying into my hair. We would cry together until we fell asleep. She really did love me."

"I'm sure she did. She didn't know what she was doing—it's a sickness."

"One day she was drunk and I was real scared. I wanted to get to the potty, but I was too little and she was too drunk to help me up. I was in the kitchen begging my mommy to help me, but she laughed at me and then pushed me down, making me cry. Then I wet my pants! I was so afraid."

"Daphne, if this is too painful—"

"She threw her cigarette at me. I should have run away, but I was little, and I was afraid. She was going to beat me . . . hurt me. Her face was red, her hands were fists. I could feel the blows even before she started. So I hit back. I hit her hard into the wall. Then I hit her head into the wall, over and over. When I stopped she was dead and there was blood. Blood all over the wall. Blood all over the floor."

"You're confused, Daphne. It's a confabulated memory. The memory of your mother has mixed with what Frankie did to the boys in the fraternity house. She used Gil's power to kill them. It was never you."

Daphne looked up at her, tears dripping from her eyes. "It was me!" Taking a barrette from her hair, she put it on the porch rail; then she sat back next to Elizabeth. "Watch." Then the barrette shot off the rail, rocketing across the yard and burying into a tree with a loud thunk. Elizabeth jumped with surprise.

"I won't hurt you! Please don't be afraid."

"I'm not. It's just that I thought . . . you did that?"

"I've always had the power. Maybe Gil did, too—maybe he got it from me—I don't know. But I did kill my mommy, and when those boys tried to do that to me, I couldn't help myself. I'm so sorry."

Elizabeth pulled her close, and cried with her. She thought of the dead boys and of the power Daphne had used on them. She was the equal of Gil at least, and it must have been her that saved Luis when he fell from the skybridge and defended them against Gil's last attack. Should someone with that power walk among them? Elizabeth was frightened, but Daphne had never harmed anyone before. Besides, if she told anyone about it, they would treat her like a freak. Would the government lock her up, study her like a specimen in a jar? Daphne had locked herself up in her own mind for years, and now that she was free Elizabeth couldn't do it to her again. No, she would never tell anyone. It was a terrible responsibility, but she trusted Daphne.

They cried together for a while, and then they rocked until the Birnbaum's van drove up, honking.

Ralph rolled out in his chair, shouting to Dr. Birnbaum.

"Hello, Dr. Bin-bam. Lookee what I got. It's just like yours only different."

Dr. Birnbaum leaned out the passenger window. "It's a beauty, Ralph."

"I can't keep it on account they didn't cut off any of my arms or legs. I was kinda hoping they would, but they borrowed it to me anyway—it's a loaner."

Archie and Yu came out, carrying Ralph's luggage, and Mrs. Birnbaum came around to slide open the van door. Shamita, Karon, and Wes followed, helping load the luggage. Meanwhile Ralph drove back and forth on the porch in front of Elizabeth and Daphne. Wes talked briefly to Dr. Birnbaum. Then Dr. Birnbaum shouted at Ralph.

"It's time to go, Ralph. We've got a plane to catch."

"Well okeydokey then." Ralph stood and limped down the steps toward the van.

"Ralph, aren't you forgetting something?" Dr. Birnbaum said.

Ralph paused, leaned back, folding his arms across his chest, and pursed his lips. Then his hand shot out and he thumped himself on the head. "How could I be so stupid?" Back up the steps he limped, then grabbed the chair, lifting it off the ground.

"Careful of your stitches!" Elizabeth shouted.

Wes rushed to help him, but Ralph had little problem carrying the chair down the stairs to the van. Then he pumped everyone's hand, hugging Elizabeth. When he got to Daphne he looked sad.

"I'll come back and visit when they're done sperimenting on me. Maybe you could come live with us, too."

Daphne hugged him long and hard. "I love you, Ralph. You were important to me."

Now Ralph looked embarrassed, and Elizabeth was amazed at the range of emotions he was showing. Quickly, he was back to exuberant.

"Well okeydokey then, let's get the show on the road."

Climbing in the van, he slid it closed from the inside, waving out the window as they drove off. As they left, Ralph's voice could be heard over the drone of the engine. "Got any gum?"

Shamita and Karon left next to visit Len in the hospital. When they were gone Wes took Elizabeth aside.

"What did Daphne want?"

Elizabeth didn't want to lie to him; secrets had no place in the kind of relationship they were building. But if Daphne was to have any chance at a normal life, no one could know about her ability.

"She's still upset and blaming herself, but I think she's getting past it."

"We'll all leave this place with bad memories."

"Yeah. But good ones, too," she said, thinking of the nights they spent with the savants eating pizza and watching movies, walks to the park, and Sunday mornings in church.

Archie and Yu came down the steps whispering, then approached side by side. Yu did the talking, while Archie nervously pushed his glasses up and down his nose.

"We're kinda thirsty. Maybe we could go get a Slurpee? Archie and I know the way."

Elizabeth watched Wes's face fall—Archie and Yu had been corrupted by Ralph.

"All right," he said. "We'll all go."

Elizabeth waved at Daphne, who wiped the tears from her face, then hurried down the steps. She smiled briefly as she passed, then ran to catch up with Archie and Yu. Wes took Elizabeth's hand and followed, but then stopped, looking at something pink sticking in a tree. Twisting and pulling, he managed to free it.

"It's a barrette—someone hammered it into the tree."

Elizabeth feigned surprise, then took his hand and pulled him along, following the savants down the block.

Available by mail from

TOR FORGE

CHICAGO BLUES • Hugh Holton
Police Commander Larry Cole returns in his most dangerous case to date when he investigates the murders of two assassins that bear the same M.O. as long-ago, savage, vigilante cases.

KILLER.APP • Barbara D'Amato
"Dazzling in its complexity and chilling in its exposure of how little privacy anyone has…totally mesmerizing."—*Cleveland Plain Dealer*

CAT IN A DIAMOND DAZZLE • Carole Nelson Douglas
The fifth title in Carole Nelson Douglas's Midnight Louie series—"All ailurphiles addicted to Lilian Jackson Braun's "The Cat Who…" mysteries…can latch onto a new *pur*rivate eye: Midnight Louie—slinking and sleuthing on his own, a la Mike Hammer."—*Fort Worth Star Telegram*

STRONG AS DEATH • Sharan Newman
The fourth title in Sharan Newman's critically acclaimed Catherine LeVendeur mystery series pits Catherine and her husband in a bizarre game of chance—which may end in Catherine's death.

PLAY IT AGAIN • Stephen Humphrey Bogart
In the classic style of a Bogart and Bacall movie, Stephen Humphrey Bogart delivers a gripping, fast-paced mystery."—*Baltimore Sun*

BLACKENING SONG • Aimée and David Thurlo
The first novel in the Ella Clah series involving ex-FBI agent, Ella Clah, investigating murders on a Navajo Reservation.